aya Blake's hopes of becoming a writer were born
hen she picked up her first romance at thirteen. Little
d she know her dream would come true! Does she
ll pinch herself every now and then to make sure it's
t a dream? Yes, she does! Feel free to pinch her, too,
a Twitter, Facebook or Goodreads! Happy reading!

anadian **Dani Collins** knew in high school that she
anted to write romance for a living. Twenty-five
ars later, after marrying her high school sweetheart,
ving two kids with him, working at several generic
office jobs and submitting countless manuscripts, she
ot The Call. Her first Mills & Boon novel won the
Reviewers' Choice Award for Best First in Series from
RT Book Reviews. She now works in her own office,
writing romance.

THEIR DESERT NIGHT OF SCANDAL

MAYA BLAKE

CINDERELLA'S SECRET BABY

DANI COLLINS

MILLS & BOON

First published in Great Britain 2022
by Mills & Boon, an imprint of HarperCollins*Publishers* Ltd,
1 London Bridge Street, London, SE1 9GF

www.harpercollins.co.uk

HarperCollins*Publishers*
1st Floor, Watermarque Building,
Ringsend Road, Dublin 4, Ireland

Their Desert Night of Scandal © 2022 Maya Blake

Cinderella's Secret Baby © 2022 Dani Collins

ISBN: 978-0-263-30099-4

09/22

MIX
Paper from
responsible sources
FSC® C007454

This book is produced from independently certified FSC™ paper
to ensure responsible forest management.
For more information visit www.harpercollins.co.uk/green.

Printed and Bound in Spain using 100% Renewable Electricity
at CPI Black Print, Barcelona

THEIR
DESERT NIGHT
OF SCANDAL

MAYA BLAKE

MILLS & BOON

CHAPTER ONE

SHEIKH TAHIR BIN HALIM AL-JUKRAT had dealt with his most senior aide long enough to know the older man's tells. Yet Ali insisted on playing these games with him. Tahir watched him fidget with the papers in his leather-bound folder, straighten corners that didn't need straightening, place the expensive Montblanc pen Tahir had gifted him two Christmases ago precisely in the centre of the top page before moving it a fraction of an inch.

Given the chance, Tahir suspected the other man would've conducted a microscopic inspection of each fingernail for dirt and brushed invisible lint off his tailored suit before stating what was obviously on his mind.

'Are we done here? I'd like to get on with my next appointment before I leave for Zinabir,' Tahir said after a full minute, attempting and failing to keep impatience from sharpening his voice.

Ali gave the merest grimace, an action not many would've noticed.

Tahir noticed.

He noticed everything. Because these days, he couldn't afford to be oblivious to anything. Not any more.

Those carefree days when he'd freely trusted, and tossed out benefits of the doubt like candy at a toddler's party, were far behind him. Smothered to death by a far too close brush with a different fate. A fate averted at a steep price he'd never be able to fully repay in this life.

In his quietest moments, Tahir couldn't help but hope he would be able to repay it in his next. Hoped to have done enough in this life to erase the deep disappointment from his father's eyes when they met in the afterlife.

Until then...

He tightened his gut against the surfeit of emotions triggered by thoughts of his father.

'Not quite, Your Majesty,' Ali replied, shifting the pen yet again.

Tahir suppressed a sigh. 'What is it, Ali? Has my brother landed himself in the papers again?' His brother, Javid, much to Tahir's constant disgruntlement, was 'living his best life', which inevitably meant dragging Tahir's treasured homeland of Jukrat into the spotlight just for the hell of it. Luckily for him, Javid hadn't done anything scandalously outrageous enough...*yet*...

Infuriatingly, his younger brother had learned to skate close to the line without stepping over it. For now, Tahir had let him be because, when he cast aside his playboy ways long enough to do his duty, Javid was the most astute diplomat Tahir had ever come across. He could saunter into near-crisis international incidents and un-ruffle feathers with jaw-dropping proficiency.

Unfortunately, it was the same brilliant technique his brother used to seduce the clothes off some of the most beautiful and influential women in the world. On a regular, tabloid-salivating basis.

Tahir himself preferred much more discreet liaisons and not just because his spotlight was much brighter as the unmarried ruler of Jukrat, but because of another viciously learned lesson from *that* incident twelve years ago.

Dragging himself away from another unwanted memory jaunt, he fixed a gimlet stare at his aide. 'I don't have all day.'

Ali cleared his throat. 'My apologies, Your Majesty. No, this isn't about your brother. His Royal Highness the Prince is behaving himself.'

'Then what is it? Spit it out, Ali.'

'The palace guards have reported a…visitor who insists on seeing you.'

He frowned, the statement as peculiar as the tone of voice his aide was using. Reluctant. Pained. Almost…trepidatious. 'Correct me if I'm wrong, but isn't there protocol for assessing visitors? Protocol you yourself had a hand in drafting a decade ago?'

'There is, sire.'

Tahir exhaled, impatience growling to be freed. 'Then I fail to see the problem. I fail to see why a random visitor at the palace gates should raise this level of concern with you.'

'The problem is that she's been camped at the gates for three days. And attempts to turn her away aren't working.'

Tahir pinched the bridge of his nose, started to open his mouth to dismiss this subject altogether, then tensed as a dart of *something* speared him. 'She?'

'Yes, Your Majesty. The visitor is a woman.'

Tahir stopped himself from rolling his eyes and stating the obvious. 'There must be some reason you're furnishing me with this information?'

'It's her identity, Your Majesty. I had palace security double-check it this morning after she finally told us who she was.'

That faintest tendril of unease grew into an icy breeze down his back.

He resisted the urge to bunch his fists, instead lacing his fingers on top of his desk, inhaling long and slow. 'Have you known me to enjoy mystery or intrigue, Ali?'

His aide cracked a microscopic wry smile before shaking his head. 'No, Your Majesty.'

'Then I caution you to avoid it now,' he replied tightly.

Ali cleared his throat, moved his pen another fraction, then, 'The visitor is a Miss Lauren Winchester, Your Majesty—'

Tahir jerked upright, sending his chair skidding back on the polished floor.

Suddenly, the vast office felt like an airtight cage, closing in on him with alarming speed. A glass cage where all his emotions were on display. Shock. Shame. Fury. Despair. Everything he'd suffered during those three harrowing days in England. *When he'd been at her mercy.*

'What did you say?' he demanded, his voice, unlike the turbulence coursing through him, thankfully bled of all emotion except chilling fury.

Now he understood his aide's hesitancy. Just as he fully grasped the term 'shoot the messenger'. Because he was furious with Ali for dropping this forbidden name into his life. For breathing it into existence in this space of measured contemplation and incisive forward-thinking. In this imperial domain where every brave and worthy decision about his kingdom was taken with a level head.

'I'm sorry, sire. We tried to make the problem go away but…'

His eyes narrowed. 'But what?'

Ali shrugged. 'She's been careful to make an appearance at the right times. She knows the protocol well enough not to stray outside the parameters of the law, like some occasional protestors do.'

Of course, she did.

Lauren Winchester had a sharp, brilliant mind.

It was the first thing he'd gleaned about her when he'd strayed into that geo-politics Q&A at his university in England twelve years ago. He'd lingered in the back, watching the woman who faced away from him run rings around some of the most learned professors and gurus in the field.

At first, he'd been intensely fascinated with her argument; with her husky, impassioned voice that spoke truth to power. Then the glorious, waist-length tumble of blonde curls he'd itched to sink his fingers into. The slim, elegant hand that had periodically gesticulated and flipped her hair over her shoulders, giving him brief glimpses of her smooth, elegant neck.

Then, after a thoroughly engrossing hour, she'd risen. Turned.

He'd seen her face.

And he'd been enraptured…

Three short months later, she'd turned his world upside down.

His father had branded him a disgrace, his mother giving him a wide berth because he'd stopped being useful to her. Friends and family alike had treated him like a pariah. His banishment to the desert had been a welcome reprieve, a place where he could unmask his shock and bitterness without prying eyes alternately judging and pitying him.

That year-long cloistering had cured him of many things. Had forged a new path he'd never looked back from. And if he'd caught traces of disappointment in his father's eyes occasionally before his death, well…that was a stain he'd had no option but to live with.

All because of Lauren Winchester.

Against his will, his gaze strayed to the wide window, despite it not overlooking the palace gates. Security protocol dictated his office be placed in the centre of the vast Moorish castle that was Jukrat Palace. That way he was protected from people like Lauren Winchester and the many fervid subjects who camped at his palace gates, hoping to catch a glimpse of the Sheikh or under the misguided impression they could gain access to him by simply turning up.

Unlike his mother, who'd been carefree and naive enough to make impromptu trips to the palace gates, much to the adulation of her subjects, until a near-assassination attempt had put paid to all that, Tahir's appearances were ruthlessly vetted and strictly scheduled.

Of course, a woman like Lauren Winchester would believe she was above such strictures.

Hadn't she been...once upon a time?

Tahir pivoted away from the question and from the probing gaze of his aide. Every cell in his body vibrated with the unequivocal need to issue the command to turn her away, but when he opened his mouth, entirely different words emerged. 'Did she try to schedule a visit through the usual channels?'

'Not that I've been able to verify,' Ali answered.

Because she knew it was futile or because she believed it was beneath her?

Tahir's lips flattened. 'You could've dealt with this without my ever learning of it,' he rasped, still half enraged at his aide for dropping this unsavoury subject into his lap. 'What were you hoping to achieve by telling me?'

Ali's eyes widened in alarm and surprise. 'Umm... well... I believe it's prudent to not dismiss the political positioning of this considering her father's role in the British government. It may prove useful in the future.'

Political positioning.

Would that any of that mattered to him regarding Lauren Winchester. The only positioning he'd been interested in during those youth-flushed days at university had been her beneath him, her sinful lips, beautifully greedy hands, and bottle-green eyes encouraging him to lose himself completely and utterly.

And he had.

Much to his deep regret when her true nature had revealed itself.

Political positioning.

He silently sneered at the words, but slowly a different emotion shook free of the miasma, tunnelling through to take centre stage. Reminding him of every vow he'd made to himself twelve years ago.

He glanced once more at Ali, wondering whether there was an argument to be made for not dismissing his words out of hand.

There was a reason Ali was firmly sealed within Tahir's inner circle of trusted aides and advisers. Often the man wore both hats because he possessed an astuteness many underestimated.

'Is that it?' he prodded. 'Or is your penchant for mental chess hoping this would lead elsewhere?'

Ali delivered another of his rare wry smiles and shrugged. 'Some situations need a definitive check or checkmate. I'm merely facilitating an avenue for closure if it's required.'

Closure.

A fancy term peddled by psychologists for those too weak to put their problems behind them.

But...*had* he moved on? Was this unasked for but perhaps opportune situation what he needed to lay the despicable set of events to rest once and for all so he could pursue another subject his advisors were feverishly interested in—the task of picking a bride, producing heirs and fully securing his place as the ruler of Jukrat?

Tahir jerked to a stop when he realised he was pacing; he'd prowled from his desk to the far side of his impressively large office and now stood in front of his father's portrait.

He met the stern-faced, steely eyes of the previous sovereign of Jukrat, an unforgiving man who'd ruled with an equally unforgiving hand. A man who'd never given quarter, never mind suffering fools gladly, even when that fool was his own firstborn son.

Would his father approve of the decision slowly unspooling in Tahir's mind? Or would he see it as another display of the gross error of judgment he'd scathingly condemned him for twelve years ago?

Ali's throat cleared. 'Sire? Do you have instructions for me?'

Closure.

Now the word was seared onto his brain, there was no shaking it free. He hadn't asked for nor desired this particular creature to wander into his lair. But would he be an even bigger fool to let her slip away? To let this wrong go unanswered?

His father might have disparaged him for what Tahir had let happen, but from that time to this, no such slurs had dared crossed the lips of friends or foes alike because he'd lived an exemplary life steeped in a single-minded dedication to duty, shrewd alliances and rigid personal discipline.

Yet somewhere deep within his own psyche the incident chafed, like a burr he'd been unable to root out despite his best efforts.

So…

No, came the bracing answer. He could not let this go unanswered.

'Cancel my remaining appointments. And bring Lauren Winchester to me.'

Tahir wasn't sure what he'd expected in the woman he hadn't seen in a dozen years. Precisely because he'd trained himself never to dwell on Lauren Winchester.

What confronted him ten minutes later, when the tall,

sveltely shaped woman was ushered into his presence, was at once disturbing and curiously even more *charged* than their first meeting.

The first thing he noticed was that she was the worse for wear for having camped outside his palace gates purportedly for days. Her pale peach knee-length dress was smudged with dirt and the dark gold hair she'd once worn in tumbling waves was tamed now, half hidden beneath the white scarf she'd wrapped loosely over her head and shoulders.

The second searingly visceral thing he noticed was that—the first observation notwithstanding—Lauren Winchester hadn't lost an iota of her allure. If anything, she was more stunning.

Features once caught in the final flushes of girlhood had blossomed into true womanhood, her heart-shaped face with more pronounced cheekbones drawing attention to the worldliness and intelligence that sparked in her eyes.

When his focus dropped to her mouth, Tahir had to clench his gut against the impact of its sensual curve. Pale pink lips tinted with the faintest hint of gloss, which might as well have been painted the deepest scarlet for all the punch it packed, for all the memories it fired through him as he lingered there.

But above all those significant changes, it was the final thing that disturbed him the most.

She was...*contained* where once she'd been effervescent, bursting with youthful outrage and unquenchable passion. There was a guardedness about her that he knew instinctively went deeper than the warranted trepidation filming the eyes locked on his.

It was as if the wattage of her illumination had been turned down.

Deliberately? Self-inflicted or by another's hand?

He pursed his lips. What did he care?

He remained motionless, as steely eyed as his father's portrait before him as he watched the woman who'd betrayed him cross the expanse of his official domain, the seat of his power and the space within which he reminded himself daily to be a better man than he'd been twelve years ago.

She stopped at the respectable, reverent distance he knew would've been drilled into her. These days, very few people were granted access, never mind allowed to get within touching distance of His Majesty, the Sheikh of Jukrat. He was the ruler who'd taken the passable province his great-grandfather had painstakingly nurtured, and his grandfather and father had then wielded into a respectable state, so that he, Tahir, could elevate it into a formidable, globally recognised and revered sheikhdom.

To drive home that unassailable fact, Tahir remained behind his desk.

Waited until those eyes that had once hypnotised him with their many mesmerising shades of green travelled up from the priceless Jukrat woven rug on which she stood, to meet his.

Waited until those plump, sinfully curved lips parted on a short breath. Then, 'Hello, Ta…um… Your Majesty.'

Every muscle in Tahir's body clenched tight, the fire racing through his veins as unwelcome as it was acutely disturbing.

At least one thing hadn't changed.

Her voice still held the husky, melodic texture, like the dark honeyed, far too rich and deceptively potent drink his mother had loved. Like the deep, hypnotic tones of a distant bell he wanted to ignore but found himself anticipating nevertheless, a part of him breathlessly poised for the next toll. And the next.

That involuntary reaction further irritated him, enough to make his fingers press deeper into the rich polished wood of his antique desk. To make him conscious of every exhale in the effort to rid himself, immediately, of the weakening sensation.

When a full minute went by without him responding, because he hadn't invited her to be sociable, she went a shade paler, then forced herself to speak again. 'Thank you so much for seeing me.'

'Don't thank me too quickly, Miss Winchester. I may have brought you here just for the pleasure of telling you to go to hell.' His voice, thankfully, was chilled enough to freeze an impressive swathe of his beloved Jukrat Desert.

Her eyes widened in alarm before they swept away, back to the floor.

In any other woman, Tahir would've taken that look for awe and reverence, for appreciation of his station and power.

But unless Lauren Winchester had undergone a personality transplant, he knew it was a false, calculated move. Born of subterfuge? Of desperation? Or even again, a deliberate erasure of a fundamental part of who she'd once been?

Why that thought grated something rigid and knotted inside him, Tahir refused to dwell on.

The slick appearance of her tongue, wetting her lips, focused him far too viciously on what it'd felt like to kiss those lips. To plunder until they both groaned with desire.

'I hope you don't.'

'Why?' he bit out, willing his body's rude, primal awakening under control.

'Because I had to come. I had no choice.'

Now *this* he understood. This argument he could dispense with easily. As Sheikh, he lived with a daily balance of choices. 'Of course you did. Good or bad. Wise or foolish. There's always a choice. Presenting yourself at my palace gates was risky. Presenting yourself before me now is stupendously foolish.'

A look flashed through her eyes and his muscles reacted again, this time with memory, as if rousing themselves in recognition of an old friend.

Except this woman wasn't a friend. She was *Delilah*.

She'd carefully cultivated his weakness—an intelligent, fiercely forward-thinking woman with a breathtaking, traffic-stopping body—and used it against him, then tossed him to the lions without a second thought.

'I… I tried emailing. I also tried calling.'

Tahir's lips twisted. 'That is either an outright lie or you were purposefully vague enough not to have been taken seriously by my palace staff.'

He suspected the latter. 'I couldn't say what I wanted…' She paused, took a deep breath, and Tahir willed his gaze not to drop lower to her chest. To the supple breasts he'd once cupped in his hands, those pale pink nipples he'd feasted on like a starving man granted a feast that would sate for a while but never fully satisfy, making him a slave to his lusts. *To her.* 'This matter is private,' she finished.

He ignored the sharp curiosity her response triggered. Curiosity was what had led him down the path to near-destruction twelve years ago.

'Tell me, Miss Winchester, does your Queen invite strangers in who turn up at her front gates demanding to speak to her?'

She flinched at his formal address. Then her lips, *still* sumptuous, *still* far too distracting, pursed. 'Of course not. But like I said, I had no choice.'

'You could've left. Returned to whatever hole you crawled out of.'

She gripped the strap of her handbag until her knuckles turned white, her nostrils quivering as she inhaled slowly. 'I couldn't,' she whispered urgently. 'This is important.'

He ignored the effort it took to stop her words from sneaking beneath his armour. But he managed it...*just*. 'My great-grandfather was assassinated by one of his subjects invited in from the palace gates. Did you know that?'

Her head shot up, eyes widening, her gaze direct and curious. 'What? No, I...didn't. I'm...sorry—'

'Oh, yes. My mother, too, came close to an unfortunate brush with harm by believing all her subjects were benign creatures she could indulge at her whim. She was cuddling a subject's infant when the attempt on her life was made. So you see how pandering to random strangers who turn up at my palace gates is ill-advised?'

She sucked in a quick, affronted breath and swiftly shook her head. 'I'd never... I wouldn't do such a thing! Surely you know that?'

'Do I? What I know is that the last time we were together, you betrayed me and walked away without a backward glance. True or false?'

Her lips were no longer thinned in outrage. They parted as she attempted to suck in a breath. Her face was devoid of colour and her eyes were dark pools of false shock as she stared at him. 'I... I'm... I can explain—'

'True. Or. False?' he demanded; his throat raw with emotions he could barely contain.

Again, she shook her head. Denying him or denying herself? 'I'm sorry.' Hushed words, whispered into the chilled silence of his regal domain.

He took his time strolling to her, needing every nanosecond to grapple his emotions under control. A dozen feet away, he stopped. 'Look at me,' he ordered, every right bestowed on him as the ruler of his prosperous kingdom throbbing in his voice and brooking no disobedience.

Slowly, her head lifted, her lushly fringed eyelashes. Then those green pools were snagging him again, luring him into their endless depths. He resisted. Because he was no longer the clueless fool he'd once been.

And Tahir Al-Jukrat took pleasure in uttering the three simple words. 'Apology *not* accepted.'

Her throat moved in a swallow and for a flash of a second, Tahir mourned the vibrant woman who'd gone toe to toe with him; their intensely stimulating conversations lasting well into the early hours of the morning, when the only thing that'd worn them out further was the marathon sex culminating it.

Despising the heat billowing freely inside him at the memory, he folded his arms and pierced her with another look.

'I understand that you're angry—'

'You do, do you? Or are you merely trotting out platitudes in the hopes that I'll be placated long enough to listen to whatever reason has brought you here? What is it? A bureaucratic favour of some sort? I'm assuming you followed your passion and went into the public sector?'

He prided himself for having never once been tempted enough to look her up. Lauren Winchester had taken far too much real estate in his head during his year-long internment in the desert for him to waste further time on her once his punishment was complete, especially with his father's disappointment branded into his soul. No, his time was better spent pursuing the goal he'd temporarily lost track of—following his forebears' footsteps and cementing the foundations needed to become the sovereign ruler of his beloved kingdom as his destiny dictated.

'Yes, I did…in a way.'

He resisted the urge to ask what she meant, focusing when she spoke again.

'But I'm not here on my own behalf.'

Several turbulent emotions spiralled through him, making him wonder if perhaps he should've reconsidered this meeting. Because he seemed patently ill-equipped to deal with the notion that she hadn't come here to beg his forgiveness. Or even seek an audience with him on her own behalf.

She was here…*for someone else.*

His gaze dropped to her fingers. Her *ringless* fingers. But the observation did nothing to ease his agitation. Lauren Winchester not displaying conventional signs of matrimony didn't mean she hadn't beguiled another unsuspecting fool.

Tahir recalled her family circumstances. A set of arrogant parents, especially a father whose lofty cabinet minister position he bandied about like a threat. A younger brother who believed the sun rose and set on his good looks and upper-class connections. He'd been frequently stunned at how different Lauren had turned out compared to her family.

Only to discover she'd been better at hiding her true nature…

Now she was here. To seek a favour for a lover? A husband? Someone significant enough to merit a three-day sit-in at his palace gates when he, Tahir, had only received a callous dismissal?

Wrestling the bitter memories back under his iron-willed control, he made the *other* snap decision he should've made when Ali informed him of his visitor's identity. To place this woman firmly back in his past where she belonged.

'You and I have no business together, Miss Winchester.

You'll be escorted out of my palace. I strongly recommend you do not return.'

She gasped, her eyes growing wide and imploring as Tahir pressed the intercom to summon Ali. The sound of the doors opening promptly made her take a single, desperate step towards him.

'I beg you to hear me out.'

He directed a grim smile at her. 'I suggest you do not come any closer. My security turns rabid at such behaviour.'

She froze and, somewhere deep within him, he experienced a sliver of satisfaction that was infuriatingly snuffed out instantly by disquiet.

And then that emotion too whittled away as her chin rose, scornful fire sparking in her eyes. 'So you truly only brought me here to waste my time?' she sniped.

He shrugged. 'I don't need to explain myself to you, Miss Winchester. I had five minutes to toss away on someone I once knew. Those five minutes are over. As for wasting your time, you were already doing that at my palace gates, were you not?'

She opened her mouth but Ali's appearance at her side and the ever-alert guards just inside the door effectively silenced her.

But those eyes…those expressive, unforgettable green eyes that were alive now she'd decided to shed her trepidation continued to spear daggers into him.

Rousing something to life inside him.

A unique, white-hot blaze she alone had been able to create within him. Tahir had searched for that spark with other women over the years. With each failure, he'd resented its creator and its absence even more.

As he watched her now every cell in his body seemed poised for her next reaction. Waited for her clever tongue to cut him down. Instead, she deflated with whatever weighed her down.

'Please. Ta… Your Majesty.'

Please.

More than her disingenuous *I'm sorry*, this word gave him pause.

Hadn't he promised himself during that interminable year in the desert that one day he would hear her beg for his mercy as she was doing now?

But it wasn't enough. What this woman had put him through, everything he'd lost—respect, integrity, his father's pride in him, the ridicule of his peers, even his mother's fiscal quid pro quo version of affection, something he'd never thought he'd miss until even that was denied him—had been because she'd refused to utter a few, simple, *truthful* words…

'Your Majesty, it is time,' Ali said into the charged silence.

Tahir's gaze shifted to his aide and read the speculation in the older man's eyes. He didn't answer. He stepped away from his desk and, without a word to either of them, strode out of his office.

Tense seconds later, he heard her hesitant footsteps. Then they picked up speed as he lengthened his stride towards his private quarters.

With one simple gesture, Tahir knew he could have her removed. But the cloying need to hear more of that begging, to salve the wound she'd torn open with her presence, stayed his hand.

Ali, clutching his infernal leather-bound file, strode alongside him. 'The helicopter is ready to take you north, Your Majesty,' he murmured.

'Good,' Tahir clipped out.

'Will you be staying the whole two weeks, as previously arranged?' he asked, casting a speaking glance over his shoulder.

Tahir's teeth gritted. 'Nothing has changed.'

'Very good, Your Majesty. In that case, the meetings with the region heads will proceed as scheduled tomorrow. Then in the evening you have…'

Tahir half listened as Ali droned on, his ears maddeningly pricked to the other set of footsteps following him. She would be stopped soon enough.

No one was permitted entry into his private quarters or anywhere in the east wing of his palace without his express permission. And he had no intention of giving it, he reassured himself as he turned down another hallway that led outside to where the royal helicopter waited.

'Wait! You can't… I'm with…him. With His Majesty,' he heard her stutter in a rush as she was predictably detained.

Tahir continued walking, welcoming the blaze of the sun on his skin when he stepped onto the flat stone concourse that abutted the immaculate lawn of his private residence, and willing it to eclipse the blaze and disquiet spiralling within him.

When his pilot gave a brisk salute, Tahir nodded his readiness.

Then, over the rising sound of the rotors, he heard her. 'Please! Your Majesty, wait! I need your help to save my brother!'

And he froze.

Lauren had learned early on in life never to show weakness.

To do so was to open herself up to cruel ridicule. From her father. From her brother. With her mother looking on and not saying much in her daughter's defence. When a tearful Lauren had demanded to know the reason behind their treatment, her mother had merely shrugged and clipped out, 'Life is tough, Lauren. Learn to grow a thick skin or you'll always be a target.'

She'd been eleven. That was the last time she remembered crying.

Two decades on, with four menacing guards barring her from Tahir Al-Jukrat's fast-receding figure, she was at grave risk of succumbing to tears.

She'd known this trip wouldn't be easy.

Patches of her shoulders and back were raw from sunburn, her throat was parched—her water bottle having dried up hours ago. Her clothes were sticky with sweat and dirt, and her feet throbbed from standing outside the palace gates for three sun-baked days in a row.

The harsh lessons taught by her unforgiving father were what had hardened her spine long enough for her to remain at the gates, to keep making her hourly requests until they'd been heeded.

Until moments ago, when the last of her reserves had been depleted.

Well…that and the obscure threats that had followed her for twelve years. The suspicion that her father knew more than he'd let on about what had happened with Tahir. Wasn't above holding another scandal over her head to make her toe his line.

Watching Tahir stride towards the helicopter in preparation to fly goodness knew where, she'd felt the last whispers of hope drifting away like dandelion seeds blowing in the wind.

Her desperation-soaked voice had stopped him in his tracks.

But that meant nothing. She'd hoped to ease herself into her reason for being in Jukrat. To calmly state her reason for planting herself outside his palace gates, guilefully insisting that they'd be wise not to turn her away because the

Sheikh would want to see her, until his guards had had no choice but to relay her request to a higher authority.

All this could mean nothing because Tahir had despised Matt long before he'd come to despise her. Her brother's indolent, entitled attitude to university life in particular, and to life in general, had grated on the intelligent, focused and ruthlessly hardworking Prince Tahir.

Even back then, the dynamic prince who'd taken her breath away from their first meeting had held a set of values and rigid beliefs that'd secretly awed her. Those values had been in direct contrast to Matt's, who'd believed in skating through life on family connections and cronyisms.

In fact, hadn't Tahir condemned her whole family to hell that unforgettable night when the Winchesters had closed ranks against him? When she'd let herself be talked into taking *the only option for the family*?

Self-loathing swelled inside her as she watched tension vibrate in his shoulders, watched the muscles in Tahir's neck stand out as he absorbed what she'd said.

Lauren would've given a limb not to be standing here surrounded by menacing-looking men, at the mercy of the Most Revered Sheikh of Jukrat, as one of his many titles loftily proclaimed him.

But her father's Save-Matt-or-Else had given her little choice, despite all signs pointing to her brother's guilt.

Her family was her cross to bear.

Perhaps it came from being adopted by parents who'd believed they could never have children naturally, only to discover a year after adopting Lauren that their miracle, much-longed-for biological child was on the way. From knowing, deep down in her soul, she'd never felt as if she belonged. She knew it was why, as a child, she'd gone the extra mile to prove she was worthy of the Winchesters' choice when they'd plucked her out of dozens of care-home babies. To gift her an enviably wealthy and comfortable life, with every advantage at her fingertips. Advantage Lauren had been careful not to squander.

She'd repaid their choice by being a dutiful daughter, an exemplary student, even a stellar professional when her father had steered her—that thinly veiled but ever present 'or else' hanging over her head—into giving up the career she'd foreseen for herself.

While she deeply resented the threat, it was for that child who still craved a family—a desire she hadn't quite been able to abandon—that she'd swallowed her trepidation and shame to come here. Face the man she'd wronged.

Eyes glued to his back, terrified he would start walking again, leaving her to the mercy of his guards, she opened her mouth to plead once more.

Without turning, Tahir gave clipped instructions in Arabic to his aide. The older man nodded and approached the pilot, whose gaze swung to Tahir, then sprang out of his seat.

Lauren watched Tahir slide into the pilot's seat, her last shred of hope plummeting to the marble terrace beneath her feet. When the whirring rotors began to spin faster, she blinked back tears. She was mentally preparing telling her parents she'd failed when the aide approached her.

A nod at the bodyguards had them stepping back, but she didn't fool herself into thinking they wouldn't react if she so much as moved a muscle.

Her gaze met the dark eyes of Tahir's aide as he stopped in front of her. 'If you wish to continue this meeting with His Majesty, you should get on the aircraft, Miss Winchester,' he said in a carefully neutral voice.

Her mouth gaped. 'What?'

He tilted his head almost regally towards the chopper. 'I suggest you do so now, before he takes off.'

Lauren's gaze darted to Tahir, who was cycling through his pre-departure procedure, eyes glued to the controls, competent fingers flicking switches. Completely and utterly ignoring her. 'I…where is he going?' she enquired around a desert-dry throat.

The aide regarded her steadily. 'Does it matter?'

Three pertinent, terrifying words.

She swallowed again, desperately suppressing her anxiety as she clung to that last seedling of hope. Clutching her purse tighter, as if it would save her from the unknown, she sucked in a breath and sprinted past the aide.

The evicted pilot stood by the rear door. When she reached him, he stepped aside to let her enter the rear compartment.

Lauren boarded. He slid in beside her and slammed the door shut.

And between one breath and the next, the helicopter was airborne.

CHAPTER TWO

LAUREN COULDN'T SEE Tahir because the compartment was cut off from the cockpit. It was deliberate, she knew. He'd switched places with his pilot because he hadn't wanted to share the space with her.

Lauren tried not to let the knowledge burn or take anything personally. The sole reason she was here was to plead for Matt. Nothing else.

At least she had a sliver of a shot remaining.

The pilot's rigidly neutral look suggested he wouldn't be forthcoming to any questions from her, so she contented herself with staring out of the window.

Yanira, Jukrat's capital city, was spread out in a wondrous splendour of shiny ultra-modern and traditional: spectacular ancient mosques with large golden domes juxtaposed with soaring skyscrapers, and the sparkling, sandy white beaches that bordered the realm to the south.

Nestled snugly between its larger neighbours of Saudi Arabia, UAE, and the Kingdom of Riyaal, the oil-rich Kingdom of Jukrat, while small in geographic size, enjoyed the same opulent status as its compatriots.

Had she been here under different auspices, she would've taken time to explore; delighted in taking her first holiday for over five years. Escaping her father's stranglehold on every corner of her life and the increasing pressure of fitting into the mould he was determined to push her into alone would've been worth it.

But she couldn't. Somewhere in the city below her, her brother was in dire straits. Despite her father's warning, and despite the fact that she'd never got her younger brother to warm to her, to forge the type of sibling bond she'd yearned for as a child, she couldn't turn her back on Matt.

Her eyes burned, from the long flight from England, lack of sleep and the emotions churning within her. Her last phone call to her parents yesterday hadn't gone well. They'd been disappointed at her lack of progress.

Lauren had felt an unfamiliar sprig of anger. No, that wasn't quite accurate. Lately, offshoots of frustration-laced anger had taken her unawares, the calm poise she'd practised for years around her parents developing hairline fractures.

Certainly, their cavalier assumption that Tahir, the man they'd forced her to shun, would hear her out had knotted fury inside her. Anger she struggled to shake off. Except she had to. She couldn't fail.

The aircraft banked sharply. Her stomach dropped for terrifying seconds before the chopper adjusted. And she saw where they were headed. Lauren swallowed the apprehension rising once more, her gaze glued to the mesmerising expanse of dark gold sand.

The connotations of their destination didn't let her dwell on one of nature's most beautiful creations.

Tahir was taking her into the desert.

A shiver danced up her spine, bringing with it rising despair.

She wasn't a damsel in distress. Never had been. But the sense of utter helplessness, of being completely at Tahir's mercy, sank into her like a rock in a pond. She had to cling onto the belief that the man she'd known twelve years ago hadn't completely changed.

Despite what you did?

Guilt scythed through her, tightening her fists in her lap, even as she held onto the thin hope that Tahir hadn't turned her away. Yet.

But what if he did?

She pursed her lips. She'd fight that battle if it arrived.

She was affirming that to herself when specks of white dotted the sandy vista. Rapt by the sheer, deadly beauty of the desert, she watched the specks turn into a large sprawl of Bedouin tents, varying in size from small, individual camping-sized ones to some large enough to house several families. Each one had their highest points tipped in the same gold she'd seen in Jukrati mosques and temples.

Brought back down to earth by their landing, she watched a group rush towards the aircraft, hands raised in rapturous greeting of their Sheikh.

On a wild frantic whim, she fished out her phone. Stared in stomach-dropping dread at the no signal icon displayed on the screen.

The sound of the door opening drew her attention to Tahir as he stepped out to greet his people.

Laser-sharp eyes zeroed in on her, dragging up a foreboding shiver.

None of her family or friends knew her exact whereabouts.

She might have boarded his helicopter of her own free will, but in doing so she'd placed herself completely at the mercy of Tahir bin Halim Al-Jukrat.

The man she'd wronged so devastatingly twelve years ago.

Tahir watched her over the heads of his subjects, the thought he'd had en route, that he should've left her on the helipad, slowly morphing into a shrewder plan.

The initial reason he hadn't had her escorted out of his kingdom was because he'd been curious. That note in her voice...

Desperation.

The kind he'd experienced once upon a time. When he'd been in her position. When he'd pleaded for her support.

And she'd turned her back on him.

But that had given way to something else.

The greater need for retribution. He'd thought he resented her being here on someone else's behalf rather than on her own quest for his forgiveness. He despised her even more that that person was her self-absorbed brother.

His lips twisted as he gazed over the endless dunes of Zinabir, his home for the next two weeks. The soaring cream-coloured tents with their gleaming gold turrets he'd flown over should've calmed him.

He'd been looking forward to swimming in the clear lake nestled beneath his favourite mountain at his final destination; to the whispered seduction of the wind weaving through the dunes at dawn.

Instead, he was submerged in the chaotic emotions only this woman evoked in him. But...no matter. She'd handed him the perfect opportunity to settle their past once and for all. Perhaps it was even karmic that it happened here, with the very tools his grandfather had taught him with.

He smiled grimly and took satisfaction in watching her eyes widen. Took satisfaction in watching her pink tongue slick over her bottom lip, that nervous tic dragging heat to his groin.

Oh, yes, Lauren Winchester would definitely rue stepping into his web.

Charged emotion pulsing through him as his plan unfurled, he raised an eyebrow at her, daring her to take up his silent challenge.

She remained in the helicopter, frozen in her seat, not exactly prey because Lauren Winchester, no matter how much she'd changed, would never be a victim. But the look in her eyes said she knew she was at his mercy.

A primitive sort of pleasure wove through him, settling his intentions into his bones with satisfaction he hadn't felt in a long time.

He saw the moment she took note of it.

Her nostrils flared in peril-scenting. Had he been close enough, he suspected he would've seen the pulse fluttering at her throat.

Fight or flight tension held her in its talons. Except flight was no longer an option. By boarding his aircraft and allowing herself to be flown across an arid and unforgiving desert, she'd sealed her fate. And the truth was hitting home. Hard.

As he indulged in the sights and sounds of the familiar, his brain considered just what had brought her here.

Did it even matter? Twelve years of silence, then appearing when she needs something. Just like Mother—

'So, you brought a guest?' The head of the nomadic Zinabir clan and one of his regional advisors enquired, mercifully drawing Tahir from the bitter thought of his mother.

Without removing his gaze from Lauren, he answered, ignoring the curiosity in the older man's words. 'It was an unavoidable situation.'

'And is this *situation* to remain in the aircraft for the duration of your stay or do you wish her relocated?' Faint amusement now laced the old man's words. 'To your quarters, perhaps?'

The knot in Tahir's gut hardened.

Once upon a time, he would've given those very instructions, would've taken pleasure in introducing this woman to this part of his kingdom. He would've relished seeing her interact with his people.

Then when they were sated with food and wine and healthy debate, he would've taken pleasure in seeing her spread out on the priceless Jukrati rug that decorated the foot of his wide divan bed, her eyes wide and her body open and willing as they pleasured one another.

Perhaps thereafter, he would've sought out her thoughts on his way of life and his rule—the ways favoured by his grandfather that blended a modern parliamentary system with regional semi-autonomy that his own father hadn't favoured. Ironically, it was spending time in the desert that had prompted Tahir into returning to that system when he ascended the throne. A way he'd discovered was welcomed and actually worked.

So, perhaps Lauren was to be credited—

No. He halted that train of thought in its tracks, dragged his gaze from her to address his advisor. 'Have her shown to the guest tent and meet me in the council tent.'

'As you wish, My Sheikh.'

Striding away, he headed for one of the larger tents to the north of the oasis.

Lauren Winchester would be dealt with soon enough.

Lauren breathed a sigh of relief an hour later once the cheery women left and she was alone in the tent.

Those wild, curiously excitable minutes earlier when she'd clashed gazes with Tahir still hadn't subsided. On the contrary, with each passing second, she felt as if the invisible sword of Damocles were swinging closer, and not even her usual pragmatism had grounded her.

That gaze had spelled out that he had a plan for her. One that most likely had nothing to do with her own reasons for being here…

From the avid stares and whispered, lyrical Arabic she'd been subjected to, it was clear Tahir hadn't divulged why she was here.

The last thing her parents wanted was for Matt's situation to be made public. Not that it could be kept a secret for ever, she thought bleakly.

She went to the low coffee table where her bag sat. With more hope than expectation, she pulled out her phone and touched the screen.

As expected, the bars were flat, phone signal non-existent. She couldn't get in touch with her parents yet, but she could compose her thoughts and jot down everything that'd happened so far, starting with her arrival in Jukrat. That way the moment she got the service returned, she could set the information wheel in motion.

And while she was at it, she could draft a few speeches for when Matt's predicament became public knowledge.

As communications adviser and special aide to her father, it was what she was good at, after all.

Crossing one of the four exquisitely woven floor rugs, she perched on the edge of the low divan. She was in the middle of composing her thoughts when she sensed his keen scrutiny.

Her head snapped up.

He stood tall and proud; laser-beam eyes fixed squarely on her.

Lauren scrambled upright, more disturbed by being the subject of his regard while sprawled all over the divan than by apprehension of his presence. Especially when they were alone. And the air hummed with emotional undercurrents she didn't really want to examine.

Her gaze darted to the tent opening, and the outline of a guard just beyond the doorway.

'I wasn't aware knocking wasn't a thing in Jukrat.'

She was sure she'd imagined the faintest twitch of his lips when his stern facade hardened a second later. 'Technically there are no doors to the tents. But my presence was announced. You didn't respond,' he stated imperiously.

'So you just let yourself in?'

His nostrils flared the tiniest fraction and his gaze flicked to the sterling silver Moorish tea set and tray of untouched refreshments set on the table on the other side of the tent. 'Hydration in the desert is essential. Disregarding it is foolish. Why have you not eaten or drunk anything?' he growled.

She started to shrug then winced when her sunburnt shoulder chafed beneath the scarf still tangled around her shoulders. 'I didn't have an appetite.'

His gaze dropped to the phone. 'Feeling separation anxiety from your social media?'

Her lips firmed, even though something inside her shrivelled at the confirmation that he'd never believed she hadn't sold him out to the tabloids. 'No. But I would like mobile service…if it's possible.'

'Why?'

'Because there are people waiting to hear from me.'

His gaze grew a touch icier, his body stiffening further. 'Such as?'

She licked her lips, unsure why she felt as if a lot rested on the answer to this particular question. 'My parents? Matt?' The ice receded a little but not enough to make her breathe easier. When he merely continued to watch her, she cleared her throat. 'But now you're here, can we talk?'

'I'd rather not engage with you while the threat of dehydration looms.'

Before she could take proper stock of what he was doing, he was striding to the antique desk set in one corner of her tent. The bell he picked up rang only twice before a young man entered. He relayed instructions and the servant nodded with a smile and hurried away.

'What was that all about?'

He poured a glass of water, strode back, and held it out to her. 'Drink.'

Her lips pressed tight. 'I'm aware I'm here by your favour but I really wish you wouldn't toss commands at me like I'm a dog,' she snapped.

'We all wish for things we can't have, Miss Winchester. I don't wish for your foolishness in not taking care of yourself properly to inconvenience me. If you pass out from dehydration or heatstroke, it would be most unwelcome. Drink.'

Put like that, and accepting how parched she was, Lauren took the glass from him, extremely careful not to touch him in the process.

As he'd made stingingly clear, there were some things she had choices about. Igniting the spark that had flared to life so effortlessly between them every time they'd so much as breathed the same air twelve years ago wasn't a theory she wanted to test again. Because she suspected the results would be staggering.

Unwilling to meet those mesmeric eyes, she looked around, secretly seeking signs of a woman's presence.

Tahir was purportedly single. But single didn't mean he wasn't involved with a woman. As her body seemed determined to keep reminding her, he was virile, a pillar of masculinity who could probably satisfy a dozen women without breaking a sweat—

No. She absolutely wasn't going to think about his virility. Or his charisma. Or the way his body had moved within hers with power, pleasure, and mastery once upon a time.

'Is there a reason you're staring into the water instead of drinking it?' he drawled lazily.

She jumped, silently cursing when the liquid sloshed

over her fingers. Averting her gaze because she didn't want to see his mockery at her clumsiness, she transferred the glass to her other hand, and started to shake her soaked hand. Only to startle again when firm hands grasped hers, a handkerchief appearing from nowhere.

And as she'd feared, she had her confirmation.

Fireworks shot through her bloodstream, dancing along her nerve endings with gleeful abandon, uncaring that they'd robbed her of breath. Uncaring that she had to grit her teeth to bite back the tiny moan that crowded the back of her throat. That her nipples and very sex had grown tight with a need only he had been able to trigger in her.

Damn him.

He seemed in no hurry to dry her fingers. His gaze was low and hooded, fixated on dragging the rich linen over her knuckles.

'Drink, Lauren.' The order was low. Thick. Implacable.

She lifted the glass and drank. Every last drop. Welcomed the quenching of her thirst and kicked herself for being unable to resist his effect on her. When she was done, he took the glass, his eyes pinned on her as he deliberately trailed his fingers over hers, as blatant at touching her as she'd been careful to do the opposite. His very gaze dared her to object, to protest how much he affected her.

She pressed her lips together, fighting the blaze searing inside her while projecting cool composure.

Lauren wasn't sure who won their battle of wills. But abruptly, he dropped her hand, took her glass and refilled it.

'Slower this time,' he intoned deeply again.

The rumbling-thunder voice sent sensation skittering over her body. She tried to ignore it but, with him standing so close, avoiding Tahir was impossible.

His scent filled her nostrils, reminding her how much she'd loved tracing her fingers over his warm skin, trailing her nose over it to inhale his very essence into her being. Lauren would've happily condemned her younger self for being silly and naive if the thirty-year-old version weren't suddenly struck with the very same yearning. If every molecule in her body weren't straining towards the unholy gleam in his eyes.

To counter that insane urge, she took a gulp of water, set the glass down and laced her fingers in front of her. It was a composure-harnessing technique she'd found useful lately, when the challenges of maintaining serenity in the face of her father's demands had worn her down. 'Ta— Your Majesty, I'd be grateful if you would let me discuss my matter with you.'

His lips flattened. For an interminable age, he simply stared at her.

Then, pivoting again, he went to the living area and, with the grace of the birds of prey revered in Jukrat, lowered himself onto the seat.

There he sprawled, like the supreme leader he was, his muscled arms thrown wide across the log-shaped cushions, and nudged an imperious chin at her. 'Very well,' he intoned.

Unexpectedly granted her wish, Lauren was temporarily stumped. Because it struck her then that within five minutes her audience with Tahir might be over. She would leave here with his offer to help or without it. Either way, she would…leave. Never see him again.

Why that thought suddenly dried her mouth while shoving a lump into her throat, she shied away from examining. But the answer arrived anyway, and with a force so unstoppable, she struggled to suppress the gasp that ejected from her lungs.

She'd…*missed* him.

Her breath shook out of her, the fingers meshing and

tightening as she grappled with the unbearable truth. All these years she'd suppressed memories of him. Mostly out of shame. But also, out of every might-have-been she hadn't allowed herself to savour.

Because she hadn't deserved even that.

'Are you going to speak or am I to decipher your request telepathically?'

Heat crept up her face for staring at him for so long. She averted her gaze, fervently praying she hadn't given away her emotions while she'd gaped at him.

'Matt needs your help.'

Another chill wave swept over his already taut features, but his eyes continued to burn as he stared at her. 'I gathered that. What does the Winchester golden boy need now? A lucrative deal he's unable to land? Or one he's unable to get out of? I recall he was always one to hastily embrace a too-good-to-be-true venture and regret it in the morning? Or is it more personal than that? Has he bedded someone's wife that he shouldn't have?'

Lauren felt every bite of that acid conjecture as if it were aimed at her, not her brother. Although Matt had done each one of those things.

Her brother had been shamelessly spoilt from birth, his position as the treasured child blatantly acknowledged with every transgression excused by parents who couldn't fault their biological child. Lauren had grown up knowing she was a distant second to Matt in every way. Knowledge her brother took pleasure in taunting her with.

She exhaled now, wishing with every bone in her body that she didn't have to say the next words. While knowing she had no choice.

'It's none of that.' It was much, much worse. 'Matt's been arrested here in Jukrat...' She shook her head, unable to finish the shameful sentence.

Slowly he uncoiled from his sprawl, his gaze not once straying from her face as he rearranged himself, his arms braced on his knees. 'Let me get this straight. Your brother is in trouble in my kingdom. And you came here seeking leniency for him. The same brother who treats you like a second-class citizen? The same brother you colluded with to throw me under the bus twelve years ago?'

If her mouth had been dry before, it turned into a desolate desert at each stinging indictment that fell from his lips.

'I'm aware we need to discuss what happened twelve years ago. To clear the air—'

'Are you? How very magnanimous of you,' he stated. 'A whole dozen years too late.' His tone was cold enough to drag shivers over her skin.

Lauren had withstood a lot in her life, not least her father's constant judgment, rancour, and emotional blackmail. She'd somehow found the inner strength to rise above. To hold her chin up and plough forward.

But Tahir's scathing censure, and the knowledge that she deserved the sharp razor's edge of it, was too much to withstand. She lowered her gaze, then shut her eyes. Swallowed.

'I'm sorry,' she murmured. Too weak and far too late. 'For what happened. I know I didn't do enough—'

'You will *not dare* tell me that you had no choice,' he warned through gritted teeth.

She dragged her eyes open, bit back a gasp when she saw that he'd surged up and stood mere feet from her. A pillar of righteous, entirely justified affront with fists clenched, his jaw rock hard as he glared at her.

'I didn't believe I did. Not then.' *And not now*, she added silently.

'No. Have the courage to speak the truth now, Lauren. You itched for the notoriety your brother enjoyed and selfishly brought me along for the ride. And you did so knowing full well you wouldn't suffer the same consequences I would. You knew the potential of disgrace and dishonour for me, for my family, my country and you did it anyway. Am I wrong?'

'Yes, you're wrong. And I… I don't know what to say to make you believe how sorry I am.'

Expecting another scathing put-down, Tahir surprised her by throwing his head back and letting out a bark of laughter.

'In my wildest dreams I didn't think we would find ourselves here, full circle, with the shoe on the other foot,' he said when the laughter died away. His accent had grown thicker, an indication, she recalled, that his emotions were running close to the surface.

He'd sounded like that when in the throes of passion, a reminder that arrived with far too much heat in her body.

'The irony isn't lost on me,' she whispered.

The gleam in his eyes intensified. 'Good. Then something else that shouldn't be lost on you is exactly how this is going to go.'

She shook her head, taking an involuntary step forward before she could help herself. 'I…we don't have to repeat the mistakes of the past. Please, Tahir… I'll do—' She paused, aware she was straying into unwise territory. But it was too late. He'd scented the weakness in her unfinished statement.

He inhaled sharply, his eyes darkening to molten gold. Slowly he inhaled, his body uncoiling like a majestic creature rising from its aeons-long slumber. In his dark golden robes, with those gleaming eyes and commanding presence, he was almost otherworldly.

Against her will, Lauren was utterly transfixed, unable to move as he prowled even closer. When he reached her, he didn't stop. Instead, he circled her, drawing ever nearer until the scent of spice, earth and man saturated her.

On his second circuit, he stopped behind her. 'Go on. Say it,' he murmured softly in her ear. 'Be brave enough to finish that sentence.'

Shivers coursed through her, the gravity of the situation drying her mouth harder and lodging a stone in her throat. Silently she shook her head.

'Shall I say it for you, then? You can deny it if I'm wrong. "I'll do anything." That's what you meant to say, isn't it?'

Digging deep to find her courage, she lifted her chin, fixed her gaze on the exquisite Moorish cabinet on the other side of the room. 'Maybe it was. But I didn't say it.'

'Why not? Because you *won't* do anything to save Matt and avoid scandal for you and your family? That's what this is ultimately about, isn't it? Are you saying there's a line you won't cross?'

Guilt pummelled her at the deep censure in those words. But in the silence thickening around them, she hardened her resolve. Keeping her gaze forward, because she wasn't quite brave enough to face him yet, she answered, 'We should discuss what happened between us twelve years ago. Maybe if we clear the air—'

She froze as he gave another bark of scornful laughter. 'What is there to say? You invited me to your home for a presumed dinner for two when your parents were away and failed to tell me a *special* kind of party was happening right under our noses. And when reports emerged of Prince Tahir being in the same location a booze-filled sex party was happening, you helped things along by providing pictures of us taken on your phone.'

She spun around then, danger be damned, because she needed to say this while looking into his eyes. Even if those eyes threatened to devour and annihilate her at the same time. 'No, I *didn't* help things along. I denied your involvement with that party.'

His jaw gritted. 'Did you? Because you seemed to be curiously unwilling to give a definitive opinion after the fact on how those pictures got into the papers.'

Because even then, she'd suspected who was behind it. Matt had denied it, of course. And her parents had warned her not to implicate her brother without concrete proof. A warning she'd taken to heart because, even back then, she'd seen how ruthless her father could be when crossed. Fear of making things worse for Tahir—because the phone that held those pictures had gone missing, along with texts they'd sent each other—had held her tongue. While the pictures and texts hadn't been overtly graphic, they'd been intimate. Passionate. Deeply personal.

The sort of thing a prince and future king wouldn't want advertised to the world. The sort of thing that caused scandals when it was.

That threat of the unknown—and the knowledge that her father wasn't above using it and other means to keep her in line—had kept her stifled over the years, much to her distress.

It was partly why she was in Jukrat, pleading for Matt, after all.

'I know you don't believe me, but I don't know how they got hold of those photos.' She sighed, the cloak of defeat threatening again. 'I tried to convince them you weren't involved. Please believe me, Tahir.'

His nostrils flared at her mention of his name. She fully expected him to order her to use his title as she'd been strictly directed by his aide. But for good or ill, she yearned to reach the Tahir she'd known back in those heady university days when she'd felt as if the world were her oyster and he were her unicorn, a fantastical myth somehow come to life and seemingly interested in plain old her.

She'd never understood what he saw in her but, by God,

she'd clung to it, treasured every second as if it would be her last. And with a simple error, it had been.

'The Lauren I believed I knew was brave. Bold. Unwavering. She believed in right and wrong.' His eyes narrowed to guillotine-sharp blades.

Except when it came to the murky business of her family. 'I know it sounds naive but... I thought it'd all blow over within days. I didn't know the newspapers would go to those relentless lengths.'

'Oh, but they did. My family lawyers did their job well, but do you realise what those pictures did to my reputation? To my father's reputation? The damage it did to Jukrat in the eyes of the world?'

Lauren felt the blood leave her face as she stared at him. At the time she'd been devastated to discover that Tahir had withdrawn from university following the relentless hounding of the press and the unsavoury things said about him. Moreover, that he'd left without giving her a chance to explain or beg his forgiveness.

And yes, her misjudgement of Matt's activities that night with his friends had been unforgivable, but she'd hoped Tahir would see things from her perspective. That her family's emotional blackmail had been equally unbearable. As usual, they'd believed Matt when he'd pleaded his innocence and Lauren had felt the force of her father's will when he'd pressed her into distancing herself from Tahir and the whole event once the tabloid press had dug their claws into the scandal.

But above all else, the desolation of losing Tahir had made her shut out the world, including tuning out what had happened to him after his departure.

Learning of the true repercussions of the scandal, of what her failure to back Tahir had done to Jukrat's reputation and to the man who'd captivated both her mind and body, had annihilated her.

'I tried to reach out.' She paused, wet her lips. 'A few months after it happened, I tried to contact you.'

His lips twisted in a macabre imitation of a smile. 'Should I tell you where I was? Give you the reason you couldn't reach me?'

She suspected she didn't need to respond. He would give her no quarter in hammering home what damage her actions had caused. So, lips firmed to stop what felt bracingly close to a moan of despair from rising, she watched him exhale long and slow.

'My father was deeply ashamed. He believed I'd let my better instincts be overruled by a woman. He'd taught me better than that, you see. Believed I was above falling prey to feminine beguilement. So when my actions brought disgrace to his rule and this kingdom, I was banished here to the desert for a year.'

This time, the noise escaped her throat, a tiny mournful sound that echoed in the horrible silence trailing his words.

Something kicked hard and true inside her. *Beguilement.*

It was the same thing she'd felt for him, starting with the deep tingling between her shoulders during the environmental symposium. She'd been looking forward to stating her case to so-called world leaders and government officials who overpromised and woefully underdelivered. She'd rehearsed her speech a dozen times and had been confidently ploughing ahead with the debate when she'd felt it.

Felt *him.*

It'd taken every scrape of composure she'd possessed to finish the debate.

Much as it was doing now.

'Here?' She cast a quick glance around her. But she knew the jaw-dropping dreaminess of Zinabir in general, and Tahir's desert abode in particular, the presence of beautiful women and attendants who waited on him hand and foot, would've meant nothing if this wasn't where he'd wanted to be. If every day, he'd been reminded of *why* he was here. Excluded from those he loved because of the shame and scandal she'd helped cause.

All because she'd selfishly wanted a special moment with him. An intimate dinner for two at her home, believing they would be alone. A moment Matt had spectacularly and callously ruined...

Telling him any of it now would sound like feeble excuses.

Too little too late.

His lips thinned. 'Hmm. It started here, in this tent we're in right now. This desert was my prison for three hundred and sixty-five days. It's almost karmic, isn't it, that you're here now? Do you believe in divine justice, Lauren?' he taunted, his voice eerily even.

She wanted to say no. But then she remembered her time with him. Those months between early summer and autumn twelve years ago had been almost transcendental. As much as she wanted to explain it away, the uniqueness of their time together had been too cosmic to reduce to a set of coincidences and pure chemistry.

He'd been the fiercest comet in her sky, blazing a mesmerising trail before he'd disappeared, leaving her looking up for ever, praying for either the sight of him or another sign to tell her he hadn't been that special. That their time together could be replicated with another man in another place.

But it never had been...

'Does it matter whether I do or not?'

His swarthy shoulders lifted in a suave, throwaway

shrug that said he didn't care one way or the other. 'Not particularly. The consequences will be the same.'

Her belly quivered alarmingly. She fought not to let him see how much his response affected her. 'What do you mean by consequences?'

'I mean I'm not the same man I was back then, Miss Winchester. I'm not simply going to permit you to waltz back into my life and let you get away with whatever you wish.'

'You make it sound as if you were a pushover back then. We both know you weren't.' Even then, he'd been a formidable powerhouse and it'd had nothing to do with the constant presence of the two towering bodyguards who'd trailed his movements all over campus. His sharp intelligence, his ability to cut through an argument to the heart of a matter and run masterful mental rings around her in the best possible way had kept her in thrall second only to his breathtaking good looks.

'No.' His gaze conducted a long, searing scrutiny that froze every cubic inch of air in her lungs and raked over her skin like the tines of a tuning fork, rousing every nerve ending to life. 'But I did let myself be distracted by...*base* things far more than was wise.'

'I enthralled you with my body. Is that what you're suggesting?' She'd meant to scoff. And yet the words came out with a traitorous sliver of excitement. Of long-denied yearning.

Yearning he heard, if the sudden gleam in his eyes was an indication.

Before she could exhale, his fingers were laced in her hair, his other hand capturing her waist. He drew her close. And she didn't resist. *Couldn't.* Because from the moment she'd walked into this palace this afternoon, that slumbering yearning had risen to life.

As much as she wanted to deny it, she'd craved this sensation of his body against hers. Of those eyes searing her face, before latching on her lips, the way they'd done countless times. The way that announced in no uncertain terms that he was about to kiss her.

'I'm not *suggesting* anything,' he breathed, his mouth so tantalisingly close that she felt his breath on hers. 'What you did to me was a fact.'

'And you hated every minute of it?' she taunted breathlessly.

One corner of his mouth quirked. 'Fishing for compliments?' Before she could deny it, he rumbled, 'I didn't, but you still proved to be a temptation I should've resisted. I should've shown you then, like now, that it would take more than sex to bring a man like me to my knees.'

'What do you mean…l-like now?'

Before she could cringe at the quivering in her voice, he was slanting his mouth over hers, dominating her senses with a kiss so deep, so hot, it melted her from the inside out.

Dear God. It was everything she'd missed; everything she'd fantasised about in her lonely bed year after year. *Everything.*

His tongue teased and plundered, stroked and suckled, dragging helpless moans from her as her hands latched onto his shoulders. He was warm, vibrant, a pillar of sexy, dogged masculinity she wanted to explore for hours. *Days.*

The hand on her waist moved to her bottom, moulding and squeezing, yanking her closer until the rod of his erection was imprinted against her stomach. Until she was straining even closer, hunger flaying her as she whimpered and succumbed to the decadence of his kiss. Long minutes passed when the only sound in the tent was their feverish exploration.

And then, just as suddenly as he'd taken hold of her, he

was setting her away, his movements far too contained as he decisively stepped away from her.

Lauren swayed, still caught in the heady narcotic of his kiss, even as she grasped his wicked intent. 'So, this was supposed to be some sort of lesson?'

When he merely raised an eyebrow, she tilted her chin, determined not to be cowed. 'Are you trying to convince yourself or me?'

His teeth bared in a devastating smile, one that was all the more lethal for not reaching his eyes. 'I've confirmed everything I need to know.'

'Which is?'

Eyes that weren't as cool as his words lingered on her face. 'That while you're alluring enough, I won't be caught in the same trap again.'

The recrimination, partly directed at himself but mostly aimed at her, finally resurrected a spark of anger. 'If you're suggesting that I did anything to make you...to disrupt your life in any way before that night, you're misremembering, I think. You've always been your own man. We got involved with each other because we both wanted to. I didn't cast any sort of...*spell* on you.'

Again he gave an almost insulting shrug that said her argument carried no weight with him. 'Maybe not. But did you foresee a moment such as this, perhaps? And facilitate easy access to me in case you needed it?'

Her mouth gaped before she could stop herself. 'You cannot be serious!'

'Look at me, Miss Winchester. Do I look in any way amused?'

Staring full on at him was like staring into a raging volcano. Mesmerising and terrifying at the same time. And no, he looked far from amused. 'The idea that I'd culti-vated a relationship with you simply for this purpose isn't only preposterous, I'd have to be a cold-hearted bitch to pull that off!'

'And yet here you are. And the idea isn't that far-fetched, is it? Isn't that what you upper-class set are known for? Public-school cronyism so they can all help each other get away with unconscionable deeds?'

She swallowed at the highly clever way he'd drawn circles around her. Again. Tahir had always had a brilliant mind. But he'd never used it against her in earnest or in battle. Until now.

Lauren felt the ground shifting beneath her and struggled to regain her footing. 'I've apologised for my poor judgment. Are you going to forgive me or not?' she demanded, her brazenness secretly stunning her.

His lips twisted. 'Much like most things in this world, forgiveness needs to be earned. Does an eye for an eye sound fair? One three-hundred-and-sixty-five-day sentence in return for another?'

She swallowed. 'You don't mean that.'

He didn't answer immediately. Instead, he clasped his hands behind his back, strode from one end of the vast tent to the other. What she saw of his profile mildly terrified her. Tahir deep in thought was a truly formidable thing. And if those thoughts were devising punitive measures against her?

Her breath caught when he faced her.

Dull embers were rousing to life in the eyes slowly journeying from the top of her head to the soles of her feet and back up again.

Lauren went hot, then cold. Hot because for a moment her senses had leapt, not recoiled, at the possibility that her punishment would be a repeat of what had just happened. Then cold because she was instantly deeply ashamed of the thought.

The twin sensations lingered, unwilling to be suppressed as he slowly returned to stop before her.

'No. As much as it would please me to hand down such a verdict, we no longer live in barbaric times. And I don't have the time to throw away on such trivial matters. But your task to earn my forgiveness *will* be done another way.'

His proximity worked a different sort of sorcery on her, making her voice tremble when she forced herself to ask, 'How?'

His tawny gaze lingered on her for a few tense seconds before he looked past her. Compelled, Lauren followed his gaze to find him watching the antique clock slowly ticking its way to seven p.m.

'Have your sleeping habits changed?'

Her internal gauge veered wildly towards hot at the question. She opened her mouth to snap that it was none of his business but bit her tongue at the last minute. 'Why are you asking me that?'

'Because if time is of the essence as you insist then you'd much prefer to get this over with as soon as possible, yes?'

She nodded, glad she hadn't told him to go to hell. 'If you're asking me if I still function on a few hours of sleep every night, then yes, my habits are still the same.' She didn't ask him the same question. Didn't want to know whether his had remained the same too, their perfect synchronicity in that department, as in several others, not something she wanted to dwell on.

Because knowing would make it harder?

She shrugged the question away as he pivoted and strode away from her. Before she could move, he was tugging on a tightly woven golden rope. In the distance, she heard the faint, deep echo of a bell.

Seconds later, the young man from before returned. Tahir spoke to him in swift, lyrical Arabic and had the situation been anything other than it was now, she would've indulged her utter fascination with his mother tongue.

Instead, she stood, palms growing clammy and her heart commencing a slow dread-laced thudding as the man nodded and left again.

Alone again he faced her. 'You'll be served dinner now. At midnight you'll be escorted to my quarters. And we will begin.'

CHAPTER THREE

'I SUGGEST YOU get as much sleep as you can. You'll need it.'

Those were Tahir's final tight-edged words before he departed, taking the life force of the atmosphere with him. Still a little dazed by the electric kiss, she'd barely registered the same trio of women from before returning.

That same soup of dread, puzzlement and excitement stirring in her belly had left no room for resentment or irritation as she was led into the sleeping area of her tent.

The scent of bath salts teased her nostrils and, drawn to the scent, Lauren went towards it. Reaching the screen, she gave a soft gasp.

A deep copper claw-footed bath stood in one corner, partially obscured by the beautifully etched wooden frame.

'Would you like your bath now or after dinner?' the oldest of the three women, who'd introduced herself as Basma, asked. The scent of jasmine and eucalyptus filled the tent. The thought of immersing herself in the water, giving herself a few precious moments to sift through what had happened with Tahir, had her waving a hand at the water. 'Bath, please, thanks.'

When Lauren refused help with undressing, Basma smiled and stepped away.

The sensation of the warm water unravelling her knotted muscles released a moan before she could stop it. Inhaling deeply, she rested her head against the high, cushioned lip of the bath and let her eyes drift shut.

Since her arrival in Jukrat four days ago, she'd lived in a state of constant stress about her meeting with Tahir.

The last thing she'd expected was that kiss. The proof that time hadn't immunised her against his visceral impact on her. That a simple touch of his body could create such...*need* in her.

It was good, then, wasn't it, that this had all been some sort of experiment for him? She needn't worry about a repeat performance.

Stubbornly ignoring the hollow in her stomach, she loosened the knot holding her waist-length hair and reaching for the sublime-smelling shampoo, washed and conditioned her hair, then fully submerged herself in the water, willing her thoughts to drift to nothing. At least for a few minutes.

The heavenly smells of flat bread and rich, spice-infused sauces finally forced her out of the bath. With impeccable timing, she'd just slipped on a satin robe and finished drying her hair when Basma appeared.

'Come. Sit. Eat.'

Lauren followed her to a low table set up in front of the seating area, holding a large array of dishes that made her mouth water as she drew closer.

The moment Lauren sank into the seat, Basma started ladling out an assortment of dishes.

'You don't need to do that. I can do it myself...' She trailed off as Basma shook her head.

'You're His Majesty's guest. It is our honour to do this for you.'

Lauren bit the inside of her cheek. If they didn't know why she was here, wouldn't she be compounding her sins by blurting out the reason for her presence?

She devoured the lentil and tomato sauce with flatbread,

saffron-laced rice and lamb cutlets, then topped it off with sugared dates dipped in honey. Her stomach almost protesting how full she was, a yawn caught her unawares as weariness dug into her limbs.

Within seconds, the trays were cleared away. Basma approached with a garment in her hand.

Lauren hurriedly swallowed a mouthful of sweet tea. 'What's that?'

Basma smiled. 'Something to sleep in.'

'Oh, no, I don't need anything. I have my dress.'

Basma's eyebrows rose, her gaze drifting to the dirt-smeared dress now tossed in a bundle on the floor near the bath.

Lauren bit her lip. She'd already accepted the tent, the bath and the food. Did she really want to cause offence by refusing one more thing?

Basma silently held out the deep aquamarine nightgown. It was sheer to the point of almost see-through and Lauren fought a blush as she took it.

The neckline was a boat-shaped design, which thankfully left one shoulder free to ease her sunburnt skin, so she chose not to complain at the diaphanous nature of the outfit.

Sending a thankful prayer that she wasn't near a full-length mirror to catch an embarrassing glimpse of herself, she hurried to the low bed set on a wooden platform and slid between the cool sheets, certain she was in for a few hours of tossing and turning.

But, within minutes of Basma turning off all but one lamp and retreating through the tent flaps, Lauren was fast asleep.

What felt like five minutes later, a gentle hand was nudging her awake.

She blinked, momentarily oblivious to where she was

as she mourned the loss of the best sleep she'd had in ages. When it all came crowding back, she jerked upright, her gaze flying to her phone.

She'd forgotten to set her alarm. If she'd missed Tahir's deadline—

She breathed a sigh of relief when she saw it was a quarter to midnight. Still, she was cutting it a little close, which was why she didn't object when Basma held out another garment.

Ten minutes later, Lauren followed Basma out of the tent.

The colour Lauren wore wasn't one she would have chosen for herself. Her professional attire veered towards staid greys or deep beiges in a concerted effort to blend in.

She would've rejected the deep saffron-coloured midriff-baring top and matching flowing skirt, which was just a series of chiffon layers laid symmetrically on top of one another, if the design hadn't left most of her shoulders bare and somewhat alleviated the pain of her burns.

Dark gold fur-lined slippers too were studded with bright red stones that winked when she wriggled her feet. And when she moved, they felt like cool heavenly blankets cocooning her feet.

The light gold stole Basma settled on her shoulders completed the garment and added a modesty to the top that Lauren appreciated.

The large camp was mostly quiet at this time of night, the few solar lamps ringing the outer perimeter illuminating the tops of the larger tents. Against the backdrop of the canopy of stars above and the shadows of distant dunes in the distance, the enchanted feeling nudged a little closer.

Reminding herself that she wasn't here for the magic of the desert, Lauren hurried after a fast-walking Basma towards the largest tent set away from the others.

The two guards stationed on the Moorish-styled entrance barely glanced at them but, again, Lauren was aware of their sharp vigilance as she passed through the small hallway and into a wider receiving area.

Basma murmured to a third guard positioned at the second opening, then, nodding at Lauren, she hurried away.

The guard parted the flap to the tent.

With murmured thanks, she stepped into Tahir's domain just as the antique clock tolled midnight.

She released a strangled breath when she realised the room was empty.

Half of the lamps had been dimmed. The faintest scent of incense whispered through the air, evoking sultriness she didn't want to feel in that moment. But more acute was the absence of Tahir.

She went to the low seat in the sitting area. Sinking onto it, she stroked the weave of the soft camel hair dyed with deep reds and oranges and depicting scenes of nomadic desert life. She was tracing a nervous finger over the surface when she sensed the laser focus of a powerful gaze on her.

Tahir stood framed in one of the many openings concealed as if by magic but was really a clever contraption of screens, thick curtains, and intersecting panels.

For several heartbeats, he simply stared at her. Then he stepped forward into a pool of lamplight, and her already compromised breathing took a perilous dive. He'd showered or bathed at some point recently too. His jet-black hair looked damp and finger-combed, and, as if toying with her memory, one lock sprang forward to curl over his temple, the sight making her fingers tingle in recollection of smoothing that tendril back once upon a time.

She dragged her gaze away, but it only strayed a few inches to the thick column of his throat, revealed by the black loose-necked tunic and matching trousers that had replaced his traditional garb. On his feet were Arabian slippers too but his were soot-black with no adornment in sight.

From head to toe he resembled a merciless avenging angel, come to exact retribution for the wrong she'd perpetrated on him.

But the scoffing chuckle that should've dispatched such an absurd thought never arrived.

Nerves, she assured herself. Triggered by the unknown.

In her duties as her father's communications aide, she rarely dealt with the unexpected. Every move, countermove and eventuality were parsed to the nth degree, eliminating nasty surprises.

Alongside these nerves, however, there was something else. Something that faintly whispered of…*anticipation*. Excitement of the unknown. A sensation she hadn't experienced in a very long time, buried under the monotony of predictable routine.

Which was…even more unthinkable.

She needed to concentrate on why she was here.

He paused a few feet away and Lauren kicked herself for remaining seated. But then she accepted that, even standing, Tahir Al-Jukrat would always remain a much greater force of nature than she would ever be.

'Did you sleep?' he asked, his deep voice rooting around inside her until it latched onto something vital, stirring it and promising an even more intense rousing.

'Yes. Thank you.'

One corner of his mouth twitched, and she wasn't sure whether it was amusement at her prim tone or mockery.

Dark golden eyes watched for another few seconds, long enough to stretch her nerves much tighter before he turned and strode to the far end of the tent.

He returned with a wide round tray, its contents covered by a black silk cloth.

After setting it down, Tahir dropped into a cushioned seat across from her, reclining on it with mesmerising, captivating grace.

When he cast her a raised-eyebrow look, Lauren cringed inwardly, realising she'd been caught staring. Again.

'What is this?' She indicated the tray.

He didn't lift the cloth, simply reclined deeper into his seat. 'It's a game my grandfather liked to play with me as a child. You and I will play it.'

She frowned. 'What...now?'

'I did warn you that you'll earn the right to be heard out at my discretion and under whatever circumstances I wished, did I not?'

Cold dread slithered through her. 'I can't...you can't balance Matt's troubles on the outcome of a game!'

Again, the twitch of his lips, those cool eyes resting mercilessly on her. 'Haven't you heard? I'm the ruler of this kingdom. I own the very ground you sit on and everything in sight. But I'll give you the choice you claim not to have had twelve years ago. You can play or you can leave.'

'That's no choice at all.'

'On the contrary. You can walk away, squander your chance to make amends for your sins, perhaps even save your brother. Although I won't disagree that it's high time he reaped the consequences of his actions,' he returned with a tight edge to his voice. 'Or you can stay.'

The idea of returning empty-handed left her throat tight and her palms clammy. Even now, after Tahir had established himself as a formidable ruler, those pictures and texts would still cause embarrassment.

But more than that, the thought of walking away from Tahir...of leaving things still fraught and unsettled between them...

Is that all? Or is it something more? That illicit tin-

gling in your being perhaps? The fact that you haven't felt this alive for so long? The prospect of reliving that mind-bending kiss?

She brushed the whispered taunts away. 'I can't leave. My parents will be devastated.'

His eyes hardened. 'Perhaps I should have them brought here, let them confront their wilful blindness. Maybe then they'll finally wake up to the true nature of the son they've spoiled his whole life. But I don't care about your parents or your brother. A few hours ago, you were pleading with me to accept your apology. This is what it'll take to make me consider it. Or it is something else?' he taunted.

She frowned. 'What do you mean?'

'Your brother may be one reason for being here, but aren't you here for yourself, too?'

For a wild moment, Lauren wondered if she'd some-how telegraphed those whispered taunts to him. That hot and cold sensation buffeted her again. 'I don't know what you're talking about.'

His eyes narrowed. 'Are you afraid to test the strength of your parents' devotion to discover whether it'll with-stand your failure?'

The truth seared its way into the heart of her insecuri-ties. Into the vulnerable place where a huge question mark loomed over the love her parents claimed they felt for her. Because even before the events of that night twelve years ago had given her father leverage over her, it'd always felt as if it was a contingency-based love. The quid pro quo kind that demanded she behave a specific sort of way in order to earn it.

Growing up, she'd been shocked to discover that, while she'd never lacked for material things, most parents, rich or poor, loved *all* their children unconditionally.

Take her best friend, Paige, and her four siblings, for

instance. On the rare occasions Lauren's parents had let her visit them, she'd been struck by the overflowing, boisterous love their family shared. They'd fiercely supported and defended each other from harm without asking for anything in return.

That had been Lauren's first inkling that her own relationship with her parents was lacking. The fracture had only widened with time.

Nevertheless, she wasn't ready to admit it to the formidable man searching out her weaknesses. She lifted her chin, her heart thumping loud enough to drown out the immediate sounds outside the tent. 'Tell me what this game is.'

Something gleamed in his eyes, a mixture of triumph and dark anticipation aimed at the heart of her turbulent emotions. 'Are you sure?'

No, I'm not.

But she curled her hands into determined fists. 'The earlier we finish with it, the quicker we can...' She paused, aware she hadn't actually secured anything with Tahir yet. 'Do I have your word that you'll help me?'

His lips twisted, drawing her attention to the stern upper and far too sensual lower. Lips she'd tasted with much fervour mere hours ago. Lips she shouldn't yearn to kiss again...*but did.* 'You're losing your touch, Lauren. You used to be a much better negotiator than this.'

She pursed her own lips, the timbre of his voice and recollection of the intimacies they'd shared threatening her thought processes. 'Do I?'

He shrugged. 'Convince me that you're suitably contrite and you have my word that I'll consider your request.'

Knowing she was treading into dangerous territory by agreeing to rehash that night, that she might skate close to baring all the foolish desires she'd once harboured about him, made her insides quake. But she dragged every ounce of composure together. 'Very well. Let's get on with it.'

Her response should've pleased him. But Lauren sensed it'd done the opposite when leonine eyes narrowed on her, ruthlessly dissecting her as he uncoiled his body, leaned forward to rest his elbows on his knees.

'I've never understood this slavish devotion you have to your family,' he drawled.

Something sharp snagged in her chest but she fought to keep it from showing in her expression. 'If you don't get the bonds of family by now, then I'm afraid you never will.'

The barb hit its mark, hardened his features. 'Perhaps not. But I know they don't deserve it. Perhaps before this is over, I'll understand?'

Lauren would've sworn there was a sliver of longing in the words and in the hand he abruptly reached across the table to trail down her cheek, had it not been for the austere harshness of his features. His body was still as stiff as a marble column. Even his breathing was carefully controlled as his thumb slowly traced over her bottom lip.

Against her better judgment, she swayed towards him again, helpless beneath his touch. And watched as, a smug smile curving his lips as though he was aware he'd set off fireworks through her system, he dropped his hand and sat back.

And without ceremony, whipped off the black silk and tossed it aside.

Dazed, Lauren stared down at what he'd revealed.

Three hourglasses lay sideways, each in their own bed of deep blue velvet housed within a frame of three filigree gold plinths and gold scrollwork base. The glass looked so delicate and exquisite, she tucked her hands into her lap, mildly terrified that even breathing on them would shatter them.

Tahir held no such reservations. He plucked them out and stood each one upright with the fine sand settled at the bottom.

She immediately noted that the measures of sand were different. Why that sent another trail of fireworks through her senses, she refused to contemplate. Instead, she forced her gaze to meet Tahir's. Then went one better and raised an eyebrow. 'Are you going to tell me what this game is about or am I supposed to guess?'

He reached back into each velvet bed, plucking out three black pouches just about the same size as the hourglasses. 'You see that each glass holds a different time span?'

'Yes.'

'Would you like to know the duration?'

Sensing it held meaning, she nodded. 'Yes.'

Tahir tapped the first one. 'This one is forty-five minutes.' He tapped the next. 'Fifteen minutes.' Then the last. 'Two and a half hours.'

'What am I supposed to do with them?'

Again, he dragged out his answer, languidly tugging the pouches over each glass before reaching into the tray. The last item was a smaller tray that sat an inch off the table's surface. Tahir flicked one finger across the smooth surface and the tray slowly spun. Stopping it, he set each hourglass on top, pushed the whole thing towards her then reclined back into his seat, watching the tray until it came to a smooth stop.

'I was a curious child. Much too inquisitive for my own good, I'm told. Definitely too much for my mother to deal with at times so I was dispatched to my grandfather here in Zinabir during the holidays.'

Part of that tale held not so good memories for him, if the trace of bitterness in his tone was an indication. Searching frantically through her own memories, Lauren recalled he'd never willingly volunteered information about his mother. She'd read between the lines and concluded that mother and son hadn't been close. His desert-dry tone lent credence to that assessment.

'I wasn't a fan of routine or rules in general. And since I was used to a quid pro quo arrangement, my grandfather and I compromised with this.' He nudged his square chin at the tray.

'What was the bargain?' she asked, intrigued despite herself.

'He would answer my every question for the duration of the time in the hourglass. And I would do as I was instructed for the rest of the day.'

Something far too jumpy leapt in her chest as her gaze dropped to the shrouded hourglasses. 'Innovative, I guess. What does that have to do with this? And me?'

He arched an eyebrow, his expression so dry she felt it chafe her skin. 'You want me to spell it out?'

She forced a nod. 'Yes. Just so I'm clear on the rules.'

He spread his arms across the tops of the thick cushion, resting his ankle on top of his other knee. Lauren didn't fool herself into thinking he was relaxed. She knew this side of him too well. He was savouring whatever was coming next.

'To begin the game, you will spin the tray and select one hourglass. Whatever time you have will be yours to use as you please. I live in hope that you'll use it for one reason but I'm guessing you'll be using it for another.' It wasn't a question but a statement.

'Reverse psychology? Really?'

He shrugged. 'Prove me wrong,' he breathed, his eyes boring deep into hers. 'Prove that you're not here solely to serve your own interests.'

There was a biting bitterness to those words that dried her mouth.

He wanted his due pound of flesh but she wasn't quite ready. Besides, time was running out for Matt. He was why she was here after all.

'What about the rest of the time?'

'I'll have the same allotted time when yours is up. I have a few questions of my own. You will answer my every question without hesitation.'

She could hardly argue since it was far more than she'd expected.

'So this is like the tale of Scheherazade and the *One Thousand and One Nights* but on steroids?'

Once upon a time, his lips would've twitched at her wry joke, perhaps even prompted one of those deep-throated laughs that made her think she'd won a special prize by drawing such emotion from him.

Tonight, his gaze merely swept down for a contemplative moment before lifting again to spear hers in frank appraisal.

'That was a fairy tale which supposedly ended in lust and happily ever after. Our story won't have such an ending. It'll end with you convincing me that you regret your actions, and a possibility that I'll come to your brother's aid. Or you leaving with nothing at all.'

So use your time wisely.

Lauren didn't need to hear the words echoing ominously between them. Her gaze dropped to the tray, the lingering, unwanted excitement wisely mitigated by trepidation.

She *shouldn't* be excited by this. She dealt in the practical. The tangible, not the whimsical. And yet…something about the gauntlet Tahir had thrown sparked something within her.

Something she'd be wise not to give in to.

So what if she'd thrived on challenges once upon a time? What did it matter if this Scheherazade-adjacent task felt like one plucked right out of her deepest fantasies? Matt's life wasn't a fantasy, and this time with Tahir was far from a fairy tale.

At the much-needed reminder, she rose from the seat, tugging the stole firmly around her. 'I'm sure you'll let me know when you're free to start this task. Goodnight.' She turned and started for the door.

'Where do you think you're going?'

She paused, unwilling to admit his deep, rumbling voice triggered another micro tsunami within her. Neutralising her expression, she turned. 'You've explained the rules and I've agreed to play your game. I'm assuming you'll fit me in at some point tomorrow?' She crossed her fingers, hoping he wouldn't spitefully schedule her too late in the day.

'You're mistaken. The game will be over by this time tomorrow.'

She stiffened. 'What do you mean?'

'It means you only have twenty-four hours with me in the desert to earn my consideration. And your time started fifteen minutes ago when you entered my tent.'

Tahir watched shock flit across her face. Every expression that crossed her face was infuriatingly mesmerising. Hours later, he still couldn't believe he'd kissed her. Couldn't believe he'd disparaged himself for his base inclinations only to succumb to the theory seconds later. Hell, even now, he could hardly keep his eyes off those luscious lips.

'What?'

He refocused on their conversation. On the game he'd decided on his helicopter ride over would be the ideal tool for his retribution. 'You're wasting time, Lauren. Sit down.'

Eyes wide with shock and a charged spark he wanted to foolishly explore, she whirled with an innate grace he suspected she wasn't conscious of and drifted back to her seat.

Sinking back onto it with that same riveting poise, she frowned. 'We're doing this now?'

'Weren't you eager to get started only a little while ago?'

'Yes, but—'

Tahir reached forward and spun the tray, watched the shrouded hourglasses whirl before slowing to a stop. For a moment he wondered whether he was tarnishing the memories he'd created with his grandfather by using this tool. Just as his mother did with him, was he lowering himself by sinking into the same soulless transactional quid pro quo with Lauren?

No. It was the most effective means of reaching his goals. Nothing more.

'Choose.'

For an age, her gaze clung to his, her expressions ranging from wariness to defiance to trepidation. Then extending one fine-boned hand, she traced her fingers over the pouch to the left for a moment before, emitting a small breath, tugging it free.

Tahir had played the game often enough to know which one she'd uncovered, and even as sprigs of excitement unfurled in his chest, he muttered coolly, 'You have forty-five minutes.'

He sat back, momentarily regretting letting her go first because he knew the next forty-five minutes would be about her brother, the selfish idiot she seemed to irrationally care about. He tightened his gut against the faint spikes of sensation that reeked far too much of jealousy. 'Proceed.'

She licked her lips, leaving a damp trail on her plump flesh and sending a pulse of lust into his groin. 'Matt was arrested two weeks ago. He…was told he'd have time to organise his defence team but the court has expedited his case.' She paused, sucked in a long breath that drew his unwilling gaze to her chest and the firm breasts pushing against the material of her saffron-coloured top.

He should've instructed that she not be dressed in his favourite colour...

He wrenched himself from that distracting thought and focused, tensing as her words penetrated.

'My judicial system marches to its own drumbeat.' Tahir shrugged. 'Unlike other court systems, Jukrat has attained its level of excellence by being fair but swift,' he said without conceit. It was a system his father had fought hard for; one Tahir had strictly maintained.

Lauren nodded. 'So I've discovered.'

He refused to be affected by the alarm in her response. 'What was your brother charged with?'

Her lush eyelashes swept down, the first indication that she didn't relish the response she had to give. When her lips pursed in a futile effort to buy herself more time, Tahir's skin tightened with premonition. 'Answer me, Lauren.'

'Drug possession,' she finally said, her voice subdued.

The potent dose of poetic justice being delivered held him still for several seconds. He only roused himself out of it when she darted a glance at him.

'Your brother smuggled drugs into my kingdom?' The words felt like ice chips falling from his lips.

Until now, with his thoughts irritatingly fixated on Lauren, he hadn't speculated about the other Winchester's troubles. What he'd done was instruct Ali to make discreet enquiries into Lauren's life. He knew she worked as her father's communications chief—an ironic discovery considering how poorly she *communicated* when he'd needed her assistance twelve years ago. He'd also discovered that her aspirations had taken a back seat to her father's ambitions.

And that she was unattached.

Her green eyes widened, probably in reaction to the hard bite of his question. 'You didn't investigate?'

'I recall mentioning I have very little time to spare for that Winchester. Besides, I knew you would enlighten me.'

'Okay. Well, he said he didn't do it.'

'Of course he did.'

Her flinch at his acerbic response produced a twinge of regret he immediately smothered.

'What is his excuse, then? Let me guess. It was someone else's fault?' The question was laden with heavy scepticism he didn't bother to disguise.

And even though he saw her reluctance to confirm what they both knew was coming next—because it would be as lame now as every excuse Matt Winchester had uttered when cornered—she attempted anyway. 'He was part of a group passing through Jukrat on their way from a business trip. He thinks one of the others planted drugs in his suitcase.'

'Of course he does,' Tahir repeated, wholly unsurprised the man was still scapegoating others. Sensing there was more, he narrowed his eyes. 'And?'

'He tried to reach you, but his access was blocked.'

Tahir allowed himself a bark of bitter laughter. 'Ah. For a moment there I thought he'd chosen to man up and face the consequences of his actions.'

'With respect, this isn't funny.'

His laughter died off, anger igniting in his belly. 'No, it's not. Which begs the question, under what circumstances did you think I'd lift a finger to help your brother?'

A visible tremor went through her at his chilly tone. The same tone he'd used during their last meeting when she'd shown where her true loyalty lay. He needed to keep remembering that. To not allow those alluring eyes to sway him in any way.

At his continued stare, her gaze fell, then darted to the fine golden sand eagerly building its miniature mountain at the bottom of the hourglass.

'What makes you think I hold any sway over an independent judicial system?' he pressed when she remained silent.

'Matt's lawyer seemed to think…that you would intercede on his behalf. Because Matt was your friend once upon a time?'

Tahir had only tolerated Winchester because of his proximity to Lauren. His jaw tightened with acid regret at how misguided he'd been. 'Remind me again how that friendship ended, Lauren,' he invited.

Perhaps it was her name on his lips that darkened her eyes. Better still, he hoped, it was her deep regret of her treatment of him.

But in that instant, Tahir was glad he'd instigated this game.

Because he intended to excise a few wounds, lay haunting ghosts to rest. And after this night, never think of Lauren Winchester again.

CHAPTER FOUR

'DO WE NEED to go through it all again?' she asked, her gaze fixed on the hourglass.

'Look at me, Lauren,' Tahir demanded. Now he'd said her name, he couldn't seem to stop. Couldn't seem to stop the flashes of memory of when he'd groaned her name when he was deep inside her, her limbs wrapped tight around him as if he were her only anchor to this world.

What he'd felt in those moments…

Tahir jerked forward, physically wresting himself away from those traitorous memories. They'd been a lie. A lethal little game where the unwary paid dearly.

Not dissimilar to the game he was indulging in now. Only this time, he would emerge the victor.

When she finally dragged her gaze up, her expression held equal parts trepidation and irritation. Why that kicked up his pulse another notch, he wasn't going to dwell on. 'Answer me,' he insisted.

'What good will it do to rehash it all over again?' she answered, a whisker of desperation in her voice.

He didn't respond, allowing his silence to speak for him. When her gaze darted to the hourglass again, she expelled a rushed breath.

'You cut him off because of his…lifestyle at uni,' she relayed in a solemn tone.

Tahir shook his head, another wave of bitterness curling through him. 'The whole, explicit truth, Lauren, not the sanitised version you use to keep yourself warm at night.'

She paled and her nostrils fluttered again in that way that would've drawn sympathy and pity from another being had they not known the depths of her duplicity. Then her chin lifted, and she was gathering herself with that depth of poise he'd used to marvel at. 'You disapproved of his drinking and partying. The way he treated others.'

'Others?' he clipped out.

'Fine, you disliked the way he treated *me*. And I know you think I colluded with him that night. But...' She stopped and took another breath, while his gut turned to stone.

'But what?' he pushed. He'd waited far too long for this, had spent *months* in this very desert berating himself for being so gullible, to tolerate her hesitation.

She shook her head, her eyes flashing with green fire. 'This is supposed to be my time, isn't it? Isn't this cheating?'

His gaze dropped to the hourglass. He'd watched those grains often enough to know only a handful of minutes remained. He forced his insides to relax. 'Very well.'

'Like I said, everything happened fast. His trial is already scheduled.'

He should've felt satisfaction at the news, should've steeped himself in well-earned retribution. But the sensation was surprisingly...absent. It took another second to get why. Because in the grand scheme of things, Matt Winchester didn't matter.

The woman who sat before him, however...

Where facts, figures and the pragmatism should've ruled, she'd lured him into casting aside his hardened cynicism, into thinking their connection went beyond the physical.

She was the one who'd made him dabble in that ingredient that was, even as the young Prince he was then, detrimental to a man in his position.

She'd made him...*hope.*

Made him ponder whether relationships like the regimental one with his father and the clinically transactional one with his mother were the exceptions, not the rule. In the end, she'd proved that she was just as self-serving as his mother.

In Tahir's eyes, *that* was her ultimate sin.

'So you would like me to do what? Call the judge and tell him to let a drug trafficker go scot-free?'

She worried the inside of her lip for several seconds before she answered. 'No, of course not, but you could ask that Matt be given a little more time to get his defence sorted properly—'

'No, that is not going to happen,' he interrupted coldly.

The hands folded in her lap twisted once before she stilled the movement. 'Please...'

'Tell me, are your British tabloids still ravenous for the sort of scandal I was embroiled in?'

She gave a reluctant nod and he stopped himself from watching the lamplight dance over her glossy hair. 'Yes.'

'So why would I want to place myself in a position to draw the same unfavourable attention?'

Wide green eyes rose to boldly meet his. 'So you won't help Matt? Is that your final answer?'

He let loose a grim smile. 'Ready to throw in the towel so quickly?'

Her shoulders twitched before straightening and he recalled her grounding rituals before she took on a formidable challenge. How many times had he watched her do her customary twenty-second countdown and her deep breathing before flinging herself headlong into a charged debate, often winning in spectacular fashion?

Somewhere deep within, in a place he wasn't entirely willing to admit existed, he wondered whether that memory was partly why he'd chosen this route to satisfaction.

Her lips parted, ready to speak. He stopped her by holding up his hand, even while anticipatory fire shot through his system. 'Your time is up,' he drawled.

She snatched in a breath, her gaze shifting to the last few settling grains of sand. Her fingers untwisted, surprising him. It was almost as if she was…relieved.

'So what now? You're going to bombard me with your own questions?'

He tugged the coiled rope dangling from the ceiling. Seconds later, two attendants entered. He relayed his request and they exited.

'Now you'll drink tea with me, and we'll see where the conversation takes us. You still drink tea, yes?'

He watched her grapple with wary surprise, her wide eyes blinking before she murmured, 'Yes. But I thought—'

'I know what you thought. And you'll get your wish sooner rather than later.'

'But you feel like toying with me first?'

He shrugged. 'I recall you being partial to well-crafted coaxing. We're barely an hour into this, Lauren. Surely you don't want to be short-changed this early?'

She sucked in another breath, right before heat flowed up her smooth neck and into her face. He allowed himself another smile. 'And you still blush on demand. Interesting. I would've thought you'd be rid of that weakness by now.'

'Blushing isn't a weakness.'

'But it's a lie when it comes to you, isn't it?' he said with more bite than he'd intended. 'Because it gives one impression while hiding the truth.'

'And what is that truth? That I made a mistake *once* when we knew one another? Is that the sword you're intending to hold over my head while you play your games?'

The astringent memory he thought he'd cemented over fractured, letting loose disappointment. 'The greater sin wasn't how it started, Lauren. It was how you chose to finish it. And I think you know that.'

His words flayed her open with regret and remorse.

He'd aimed a bullseye at the heart of her guilt. And he'd scored. She wanted to ask him whether he was satisfied but she chose silence because she already knew the answer. He wasn't nearly done with her. The pound-of-flesh-taking would be the stretched-out affair he'd alluded to. But while minutes ago she was certain he was hinting at her preferences in bed, his last statement was much more pointed.

Whatever retributive foreplay he'd planned would be extensive. And ruthless.

The attendants' return with their tea was another reason she remained silent. They set out the refreshments and handed her a delicate cup filled with jasmine tea.

Somewhere within the tent, an antique clock gave a faint chime. It would all have been magical had electric tension not continued to snap between them.

Her gaze flicked to the hourglass and surprise darted through her.

While their tea was being served, Tahir had placed the forty-five-minute hourglass in front of him, ready to go.

Heart in her mouth, she watched him flip it.

Then he sat back, as if he had all the time in the world. 'Drink your tea,' he drawled, jangling her nerves further.

She took a sip, unable to stop herself from watching his strong throat move as he too drank his beverage.

In the short silence, Lauren noticed that while the camp

was substantially less busy, it wasn't quiet. 'Does no one sleep in the desert?'

Tahir shrugged. 'Nomadic life is fluid. Besides, their Sheikh is in residence, accompanied by a mysterious guest. That's bound to arouse a little more…energy.'

A fizz of amusement rose in her. 'Is this a new thing, referring to yourself in the third person?'

A glint lit in his eyes but before she could fool herself into imagining she'd amused him, the austerity returned. 'You haven't earned the right to ask that.'

And just like that, the mood dialled back to chilly. With hands that had developed a sudden tremor, she set the delicate cup onto its saucer.

He took his time draining his cup, then poured himself another after an eyebrow cocked in her direction prompted a murmured, 'No, thanks.'

Armed with his second cup, he skewered her with narrowed eyes. 'The last time we had an honest conversation twelve years ago—' his lips twitched when she winced at the qualifier, then he continued '—you already had an internship at the United Nations in Geneva with an in principle offer of a position as a humanitarian in New York thereafter. Unless you were faking the emotion, you were ecstatic about both. But, according to my report, you've been working for your father since graduation. Care to tell me why?' he asked.

Surprise and something equally disconcerting jerked through her. 'You had a report done on me?'

'I have a report done on everyone I spend more than ten minutes with. It's part of my security protocols so don't feel special.'

She sucked in a breath, digging deep to prevent the effect the drastic redirection her life had taken from those halcyon days from showing on her face. 'Things change.'

That infernal eyebrow cocked again. '*Things?* Enlighten me,' he invited, even as his focus sharpened.

Lauren reminded herself that this was what she'd agreed to, what she had to endure to help Matt. Nevertheless, opening one of the many wounds she'd cauterised for the sake of self-preservation wasn't something she relished. 'You weren't the only one who was affected by what happened. I… I fell behind a little in my studies.'

'Why?' he shot back.

She absolutely wasn't going to admit how terribly she'd missed him, how the magnitude of that night had weighed on her so heavily that the joy and enthusiasm she'd taken in her studies had evaporated. How she'd barely been able to get out of bed, never mind make it into lectures, without the glaring reality that she'd had a direct hand in him no longer being at her side, escorting her to class when his crushing coursework allowed.

'Did your conscience haunt you? Guilt has a way of doing that, I understand.'

'Do you intend to keep baiting me or would you like me to answer your question?'

He levelled a cold stare at her, and she took another breath.

'I took some time off, which meant I had to decline the internship offer. That had a knock-on effect on the New York offer. They invited me to reapply the next year.' She paused, memory searing. 'But I didn't.'

'Why not?' he pressed again.

The painful conversation she'd had with the dean replayed in her mind. 'The dean strongly hinted that I wouldn't be successful if I reapplied. Everyone knew about the… scandal and he was reluctant to endorse my application.' She raised her gaze to his. 'I suppose that pleases you?'

'That you wasted your potential because you compromised both yourself and me without a moment's hesitation? No, it doesn't.' His voice was soft and almost doubly lethal for being so.

Looking into his eyes, Lauren was startled by the veracity in them. He really was genuinely displeased by her circumstance. 'I thought you'd gloat about it.'

A single clench of his jaw. 'Which proves how little you know me. Then *and* now.' Before she could react to that, he continued, 'So the dean withdrew his support, but he wasn't the only avenue to achieving your goals. Where was the strong-willed woman who wanted to change the world?'

Reeling under her father's threat to harm you...

The equally esteem-shrivelling discussion with her father unspooled in her head. This one she wasn't ready to spill so she shook her head. 'I chose to start by supporting my father's position.'

The eyes focused on her contained enough scepticism to make a lesser woman fidget. But she'd learned to hone her emotions in public, to hide her discomfort and her desires, to blend into the background until needed.

'Does it really work?'

She frowned. 'Does what work?'

'Lying so effortlessly to yourself?'

'Just because I don't agree with your view of me doesn't mean this isn't what I want.'

The clock chimed again.

Tahir's gaze flitted over her shoulder and the muscles in Lauren's stomach tightened.

He set his cup down. His forty-five minutes had flown by, and Tahir was pushing the hourglasses towards her again. 'Choose,' he said.

Her heart skipped several beats as she reached out and chose the one farthest away from her. Drawing back the cloth, she exhaled noisily when she saw her pick.

'You have fifteen minutes. Turn it when you're ready,' Tahir said.

She didn't hesitate. She told herself she wanted to press on with advocating for Matt but deep down she wanted to sprint away from how lonely and vulnerable she'd felt after he'd left England. Left *her*.

She lifted the delicate hourglass, carefully turned it upside down, her mouth drying as she watched the first grains filter through.

'You say you won't interrupt your judicial process but last year you advocated for two of your subjects to be freed.'

If he was surprised she'd done her homework, he didn't show it. He merely inclined his head.

'Indeed, but that came with conditions I was willing to accommodate. Your brother's misdeeds don't fall under the same purview. Not even close,' he said with a definite snap in his tone.

'How can I convince you to consider it?'

He uncrossed his legs and slowly rose to his feet. Stepping away from the divan, he strolled to one end of the living room, hands clasped behind his back. Lauren tried not to let the slide of muscle beneath his tunic distract her, but it was as difficult as attempting not to marvel at a sleek predator owning his habitat.

'Tell me one thing, Lauren. Did you get involved with me back then because you knew something like this might happen? That somewhere down the line, you'd need a sheikh or a king in your corner to bail you and your family out of some such a predicament?' he demanded without turning to face her, his voice tight with some peculiar emotion. 'And remember if you lie to me, I'll know,' he warned.

Because he wasn't facing her, Lauren squeezed her eyes shut, her heart sinking. The hot, unequivocal *no* she wanted to shout out stalled in her throat. Because hadn't she heard

Matt and her parents calculating just such a thing when she'd started seeing Tahir? Hadn't she heard them loftily accommodating her fling with Tahir because they believed it might benefit them at some future date?

At the time, she'd been hurt and horrified enough to confront them. At first, her father had dismissed her protest. Lauren knew now that she should've walked away. Because by exposing how much Tahir meant to her, how unwilling she was to jeopardise her new relationship, she'd played right into their hands.

'I'll take your silence to mean yes, shall I?' he bit out coldly, his shoulders tight.

'I can only tell you that *I* didn't,' she said finally. 'It was never about your position or your connections for me.'

He whirled to face her and the fury in his face shrivelled her insides. In the head-to-toe black he wore, he was a stunningly arresting pillar of affront, like a beautiful tsunami that would devastate once it arrived but was mesmerising to watch unfolding. 'And yet here you are, asking me to save your self-absorbed, selfish brother when all evidence says he needs to be behind bars.'

'No!' She rushed to her feet. 'That can't be your final answer.' *Tell me what I need to do.* The words remained locked in her throat, mild terror at uttering them keeping them wisely hidden.

The fury seemed to drain out of him, a whisper of bewilderment flashing through the gaze that traced her face and lingered on her lips before it neutralised and resettled on the hourglass.

Lauren didn't need to look to know her time had run out.

That they'd circled back to his arena.

'For the next fifteen minutes, I don't want to hear your brother's name,' he said stiffly.

Butterflies beat an urgent tattoo against her belly, the

sense of the ground shifting beneath her feet real and disconcerting. 'What do you want to talk about, then? The weather?'

'Hardly.' His gaze dropped to her hand.

She followed his gaze, almost needing visual confirmation that she wasn't fidgeting. This was what he did to her. Made her lose her equilibrium.

'Are you married? Do you have a lover?'

A gasp left her throat. 'That's what you…' She paused, shook her head. 'Didn't your report provide an answer to that question?'

His expression grew more brooding, his jaw clenching for a tick. 'Answer me, Lauren.'

Her chin lifted, a vital need not to cower before him taking root inside her. 'I know you don't think that highly of me, but I wouldn't have kissed you if I was involved with someone else.'

His eyes darkened, his tongue resting betrayingly on his inner lip before he slanted an eyebrow at her.

She exhaled noisily. 'No, I don't have a husband. No lover. No significant other. I prefer my work to…all of that.'

He sauntered towards her, not stopping until only a few feet separated them and the very air around them was charged with snapping electricity. 'Prefer? No one *prefers* the monotony of mindless drudgery over great sex and the stimulation of challenging work. Certainly not the Lauren I remember, who worked hard and played hard. So you'll have to do better to convince me that reducing yourself to this mere…shadow is what you really aspire to.'

'Are you speaking from experience?'

He lowered his head until their cheeks were aligned but not touching. Until his scent filled her nostrils, and she closed her eyes to stop herself from launching herself at him. Begging for him to kiss her again.

'Of course,' he said after an age, then brushed her jaw with his in sizzling contact before retreating.

She was bewildered and not quite ready for his frank admission, and it caught her somewhere raw and unwelcome. Which was ridiculous because she had no right to this man. There was no value in wondering what liaisons he'd had since they parted. Whether, like many men of his ilk, he was contemplating settling down and producing heirs to carry on his legacy.

She'd been lucky enough to cycle through his orbit once upon a time and revel in the brilliance of his rapier-sharp intelligence, astonishing charisma and effortlessly powerful presence he wore like layers of skin. Her actions might have hastened her departure, but Lauren didn't doubt it would've happened anyway.

Men like Tahir Al-Jukrat were destined for the kind of dazzling, meteoric lives mere mortals could only stand back and admire in goggle-eyed awe. They wielded the very power she was here to petition for on behalf of her brother. She needed to remember that.

'Well,' she said briskly. 'That's my choice. I don't need to justify it to you.'

'Justify? Maybe not. But you have a task to complete. And I want that task to be performed by a woman not shrouded in mystery. The true woman buried beneath this stiff and inferior copy.'

That stung. *Hard.* Because damn him, it was *true.* But she didn't plan to take it lying down. 'You want me to bare my soul to you? Well, that's not going to happen.'

He stepped to the side, then proceeded to circle her, drawing ever closer until his intoxicating scent teased her nostrils. 'Nothing so melodramatic. We can start with why you're sacrificing yourself for the sake of your ungrateful family,' he tossed out, so casual it took a fraction of a second longer for the barb to spear her.

'How dare you? You don't know anything about my family.'

'I know enough about your father's previous business dealings to know the route he took to achieve his goals.'

Mild nausea rumbled through her belly. 'What does that mean?'

'It means that your choice to become a humanitarian was admirable but surprising to me because it was at the opposite spectrum of who Charles Winchester is. To be honest, I was astonished to discover you were connected to him at all.'

Lauren bit her lip. She'd never told Tahir she was adopted, not because she was ashamed of the fact. No, the reason had been deeper than that. She'd been ashamed because she'd always felt…lacking. A puzzle piece that didn't quite fit the perfect picture she'd longed for as a child.

Disclosing that to a guy as entrenched in his beliefs and heritage and steeped in destiny as Tahir was had felt like admitting a deep flaw.

'Or is it more accurate to ask what hold he has on you to make you jump to do his bidding without question?'

Panic joined the nausea, the feeling that he was skating far too close to the truth sending chilling alarm all over her body. 'I'm not sure where you're getting these outlandish ideas from. I love my parents. I'd do anything to not make them suffer the pain of seeing their son in prison. Isn't that enough? You have a brother. Wouldn't you do the same were you in my position?'

'My brother is my diplomatic envoy and the international representative of my kingdom. I'm confident he would move mountains with his bare hands before he let himself be caught in a situation like Winchester's,' he responded scathingly.

'Well, we can't all be flawless like you and your family,' she said, striving to not give away a hint of the jealousy and longing that wove through her at the unwavering certainty in his voice.

But when he faced her again, she caught shadows of bleakness and bitterness in his expression before it was wiped clean. Before she could wonder what had triggered the reaction, he was speaking again.

'Are your parents here in Jukrat? Did they make the journey with you to support their son?'

'Why do I think you already know the answer to that?' she snapped.

His lips twisted. 'So, your role is perpetual whipping post?'

She pivoted to face him as he stepped to move around her once more. 'Why are you so interested in my family dynamic? What bearing does it have on my presence here?'

The twist deepened, drawing her attention to the far too sensual curve of his lower lip. To the firm smoothness of it. To the memory of feeling it pressed in carnal pleasure against hers. 'You were about to tell me who dimmed your light.'

The statement caught her on the raw, making her belly clench against the verbal punch. She raised her chin and tried to brazen it out. 'Don't we all have lofty ideas about who and what we want to be when we're young?' She pulled off a nonchalant shrug.

For the longest time, he simply stared at her. 'Lie to yourself if you must. But don't lie to me,' he said through gritted teeth, his piercing gaze pinning her in place.

Frustration clawing through her, she threw up her arms. 'Why does it matter?'

'Because you pulled the wool over my eyes once. I don't intend for you to do so again. Tell me the real reason why, Lauren.'

Her breath shook out of her, the sound of her name on his lips snaking familiar sensations through her. She battled past it and gave him the only answer she could. 'My father can't afford any hint of a scandal right now. You probably know he's lobbying for a different cabinet position. He asked me to come, and I agreed. If I seem like a...different person from who you think I was before, it's because I entered the real world and accepted that certain ideals were best left behind.' Ideals her father had warned her off the bat he would oppose once he was in office when he'd announced his intention to seek a cabinet ministerial position six years ago. He'd cautioned her not to embarrass him... *or else*, then coaxed her to join his staff, with a promise of backing her once he left office.

Lauren had had no choice but to place her goals on ice, praying her father would be done with politics in the four years he'd insisted he intended to be minister. But Charles Winchester had tasted true power. And when his party had won re-election, he'd fully embraced that power.

Two years, she silently repeated to herself.

Two more years and she'd be free.

Until then...

She raised her gaze to Tahir's and tried not to be cowed by the penetrating look he levelled on her. 'Your fifteen minutes is also up. Shall I spin again?'

Without waiting for his answer, she returned to the divan. Until that moment, Lauren had believed herself entirely too pragmatic to rely on luck. But then she found herself tucking one hand into her lap out of view of Tahir's mocking eyes, and carefully crossing her fingers.

The other reached out, a slight trembling seizing them

as she spun the tiny roulette tray to play the game that was turning out to be far more emotionally draining than she'd anticipated. It was why she wished for the fullest time span of the three.

A relieved gasp broke free when she lifted the silk cloth, and her wish was granted.

Golden sand filled the bottom half almost to the brim and she was tempted to stroke it in gratitude. She didn't because Tahir was joining her, and the tingling in her body was absorbing all of her attention.

He settled himself opposite her, his gaze drifting from her face to the hourglass and back again. 'You seem relieved. But you forget when it ends I have you for two and a half hours too. You barely withstood the last fifteen minutes.'

I have you...

Lauren suppressed the short burst of intense fire that lit through her belly. They didn't mean anything. 'Have at it. I can take whatever you throw at me,' she responded with much more bravery than her quivering insides indicated.

If she'd expected him to be irritated or chilled by her response, she was to be disappointed. For the first time tonight, Tahir appeared...amused. True, the humour was hard-edged and faintly mocking but—she admitted as her heart lurched—it was both better and worse than what she'd suffered so far.

'Challenge accepted.'

The deeply intoned words burrowed into her, rousing even more memories. Rousing her from the state of inertia and apathy she seemed to have fallen into recently. She might have been looking directly at Tahir but in her periphery, colours and textures suddenly seemed brighter, more vibrant. The way they had when she'd been with him twelve years ago before it'd all turned to ash.

Which meant what…?

God, she was off her rocker!

Pulling herself away from fanciful thoughts, she reached for the hourglass, inhaled to steady herself, and turned it upside down.

CHAPTER FIVE

TAHIR PREPARED HIMSELF for another lengthy plea on behalf of her brother, the distaste in his mouth souring further as anxiety flashed across her face.

For a moment or two in the last fifteen minutes, he'd caught glimpses of the woman he remembered. He despised this new, unflattering, uninspired version—the one brainwashed into believing she wasn't worthy of the aspirations she'd passionately advocated for. It grated that the women-championing, aspiring humanitarian had meekly accepted the role of a glorified secretary.

He frowned inwardly.

Why was it important? He didn't...*shouldn't* care about the altered trajectory of her once promising destiny. And yet...

He shifted in his seat, berating himself to move on.

His gaze dropped to the trickling sand, noting that almost a minute had passed. 'Cat got your tongue?'

She startled, the beginnings of a blush tingeing her cheeks before her gaze darted away. A spark ignited in his groin, triggering another wave of unease. So what if that refreshing reaction still lingered despite the disappointing changes?

He watched her take a long, steady breath, her eyes lingering on the hourglass before rising to his.

'Tell me about your grandfather.'

It took a few stunned seconds for her left-field, soft-spoken request to penetrate. He stiffened, a frown knotting his forehead. 'Excuse me?'

The tiniest hint of a smile appeared; the kind that said she knew she'd surprised him. Wariness gripped him as she watched him, irritatingly patient while she awaited his answer. 'Why?' he gritted out.

She shrugged. 'I have some time.'

He cocked an eyebrow. 'And this is how you wish to spend it?' Surprise was giving way to another emotion, one he didn't want to entertain. *Warmth.*

She couldn't know his grandfather had been his favourite person in the world, that he'd treasured the days of the year he'd spent with him in the desert. More than that, Tahir needed to harden his heart against the possibility that this was a ploy to soften him up, her ultimate goal still very much in play.

His grim smile made her stiffen.

'If I discover that this is a ruse to win me to your desires, know that the punishment will be swift and merciless.'

She paled, all hints of that blush disappearing as her eyes widened with hurt. 'You think I'm asking just to butter you up?'

'Are you not?'

The hurt intensified and pinpricks of guilt burrowed into him.

He had nothing to be guilty of.

Her tongue slicked over her bottom lip and the tension ratcheted up inside him. 'Discussing Matt triggers animosity between us. I… I just thought you…we might both want a break from it.'

'And my feelings matter to you?' he asked drolly.

'Of course they do.' She swallowed and shook her head.

'Believe it or not, while I intend to keep advocating for my brother, I don't want to spend what's left of my twenty-four hours trading barbs with you.'

'Said the woman who once took the floor of a debate tournament for twenty-seven hours straight with only a handful of short breaks.'

She gave a soft gasp. 'You remember that?'

He shrugged, a little annoyed with himself for dredging up that memory. 'I've forgotten very little of my time at university.' He'd meant it to sting and to generalise, but his brain supplied other, more carnal reminders, throwing even wider the funnel of heat attacking his insides. Like how *thoroughly*, *exhaustively* and *passionately* they'd celebrated after she'd won that debate.

Briefly, he wished he'd agreed to Javid's request for his presence this week at the international trade summit in Toronto. It would've been a good opportunity to indulge in a discreet liaison—the type he could no longer enjoy in Jukrat without inviting wild speculation about his future bride—to alleviate the hunger prowling within him. Wished he hadn't broken off the years-long understanding he'd had with a certain female head of state who valued discretion and the need to blow off steam in bed as much as he did.

He suppressed the persistent tug of need and focused as Lauren responded. 'Then you'll know that the quickest way to burnout is to go full pelt right out of the gate?'

Lips thinning, he wanted to condemn her for playing games with him, but hadn't he started this very game? Hadn't he given her the very tool with which she was setting up her own offensive even though she would lose in the end?

Irritated but fractionally impressed by her tactic, he rose and headed for the cabinet tucked discreetly into one corner of his living room.

While alcohol consumption was allowed in Jukrat, it was still a young law, passed by his grandfather a handful of decades ago. More than half of his kingdom still practised a teetotal life, and Tahir respected that by not flaunting his curated alcohol collection.

Throwing the cabinet open, he made his selection and picked up the glasses.

Turning around, he froze.

The sight of her slim torso, of the long braid teasing the small of her back, of the legs she'd tucked beneath her some time in the last few minutes, all reeked far too much of another place. Another time.

He'd been granted the perfect conduit through which to deliver his retribution for what Lauren Winchester had done to him.

And he was serving her wine?

Just then she glanced over her shoulder, her eyes moving from his face to the bottle he clutched before her eyes widened, accurately reflecting the astonishment moving through his own gut.

After several beats, one corner of her mouth twitched but didn't produce a full smile, perhaps when she noticed his stillness. 'Are we moving into the drinking part of the game?' she asked with forced gaiety.

Tahir shrugged. This small misstep needn't derail his intentions. Hell, it might even lull her into a false sense of security. 'You were partial to decent vintage Shiraz if I recall.'

This time her blush flowed higher and deepened, bringing his attention to her high cheekbones and plump lips. Cementing the thought that, yes, he much preferred her this way. A combination of wit, beauty and intelligence.

His fingers tightened on the bottle, the warning that this was veering down a risky path whispering at the back of his head.

'So are we going to drink it or stare at it?'

Tahir caught the nerves in her voice, and he was unapologetic enough to admit that satisfied him.

Nerves would keep her on her toes, dissolve any illusion of sneaking beneath his guard. 'No one else within this kingdom or outside it would dare speak to me this way, do you know that?' he breathed as he returned to the seating area.

Then the reaction he'd expected fully materialised. Her lashes swept down but not before he caught the flash of defiance. 'You said you preferred plain speaking. I'm accommodating you.'

The spark within threatened to turn into a flame, channelling his thoughts towards a different, *beautifully dirty* sort of accommodating.

Yes, he really should've gone to Toronto.

But then you'd have missed her...

'To your earlier comment about trading barbs, I'm far from fragile. I'd have to be made of sterner stuff than that to rule a kingdom.'

The cue did its job of reminding her of his position.

She cast a look around her, taking in the antique furnishings, some of which had belonged to his great-great-grandfather, before returning to him. And why that mildly awed look from those stunning eyes should've fanned the flame of the infernal heat gripping him, he wasn't in the mood to analyse.

'It's...being here in this tent. It almost makes me forget—' She stopped herself but they both knew what she'd meant.

'You'll do well not to,' he cautioned, the gravity in his tone meant as much for him as for her. He couldn't lose sight of what her presence meant. Or of his destiny both within and outside the weathered camel's wool structure that formed his shelter.

She stiffened, then gave a curt nod. 'I won't.' After a moment's pause, she continued. 'So, is discussing your grandfather off the table?'

He debated his answer a fraction longer, uncorked the wine to let it sit while she tried to disguise her uneasiness. Deciding that there was nothing to be lost by divulging general information she could discover within a coffee-table book on Jukrat, he exhaled.

'My grandfather was a great man, the visionary who dragged Jukrat into the twentieth century. It's why you'll find his name plastered on buildings, airports and monuments all over the kingdom.'

Her gaze had returned to him while he spoke and now her pert nose wrinkled. 'I was hoping for more than a sound bite straight from the PR's office.'

Shut her down. Remind her this isn't a social visit.

But his gaze fell on the hourglasses. He'd left the door open by telling her a deeply personal memory, so, really, he had himself to blame.

'He gifted me those on my twenty-first birthday but I left them with him so we could play the game he taught me right up until he passed,' he found himself divulging.

'When did he die?' she asked softly.

'Eight years ago.'

Her green eyes dropped to the trickle of sand, the sight that had in turn triggered anticipation and impatience on many occasions, holding her in similar thrall. 'Why the three different measures?'

'He wanted me to learn the efficacy of quick thinking, of making well-balanced decisions, and when to bide my time.' All three of which seemed in short supply when it came to the woman sitting in front of him.

Her short, neatly manicured fingers trailed down one side of the glass and over the filigree mould, and it felt as if she were touching him.

Again, he asked himself why he'd used such personal means.

Again, he shied away from the answer.

'Have you played it with anyone else?' she asked after a long minute.

His gaze flicked to her face, unease moving through him at her careful composure because he was plagued again by the need to see her real emotions.

'Not in the direct sense,' he replied, swallowing past the curious stone in his throat as he thought of his grandfather.

Her gaze tangled with his again. 'What do you mean?'

He reached for the bottle, more for something to do with his hands than anything else. He poured a glass and passed it to her. When her fingers brushed his, he tightened his gut against the flame that flared low in his belly. Against the need to keep his fingers exactly where they were, experiencing the smoothness of her skin.

Pulling back from temptation he had no intention of succumbing to again, he filled his own glass and took a healthy sip. While the excellent vintage warmed his insides, he contemplated his answer. A pat, throwaway response that gave nothing of himself away, he decided. But even before he spoke he knew he wouldn't dishonour his grandfather's memory that way.

'I only bring the hourglasses with me to the desert. When I'm here, I reprise some of the games I played with my grandfather. It helps me...strategise.'

Very few people would dare disparage the Sheikh of Jukrat to his face. From the glimpses of the old Lauren he'd caught in the last few hours, Tahir knew she was one of those brave souls. So perhaps that breath locked in his diaphragm was in anticipation of a bolder challenge.

But all she did was raise her glass, sip the wine, and nod. As if she wholly understood what amounted to having conversations out loud with a man who was long dead.

'It's an effective way of drilling down to the bare bones of a problem. I do that all the time but with cue cards and the timer on my phone, not exquisite hourglasses like these.'

He narrowed his eyes, drilling through her words to find hidden meaning or mockery. When he didn't, something unknotted inside him.

'But I'm guessing it's also a way of remaining close to him?' she added.

It was, but he wasn't about to admit how much he missed the old man's counsel. His father had cut him off from all avenues of support to teach him a lesson during his banishment. That missed year with his grandfather hurt the deepest. A year he'd never get back thanks to Lauren.

The abrasive reminder pulled him back from the temptation of finding kinship with the woman who'd betrayed him.

Nearly forty-five minutes had passed. Did she intend to use up all her time discussing everything but her brother?

'Fritter away your time if you must but it won't be on personal questions about me.' He injected enough ice in his tone to make her stiffen.

She blinked and looked away, but not before he caught the flash of hurt. He didn't care. This situation was entirely her own doing.

'Fine.' She cast a furtive gaze about before meeting his. 'I have a copy of Matt's police report. Would you read it and—?'

'No.'

Her nostrils flared with vexation. 'No? Just like that?'

'There's no point. I'm nowhere near convinced helping

him is in my best interest.' He didn't feel inclined to add that he'd had Ali acquire the report and read it to him over his satellite phone when Lauren had returned to her tent for dinner. Nothing contained in the document had convinced him Winchester was innocent.

'But—'

'Didn't we agree that the only way to sway me would be for you to make personal amends? Not with official documents or appeals from absent parents. Only you, Lauren.'

Something about her name rolling off his tongue sent another sensual wave through him. Damn, he was really hard up if that was enough to trigger arousal.

He watched her jump up, his jaw gritting when she commenced pacing in his living room. The layers of material forming her skirt swayed with each movement, granting him a view of supple hips and firm buttocks hidden beneath folds of chiffon. He also knew without parting those folds the killer legs currently shrouded from his gaze. Legs that had held him captive as he thrust hard and true inside her.

She pivoted when she reached the rug-covered wall, her movement understated grace and elegance but no less riveting.

His eyes dropped to the fingers curled around the wine glass she held.

Some part of his psyche seemed bent on torturing him because, with clarity that would probably baffle scientists, he recalled those hands greedily reaching for him, her short nails scouring his back as she lost herself in sexual pleasure.

Lauren had been by far the most responsive lover he'd bedded. As much as he wanted to convince himself otherwise, it'd been a vital part of what he'd regretted most about her when he'd walked away.

Because, what...? He'd retained some lofty idea that

their involvement would've extended beyond the boundaries of their university lives?

When his entire future had been mapped out since he'd taken his first breath? Back then, a part of him had mocked his belief that things could be different, while another part had been rebelliously hell-bent on finding out for himself. That part still resented her for taking his options away.

In an irregular move, his feelings about that must've shown on his face because she stopped mid-pace, her striking eyes widening. 'W…what are you doing?'

He forced his muscles to relax and raised an eyebrow. 'I thought it was obvious. I'm looking at you. It's hard not to when you're parading in front of me.'

'I'm hardly parading,' she threw back tartly but her tongue darted out to slick over her bottom lip, a nervous, tempting impulse she still retained.

He waved a hand at her. 'Continue. I recall you do your best thinking on your feet. Don't let me stop you.'

The glare she threw at him almost provoked a smile. 'And I remember you like to bait your opponents before delivering the coup de grâce. Is that what's happening here? Are you *relishing* this?'

'That depends.'

'On what?'

'On if we're discussing foreplay or something else,' he drawled.

Her mouth gaped for several amusing seconds before she snapped it shut. 'You *are* toying with me.'

'Am I?'

'Yes,' she hissed, her chest rising and falling, dragging his attention to the perfect mounds.

'Why would I do that?'

'Because I'm certain the last thing you'll want to be discussing with me is…is *sex*.'

The last word was hushed, and despite her blushing furiously there was a wariness to the word that punched another billow of heat through him. 'You say it like it's a dirty word.' His eyes narrowed. 'Has it become one to you?'

'If you're asking me if I've grown prudish, the answer is no. But there's a time and a place—'

'Like the middle of the night, over a glass of wine when certain subjects are off the table?' he finished drolly. 'It seems like the perfect time to discuss why there's no man in your life. Your name and position alone should have them lining up around the proverbial block,' he said, gut clenched against the acrid sensation that felt a lot like jealousy.

'You're wrong. Besides, I wouldn't want a man who was attracted to me simply because of my surname. Is that how you pick your lovers?'

'We're not talking about me, Lauren.'

Her fingers tightened momentarily around the glass as she turned away. Then he caught her wince as her stole slipped off her shoulder.

'What's that?' The question ejected out of him.

She frowned. Then followed his gaze to the distinct redness on her shoulder. 'Oh, I got a little sunburn.'

He didn't realise he'd jerked to his feet until he was moving towards her. When he saw the extent of the burn a wave of fury rolled through his gut… 'Were you given anything for it?'

She shook her head. 'It's nothing.'

His jaw gritted. 'It's not nothing. And you shouldn't keep it covered.' Reaching for the wrap, he tugged it away and flung it on a nearby seat.

Whirling, he strode out of the living room, along a series of hallways to his bedroom. Retrieving what he needed, he returned.

'Come here,' he said.

She remained where she stood. 'Stop ordering me about.'

'Come here, Lauren, or I'll confine you indoors for the remainder of the time while I get on with my day.'

She took her time to weigh his words while the concern-laced fury swirled in his belly. Fortunately, she realised it wasn't a bluff. With far too arresting movements, she glided back to the divan.

With the wrap out of the way, he couldn't stop himself from taking in her slim torso, the proud protrusion of her breasts, her trim waist and where her hips started to flare.

Whatever else had happened to her, Lauren Winchester hadn't lost an ounce of her allure. That confirmation fired straight to his shaft, swelling it with breath-stealing swiftness.

Begrudgingly thankful his tunic masked his reaction to her, he waited for her to sit, then crouched beside her. And immediately realised he'd compounded his situation when the sublime scent of jasmine, eucalyptus and woman filled his senses. He reached blindly for the tub while attempting not to greedily breathe her in.

'What is it?'

For a charged moment he thought she was addressing his state, but a glance saw hers moving from the container to his face. 'It's an organic balm prepared by the Zinabir women. I believe the base ingredient is aloe.'

She reached up and dragged her plait over one shoulder, her fingers gathering any stray strands away from the exposed skin. 'It smells amazing,' she murmured.

She smelled amazing. Intoxicating.

So much so he wanted to dip his nose into the smooth curve of her shoulder, inhale long and deep. Trail his tongue over that same path, feel goosebumps prickle to life against his lips.

Instead, he tossed the lid on the table, dug his fingers

into the balm and applied it onto her reddened skin. Any attempt to be clinical and detached failed immediately, her silky-smooth skin dragging him back yet again to a time when he'd had free rein to touch and stroke, taste and devour. A time when every inch of her body had been his much-relished playground.

A soft moan escaped her, and his teeth gritted harder, the sound punching through every barrier and resistance to gleefully fuel the inferno raging within.

'That feels so good,' she said huskily.

'Hmm,' was all he managed, his gaze fixated on the skin he caressed. Once he'd treated the reddened area twice, he exhaled. 'Now the other.' His voice was thicker, hoarser than he wished as he waited for her to present him with the other affected shoulder.

Tahir congratulated himself on keeping a tight leash on the groan that threatened to rip free as he tended to her. But he couldn't quite stop his fingers from drifting over the delicate shell of her ear and the spot beneath, confirming his thought when she shivered wildly.

'You're still sensitive here,' he croaked before he could catch his words.

Stunning eyes dark with lust met his. For tight seconds, they were locked in desire's maelstrom. Her nostrils quivered and the tiniest sound rippled from between her lips.

'I thought you weren't going to succumb to my charms ever again?' she taunted on a breathless whisper, even as her eyes devoured his mouth.

Effectively called out, he felt the lash of shame, but even more disconcerting was the urge to reverse his edict. To keep stroking that sublime skin, coax more delightful sounds from that beautiful throat.

Tight-jawed, he closed the lid to the tub with more force than needed, tossed it away and placed several necessary feet between them. 'That should give you some relief,' he said tightly.

She continued to watch him for a spell, then, her composure annoyingly restored, she murmured, 'Thank you.' A hint of a nervous smile curved her lips as her gaze glanced off his. 'It feels better already. You're right. It wasn't nothing. I don't know why I said what I did when you—'

His waved hand silenced her. 'You know why. You're just afraid to address it. But no more.'

Her head jerked up, surprise colliding with the beginnings of wary annoyance. 'Excuse me?'

'Wrong again. No more excuses.'

Her lips parted, no doubt to offer a scathing rebuttal, but the appearance of his young attendant hovering near the entrance stopped her. The message delivered had Tahir frowning, then feeling a touch relieved.

He glanced at the hourglass to see there were minutes left. 'Your time is almost up. I'm told my brother wishes to speak to me, so you get a little leeway while I take his call. We'll pick this up again when I return.'

Lauren watched him stride out, all broad shoulders and immutable power, with her mouth agape.

What the hell had just happened?

She didn't regret not pressing her claim about Matt. The strategy to bide her time was one she knew well. Sometimes the best way to create forward momentum was to first take a step back.

But the last thing she'd expected was for Tahir to spin even more circles around her.

Why was she surprised though? Hadn't he been the toughest, most astute strategist she'd ever come across?

Exhaling to alleviate the stress cramping her muscles, she told herself she was relieved he'd gone, but it was a lie.

As shameful as it was to admit, she'd never felt more alive than when he'd challenged her or irritated her with his insistence that she was a shadow of her former self.

As if she didn't know that. As if she didn't look at herself in the mirror each morning and drop her gaze in regret.

Eyeing the hourglass, she shook her head at the faint hollow in her stomach. Her intentions had backfired. She'd wasted two and a half hours in the process.

But beside that unnervingly bleak sensation coursing through her was a more dangerous one. She twisted her head to stare at the sheen on her left shoulder, the aloe working its magic, and suppressed another moan as she relived the last few minutes.

Tahir's touch had been electrifying, not diluted one iota by their butting heads—cerebrally or carnally. It was bad enough that she'd let out that moan. Worst still, she'd wanted him to keep going, to pick up her taunt and act on it. Tug her into his arms and kiss her again. *She'd craved it.*

She rose and retrieved her wrap and half-finished wine, ignoring the voice mocking her for shutting the door after the horse had bolted.

She paced, hoping the movement would clear her head. But it was no use. The heat in her pelvis continued to grow, sexual need building until she gave a frustrated groan.

For years she'd easily blocked out interest from the opposite sex.

Sure, she'd gone on a few dates, had even had a brief relationship with one or two men who'd sparked her interest for more than a few weeks. But inevitably, things had turned lukewarm and then fizzled out entirely.

Now she wished she hadn't called time on dating when she'd turned thirty. Maybe if she'd taken care of her sexual needs, she wouldn't be feeling this wound up by a simple, impersonal touch from Tahir.

But had it been impersonal?

Wasn't the fever rampaging through her that much hotter because she suspected he'd been affected by touching her too?

So what?

The Tahir she remembered had been a full-blooded male with a healthy interest in the opposite sex. An interest returned a hundred-fold. One minute in his presence had confirmed he'd grown into his masculinity, a powerful sexual being who only needed to lift a finger to have women crawling all over him.

She was nothing special to him. Especially after inadvertently embroiling him in scandal.

Renewed guilt doused the fever in her blood. She was contemplating how best to recommence her reason for being here when the young attendant returned.

'His Majesty would like you to join him,' he said.

'I...where is he?'

'Nearby,' he replied.

'Wait,' she said when he turned away. 'Is there a phone I can use? I need to make a call.'

He shook his head. 'There is no mobile service in the desert.'

Lauren pursed her lip against pressing further. Surely if Tahir was speaking to his brother, then he had a means of communication?

Suspecting the servant's response was a tailored one, she refrained from pressing. 'Okay. Thank you.'

It was still dark outside, but the camp was slowly rousing, the sounds of pots and pans and strong coffee filling the air.

A quick calculation summed up that she'd, surprisingly, been in Tahir's tent for over six hours. It'd felt like minutes!

They walked past the tents and up a small hill. While

she couldn't immediately see it clearly, Lauren could just about make out the outline of the mountain she'd seen from the helicopter looming in the distance.

And like the mountain, at first, she didn't see Tahir but her senses screamed that he was close. Halfway up the hill, she saw him, a towering figure framed against the dark sky. A shiver coursed through her, even as she berated herself for being melodramatic.

When she reached him, he didn't turn to greet her. What she saw of his face was fierce, deeply contemplative. Intuition hinted that it had nothing to do with the words he'd thrown at her before leaving the tent.

This was about something else.

'Is everything okay?' she ventured after a full minute had passed in silence.

His lips tightened. 'There's a situation brewing in Riyaal,' he said. 'It may be nothing or it could develop into something if Javid and my trade minister aren't successful in handling it.'

Javid was his younger brother, she recalled. The irreverent playboy Prince, known as much for his ability to charm women out of their underwear as for his exceptional skill in diplomacy. Lauren had wondered how that didn't create a huge conflict of interest every time she'd skimmed his hedonistic exploits in social media. 'Was that what the call was about?'

Tawny eyes swung to her, his eyes narrowing. 'Why, Lauren, you sound as if you care.'

The barb hit its mark, making her wince deep inside, but she was damned if she would give him the satisfaction. 'You sent for me. I'm here. You can pretend that I do care, see where that gets you.'

A gleam burned in his eyes. Under different circumstances, she would've termed it admiration, perhaps even respect. But it was gone an instant later, the austere expression back in place.

Turning away, he presented her with his profile once more, his gaze on the horizon. 'Perhaps, but for the next few moments, I wish to pass the time another way.'

She cursed herself for the way her pulse leapt. 'How?' she asked, thankful her voice wasn't as foolishly excitable. 'What's happening?'

He didn't answer, merely nudged his chiselled chin at the view.

Lauren followed his gaze and saw nothing but a dark grey landscape. About to ask what she was meant to be looking at, she swallowed her words when he raised a hand. The movement wasn't the imperious gesture she'd been subjected to a few times since her arrival. It was a…gentler motion, an anticipatory one that urged patience.

She redirected her focus to the inky landscape.

Then gave a soft gasp when the thinnest slash of orange broke through the grey. As she watched, the line continued to stretch horizontally across the bottom of the sky, a living painting come to life right before their eyes.

All around them, the desert held its breath in awe of nature's splendour.

Utterly mesmerised, Lauren barely saw Tahir lower his hand, but she didn't need to look at him to know he was equally riveted, perhaps even more so because the ground on which he stood was in his blood, his connection to land and sky and sand absolute.

Slowly, the sliver became a streak, then a forceful kaleidoscope of colour until the yellow took control, the sun's rays stretching fingers of benediction over the earth.

Sand dunes slowly took majestic form, undulating to life for countless miles as the new day burst into being.

'My God,' she breathed, humbled and alarmed in equal measure because Tahir had shared this with her.

Something moved within her, dangerously skimming far too close to vulnerable parts that needed to be kept barricaded.

He could've left her in the tent, and she would've been none the wiser.

Instead, he'd...

She turned to find him staring at her with an intensity that almost made her stumble back in shock.

Heat. Fury. Contemplation. Censure. *Desire.*

They all blazed in a furious mix, much like that kaleidoscope before the sun burst through just now. Lauren swallowed. She tried to tell herself it was the trick of the light, but the lie barely formed before it crumbled beneath the force of his stare.

Aware that some of those emotions might be reflected on her face, she averted her gaze. But like a sick compulsion, her eyes reconnected with his seconds later. 'Thank you for showing it to me. It's beautiful. But...why?'

For several heartbeats he didn't speak. Then his regal head turned, his eyes piercing her with a gimlet stare. 'Because it's worth sharing with friend *or* foe. The former because my kingdom is beautiful, and they'll appreciate it. The latter because they'll appreciate that my heart, my duty and my destiny is tied to this land, and I'll do anything to defend it.'

She was still processing the weighty response when his teeth bared in a smile that was at once breathtakingly beautiful and nape-tingling in its warning.

'Very soon you'll need to decide which one you are, Lauren.'

Her snatched-in breath stayed locked in her throat as he strode away from her, a tall, magnificent figure who commanded attention and received it, every tribesman, woman and child pausing as he approached.

Many exchanged smiling greetings and received one in return, but his stride barely broke as he headed for his tent.

Once he'd disappeared and she could breathe again, Lauren returned her gaze to the sunrise, now a gorgeous landscape of yellow, gold, brown and blue.

Friend or foe.

She knew which one she wanted to be. But was beginning to fear that, whatever she did, Tahir would always regard her as an enemy.

That insight took some getting used to, keeping her on the hill several minutes more until the reminder that she had a task to perform regardless of her own personal feelings sent her back down to the camp.

She entered Tahir's tent and drew to a stop. Attendants were packing his belongings, some monogrammed cases already stacked beside the entrance.

'You're leaving? I... We had an agreement!' As much as she wanted to attribute the hollow sensation inside her to Matt's predicament, she knew it was for her. She wasn't ready to be done with him. Wasn't ready to leave Tahir. The truth shook through her as his lips twisted in a sardonic smile.

'How quickly you doubt me.'

She frowned. 'Doubt you? Your things are being packed. I...if I'm wrong and you're not leaving, then tell me what's happening.'

His eyes glinted at her firm insistence. Lauren caught the attendants' shocked looks at her addressing their Sheikh with such bolshiness but she didn't cower or apologise. They *did* have an agreement.

'Zinabir was only meant to be a pit stop. It's customary for me to spend one night with my people here before I move on.'

'Move on where?' And did that include her or—?

'My final destination is further north. And before you throw even more of that indignation my way, yes, Lauren, you're coming with me.'

CHAPTER SIX

AFTER A LAVISH BREAKFAST of honeyed dates, roasted oats in natural yoghurt and strong, aromatic coffee that did its job of caffeinating her, they prepared to leave.

With nothing to pack besides her freshly laundered dress currently folded into the handbag slung over her shoulder, Lauren was ready in minutes.

What she wasn't ready for was the huge camel eyeing her with dark caramel eyes as it chewed on freshly cut grass.

She'd seen Tahir's belongings being loaded onto two four-by-fours and watched in stunned surprise as half his bodyguards drove away with them. The remaining four were now seated on their own beasts, and Lauren felt as if everyone in the camp was watching her.

Even curled up on the ground, the creature looked hugely intimidating and deeply bored all at once. 'Care to tell me why we're not in the SUV with your other guards?' she asked Tahir, who stood imposingly a few feet away having just finished conversing with the camp's leader.

'It's very simple, Lauren. My kingdom, my rules,' he stated with such simple but implacable authority, it resonated deep in her bones. 'But if you're feeling unduly inconvenienced just say the word and I'll have you flown back to the capital.'

She bit her lip, eyeing the creature that looked even

larger up close. 'I'm… I only hesitate because I've never ridden a camel before. I… I've heard they bite.'

'Only if they don't trust their rider. Show her you're trustworthy and you won't have a problem.'

'Her?' she repeated tentatively, a little less nervous at the thought of riding a female camel.

'Don't let her gender fool you. The females are often the feistiest.'

She'd taken a tentative step towards the animal who was eyeing her steadily when she felt Tahir's presence behind her.

Strong hands wrapped around her waist, and she was drawn back against a hard, solid chest. Warmth flowed over her skin, suffusing her in heat she wanted to stay in for ever.

'Are you ready?' he murmured in her ear, his breath causing another shiver to steal through her.

'As I'll ever be.'

Was it her imagination or did he give a very faint chuckle? She didn't dare turn to investigate because she risked him seeing what his proximity did to her. How every atom of her jumped in excitement and strained towards him.

Without warning, he hoisted her up and into the saddle. Suppressing a yelp, she clutched the pommel and fought not to slide right off.

'Lower your centre of gravity, tighten your legs and move with her. She'll do the rest.'

'Just like that?'

His eyes locked with hers, a sombre look drifting through the tawny depths before they hardened. 'Sometimes the simplest solution is to let go and let be. And sometimes it is not.'

Her nape tingled, certain his response was aimed at far more than riding a camel, drenching her like a rogue wave.

She swallowed as his gaze stayed on her for a fraction

too long. Then, freed from it, she watched him swing effortlessly into his own saddle, his innate grace and absolute masculinity almost too overwhelming to witness.

A click of his tongue and murmured words and both his camel and hers moved, their smooth undulating gaits settling into a pleasant rhythm once she got used to it.

When the well-wishing cries of the desert tribe faded away, they settled into a semi-charged silence. They were fully immersed in his two-and-a-half-hour time slot, and she was reluctant to raise any subject that might trigger more of his probing questions.

'How will we know when your time is up?' She couldn't immediately see the hourglasses or the case they'd come in.

His gaze slid from the horizon to her, one eyebrow arched in mocking contemplation. 'Feeling anxious?'

She shrugged. 'As you said, rules are rules.'

'I'll let you know when it's your time. Unless you doubt my honour?' he finished with a bite that lanced through her.

'No, I don't doubt you.' And she didn't.

Something shifted in his eyes. She wanted to tell herself that her words had touched him, but his lashes veiled his expression, his profile veering from her a second later, stopping her from verifying that thought.

And because she couldn't let it go, because some vital place inside her seemed hell-bent on satisfying that peculiar curiosity, she continued. 'Your people love you.'

His gaze snapped back to her, his brooding eyes narrowed. Searching. Assessing.

He'd warned her against playing him. Against attempting to soften him up for her own and for Matt's advantage. It stood to reason he would be sceptical of her unsanctioned observation.

'It's true,' she pressed on steadily. 'I've only been in Jukrat a handful of days, but I've heard the way they talk about you, the way they respect your rule. I'm not trying to kiss your ass. It's just an honest observation. You have a lot to be proud of.'

'They didn't always feel that way,' he offered after a handful of minutes had passed when she'd thought he would ignore her.

She waited for the hard look in his eyes to soften. For his clenched jaw to ease. Because she suspected that she was culpable for it.

'I didn't always live up to my father's expectations.'

Guilt was a living flame searing her insides. 'Because of what happened?'

His lips thinned but then, surprisingly, he shook his head. 'That was the straw that broke the camel's back, as it were.' He glanced down briefly at his camel, his mouth twitching when the creature turned its head to fix him with a censorious gaze. He clicked his tongue and the animal faced forward again.

'He was a hard taskmaster, probably because he had large shoes to fill after my grandfather's rule and felt he needed to be overly stringent with me. I lived with the threat of letting him down from infancy until he passed.' There was an uncommon bleakness to his tone that sent a wave of sympathy through her.

She lived with that threat every day too, but she wasn't a powerful ruler, much adored by her kingdom. 'But...you're accomplished in many ways. Even twelve years ago you were more or less the person you are now.'

He slanted her another assessing look. 'You don't think I faked it till I made it?' he asked, thick sardonicism in his tone.

'No,' she answered truthfully. 'I believe you'd boil yourself in hot oil before you faked a single thing.'

He stiffened in his saddle, but a glimmer appeared in his eyes, his chest moving as he sharply exhaled.

'How well you think you know me,' he murmured, again after a handful of minutes, his words infused with charged emotions.

'Am I wrong?' she asked, despite sternly berating herself for her runaway tongue.

'No. I abhor subterfuge of any kind,' he confirmed, implacable power in his tone.

She swallowed. She considered laying it all bare, telling him why she was caught between a rock and a hard place, but wasn't it twelve years too late? Pushing the disquieting thought away, she refocused on their discussion.

'So your life was an endless series of hoop-jumping, but surely there was some sort of balance?'

He sent her a droll look. 'You're wondering if the stick was mitigated by the occasional carrot?'

'Wasn't it?'

She didn't see it this time, only sensed the bleakness tingeing the air.

'He reserved his affections for others. One person in particular. A person who didn't particularly welcome it.'

Having been a subject of blatant favouritism, Lauren could hazard a guess. 'Your brother?'

'No.' The terse response came without further clarification.

'Who, then?'

A firmer flattening of his lips, then, 'My mother,' he rasped.

She frowned, recalling that while he'd spoken of his brother and father, he'd rarely mentioned his mother. In fact, was it only yesterday he'd spoken of her? She felt as if she'd lived a year since they'd met in his office.

'Does she live with you at the palace?'

'No.'

The finality of the answer made her wonder if she'd drawn a bad memory. 'I'm sorry, she's not…is she still…?'

'Alive? Yes, very much so. She moved to Paris after my father died. We meet once or twice a year for the customary stilted lunch or dinner when she stages a maternal performance neither of us believe in.'

Lauren winced at the acerbity in his tone. 'Why staged?'

His nostrils gave the briefest flare, then he was back in supreme control. 'Because my mother exists solely to bargain her way into more of whatever she desires.' He caught her puzzled frown and elaborated. 'She isn't the kind of mother who gives anything for free, be it her duties as Queen Mother or her affection for her children.'

'You mean she had to be *paid* to love you?' she asked, disbelief bleeding through her voice.

Another stark look flashed across his face. 'Is it love if she had to be paid to bear me or my brother?'

'How do you know? Did she…did she tell you?' The thought of that was abhorrent, even worse in her opinion than being abandoned at birth by a mother who wanted nothing to do with you. At least in her case, she'd been given up to the authorities in the hope that she might be given a better life.

'There was documentation to that effect. She received a sum for delivering her firstborn and another for her second. From then on, each achievement, great or small, was transactional. I learned that to get her attention, I needed to give her something in return.'

'Something like what?'

'As a child it was mostly a sacrificial transaction. One appearance at a school recital meant she was free to skip the next two or three. As an adult, it was more…materialistic.

Attending a handful of important state functions usually cost me a villa in Spain or an upgrade on her private jet.'

She sucked in a stunned breath. 'That's...deplorable.'

'Is it?' he parried with a curiously flat tone. 'Or was it a valuable early lesson that everything comes at a price?'

'Surely you don't believe that?'

Leonine eyes cut to her, their depths holding no give. 'Isn't that why you're here? You may delude yourself that it is out of duty for your brother, but haven't others bargained with that duty to drive you to me when it was perhaps not your own choice?'

His intuitiveness floored her, as did the cutting comparison to his mother. But in truth, she could deny neither.

She was still floundering when he clicked his tongue and muttered to his mount. The camel kicked into a light trot, signalling their conversation was over. Hers followed, uneasy silence descending as they headed north.

Just as she feared her nerves would snap at the tension between them, a stunning, immense riad-style villa came into view. With soaring gold sun-shaped domes and ochre exterior walls, it blended seamlessly into the desert.

As they drew closer, she saw further graceful arches and wide terraces, the breathtaking Moorish villa a feast for the senses. Guards were posted at the entrance and at various discreet points along the storeyed terraces, but it didn't take away from the beauty of Tahir's desert residence.

It was only as Lauren's gaze shifted back to Tahir's broad shoulders that she realised they were bypassing the entrance and skirting the villa altogether.

Another handful of minutes later, they approached a wide cluster of palm trees and what looked astonishingly like...a large, sparkling body of water.

She reached him just as his camel was settling itself on the ground and Tahir was sliding out of his saddle.

'Where are we?'

'My private oasis. We'll go inside once we're done here.'

He murmured to her mount and the creature lowered itself. Her breath locked in her throat when he reached for her. As before, he wrapped his hands around her waist and lifted her off the beast, but this time they faced one another, and the strong compulsion that seemed to have become part of her commanded her gaze upward to clash with his.

For breathless moments, they simply stared at one another, his hands holding her captive while her heart banged hard against her ribs. Perhaps it was a trick of the light, but everything inside her froze in anticipation as his head descended a fraction, those far too sensual lips drawing tantalisingly closer.

But in the next instant he was setting her free, jerking away from her before striding towards his guards. One of them approached with a large basket and set it down on a flat rock a few feet from the edge of the water as she took a better look at her surroundings.

Several tall boulders formed a natural barrier against the elements on one side, while palm trees framed the remaining area, creating a circle of rock and trees with the sparkling spring a welcoming respite stop.

The spring itself was about the size of two Olympic-sized swimming pools and as she approached it she could see clear to the bottom of the turquoise-coloured water.

'I usually come to cool off here to complete my journey,' Tahir murmured from behind her.

She startled a little, unaware he'd approached while she'd been lost in the wonder of the little oasis. Then all she could think of was him, his proximity wreaking havoc on her senses.

'It's beautiful. It feels like a special place.' A place for lovers. For a sheikh to relax with his sheikha. To forget about duty and obligations and destiny and simply…be.

And because she knew such a place would never be for her with a man like Tahir, she cast around for a way, *any* way to distract herself from the acutely depressing thought.

But then he stepped away, and she saw that they were alone. The bodyguards had left. It was most likely because there was only one entrance to this magical place, and they were confident their sire wouldn't be in any danger.

'This is the only place I'm truly alone.'

'Do you want me here?' Her gaze went to where the contents of the basket had been spread out on a large picnic blanket. Somehow, the hourglass was still upright, the passage of time relentless. Peering closer, she saw that there was about a quarter of the portion remaining. 'You can have the rest of the time on your own.'

'I said twenty-four hours together. Nothing has changed.'

She swallowed her disquiet. 'What would you do if you were here on your own?'

A glimmer started in his eyes, and she watched, breath held tight in her chest, as it grew to a spark, then a flame. She was half relieved, half disappointed when his lashes dropped but it was only so he could conduct a searing scrutiny of her body, in a way that left little doubt as to the direction of his thoughts. The sensations roiling through her gave way to hot, scalding jealousy. Was he thinking about the last time he'd been here and, specifically, who he'd been with?

'Never mind. I don't think I want to know.'

Both eyebrows slowly rose. 'Oh, but I think you do,' he drawled.

'What you do and who you do it with is none of my business.'

'Then why ask?'

She floundered, then threw in a shrug. 'I was just making conversation.'

'You've come this far. Don't be a coward now, *habibti.*'

Habibti. She knew that word. It was an endearment she hadn't heard in a dozen years. Last whispered hotly in her ear, right before a hoarse roar signalled his climax swiftly on the heels of hers.

Darling. Sweetheart. Treasured one.

The spark of heat in her blood became a blaze, charged by the memory and his deliberate taunt. Calling her a coward was meant to rile her. She knew that. She shouldn't have fallen for it.

And yet she let him stoke the fire. Let her nostrils flare in a fruitless exhale of her irritation. 'Call me a coward again. I dare you. *Your Majesty.*' She let her own taunt linger in his title, felt a bolt of satisfaction when his eyes narrowed.

'Here in this place, I'm Tahir to you. And *you* can be your true self. No inhibitions.'

Those last two words turned that blaze into an inferno. Something dangerously sultry and seductive that magnified the thumping of her heart; intensified the sweet, heavy scents weaving through the air. The very tangible thrum of lust winding around them.

Without waiting for a response—or because he wasn't about to be affected one way or the other by whatever she did next—he strolled with sure, lithe strides towards the waterfall.

'You asked what I normally do here when I'm alone. I would normally swim naked. But so as not to excite your very English sensibilities…' He deliberately trailed off, absorbing every ounce of his attention as he pulled the strings of his trousers and the linen material dropped to pool at his feet.

Lauren was half ashamed of the dart of disappointment when she saw the boxer shorts he wore beneath. The other half of her was desperately pleading with herself to stop her blatant ogling of his magnificent body.

As was evident from watching him this last half-day, the years had only built on the already perfect specimen that was Tahir Al-Jukrat.

There was no spare flesh on his body, just a physique honed by genes and discipline and a masculinity gifted by an impeccable lineage.

The blazing sun threw every bare inch of him into perfect, bronzed relief and a full-bodied shiver tingled through her, a deep craving to touch seizing her with such power that she needed to yank her gaze away to stop herself from doing the unthinkable. From surging up and closing the distance between them, letting her fingers explore the chiselled planes and muscled valleys. From scenting and tasting and feasting as she never had before.

A loud splash jerked her free of her desperate craving to find Tahir submerged in the crystal-clear water. He dived beneath the surface, causing barely a ripple. She held her breath, watching with rapt attention as half a minute passed before he broke the surface at the far end.

'Are you just going to sit there?'

His deep, sexy voice carried across the water, made all the more electrifying by the look he cast her.

Lauren chewed on her lip.

A swim with the sovereign ruler of Jukrat. Something to tell her grandchildren decades from now when she reprised the twenty-four-hour game she'd engaged in with Tahir.

For the sake of her brother.

Guilt rippled through her chest. She hadn't given Matt a thought in the last hour. Watching Tahir's lazy, powerful strokes as he swam back to her, she knew she wouldn't be thinking about her brother for the duration of the time in the hourglass.

'I don't have a swimsuit,' she said, clinging to the feeble excuse.

He resurfaced a few feet from her, throwing his head back to dislodge the wet strands from his eyes. The move threw his face and throat into sun-worshipping relief, and it was so sexy, Lauren couldn't help but stare in awe. Even when his gaze settled on her, when he drifted closer, his eyes darkening with the desire he seemed to be giving free rein to, she couldn't avert her gaze.

'Are you going to let that stop you?'

She grimaced at the thought of swimming in her underwear. But the superseding thought was that she would be minus the cover of her clothes, in the presence of the most dynamic, physically arresting man she'd ever encountered.

And why that only sent spirals of fevered anticipation through her veins.

She'd covered her head and shoulders with the wrap before they'd left the camp and now the sun had risen higher, it was a relief to discard it. Especially when Tahir's gaze heated up as it raked the skin she bared.

Breath hitching, she dropped her gaze from his, striving not to be overwhelmed as she eased down the zip beneath one arm and drew the top over her head. Rising to her feet, she pulled off the skirt and tossed it away.

Tahir's gaze was still locked on her when she sent a furtive glance his way, and she couldn't stop the flow of heat to her face at the stamp of arousal etched into his.

With a smooth dive, she plunged into the water, with hope she suspected was futile that it would dissipate the reciprocal sensations moving through her.

For a few moments, she was overcome with a different sensation.

Her bath last night had been heavenly, but this was pure bliss. Copying Tahir, she swam underwater until her lungs demanded oxygen.

When she surfaced, he was resting against the rock she'd just dived off, his elbows propped behind him as he watched her.

She told herself the distance was wise. And yet, a few minutes later, she found herself drifting towards him, her gaze locked on him.

'Enjoying yourself?' he drawled, a glint in his eyes.

She was, and again that dart of guilt assailed her.

The glint disappeared, his eyes turning brooding again. 'This is my time, and I will not permit self-flagellation. Especially when the cause is your brother,' he growled.

'You mean to command my emotions now?' It slipped out before she could stop herself, that thrilling urge to challenge him a lure she couldn't resist.

'You think I cannot?' he returned. Before she could respond, 'Come here, Lauren,' he growled, eyes fixed on her with rabid intensity.

She shook her head but even that action was too feeble for her liking.

He didn't address her refusal, merely continued to stare at her with heavy, imperious expectation.

Wondrously compelled, she complied, her actions almost independent of her stunned thoughts. She reached him, and witnessed the infuriating satisfaction etched in his face.

Spinning her around with speed that snatched her breath away, he lifted her from the water, settled her on the flat rock and dropped his forearms on both sides of her hips.

Lauren fought the urge to fidget, fought the urge to demand he put those hands on her. Because in that moment, nothing else mattered but satisfying the clarion call of her body, the demand to lick off those droplets of water saucily clinging to his lips.

She must have made a sound or licked her own lips; Lauren couldn't summon the cognition to verify. His eyes dropped to her mouth, his jaw clenching tight as he exhaled harshly.

Gripping the backs of her thighs, he parted her legs and situated himself between them. The hard, packed torso brushed her inner thighs as he moved closer. Heated eyes scoured her body once. Twice. Then a low growl rumbled from him. 'I have to taste you again.'

Anticipation shivered through her as she too exhaled. 'Please,' she whispered, too far gone to contemplate the consequences of that one, betraying word.

Flames burst to life in his eyes, sending out a loud warning that she might not be the same once he was done accepting the invitation she'd issued.

'Be sure, Lauren,' he added, as if he'd divined the inner caution.

In answer, and because her roiling senses had deprived her of speech, she draped her arms around his neck, then lowered her head until their lips were less than an inch apart.

The invitation was clear. Unequivocal.

He seized it.

The hands she'd craved clutched at her hips, digging in and branding her and holding her in place. At the same time, he surged up and captured her mouth with his in a deep ravishing that had her moaning with pleasure.

His tongue swept into her mouth, tangling briefly with hers before he nipped at her bottom lip. Her tiny cry drew an animalistic groan from his throat. Then he was swirling his tongue over the delicious hurt, creating whirlpools of desire that swiftly turned into ravenous cyclones. Her fingers tunnelled into his wet hair, gripping tight as she strained closer.

Her breasts pressed into his chest, the diamond-hard tips causing decadent friction that intensified the flames leaping through her blood. Between her legs, damp heat mounted, her clitoris plumping in needy longing.

Again and again, he nipped and licked and devoured.

Again and again, she shuddered in delight, her senses soaring. She'd lost sense of time when he raised his head, pulling back a fraction.

A whimper escaped her. 'More,' she pleaded. Drunk on desire. Drunk on him.

For an eternity, his gaze drilled into hers, seeking something she couldn't quite name. After another eternity, he dragged her arms from his neck and planted them on the rock.

'Don't move,' he commanded.

She was about to protest the distance between them, her breath strangled when he surged forward, his mouth locating the pulse throbbing at her throat. Another helpless cry fell from her lips, echoing over the water before surging back into her. Her vision grew hazy, delight dancing through her.

Languidly, he explored her pulse, basking in the furious desire he'd created in her.

His fingers moved to her bra strap. Still trailing his lips over her skin, he lowered one, then the other. Firm lips brushed her collarbone and a deep sigh escaped her.

She'd missed this.

Missed *him*.

This mindless pleasure only he had been able to invoke in her. It dawned on her then that the reason she hadn't been able to commit to the few relationships she'd tried out was because they'd never come close to what she'd experienced with Tahir. Neither time nor experience had brought the sort of exhilarating combustion just being in Tahir's presence had provoked. And so, she'd given up even before it'd started...

For one heart-thumping moment the power of that realisation threatened to wrench her from the euphoria engulfing her. But then his masterful lips trailed lower, over the crest of her breast, and she was lost. In sensation. In stomach-clenching anticipation as he dropped kisses over her flesh, everywhere but where she needed him most. The hard peak furled tighter as she clenched her fingers in his hair, urging him to her nipple.

It was only because her rapt gaze was fixed on him that she caught his fleeting, wicked smile. But his face grew serious again, the hard edge of arousal making him even more breathtaking. Making her insides melt with disgraceful ease.

She was watching him when those lips closed over one rosy peak. He boldly suckled her, swirled his tongue in decadent flickers that arrowed sensation straight between her legs.

Lauren gave herself up to the pleasure, panting when, after mindless minutes, he firmly urged her backwards to lie flat on the stone.

Brooding eyes skimmed greedily over her, setting off further fireworks wherever it touched.

'You look like the most decadent sacrifice, *habibti*.'

She wanted to ask if such a sacrifice was worthy to erase the turbulent episode of their past.

But desire and emotion she wasn't willing to name clogged her throat. Perhaps that was a good thing because she didn't want to ruin this moment. Didn't want to halt this incredible experience that might very well be her last.

Right now, Lauren was fully intent on being selfish. On

not allowing thoughts of Matt or her parents to impinge on this moment.

She took it without shame or rancour. Because it was possible this might be what she needed to move on. To form better relationships in the future.

Her actions had prevented them from reaching the natural conclusion of their last affair. Perhaps this was the closure she needed.

Or maybe you're deluding yourself.

She shied away from the taunting voice, happily gave up thinking as Tahir spoke again.

'A sacrifice I won't deny myself,' he concluded thickly, his hands tightening on her inner thighs. Right before he parted her to his searing gaze.

For another interminable age, he simply stared down at her, his tongue moving languidly over his bottom lip in shameless, ravenous anticipation.

'Tahir.' His name was a croak of helpless need that had his nostrils flaring in satisfaction and triumph. That had his broad shoulders squaring as if accepting his regal due.

'Yes, *habibti.* You will say my name like that, scream it when I bring you pleasure.'

Another imperious command she had no trouble obeying.

And when he lowered his head and boldly tasted her, she cried out, her head rolling back as desire rippled in relentless waves through her.

He teased and tormented, savoured and pleasured her until his name was an anthem, her hands blindly seeking his broad shoulders as he pushed her to the brink.

The sweet torment intensified as he kept her there, repeatedly denying her release until she was a mindless mess.

Only then did he grant her the climax that had her

screaming his name, her nails digging into his flesh as bliss washed over her.

Eyes squeezed shut, her breathing rapid enough to cause alarm, she felt him climb onto the rock beside her, gather her close.

Still drunk on her release, she burrowed into him, the warmth and scent of his skin filling her with further delight.

But soon the silence encroached, the fractious past and unstable present splintering the air in the aftermath.

She wanted to raise her head, look into his face and decipher what he was thinking but, again, she feared what he would read in hers.

So when, without speaking, he slipped off the rock and lowered them both into the water, she told herself it was for the best. When he swam to the other side, heaved himself out of the water and began to dress, she convinced herself there was no reason to be upset.

And yet, upset she was as she too dressed, and they picnicked in silence. As she let him lift her back onto the camel to complete their journey.

He shouldn't have done that.

The grim conclusion settled deeper into Tahir as they dressed. For starters, he'd created a memory he'd now always associate with Lauren at a place special to him.

He'd given in to temptation.

He exhaled in self-loathing and self-recrimination.

Mere hours after he'd proclaimed such a thing would never happen, he'd jumped into the fire of desire that now threatened to consume him. He grimaced and adjusted the painful throbbing of his arousal. To compound his sins, he couldn't stop glancing her way. Couldn't stop his eyes lingering on lips reddened from his kisses. From examining the faint marks he'd left on her neck with his heavy caresses as she half-heartedly nibbled fruit from their picnic spread.

Steering his gaze away for the umpteenth time, he willed calm into his body, dredged up all the reasons why tangling with her was a bad idea.

But those reasons felt hollow when all he could concentrate on were her moans, her eager responses and those greedy hands on his body.

Tahir was relieved when he finally guided her to his riad. *Home.*

Yet another place he was bringing Lauren to that held the potential to etch memories he didn't want added to the fabric of his life.

The solution is easy. End this now. Send her away.

His unfettered growl made the camel corralled nearby grunt uneasily.

Reaching out, he smoothed his hand down the camel's side. 'Easy, *habibti*,' he murmured, then grimaced. Another endearment he couldn't utter without thinking about her and what had just occurred.

Her uninhibited responses. That tinge of wonder that made him speculate what sort of relationships she'd been in that could've left such traces of innocence.

He growled again as another sensation stirred within him.

Jealousy.

Ridiculous, he told himself. He was a sheikh, the supreme ruler of a prosperous kingdom.

True. But he'd been drawn to this one right from the start.

Yes. And she betrayed you. Remember that.

Curiously though, the insistence was less powerful, the hint of a question at the end of that warning disturbing enough for him to quicken his steps, hoping it would dispel the thoughts pursuing him.

Yes, Lauren might have betrayed him. They would never be friends but how many of his past lovers had he been friends with?

His jaw clenched as he summed up the number on one hand. As his mother had taught him, he'd ensured his liaisons were transactional. Guaranteed pleasure on both sides, followed by a tasteful gift and assurance that the involvement would remain discreet.

And that was a thing to be proud of? Like baring the details of his relationship with his parents, something he'd never discussed with anyone but his younger brother?

He swallowed as his discomfort intensified, as the true depths of his revelations settled on him. Lauren was the only woman he'd acted out of character with. Should she choose to make public the intimate details he'd shared with her as she had twelve years ago, he would deal with it.

With compulsion he was starting to resent, his gaze swung back to her.

What was it about this woman that made him act out of character? It couldn't simply be her ravishing body. Her brilliant mind had also been a thing of awe.

But he'd met equally brilliant people in his time as Prince and many more since he took the throne. None of them had impacted him so deeply.

So what was it…?

He gladly gave up pursuing his chaotic thoughts as he walked through the gates of the sprawling riad.

This time when he helped Lauren off her camel, he ensured there was minimal contact, striding off the moment her feet touched the ground. He curled the hands that itched to touch her, relive those moments at the springs, and took a step back.

'You'll be shown to your rooms to refresh, but the game isn't done. See you in ten minutes.'

CHAPTER SEVEN

LAUREN WATCHED HIM walk away, her thoughts churning faster with each step he took away from her. As at the camp, beautifully dressed female attendants surrounded her, the matron introducing herself as Nesa.

Unlike the desert, however, these women were less smiley, the contemplative curiosity in their eyes more solemn than their nomadic counterparts. They also moved with purposeful briskness, ushering her away with quick, firm strides.

Lauren felt like a goldfish in a bowl as she trotted after them, her eyes goggling at her stunning surroundings.

Several arched mosaic-tiled hallways bordered large courtyards overflowing with potted palms, cacti and colourful groupings of seats.

After the sixth such courtyard, she knew she'd need a map to navigate her way around the villa.

They finally stopped before a set of soaring double doors made entirely of what looked like carved petrified wood. Had she been alone, Lauren was sure she'd have run her fingers over it, explored the gentle bumps and dips carved by time and the deep gold handles in wonder.

But then she was being ushered into a breathtakingly beautiful private living room. On the floors, large, exquisite Persian and Berber rugs muffled the sound of their footsteps. The ocean-blue colour scheme was repeated in the velvet sofa, the multitude of cushions and benches stationed around the room and the mosaic patterns etched into the walls and ceilings.

A queen-sized bed was equally exquisite, with posts and white muslin curtains currently drawn back and held by silk woven rope. On the opposite side of the dressing room, she was beckoned by another colourful room.

The walls of the bathroom were painted a jewelled peacock green with gold and copper accents including a large tub that made her yearn for a dip. Dragging her gaze from the inviting sight, she followed through into a dressing room, slowing to stop at the sight that greeted her.

No.

Tahir wouldn't be so crass as to direct his staff to show her into a room that belonged to a lover or concubine.

Nevertheless, she needed to be sure. The mixture of dread and jealousy stirring in her stomach would only grow if she remained silent.

'I think there's been a mistake. These clothes...' She paused, wondering how to couch her words without causing offence. 'They're not mine.'

'His Majesty's residences maintain a certain standard,' Nesa replied. 'I'm sure he wouldn't like for any guest to feel...inconvenienced.'

Lauren sensed criticism within the words but strove to rise above it.

Delivering a saccharine smile of her own—a talent she'd honed from years of dealing with sketchy politicians with hidden agendas—she nodded. 'Thank you for the consideration.'

Nesa inclined her head, and just like that the matter was settled. They showed her the balcony with the trellised pergola that boasted even more areas for relaxation and after another stolen minute admiring the jaw-dropping views of mountains and sand dunes, she returned to the bedroom, freezing when she saw the phone on the bedside table.

'Do you have mobile service here?'

Her heart fell as Nesa shook her head. 'No, but the land-line works.'

She barely heard Nesa say she would fetch her in five minutes. The moment Lauren was alone, she hurried to the phone. Heart in her mouth, she lifted the receiver and dialled the familiar number.

'Hello?'

'Lauren?' Her mother's cultured tones held underlying censure and disapproval. 'Where have you been? The staff have been trying to reach you at your hotel since yesterday.'

The staff.

Not her. Not her father. No enquiries as to whether she was okay.

Despite three decades of the tangible distance she'd always felt from her parents, her stupid, vulnerable craving for acceptance made it hurt that neither of them had bothered to pick up the phone themselves.

She gripped the handset tighter and buried the hurt, as she was used to doing. 'There was no time to let you know where I was going.'

'And where did you go?' Alice Winchester enquired. 'Did you manage to make progress with Matt's case?'

'Not yet.'

'Not yet,' her mother echoed, a distinct chill in her voice. 'You've been there four days.'

I'm not a miracle worker, she wanted to snap. She bit her tongue just in time to hear her mother sniff.

'Poor Matt must be beside himself.'

'Have you spoken to him?'

A throb of silence passed before her mother answered, 'I've been told he's not allowed phone calls.'

It wasn't true. Her mother simply hadn't been able to fit in a call to her jailed son around her schedule. Or more likely, her father had forbidden her from contacting Matt in case word got out.

'We'll have ample time to speak when he gets home. You are making sure that happens, aren't you?' The question was pointed, the ever-present implication that Lauren wasn't allowed to fail heavily underscored.

Her gaze went to the empty doorway, for some absurd reason picturing Tahir standing there with another brooding look levelled her way. Heat snaked through her, her mind delving back to what had happened at the springs, how much she'd given up to him, consequences be damned—

'Lauren? Are you there?'

She started guiltily, controlling her erratic breathing as she answered, 'I'm here, Mum. And…yes, I'm working on it.'

'Good. Your father will be glad to hear that. We really need to put this unpleasant business behind us as soon as possible. Let us know when you're both on your way home.' The final words held a throb of hope laced with guilt, and she wondered whether her mother felt more than she was projecting.

Before Lauren could be certain, the line went dead. She replaced the receiver as Tahir's words from last night echoed in her mind.

'…why you're sacrificing yourself for the sake of your ungrateful family.'

The question prodded harder as she stared at herself in the bathroom mirror.

Her braid had come loose during her swim. Locating a brush, she dragged it through the tresses until they flowed over her shoulders. Aware that the minutes were fast ticking down, she hurried to the dressing room and plucked out the first outfit she saw.

The cobalt-blue skirt was the same layered Jukrati design she'd worn last night, but with a wide-sleeved matching top. The material was a soft, light and airy linen, the exaggerated boat-shaped design of the top allowing for her healing shoulder burns not to be aggravated.

Sliding on slippers in the same hue, she dug out her lip gloss from her handbag and applied a light sheen before leaving her bed suite.

Nesa was waiting on a delicate-looking scroll bench outside her rooms, her arms folded neatly in her lap. When she saw Lauren, she rose and politely gestured towards another arched hallway.

They passed Doric columns and walls decorated with Arabian lanterns that threw artful shapes onto the walls, making the whole space a feast for the eyes and the senses.

Another myriad hallways, tiny alcoves and courtyards later, they arrived in the largest space she'd seen yet.

It was a garden courtyard, the largest one she'd seen so far and it was stunning, the peacock-green walls and trees decorated with miniature Turkish lamps that would be spectacular in the evening. In true Jukrati style, low divans and long benches festooned with bright-coloured cushions were positioned in careful arrangements. In one corner, a small fountain tinkled pleasantly, adding a relaxing ambience to the space.

Seeing Tahir seated at one of the tables didn't exactly aid that relaxation though. Hysterical butterflies took wing in her belly, their agitation intensifying the closer she got to him.

He'd changed attire too, and if his all-black garments from last night had given him a larger-than-life presence, his all-white tunic and trousers now lent him a towering aura that was far too breathtaking.

He watched her for a beat before he spoke. 'You spoke to your parents.'

It wasn't a question. Anger and hurt—most likely a residue from her phone call with her mother—lashed within her. 'You're monitoring my calls?'

'Do I need to remind you again of my security protocols?' Before she could answer, he continued coolly, 'A call was logged to England. The content of your call wasn't monitored. I drew the natural conclusion.'

As quickly as it rose, her temper dissipated. 'Okay. Yes, I spoke with my mother.'

One eyebrow slowly rose. 'By your tone, the conversation didn't go the way you imagined it would?'

She wanted to snap at him not to make her relive it. But that was as good as admitting things were bad. That she was burying her head in the sand. And…she was tired of doing that. Tired of fighting on endless fronts.

'No, it didn't.'

He stared at her for an age, then, without breaking eye contact, he raised his hand. Seeming to materialise out of thin air, a smiling young man stepped forward with a tray of refreshments. 'Lunch will be served in two hours. In the meantime, have something. You barely ate the picnic food.'

The reminder of their torrid episode at the springs drew heat into her face. She remained silent as a bountiful spread was laid out on the table.

Then the now familiar hourglass tray was delivered on a hand-painted pedestal and placed next to her chair.

'Shall we resume?'

He was sticking to the letter of their game, but she had a strong feeling he would be counting the minutes until he took full control again.

When she lifted the silk cloth, a mere fifteen minutes stood between her and his wish. Resolutely, she flipped the hourglass. And took a different tack.

'Are you going to tell me what the problem is in Riyaal?'

For the longest time, his lips firmed. Just when she thought he'd refuse to answer, he did. 'My cousin is being obstinate about our trade talks. Apparently, he's decided the terms aren't quite to his liking even though we agreed on them months ago.'

'And you can't hold him to them?'

Tahir exhaled in frustration. 'I've just learned he's made bad deals with a few other states, made promises he couldn't keep and now it's beginning to impact his deal with me.'

'How?' she asked, a little too eagerly.

'His levies are crushing him, and he's making threats about passing them on to me.' He paused, his eyes narrowing on her. 'How would you deal with this?'

Her eyebrows shot up while eddies of warmth sprang up inside her. 'You want my input?'

He shrugged. 'I find that not every answer can be arrived at with linear thinking. The obvious answer is to refuse and let him stick to our original agreement, of course. But perhaps you have another solution?'

'You automatically assume my reasoning is going to be radical?'

A twitch that wasn't quite a smile flashed at one corner of his lip. 'I recall a few instances when you've adopted such a stance successfully.'

Tahir watched her contemplate his response.

Did she realise she was drawing closer? That the spark she'd claimed she'd wilfully abandoned was right there in her eyes? That she'd adopted that challenging posture that made his blood rush a little too fast through his veins because he knew he was in for a heated debate with a woman who thrived on such verbal skirmishes?

This was the woman he remembered. And for good or ill, the impulse to reawaken her was why he'd summoned her parents to Jukrat. For his own peace of mind, this matter would be settled once and for all with the woman who wasn't a shadow of herself.

Is that the true reason?

Tahir held himself still and reassured himself that it was.

But it was a lie that shook through him with far more fervour than he welcomed. 'Let's hear it, then,' he said briskly, hoping his stern tone would shake off the other disconcerting emotions weaving through him.

Lauren berated herself for her foolish heart skipping several beats. Tahir was merely seeking an opinion—probably one of many—not planning to base his entire life model on it. Nonetheless, she couldn't quite halt the thrill snaking through her.

'Has he done something like this to you before?'

'In varying degrees but nothing this drastic before now.' Tahir's lips twisted. 'Unfortunately, more often than not, asking Adnan to keep a promise is like placing a sweet in a toddler's hand and asking them not to eat it.'

'What are you going to do?'

A chilling smile curved his lips, triggering the reminder the blood of marauders ran through his veins. 'I've tried the velvet gloves, perhaps it's time for the steel hammer.'

She pursed her lips. His eyes narrowed on her. 'You disapprove,' he surmised. Then before she could respond, he pushed. 'You have an alternative?'

'Maybe.'

'I'm listening.'

Why did that please her enough to make her heart leap? 'Put him in a position where he has no option but to do the right thing.'

He grimaced. 'How? He's as intransigent as they come. He digs his heels in even when it's not necessary just to be bloody-minded.'

'People like that often do it for the attention. He probably craves yours.'

'I can't pander to him just to make him behave himself,' he grunted.

'But dragging things out indefinitely will not just hurt him, it'll hurt you too in the long run. Make him an offer he can't refuse.'

A frown creased his forehead for a full minute. 'He's found himself in this position because he's brash and impetuous. His policies often fail because they're rarely thought through efficiently.'

'So he could benefit from some guidance? From someone like your brother? In a different advisory role, perhaps?' His lips flattened and Lauren knew he didn't like the idea. 'You won't have to lose your brother's diplomatic services. But having a man like Javid in his corner might be just what brings him around?'

Slowly his scowl cleared. 'I may not have had much time for him when we were younger, but he got on well enough with Javid. And there's no reason why Javid can't continue his duties alongside. Perhaps that might even curb some of his less salubrious activities,' he mused with a throb of satisfaction in his voice.

'There you go, then. Problem solved.' Lauren wasn't aware she was smiling until his eyes scoured her face and dropped to linger on her mouth.

'Indeed. How alive you come when you're in your element.'

Something passed between them…a potent connection

that stole her breath for several seconds before delivering a heart pounding she knew she should ignore.

But on the tail of it, that disquieting sensation lingered until she knew she had to air it. 'Tahir…this latest thing with Adnan isn't happening because of…my presence, is it?' His nostrils flared, and she wanted to kick herself for ruining the atmosphere. 'I'm sorry, but I have to know—'

'Whether he's caught wind of my ex-lover's arrival and believes I'm distracted?' His lips firmed. 'Probably. Spies don't just exist in movies and novels.'

'But you don't know for sure?'

'Leave me to handle my cousin. But be assured that neither he nor your brother will interrupt the remainder of our twenty-four hours,' he clipped out.

Frantically, she tore her gaze from him, feigning interest in the beauty and magic of the place so he wouldn't see how affected she was by the reminder of their limited time.

But then she forced herself to be realistic. It would take more than half a day to erase what had happened twelve years ago, especially when she hadn't come fully clean.

Biting her lip, she concentrated more on her surroundings, letting them wash over her. 'It's beautiful and peaceful here,' she murmured, tactfully changing the subject.

A throb of silence passed, during which his gaze remained fixed on her, before he replied. 'It wasn't always.'

Her heart thudded heavily in her chest. 'Because of your banishment?'

'Yes.'

Lauren decided to forge ahead to the subject that weighed heavier on her mind and heart with each passing minute. 'I hate that I contributed to turning something you loved into an unpleasant memory for you.'

He looked around him for several seconds before he

answered. 'It was a good lesson in not taking things for granted or at face value.'

That stung far more than the pragmatism in his response should've elicited. 'Maybe. But did you really need another reminder? And did that reminder have to be this one?'

'We can't change the past, Lauren,' he said with a finality that shook her to her very bones.

'No, but you can consider forgiving it,' she murmured.

His nostrils pinched but he continued to regard her like a specimen under a microscope. 'Convince me that there's more than one reason for you being here. Do that, and I'll consider it,' he countered smoothly, one contemplative finger trailing the lip of his coffee cup. But underneath it, there was fierce tension that jangled her nerves.

What he was asking of her…

She'd bared so much of herself and been hurt in the process by the family that should've loved her.

But wasn't she tired? Wasn't enough quite enough?

Lauren dragged her gaze from the sensual motion of his finger and sucked in a breath. This time, she wasn't frantic at the relentless passage of time. Because while her first reaction was to say *no* to this question, deep inside, another response burned within her.

Of course, he gleaned that with his next words. 'You won't be betraying him by admitting Matt is long overdue a few life lessons. And you're equally overdue a little reconditioning of your own.'

She played it cool, arching a lazy eyebrow. 'Such as?'

'You throttle your ambition and desires for a family that doesn't appreciate you. At the risk of repeating myself, you're wasted on them. Your talent, your passion.' His burnished gaze raked her face, lingering on her mouth. 'Your beauty.' The thick, peculiar note in his voice burrowed deep inside her, warmed her where she'd grown used to being so cold it'd become a part of her.

But the thawing was painful, the admission that change was needed lodging a huge lump in her throat. 'You can't change your family. You know that as well as I do. What would you have me do?' she tossed back, not quite ready to confront the solution that shrieked in her head.

He regarded her steadily with far too much circumspection in his gaze. 'You know, Lauren,' he delivered without pomp or gloating. 'You've always known. You were abandoned by your mother so you're afraid you'll be abandoned again.'

She gasped. 'You know I was adopted?'

Tawny eyes met hers and she saw neither judgement nor rejection. 'Yes. Matt told me years ago,' he replied, then, before she could absorb that news, he was moving on. As if it was no big deal. 'You're strong. Don't subdue your own strength just to make them feel stronger. Step out from the shadows. Remind yourself how it feels to bask in the light. How it feels to let go and just…feel.'

It spoke volumes of her need that she was immediately thrown back to their time at his oasis when she'd vowed she wasn't going to think about the pleasure he'd given her at the springs. Not just physical pleasure but a connection she hadn't felt in years.

Dear God, she wanted a repeat performance. Wanted reprieve—and not just a temporary one, her heart insisted—from those shadows he spoke of.

She pushed away the lingering guilt over Matt.

She would never be in this place again, would probably never share space with Tahir, so why not let the time unfold without the angst and tension? Why not come clean with everything and let the chips fall where they might? Drawing a deep breath, she looked him in the eyes. 'Those shadows you talked about…some of them were because of you.'

He stiffened. 'What?'

'I…you probably don't remember but there were texts…besides the photos?'

His eyes darkened to burnished gold. 'I remember.'

She gasped softly. 'You do?'

'Yes. What about them, Lauren?' he pressed, a sharp edge in his voice.

'My phone went missing…after the pictures were leaked. I never found it. But…' She paused, unable to put her suspicions into words. To do so would be to damn her family definitively.

'But you think you know who has it? Let me guess, one of your family?'

Anguish mounting, she nodded.

He exhaled slowly, his expression growing livid. 'Let me get this straight. You thought they may have got their hands on something that would cause a nuisance and you let them hold it over your head?'

Her hand tightened around her cup. 'It was more than a nuisance. You were already caught in one scandal and—'

'And the far worse damage was already done, Lauren.'

'No, it wasn't. I couldn't risk it.'

He shook his head. 'Pictures of a prince doctored to suggest he was involved with a sex and drugs party are a world away from a few racy texts exchanged with his lover, don't you agree?'

'Then why do you look so angry?'

He muttered an Arabic imprecation under his breath. Then he was cupping her nape, drawing her close. Hot, demanding lips sealed hers, his tongue breaching her lips to dance sinfully with hers in a kiss that left them both breathless when he pulled away several minutes later.

Senses spinning, every cell in her body hungering for more, she pressed her fingers against his throbbing lips before demanding, 'What was that for?'

'It was a choice between that and putting you over my knee and spanking the hell out of you for diminishing yourself in a misguided notion that you were saving me. This king is perfectly able to handle nuisances like that.'

Her mouth gaped, and she wasn't sure whether his words scandalised her or turned her on. 'I…you're unbelievable.'

An enigmatic expression flitted through his eyes. 'And you're forgiven,' he clipped out. Before her heart could leap with joy, he added, 'For that at least.'

The bubble of hope dying inside, she veiled her gaze.

Until he grasped her chin, nudged her to meet his eyes. 'Back to our previous discussion. Are you ready to shed those shadows?' he demanded thickly.

She wasn't but the temptation to *just feel* as he'd urged was irresistible. 'Does that mean we dispense with the hourglasses?' she asked eventually.

He shook his head, and she watched the sunlight dance over the gloss of his jet-black hair, watched it create intriguing shadows over his face. 'Oh, no. Those stay. Far be it from you to level an accusation of inequality on me come morning. Besides, I suspect you're quite enjoying our little game?'

Heaven help her but she was. With vibrant new clothes, her surroundings and the breathtakingly powerful, charismatic King for company, it was as close to the fairy tales she'd devoured as a child as she imagined she would get.

She didn't want to think about her present or her life back in London. She wanted to remain locked in this moment with Tahir, when the only thing she needed to concentrate on was when those elegant hands would pluck the next silk covering off the hourglass, and what that might hold in store for them.

'Fine,' she said as the last grains of sand signalled the power switch. 'I'll do things your way. For now,' she tagged on weakly.

The gleam in his eyes was far too dangerous to her health. She curled her fingers around her cup, willing the heat to ground her. All it did was call attention to the wave of flames rolling through her when he leaned his strong, bare forearms on the table after turning the hourglass.

'There's an event happening tonight. You will join me.'

'Considering we're joined at the hip till midnight, I don't think I have much of a choice, but okay.'

His gaze lowered for a moment, as if seeking the non-metaphorical hips she referred to. When they rose again, the gleam had intensified.

'What is the event?' she asked hurriedly to smother the feelings rampaging through her.

His lips twitched, the first genuine hint of amusement that wasn't wreathed in censure or mockery. 'I'll leave you to discover it on your own tonight, I think.'

Very few things surprised her any more so when the element of surprise became a possibility, it was always a thrill. Or was she just feeling this way because of the man delivering the surprise? 'How will I know how to get ready, then? What to wear?'

A look crossed his eyes and was gone before she could decipher it but his gaze remained as fiercely incisive. 'While you are under my roof, you need not worry that you'll lack for anything.'

There was courtesy in those words. But there was also the undeniable belief in his power and might, which was…intoxicating. And a little perturbing because Lauren would've thought she was the last person to be attracted to such raw power.

But truly, wasn't Tahir much more than that? Weren't the intriguing layers of his personality what had drawn her to him twelve years ago?

Still drew her to him now?

Watching him rise to his feet dispensed the need to examine the last question. 'Come.'

'Where are we going?'

'Does it matter? It's my time, is it not?' he said, then, catching her questioning look at the hourglass, added, 'We'll be back in time.'

She rose and fell into step beside him.

Then Tahir did the last thing she'd expected. He showed her his desert palace, trailing her through exquisite miniature orange and lemon groves, an all-white meditation room, a receiving hall made entirely of blue-veined marble, cobalt-blue pillars and a giant beaten silver fountain stunningly lit by a soaring chandelier that made her jaw drop. But her favourite room by far was the windowless library. It was lit by another grand chandelier, but all four walls held floor-to-ceiling shelves stacked with books.

'The lack of sunlight is to protect the books,' Tahir murmured, standing close to her as she spun slowly on her heel, her head thrown back to better admire the incredible space.

Drawing closer to one shelf, she read the spines of a few books and gasped. 'Some of these are…over two hundred years old.'

'My father was zealous about acquiring first-edition masterpieces. Every royal residence has such a library, but this is the largest.'

'I could spend an eternity in here,' she murmured, then her breath caught all over again when she saw the glimmer in his eyes. 'This is where you spent most of your time during your year here, isn't it?' she asked, regret tingeing her voice.

'Yes,' he responded simply. 'And before you pity me, I gained a lot of perspective during that time.'

She bit the inside of her lip. Had he gained other things too, like the hard edge she didn't remember him having twelve years ago, or had that come from ruling? And, considering most of his counterpart Arabian Peninsula monarchs and sheikhs were long married by Tahir's age, she wondered if her actions twelve years ago had contributed to his unattached status.

'Why aren't you married?' She blurted words she totally hadn't meant to ask.

He stiffened, anger flashing through his eyes before it grew cool and neutral. 'You think you had something to do with that?'

Her heart pounded hard. 'Did I?'

His lips slashed in a wide smile that didn't quite reach his eyes. 'You give yourself too much credit.'

The words stung. Deeply. But then she only had herself to blame, didn't she? Needing space, she wandered away on the pretext of admiring the rest of the library, but she could barely focus, both from the prickle of tears clouding eyes and from the fact that Tahir, having delivered that low blow, had seemingly shrugged it off, and was back to host mode, tracking her movements until she wanted to scream.

It was a relief to leave the library and step out into the fresh air on the second level. Tahir led her to an immense open terrace, drew her to the northern edge and pointed to the distance. 'That is your surprise,' he said.

Lauren stared at the horizon but all she could see were distant mountains and endless sand dunes. But squinting, she saw what he was pointing out. The faintest billowing

of a cloud that hung too low to be in the sky. 'My surprise
is an approaching sandstorm?' she asked, confused.

One corner of his mouth twitched. 'No, it's not a sandstorm, but it'll be here in a matter of hours,' was all he said
before they were interrupted by a young staff member bearing the hourglasses.

Tahir took them and set them on the table.

As if caught in the strange time warp, they watched the
grains run out, Lauren feeling as if something vital was
slipping away. When the glass finally emptied, Tahir covered it again, spun the tray and watched as she made her
choice again.

Forty-five minutes.

On they toured, each room in the palace more spectacular than the last, each revelation making her gasp in wonder. But the strange sensation lingered, the notion that *she*
was running out of time, not Matt. That unless she acted,
she would regret it.

As much as she tried to push the sensation away, it clung,
growing stronger and tighter by the minute. It was still there
when the servant made another appearance, murmuring
to his liege in Arabic. When he left, Tahir turned to her.

'Come, our lunch is ready.'

She followed him, acutely aware that he'd never answered as to why he hadn't yet married.

Lunch was an indulgent feast, Tahir content to spend his
forty-five minutes introducing her to his kingdom's delica-
cies, a pleasurable pastime heightened by the visual passage
of time. And by the increased level of excitement within
the palace as their meal grew to an end.

When it was time to choose again, Tahir's eyes gleamed
with brazen satisfaction as she drew the silk from the two-
and-a-half-hour hourglass. His gaze rested on the contrap-

tion for long seconds before snagging hers. 'Between us we have five hours. That is more than enough time.'

'For what?'

'To do whatever we want.' Tahir rose to his feet. 'But I suggest you return to your rooms. Your attendants are waiting for you.'

With another intense look, he left without further elaboration.

Lauren discovered the reason for the staff's excitement one hour later when she heard the growing sound of musical cries, steady drumbeats and the peculiar lyrical clicking she discovered were from finger cymbals striking in rhythm.

Standing on her terrace, she watched the large crowd edge the western plain of Tahir's villa, their voices raised in decadent, spine-tingling music as several performed jaw-dropping acrobatic moves.

'What…who are they?' she asked Nesa, who'd spent the better part of the last hour primping and styling Lauren's hair and make-up, all without giving away what it was she was getting dressed for.

The woman, who'd been courteous but slightly aloof, now gave a small smile, her gaze warming. 'They're a group of nomadic traders and performers. They always pass through when His Majesty is in residence.'

Lauren's gaze flittered over the gaily dressed crowd, her own excitement building at their carnival-like exuberance. 'How long will they stay?'

'Just one night. Which makes it even more special.'

Lauren found herself nodding, aware she was experiencing something unique. She looked down at her own clothes.

It was another saffron-coloured outfit, but even more elaborate, with a wider band of jewelled stones etched into the neckline and the hem of the top that sat just above her belly button. The skirt was heavier too, again with rows of crystals marching down the long overlapping slits on the sides that parted to show a bit of leg when she moved.

Her shoulder burn was much better, and the light chiffon wrap protected her from the worst of the sun's rays. Her hair was caught up in an elaborate style of coiled braids and jewelled pins and she didn't need another look in the mirror to recall the understated but stunning make-up Nesa had created to make her eyes look huge and her cheekbones stand out. Somehow her favourite perfume had also been conjured up and she only needed to move a fraction to catch the scent of the fragrance.

Her gaze once more swept over the crowd and, for some unknown reason, her heart raced faster as she wondered if Tahir was down there, greeting his visitors.

'His Majesty would like you to join him downstairs,' Nesa said, as if she'd read her mind.

Several deep breaths, hallways and courtyards later, Lauren stepped into an immense, open-air receiving room. Consisting of several seating areas partly sectioned off by muslin curtains, it gave the aura of privacy while also holding a large gathering. Diamond-shaped black and white mosaic tiles drew the feet into the heart of the room while small fountains provided a soft background of serenity.

But serene was the last thing she felt as she approached the man who stood to one side of the room, his hands tucked behind his back. He was dressed from head to toe in a white kaftan, *thawb* and *keffiyeh*, the only contrasting colour the black rope holding his turban in place. With his height and breadth of shoulders, Tahir took up the whole room, commanding every scrap of her focus as his gaze latched onto her.

Lauren barely saw Nesa melt away as Tahir's eyes grew heated, gaining ferocity as they travelled over her, lingering for long moments at her neckline, the bare skin at her midriff, then finally on her glossed lips.

'My colour looks good on you,' he rasped, an indecipherable note in his voice.

Her eyes widened. 'Your colour?' Why did she sound breathless? 'You chose this colour for me?'

The barest hint of a smile twitched one corner of his mouth, then he was back to ferocious intensity again, even as one thick shoulder lifted in a shrug. 'Someone on my staff knows my favourite colour and has rightly guessed you would do it justice.'

Before she could read too much into that, he was breaching the gap between them, driving her breathless. 'You've seen the crowd outside?'

She flicked her gaze over his shoulder, towards where the sound of revelry was steadily increasing. 'It must be nice to have your own personal carnival,' she said, attempting to tease. Anything really to lighten the atmosphere that seemed laden with...*something*.

'They're their own entity. They merely grace me with their company for a time.' Again, there was a peculiar note in his voice, his gaze lingering on hers after he spoke, enough to make further sensation tingle down her spine. 'I also know it's best to welcome them now rather than later, before things get a little...out of hand. You'll come with me.' He held out a hand in an imperious gesture that left little doubt as to his desire.

But the shock of the request stilled her. 'You want me to meet them with you?'

Something flashed in his eyes, gone far too quickly. 'Do you object to that?'

'I don't, but...' She paused, tried to reframe the jumble of words scrambled further by her wildly insane heartbeat and the intensity of the surreal feelings tumbling through her. 'Isn't it against some sort of protocol? I'm...nobody.'

This time the light arrived, burned brighter. And stayed, laser beams tearing beneath her skin, burrowing where she wasn't sure she could prevent him from landing. 'You're not nobody,' he rasped, his voice low. Intense. 'You never have been.'

Something deep, visceral, moved within her. 'Tahir.'

His nostrils flared at her uttering his name as if it moved something within him too.

Connection.

The craving throbbed hard and insistent inside her as his hand extended further, imploring and impatient at once. 'We're keeping my guests waiting. Will you join me or not?'

Any objection she had, feeble as it was, evaporated. She told herself it was because he'd couched his invitation as a question this time, that their situation demanded she stay by his side, but she knew she would've gone regardless. That unstoppable pull was binding her stronger and, try as she might, Lauren couldn't fight it. In truth, she *didn't* want to fight it any longer.

She slid her hand into his, surrendering to the wild tingles that raced up her arm as he led her to the wide doors into another courtyard and then outside where the revelling crowd cheered at the sight of their Sheikh.

Where she attempted to hide her self-consciousness as unabashed gazes swung to her and stayed, her presence by Tahir's side attracting the attention she knew it would.

Since Jukrat was a bilingual country, many of the performers responded to Tahir's introduction of her in English. She tried not to be touched by the consideration, tried...and failed not to be moved by the festive atmosphere.

An hour later, after sampling more food and being treated to more jaw-dropping performances, she retreated to the terrace, clutching a silver goblet of wine someone had thrust into her hand at some point.

As it'd done for the better part of the evening, her gaze didn't have to roam far to land on Tahir, his words echoing in her mind.

You're not nobody. You never have been.

She knew she was a fool to personalise words she should be keeping at a distance. But then wasn't she a fool when it came to Tahir? Wasn't she, somewhere in her deepest, most secret place where her wishes wouldn't die, hoping that this pseudo fairy tale she'd found herself in would have the same ending as the one told in books?

She pressed her lips together, frantically reaching for common sense. For something solid and pragmatic to hang onto. But the combination of music, laughter and revelry, *and Tahir*, made that impossible.

'Lauren.'

She jumped, unaware he'd approached, was peering intently at her, those eyes burrowing into her secrets again.

'There's something on your mind. Tell me,' he commanded, his voice a meld of deep sensuality and concerned demand.

It was almost as if he cared.

She tried to shrug away the emotion settling on her shoulders. But the evening had been far too special to insult it with trivial dismissiveness. 'It's foolish, I know, but I don't want this—' she turned and waved her hand at the spectacle of music and dancing and exotic scents and laughter '—to end. I want to live in this moment for...' *ever*. The last word stuck in her throat because she knew even as she uttered it that her wish was as ethereal as the breeze whispering over her skin.

'There's a reason you don't want to return to your old life. Say it, Lauren,' he pressed again.

Her gaze flew to his, and locked. 'Because I don't want to go back to feeling…lost.' Whispered words that seemed to spill from deep within her soul without any prompting. But once they were said, she felt something crack within her, something she'd once thought sacred but now knew was perhaps not as treasured.

Tahir nodded, the look in his eyes reflecting deep comprehension that scared her a little. It was almost as if he'd anticipated this, as if he'd known every secret buried in her heart. 'And you won't. Because it's time to face up to it. You only felt lost because you didn't want to accept the way to your freedom. Change is hard. But it's also freeing. You've hidden yourself away for too long. Isn't it time to reach for what you truly want?'

When had he drawn so close? She could reach out, press her hand against that hard, muscled chest, feel his heartbeat…

Without conscious thought, she did just that.

His heart slammed hard against her palm, the strong, steady echo mesmeric in its rhythm. Beneath her touch, his chest expanded as he inhaled deeply. As he stood still and she touched him, the unattainable King who seemed to be in her grasp. Whose eyes swirled with the same arousal eddying through her.

'Lauren.'

There were a thousand questions in her name. But there were only a handful she wanted to answer. 'Freedom, at least for tonight, sounds good,' she said.

His heart seemed to trip, then beat just that little bit faster. Had she not placed her hand right there, she wouldn't have known her response affected him that much. But she did. And its effect was…powerful. Metaphysical. Vastly moving.

In another instinctive movement, her fingers curled,

grasping a handful of his tunic to stop him from stepping away, from leaving her. They were in public, and she was all but pawing the Sheikh of Jukrat. But like everything else when it came to Tahir, it unravelled wild and untamed outside her control. As if her very soul dictated and directed her wishes before her brain could argue the toss.

A glance into his face showed her actions hadn't displeased him. He was just as unconcerned about who witnessed her bold touch.

Instead, amusement mingled with weighted arousal and thick anticipation. Which then morphed into ferocious intent the longer she kept his gaze.

'Tell me what you want, Lauren,' he demanded hoarsely.

She knew what he was asking. It was what she'd spent every second denying from the moment she'd stepped into his office…was it only yesterday? She'd lived ten lifetimes since those tense moments.

So why not one more? It would be short, of course. But she would be in his arms. She would kiss those sensual, masterful lips. She would experience those hands on her body, his thick shaft moving inside her. All that sublime power unleashed on her.

She swayed closer, her tongue gliding out to wet her lips as desire moved like honey through her veins.

He made a sound in his throat, a cross between frustration and warning. The hand imprisoning hers on his chest squeezed, a firm insistence that she answer.

'I want the freedom…to be with you.'

To find myself with you the way I did twelve years ago.

CHAPTER EIGHT

SHE DIDN'T SAY those words out loud, of course. She was many things, but she wasn't a fool, and the last thing she wanted was to throw the anvil of that reminder between them. Not now. Not when he'd steered her into believing she could be something different. Something more.

That the kernel of *something* she'd refused to nurture because it resembled betrayal wasn't that at all. It'd been self-preservation. A compass that had refused to stay hidden because it was vital to who she was meant to be. Tahir had forced her to dig it free. To dust it off and dare to look at where it pointed.

He'd given her that.

And if he wanted her as much as she wanted him... wasn't that just the icing on the cake?

'Take me to bed, Tahir,' she breathed, every emotion she'd felt for this man shaking through her. 'I want you,' she added, just so there was no confusion.

She gasped when he immediately wrapped one muscled arm around her, pulled her close to plaster her to his body.

No, the Sheikh of Jukrat didn't care who witnessed his heated interaction with her.

Why that thrilled her from the roots of her hair to her very toes, she was thankfully saved from exploring when he lowered his head and sealed her mouth with his. His tongue swept inside, stroking hers with slow, firm glides that tunnelled desire straight between her legs. Even before she released his tunic to wind both hands around his neck, her panties were damp, her clitoris swollen and needy, her arousal a tsunami already threatening to sweep her away.

Lauren barely felt him move her backward, didn't care where he was taking her. The cool touch of a solid wall behind her was immediately ameliorated by the hard, living flame of Tahir's body caging hers.

He feasted on her with animalistic intensity and relish, raw sounds rasping from his throat as he plundered her mouth. His fingers drove into her hair, firm fingers angling her head for better access.

And she gave it to him. Gave her all to the searing kiss that felt as vital as breathing, the fire of it sweeping through her, branding her.

One hand dropped to claim her hip, to drag her even closer so she couldn't mistake the force of his arousal against her belly. Lauren moaned, need building until she believed she would combust.

But then, Tahir moved again, lifting his head to place a little distance between them. Fevered eyes raked her face, lingering on her swollen mouth before he exhaled audibly.

'As much as I want to take you right here, right now, I don't think my people are ready to be scandalised by their Sheikh in such a manner, do you?' he rasped.

'Won't they mind you leaving them?' she asked, even though she was more than willing to be done with the celebration.

'They've had more than enough of me. Now it's your turn.'

The intent and promise in his voice melted her from the inside out, the thought of wasting any more time dragging a frustrated moan to her throat. Luckily, she managed to swallow it back down, but Tahir's nostrils flared nonetheless at whatever he read in her face.

'You would drag a man to his doom, *habibti*,' he declared thickly.

'Then it's a good thing you're not just any man, isn't it?' She didn't know where she found the wherewithal to tease but greedy flames of excitement lit through her when he gave a helpless groan.

His fingers encircled her wrist, dragging her from the wall. Guards and servants bowed and stepped back as he strode through the villa.

Expecting him to use the main courtyards and hallways, she was surprised when he headed for the far end of the eastern wing.

The sound of music and laughter faded as he stopped beside an inner wall covered by a towering vine in the farthest courtyard. Despite the few lit lamps, she didn't see exactly what he did, but she gasped when a section of the wall gave way to reveal a long, semi-lit passage.

'What…where are we?' she asked. Her voice shook, not because she was afraid, but because this was far too much like the fairy tales she'd discarded decades ago but, it seemed, still lived somewhere in her heart.

In the semidarkness, she caught the wicked flash of his eyes as he looked down at her. 'When my great-grandfather built this villa, he incorporated a few… interesting designs.'

'Like secret passages?'

His lips curved, his teeth flashing as he smiled. 'Among other things.'

They walked for a full minute, bypassing a handful of entrances before he stopped at one. When he pressed on another discreet panel, it sprang open to reveal a long, familiar-looking hallway.

'Is that…are we near my room?'

'Yes. Your suite connects to mine, and we share this wing,' he said, as if it was the most natural thing in the world. And perhaps in his world such a thing was natural. In truth, she'd discovered so many different things after less than twenty-four hours in Tahir's orbit that demonstrated just how much she'd kept a shroud over herself.

And...she was eager to embrace it all.

When he lengthened his strides, she fell in beside him. And when he nudged the imposing door open and stepped into his suite, she girded her loins and stepped into the experience.

Tahir's suite was unashamedly masculine, the bold terracotta colour scheme broken only by thin accents of gold. But interspersed with it were the usual splashes of equally bold colour she was beginning to associate with all things Jukrati.

Brocade sofas were positioned in the vast room with exquisite paintings and indigenous tapestries gracing the walls. But it was the emperor-sized bed that held her attention.

It was a work of art.

It was erected on an immense raised platform, the headboard a magnificent creation of dark ebony petrified wood, carved and polished into a masterpiece she would've loved to study, had Tahir's hand not trailed up her arm and shoulder to clench in her hair, his other arm banding her waist once more. A shudder rushed through her at the passionate hold, her body blindly pivoting into his as he angled her head for another dominating kiss.

They kissed until she was breathless. Until she firmly believed she would climax from the magic of it alone. Her head was still spinning, her senses screaming when he broke the kiss and whirled her around.

He drew her hair back from her neck and trailed kisses

down her spine, his hands wreaking equally delightful devastation. When his hands framed her hips, she turned to watch him.

The sight of Tahir on his haunches behind her, his gaze searing every inch of skin it touched, was enough to make her sway on her feet. One hand reached out to steady her, then, the moment she stilled, he tracked the backs of his hands up her legs, slowly, in an unhurried exploration that had her panting in under a minute.

'Your skin is like the warmest silk.' He reached the curve beneath her bottom and stroked the line from the outside in, pausing just before where she was hot and damp and almost embarrassingly needy. His nostrils flared and Lauren watched him visibly swallow. 'And you smell intoxicating.'

Firmly, he nudged her legs apart, the thumbs stroking her inner thighs skating tantalisingly close to her apex. When his lips parted hungrily, she gave a needful moan, breaths shuddering out of her as her need built and built.

'Do you want me to pleasure you? Taste this beautiful gift you're offering?'

The tremor coursing through her turned her nipples to hard points and there wasn't a single cell in her body that didn't screech *yes* to his husky query. 'Please, Tahir. I need you.'

His whole body seemed to surge at her response, an animalistic growl leaving his throat as he gripped her thighs harder, held her captive as he rolled forward onto his knees. And delivered on his promise.

Her eyes clamped shut, pleasure overflowing. It felt like the most natural thing in the world, to reach back, spear her fingers through his hair and hold him to his task. And from the healthy grunt he gave, he more than approved her enthusiasm.

Thick curses left his throat as he lapped at her, the ex-pert swirls of his tongue at her core and over her clitoris driving her deeper into insanity until, with a cry torn from her throat, Lauren exploded in a heady climax.

She struggled to catch her breath as stars darted and tumbled behind her eyelids, as she felt him surge to his feet, a firm hand at her back to tumble her into bed.

When she finally dragged her eyelids open, it was to the sexiest striptease from the Sheikh of Jukrat, his eyes latching onto hers as he slowly stripped.

Once naked, he prowled onto the bed to crouch over her, and Lauren truly believed he was the most spectacular sight she'd ever seen.

And because it'd been so long, because she'd yearned for him so, she shamelessly explored him. From his taut cheekbones to the square jaw clenched tight to control his arousal, to the glorious landscape of collarbone, chiselled pecs and sculptured abs, he was a living, breathing tapestry of masculinity she wanted to revel in until time stopped.

Need built again, demanding satisfaction. So when, with a growl, he captured her hands and pinned them above her head on the bed, his eyes staring intently into her eyes for a minute before he swooped down to capture her mouth again, she let him, swopping one heady experience for another with an eagerness that mildly alarmed her. And then that too was washed away, obliterated by the body pressing down onto hers, the wicked tongue that had just made her come so spectacularly stroking hers, ratcheting up the fever in her veins.

They kissed until her lips burned with passion, until her legs were wrapped tight around him, her body molten and ready.

With almost driven purpose, he tore his lips away to stare down at her once more, savage desire etched into his face. 'You wreck my control so effortlessly,' he charged, then he shook his head. 'I should be immune to you. Should be done with this fever you invoke in my blood,' he finished with a hoarse growl. But even as he spoke, one hand was moving over her body, capturing her breast and moulding it, his nostrils flaring as he toyed with her nipple.

'But you're not,' she dared to counter, feminine power weaving through her with an intoxication she could see becoming addictive, very quickly. But then, she didn't need to worry about that, did she? In a handful of hours, this would be over. Whether she succeeded or failed, her life was back in England.

With her family…

That punch of rejection struck again. The arrow-sharp hunch that, whatever happened here, she wouldn't return home the same. That the Lauren she'd been when she boarded the plane a handful of days ago had irreparably changed.

'Lauren.'

The snap of her name drew her from her morose thoughts.

'I am the only one you will think about,' he decreed with an arrogance that should've annoyed her. But how could it when she wholeheartedly wished the same? When she didn't want to think about what tomorrow held for her?

'Yes. Only you,' she breathed.

His eyes flared with satisfaction, then darkened dramatically as she rolled her hips against the power of his erection that throbbed insistently between her legs.

'Tahir.' His name was like the finest wine, full-bodied and languorously savoured, the extra pleasure of it the look on his face as she said it.

A shudder raked through him.

Then he was moving, tugging open a hidden compartment on the side of the bed she hadn't even noticed. He reared onto his knees and tore open the packaging on the condom he'd retrieved. Jaw clenched hard once more, he rolled it on.

She started to draw down her arms, to reach for him, to caress the hard rod of his manhood. But he recaptured her hand, holding her effortlessly with one as the other clutched her hip.

'Enough, *habibti*. You can explore to your heart's content later. Right now, I must have you…need to be inside you,' he said with a jagged gruffness that transmitted straight to her blood. The thought that he was far gone for her was a heady thing indeed.

But, as she knew he would, he claimed his power back, delivering a searing kiss before, positioning himself at her heated core, Tahir drove slowly and relentlessly inside her.

Her moan was deep and long and soul-shaking, the pleasure of his possession shaking the foundations of her being. 'Oh, God!'

He stilled; his eyes molten as he stared down at her. 'So tight. You feel…' He shook his head once more. 'How long since you took a lover?' he rasped tightly.

Heat rushed up into her face, her eyes widening. 'What?'

Kisses trailed from the corner of her mouth to the shell of her ear. 'Your delicious snugness tells a story.'

As if to relay how much he relished that story, he moved, rolling his hips in a sublime undulation that had her whole body surging in appreciation.

'How long?' he pressed when all she did was try to hang on.

'Tahir…' She paused, knowing he wouldn't let this go. 'A few years…' she managed to slur.

Triumph blazed in the eyes that met hers, as if her celibacy was a trophy he'd won. And perhaps it was. After all, hadn't the very rare sex she'd indulged in after Tahir been a perfunctory act, even a last-ditch means to find connection that never materialised?

'Is your ego adequately stroked, Your Majesty?' she murmured, then, with a wicked urge to retain some ground, she rolled her own hips.

An unguarded groan left his throat, his breathing turning agitated. Then as if a switch had been flicked, his grip on her hip tightened, his strokes gaining a rapid and relentless rhythm that had her tossing her head in lust-filled abandon.

'Yes! Oh, yes,' she cried. Her throaty pleas seemed to trigger him into faster movement. His possession grew frenzied, his eyes as wild and untamed as his beloved desert.

Long after sweat had slicked both their skins and her throat had grown hoarse, he was drawing further demands of her body. And she granted each one, tumbling from one release to the other until, with a guttural roar, Tahir finally achieved his own.

CHAPTER NINE

TAHIR DIDN'T FIGHT the sublime sensation stealing through his veins. But as their bodies cooled and a drowsy Lauren drifted off into sleep in his arms, he braced himself for the storm of emotions and questions rushing at him.

Curiously, regret stayed muted in the background, a mirage content to keep its distance. He didn't mind. He didn't regret what had just happened. What troubled him most was the seeming...*inevitability* of the whole thing.

Somehow, he'd known in his bones in those moments after she'd blurted out her plea on his helipad that they would end up here, in this position, their limbs tangled around each other in post-coital abandon. Were he the type to believe in the cosmic, he'd think this was written in the stars. That true control wasn't his when it came to Lauren Winchester.

But he wasn't such a type. He'd suspected this might happen. He'd resisted but, ultimately, he'd been unable to stop it. Because he hadn't wanted to, despite all signs pointing to it being a bad idea?

He clenched his jaw, fighting the implication that he was so weak-willed when it came to this woman.

But wasn't he? He'd barely managed twenty-four hours before succumbing to her allure. They'd fallen into bed while the serious issues of her remorse and his forgiveness remained in the balance. Hell, he'd devolved into playing *tour guide*, showing off the very place she'd had him banished to, then compounded it all by inviting her to greet his guests at his side.

He hadn't even spared more than a fleeting thought for the rampant speculation he would be inviting by that last action.

All because he'd yearned to see her come alive and would've done anything to achieve it?

He exhaled, attempting to escape the discomfort of his own thoughts. He knew before morning his advisors would be demanding to know the same thing—what had he been thinking? But they wouldn't stop there.

They would probe and nuance-seek his actions to death. Or until they were satisfied it wasn't a harbinger of some other decision.

He shifted, his mind attempting to sidestep the unfeasible thought that wanted to sprout. Except that task, too, seemed impossible. Come midnight, questions would come. For answers he didn't have.

Or did he?

Discomfort warred with anticipation, producing a disconcerting mix.

Against him, Lauren moved, sighed and curled her hand over his chest.

He needed to get up, vacate the room or move her to her own bed.

But…his gaze tracked across the room to the hourglass his valet had delivered here hours ago at his direction. They were still caught up in the game, weren't they?

And which part of the game is this?

The part where he abandoned everything his grandfather had taught him for the sake of a woman? The part where he could hear his own father's condemnation even from the beyond?

He gritted his teeth tighter. Wasn't he above that, though? His father had had his own flaws. He'd been too strict. Too set in his ways to bend and move with the times. To bend and move for his children. His marriage had barely survived what he himself had preached.

Wasn't Tahir entitled to his own opinions? His own path? His own mistakes?

Plural?

Disconcertion grew. Wasn't one mistake with this woman enough?

Or was he being disingenuous? Now he knew more about the circumstances of her past, could *he* find it in himself to bend a little, the way his own father hadn't quite been able to?

The voice echoing a response within him was far too strong. Far too definitive.

But he couldn't rush into decision. Didn't he owe himself the right to be a little circumspect? Or was he pushing for time on a situation he'd already decided on?

He tried to tune out the voice mocking him that he'd already forgiven her completely and was playing for time. That he was reaching for circumspection far too late. He'd thoroughly spent himself with Lauren, given in to incandescent passion that still seared the edges of his senses.

Passion he wanted to relive all over again. And again.

It was that all-consuming need that finally drove him from the bed and past the hourglass that was slowly dwindling the last of Lauren's time. Time she'd given up to be with him. He shook his head, unwilling to read more into it.

And yet he couldn't prise his gaze from the whispering falls of sand, from the sensations moving within him, urging him to seize this moment before it passed.

Before it was too late…

His gaze drifted back to the woman laid out on his bed. Need punched through him one more time, and he had to lock his knees to stop himself from stalking back to the bed, waking her…

No.

Sex was addling his brain. Throwing on a dressing gown, he stepped out onto the terrace, choosing to let Lauren sleep.

Hell, he welcomed it to sort through his own thoughts. The sun had gone down, and his nomadic guests would be readying to leave so they could arrive at another oasis before midday tomorrow.

For a single moment, he envied their freedom. To do as they wished. No greater responsibility than fulfilling their next desires. With whomever they chose. Without consequence or duty or politics dictating their actions.

He…yearned for that.

Forgive her, and you can have it…

The voice whispered on a breeze, ruffling his hair and further unsettling his emotions. Was it a lack of sleep directing his thoughts this way?

A sharp intake of breath brought all his thoughts crashing to a halt.

But he didn't turn around. Because in that moment, Tahir knew the thing he yearned for the most was the woman rousing from his bed. The woman he sensed coming closer.

Her scent, mingled with the sweat and sex they'd heartily indulged in, reached his nostrils before she did. He attempted to brace himself but that infernal emotion punched through him again when she slid her body…her *near naked* body, against his.

'I didn't mean to fall asleep,' she murmured, her voice

sleep-husky, sexy and far too alluring to be borne with the types of thoughts he was having.

'It was your time to do with as you wished.'

He felt her stiffen ever so slightly and felt a tinge of regret for dragging up the reason for their game. The culmination of which he was still unsure how to deal with.

He pushed that thought out of his mind for the moment, and, because he seemed incapable of resisting her, he wrapped his arm around her waist and tugged her between him and the stone balustrade of his terrace. Then almost wished he hadn't when a quick glance down confirmed she was draped in nothing but the saffron silk wrap she'd worn over her attire this evening.

Instantly, he felt his body rise, his blood thrumming quicker through his veins.

'The sand ran out a minute ago. I turned it so it's your time now,' she murmured, her far too tempting lips so close. So sumptuous.

'Then I have in mind exactly what I wish to do.'

He scooped her up, revelling in her gasp and the way her arms instantly curled around his neck.

Addictive.

Obsessive.

Dangerous.

All words that pounded through his brain, attempting to pull the brakes on something he suspected was already too late as he strode in sure steps past secret, darkened hallways and courtyards to another treasured destination.

There, he listened to her gasp again, watched pleasure unfurl on her face as she glanced around her.

'Where are we?'

'My private bath chamber.'

Her eyes widened. 'Another one?'

'No one uses this one but me.'

He let her body slide down his until her feet dropped next to his. Then he was sliding his fingers into her hair, capturing her nape and dragging her closer.

'I haven't had nearly enough of you,' he grunted, the confession torn from his soul.

Her green eyes latched onto his and he could've fooled himself that he saw adoration in there. Perhaps even the same yearning that swelled like a billowing sandstorm through him.

He convinced himself it was a trick of the light as he lowered his head. As he took her lips, felt hers cling to him and tried to swat away the emotions battering away at him.

This was nothing more than sex.

Two and a half hours. He would use all of it. Indulge to his body's content.

Then he would get back on track.

His infernal yearning *would* be contained.

Her throat was raw from screaming in ecstasy. The moment Tahir had assured her they were entirely private and wouldn't be either heard or disturbed, Lauren felt as if a passion tap had been turned onto full.

Except she was beginning to suspect it wasn't merely passion. Passion wouldn't have triggered the sort of panic she'd felt when she'd woken alone, afraid she'd frittered her precious time with Tahir away with sleep.

Her precious time?

Yes, those three words had been equally terrifying. Because again, Matt had failed to feature in her thoughts, and, worse still, her guilt had been minimal.

She had been thinking entirely of herself. Of the hairline cracks in her heart she suspected had occurred a very long time ago. Twelve years, in fact, when she'd walked away from Tahir Al-Jukrat. Cracks that had grown wider with each moment spent in his presence, leaking emotions she feared she couldn't contain for much longer.

'Am I losing you?'

Thick words that dragged her attention back to the present. To the man stretched out beside her on the blanket beneath the stars, one hand on her hip while the other fondled her breast.

Dear heaven, but he was magnificent. Despite the sun having set, there was enough light to make out the chiselled perfection of his features.

No, but I lost you.

She swallowed, for a split second terrified she'd spoken the words aloud. But the quizzical, watchful look in his eyes said he was awaiting an answer.

'I'm right here,' she said, attempting lightness she didn't feel.

The look in his eyes didn't change. 'Are you?' he mused, the tiniest hint of an edge in his voice. 'I find myself in the peculiar circumstance of wanting to know what a woman is thinking.'

Panic flared higher. She couldn't tell him her true feelings, of course. That would be like baring her jugular to a predator. 'I'm thinking that I have a question I'd like to ask.'

One corner of his mouth lifted, amusement mingling with languid satiation on his face. A part of her felt awe for reducing the supreme ruler of Jukrat to a satisfied, post-sex haze. But the greater part of her was still caught in alarm at the passing of time. At the heavier weight of her emotions with each passing second. At the keen knowledge that their twenty-four hours would end with having changed on a fundamental level.

'I'm not entirely sure how to take asking permission before asking.'

She hadn't consciously framed the question. It seemed

dragged out of her soul, perhaps a puzzle piece she wanted in place for herself. 'Did you ever manage to repair your relationship with your father?'

His touch tightened on her flesh for a short second before he released her. Jaw clenched, he rolled away from her. 'That is not a subject I like to discuss in bed.'

'Technically, we're not in bed,' she teased, desperate to reverse time. Wishing she didn't feel a chill in her soul when he was still within touching distance. But with every avenue seemingly paved with emotional landmines, she was stuck.

'Ah, I'm afraid the cushion of technicalities won't make me any more amenable.' Shoulders stiff, he rose from the blanket and prowled into the semi-darkened space. A second later, he was shrugging on a robe that seemed to have materialised out of nowhere but was probably tucked into all the discreet, magical corners his tents and desert residences contained.

Without speaking further, he padded to one of the giant boulders surrounding the bathing area, his gaze still averted from her. And for several minutes, a grim silence cocooned them.

'Now it's my turn to ask whether I've lost you.' Her voice was soft. Shaky. Its meaning far deeper than the obvious.

You never had him. He was a previous but temporary gift you foolishly squandered.

Feeling far too naked on the blanket, she rose too, slipped the wrap over her shoulders before folding her arms around her waist. She looked up to find his eyes fixed on her. Mild displeasure warred with something else. Yearning, possibly. Or at least a window beyond which something glinted, like a...*proffer*.

She stopped herself from reaching out, grasping it with

both hands. Like everything beautiful and magical in this time and space, it was transient. A mirage.

And yet, she remained…hopeful as he exhaled. 'I've mentioned more than once that I'm not the man you used to know.'

Her heart lurched painfully, then dropped.

But he was continuing. 'My time in the desert forged that change.' His lips twisted. 'For starters, I didn't trust a single word the print media said about anything from then onwards.' His face resettled into austere lines. 'But to answer your question, yes, I became more of the man my father wanted me to be.'

'And what was that?'

'Steeped in duty to the Jukrati people. Rebuilding the reputation of my beloved kingdom. In the end, I gained his approval.'

The words were as austere as his expression, a literal answer to a literal question. She licked her lips, fighting the urge to let it be. But she couldn't. Because, right along with everything she'd wanted for this man, she wanted him to have found peace with his father, too. 'Did he ever forgive you?'

A bleakness fleetingly shrouded his face, gone the next instant. 'I didn't ask for forgiveness, and he never indicated I would get it. But according to those in his council, he died believing I would rule Jukrat ably enough.'

'And your mother?'

His expression grew tighter. 'What about her?'

'You explained the relationship you have. But…did you ever ask her why she signed the document?'

He frowned. 'There is no excuse for agreeing to such a thing.'

'Even in arranged marriages, especially if perhaps some council of advisors suggest it?'

His expression darkened further, but just as before he seemed disarmed, as if the possibility hadn't occurred to him. Then he shook his head. 'Why are we discussing this?'

She shrugged. 'You've given your opinion, repeatedly, about my family situation. I thought it only fair to return the favour.'

'But unlike you, I've accepted the glaring truth. And moved on with my life.'

Heart caught in a tighter vice, and not wanting him to see how much she hurt for him, she dropped her gaze.

'You don't look content with my response, Lauren,' he said after a full minute.

Confused and, yes, a little desperate at how much his happiness meant to her, she let out a shaky laugh. 'Content? How can anyone be content by a father not telling his son that he's proud of him? That he loves him? And a mother who might feel more but is unable to show it?'

He exhaled harshly, the corners of his lips pinched tight. 'Perhaps because neither of them deemed me worthy.'

'That's absurd!'

He stiffened, those eyes burnishing brighter. Sharper. Drilling straight into her vulnerable spaces. 'Why?'

'Because…' She froze too, her heart caught in her throat.

Because you deserve love. You deserve to be loved the way I love you.

The truth shook her to her last cell. And it came with laughable inevitability.

Of course she loved him.

She'd loved him for twelve long, lonely years when she'd lived less than a half-life.

'Because?' he demanded tightly.

She cleared her throat of the rock of truth waiting to tumble free. 'Because every child deserves to be told they're loved, no matter what.'

The light dimmed, a harder tension seizing his body. 'Surely you know by now that receiving what one deserves is often not a foregone conclusion. If it helps, I didn't think my time here was a total disaster.'

Registering that she was clinging to straws didn't stop her from pushing. 'So *you* believe that something good came of it?'

A fierce light illuminated his eyes, turning them golden in the lamplight. 'Until recently, I imagined so,' he rasped, his lips barely moving. 'But I've changed my mind.'

A chill swept into her heart. Because she realised then her questioning had another agenda. She'd been gearing up to ask if *he* forgave her. Whether they could, at the very least, part without acrimony.

If nothing good came of his time here, then he still believed she'd taken that time from him. He'd lost a year with his grandfather because of her.

Hot tears prickled her eyes, a tumult of emotion building and building until she feared everything would come tumbling out.

But…perhaps that wasn't a bad thing? So much had happened between yesterday and today. Dared she plead her case one more time?

Before she could chicken out, she rose from the blanket. 'Tahir, I'm sorry.'

He frowned, then jerked upright from where he'd leaned against the boulder. 'You misunderstand what I meant, Lauren. I've changed my mind because there's nothing to—' He paused as footsteps approached.

When a disembodied voice spoke in low, urgent tones, Tahir frowned and answered.

Lauren wanted to shout at the intruder to go away. She needed to hear what he'd been about to say.

But striding forward, Tahir picked up a silk wrap, again

conjured seemingly out of nowhere, and gently draped it over her shoulders. For a taut few seconds, he simply stared at her, questions teeming in his eyes. But she recognised the moment he shut them down.

'I'm needed on an urgent call. But this conversation isn't over. We'll pick it up when I'm done, yes?'

Even more bewildered, she nodded jerkily, her heart leaping wildly in her chest as he tugged her close and brushed a soft kiss on her forehead.

Then he was striding away, his magnificent towering figure disappearing before she took her next breath.

He must've given instructions regarding her because, a handful of minutes later, Nesa and another attendant appeared, and she was ushered back to her suite.

Thankfully, they left her when she insisted she could dress herself.

After rinsing off and donning fresh clothes, hair brushed and the lightest make-up applied more for fortitude than anything else, she was about to head out onto her terrace for some much-needed head-clearing air when she recalled that the hourglasses were in Tahir's suite.

She debated leaving them alone, but it seemed essential that they finished what they'd started.

She was now familiar enough with the hallways on this level to navigate her way to his private quarters. Expecting a hovering aide or attendant who would let her in to retrieve the hourglasses, Lauren was surprised when she found the hallways empty.

Approaching Tahir's doors, she tentatively knocked. To no response.

Biting her lip, she turned the handle and entered.

The first time she'd entered these quarters, it'd been through the secret passage. When she'd left it, she'd been far too distracted to see which way Tahir took. Now, she saw that within the quarters were three smaller hallways, each shooting off into more rooms. She bypassed an elaborate sunken living area and went down a corridor that turned out to be guest bedroom before retracing her steps. The second led to an immense kitchen and sleek gym.

The third revealed the master suite she sought.

Heat billowed inside her as she took in the rumpled sheets and discarded clothes. The half-finished bottle of wine Tahir had opened after they'd made love the first time stood on his bedside table.

She turned a full circle in the room, desperately etching every corner of it in her brain so she could draw on it when the future grew too bleak.

When her gaze landed on the hourglass on top of a hand-carved cabinet, her eyes widened. Had they really only been gone just over an hour? She went towards the tray, her heart hammering with each step.

After this she would only have a turn or two before midnight struck. Three if she was lucky. She would continue to advocate for Matt, of course.

But didn't she matter, too?

She was *still* in love with Tahir.

Did she not owe it to herself to fight her own corner? Her own happiness? To lay all her cards on the table?

What if he rejects you?

Her fingers trembled against the filigree casing of the hourglass. But she raised her chin. She'd just been reminded, *by Tahir*, that she had hidden strength. Wouldn't it see her through?

The rejection of her parents was one thing, but the rejection of the man she loved…? The man who was everything her heart and soul desired? Could she withstand it if her hopes were dashed?

She clenched her fist, the answer too terrible to contemplate. And yet…

Could she live with herself if she didn't?

No, she couldn't.

A strange, almost euphoric resolve in place, Lauren whirled about. Then stopped. Tahir was occupied with a phone call elsewhere. Should she wait for him here or return to her room?

Here.

Decision made, she stepped out onto the terrace because being in the room where he'd made such sublime love to her threatened to scramble her brain. For what lay ahead, she needed every available faculty.

Night-time in the desert was even more mesmerising than the day. The elements of danger that lingered only heightened the brightness of the start, the crispness of the air. Eyes on the constellation, she gasped softly when a comet streaked across the sky.

She wasn't too far gone to make a wish, but she hoped with every fibre of her being that this time he wouldn't slip through her fingers too soon.

That she would be—

Tahir's deep, serious tones interrupted her fanciful thoughts, for which she was half grateful. Pulse racing, she turned, but he wasn't in the bedroom or on the terrace with her. It dawned on her that the labyrinthine layout of the villa meant he could be above, below or in a room beside her.

It turned out he was on a half-level above her, on a smaller terrace connecting to what looked like a study.

The last thing Lauren wanted was to be caught eavesdropping on a conference call.

And she would've retreated from the terrace had she not heard her name uttered by a voice she didn't recognise.

Her feet froze. Her palms grew clammy. Every instinct urged her to leave. But Tahir was responding. And with the resonance of a sonic boom, shattered every last one of her dreams.

'You've wasted both your time and mine by gambling with a weak hand, Adnan. Lauren Winchester has no bearing on the decisions I make regarding my kingdom, at present or in the future. If you think I'm distracted enough by her or you are spying on me to see what happens with her brother so you can leverage it to alter a single clause in our agreement, you're going to be woefully disappointed. Nothing has changed. Nothing *will* change. Javid has agreed to help you advance this agreement. I suggest you make the most of his expertise. That is the only concession you will receive.'

CHAPTER TEN

IT DIDN'T TAKE Tahir very long at all to realise he'd taken this call for one reason only. Distance.

An excuse to step back from the emotions bombarding him when Lauren dragged up painful subjects. So fast on the heels of his own soul-searching, he'd felt as if he were coming apart at the seams.

He'd taken the reprieve. And now every cell in his body was straining to be back there with her. To jump into the deep end and to hell with keeping his every emotion locked down tight.

In a world where everyone wanted something from him—case in point, this conversation with his cousin—Lauren had asked for nothing for herself except his forgiveness. Forgiveness she still believed he withheld because he hadn't fully conveyed it before they'd been interrupted.

He frowned, impatience digging deeper claws into him as his cousin droned on.

As he'd suspected, Adnan had played the card he believed would sway Tahir. Now he was tugging on family bonds, with mild threats thrown in about knowledge of Winchester's arrest. Tahir heard Javid's faint snort in the background. He would've laughed himself had the need to get back to Lauren not been so visceral. If this was what twenty minutes away from her felt like, how would it be when their twenty-four *hours* were up?

What would it be like if she left him…?

'…for the sake of my future heirs,' Adnan petitioned plaintively.

Future…heirs.

Tahir jack-knifed in his chair, sending an expensive paperweight skidding across his desk. Tense silence echoed from the connection, then, 'Everything all right?' his cousin asked.

Control honed since birth came to his aid as, with his heart jammed firmly in his throat, he answered evenly, 'I'm not interested in going around in circles with you, cousin. This conversation is over.'

He hung up and jumped to his feet, his urgent strides eating up the distance to his private suite. Tahir wasn't sure why he'd assumed she would be there and the tingling sensation at the back of his neck didn't help as he barked at an aide as to her whereabouts.

Miss Winchester had returned to her rooms and taken the hourglasses with her, he was told.

He found her on her terrace, seated on a trellised chair with refreshments set out. Refreshments she hadn't touched.

Was it his imagination or did her back stiffen as he approached? He couldn't quite tell in the lamplight. Cool eyes drifted his way and a small smile played at her lips.

He wanted to sweep her into his arms, kiss those lips until they clung to his. Until she was mad with the same turbulent emotions coursing through him. But he needed a level head. Too much hinged on this new, intensely unnerving turn of events.

'Ah, there you are. I brought these in here so we don't lose track of the game. I hope you don't mind.'

Tahir frowned. There was a chilled civility in her tone

he'd never heard before. He'd heard her fired up about solutions to a humanitarian crisis, heard her passionate, disconsolate, and defiant. But never these snooty cut-glass upper-class tones her brother and his cronies favoured.

Giving his head a silent shake, he strode closer, the subject throbbing wildly inside him driving his every breath. 'We need to talk.'

She waved a graceful hand at the hourglass. 'Of course. It's still your allotted time. Fire away.'

Since there was no delicate way to approach this, and because, hell, he didn't want to, he stated bluntly, 'I didn't use protection the last time. Is there a possibility that I've made you pregnant?'

Lauren felt the blood drain from her face. Of all the ways she'd imagined their next conversation going after what she'd overheard, this was the last thing she'd expected.

The hand next to her untouched glass of sweet tea trembled wildly and she was absurdly glad she hadn't picked it up to take a sip. Because she was sure she'd have shattered—

'Lauren?' he pressed. His face might have been a mask of rigid control, but electric tension vibrated from him. And his eyes…if they'd been burnished gold before, they were the colour of flaming sand now. Alive and all-consuming.

It isn't for you. It's for the situation he finds himself in. Another scandal…

The reminder was bracing enough to restore a modicum of calm. 'And what if I'm pregnant? Are you going to strike a bargain with me too the way your mother did with your father and with you?' She flinched the moment the words left her lips. Then she cursed herself for her soft heart.

For a single moment, he looked incandescent. Then his ashen features neutralised. 'Is that what you want?'

'No!'

At her forceful answer a touch of tension eased in his tight shoulders. But the majority of it remained. 'Tell me what you want.'

An hour ago, she would've cried with joy to hear those words. 'And you'll grant it? Why don't I believe that?'

His hands slid into his pockets. 'You won't know until you state it.'

'Fine. It's easy enough. I want to finish this game and return home.'

A tic throbbed at his temple. Then, 'No.'

Don't panic. 'No? Just like that? You know you can't hold me prisoner, right?'

He sauntered away and leaned against the terrace wall as if he had all the time in the world. 'I won't need to. Before we're done talking, you'll be agreeable to what I have in mind.'

'You sound very sure of yourself.'

'I've had practice,' he said without an ounce of self-doubt.

'This isn't some sort of business transaction.' The words seared her throat, her every emotion turning her insides raw.

He inclined his head. 'No, it's very personal. But it's a transaction nonetheless.'

'A transaction you think you'll win.'

'We'll both win.'

She tilted her head, dying to unsettle him as much as his calm assuredness was unsettling her. 'And how do you work that out?'

'Because I will make you my queen.'

He tossed the words out as if he were announcing what his palace chef was cooking for dinner.

Her jaw sagged to the floor and for the life of her she

couldn't pick it back up because a multitude of emotions held her captive. When she managed to speak it was to eject one stunned word. 'What?'

'You're not deaf, Lauren.'

Her gaze flicked above his head, to the stars she'd stood under such a short time ago and stopped herself from making fruitless wishes. It seemed the cosmos had taken it upon itself to deliver a poisoned wish nonetheless. Because what could be more devastating than being granted a lifetime beside the love of your life when he was doing it out of duty? 'No, I'm not. Which makes me wonder if you're the one who's gone insane.'

His whole body bristled with affront, his eyes narrowing into laser missiles. 'Excuse me?'

'You're not deaf, Tahir.' She launched his words back at him, the voice screeching at her to watch her tone conclusively ignored.

'You question whether I'm impaired because I want to keep my child and heir under my roof and my protection?'

'No, I question your reasoning as to why you think you need to do that by marrying a woman you don't want. A woman who doesn't want you back.' She tagged on because it felt vital that she clarify that lest he believe otherwise.

It was clear that clarification was over-exaggerated when his gaze tunnelled into hers, his expression patently mocking. 'You don't want me? Really? Shall I prove to you how much you don't want me?'

'Isn't that how we found ourselves here in the first place? Trying to prove some sort of point to each other?'

'I'm happy to give you a lasting refresher that would make you stop lying to yourself once and for all,' he proffered, the eyes boring into hers absolutely deadly with intent.

'No, thanks.' Her voice was prim, but her emotions were anything but.

Challenge flared in his eyes for a moment, ramping up every cell in her body in response. Then, like the imperious ruler he was, confident in his power and influence, he bared his teeth in a smile.

'Then shall we get back to the discussion?'

'I've said all I'm going to say.'

He folded his arms, and she categorically forbade her gaze from dropping to his brawny forearms. Arms she'd gripped as she'd drowned in the pleasure he'd created. Of course, her senses had other ideas.

They prompted her gaze to seek out the gap opening at the throat of his tunic, to feast on the swathe of bronze skin displayed there, then up to gorge on the lines of his strong throat. When it then travelled up to meet his, the far too knowing and abashedly carnal look he returned flared heat into her cheeks.

'Let me get this straight. You intend to return to England, where you'll give birth to my child and live with them under your parents' roof with no argument from me?'

The desert-dry incredulity in his voice made her flinch. Because, set out like that, it was as unlikely as sprouting wings and flying away from this increasingly terrifying conversation.

'All this is highly hypothetical. We don't even know if I'm pregnant,' she said, cringing at the touch of desperation in her voice.

He didn't budge from where he stood. Nor did he lessen the laser focus of his gaze. And Lauren should've hated the under-the-microscope sensation that triggered, but unnervingly being such intense focus of Tahir's gaze was...thrilling. And desperately heartbreaking.

'You didn't just have sex with a guy you met on a dating app and shared a few dinners with, Lauren. I'm a sovereign of a kingdom with the accompanying responsibilities and protocols that need to be observed. I'm not going to engage in a wait-and-see game while you weigh your options. In this matter, your choices are unfortunately limited.'

'You say unfortunately as if you mean it? And yet I don't believe you're sorry about it at all.'

He shrugged. 'I'm choosing to be practical about it.'

Practical. Protocol. Inconsequential.

Words that sharpened into little arrows and pierced vulnerable places she didn't even know were unprotected until they found their target.

Rising, she put more distance between them, whirling away to squeeze her eyes shut. Then, resenting the show of weakness, she pivoted right back to face him. 'My future choices are mine to make, not yours.'

Disappointment and another indecipherable emotion flashed through his eyes. 'Is what I'm offering you really that deplorable? Is becoming my queen such a nightmare for you?'

My queen.

The title attempted to wrap itself around her heart. She refused to allow it. He didn't love her. So she forced a shrug. 'This wasn't how I saw my life going.'

Again that flash of emotion. 'Life rarely plays out the way we envision.'

'That's not true for you though, is it? You're exactly where you want to be, aren't you?'

Slowly he advanced to where she stood. The folded arms dropped to his sides. He didn't reach for her, but he didn't need to. Her entire being was focused on him.

'Do you think you could've conceived my child, Lauren?' The words were low, deep, throbbing with a kind of possessiveness that warned that, should she answer in the affirmative, life as she knew it would be over.

She could've prevaricated. Or simply refused to answer.

'I'm within my ovulation window. But that means nothing. Unfortunately for you, you can't control things this time, Tahir. And as to whether I want to be your queen, whether I'm carrying your child or not, the answer is no.'

The answer is no.

In the short space of time between realising his blunder with protection and reaching her, Tahir's imagination had gone on a wild rampage.

He'd imagined Lauren's belly round with his child.

He'd imagined holding his child for the first time.

He'd imagined doing things differently. Better. To stop the sins of the father being visited upon the son.

Because...

Every child deserves to be told they're loved...

Those words especially, said with wide, earnest eyes, had drilled into his very soul. Had made him believe...in those frantic minutes...that he might have what it took. That, decades from now, no child of his would confess to another human being that his or her father didn't love them. Instead, they would boast of his affection. They would go through life secure in his unconditional love.

Damn it, Lauren had made him *hope* again. And this time the fall would be greater...because he loved her.

While she...

Whether I'm carrying your child or not...

Tahir couldn't even summon the power to be furious at her. He had absolutely no one to blame but himself.

'Did you hear me?' she bit out, her face still pale from his news. His *unwanted* news.

'Oh, yes, *habibti*. I heard you.'

Did she now flinch at his endearment? When she'd shuddered with delight at it a mere two hours ago? Extracting himself from the wall, he tugged the shroud over the depleted hourglass and set the tray before her.

Startled eyes rose to his. 'What are you doing?'

I don't know. But I can't bear this to end yet. 'We're not done.'

She opened her mouth and every sinew in his body strained for her next words. Because the hope she'd awakened refused to die. But all she said was, 'Fine. Have it your way.'

Her hand shook as she spun the tray.

Lauren knew he'd seen but she didn't care. He was determined to finish his game and she wasn't going to give him the satisfaction of begging him to release her from it.

But even as she went through with the sham of finishing a game that no longer mattered, her other hand dropped beneath the table to her belly.

Pregnant.

A baby... *Tahir's baby* could be growing inside her right this minute. She swallowed, the enormity of that possibility shaking through her. She'd come off the pill after swearing off dating following her thirtieth birthday. And the idea of having sex with Tahir on her arrival in Jukrat had been nigh on laughable.

A wave of dizziness swept over her, making her squeeze her eyes shut once more.

'The prospect of finishing our game is deplorable to you now, too?' he grated.

She wanted to scream and demand why he was bothering. Lauren knew she was a glutton for punishment where this man was concerned because even now, when self-preservation urged her to end this, to flee far and hide, she remained seated. She reached for the silk shroud to her left and tugged it free.

'Ninety minutes between us. That should be enough time,' Tahir said, then turned to walk away.

'Enough time for what?' she asked, the sensation of being in an alternate universe hitting hard.

He stopped, turned. In the shadows thrown by the lamplight, all she saw was his stony expression and eyes that continued to burn far too ferociously. 'You want to be free of me, don't you? You yearn to return home? You'll get your wish soon enough.'

That was how Lauren found herself in the helicopter one hour before midnight, with Tahir beside her and the hourglass counting down between them. They'd barely spoken, each wrapped up in their thoughts.

Uppermost in hers was the fact that the thing she'd dreaded had come true far too quickly. Tahir was getting rid of her. And she didn't think she could bear it.

She pursed her lips tighter, terrified she would blurt out her feelings and damn herself for ever.

When Tahir answered a call a short time into their flight, she was relieved. Then her heart was breaking all over again at the thought that soon she wouldn't hear his voice. Wouldn't experience the dexterity of his brilliant mind or feast her eyes on his towering magnificence.

She would be returning to a half-life not of her parents' making but of a love unrequited. When blurry lights winked beyond the window, she thought it was rain. Then she realised her tears blocked her vision.

She blinked them away as the aircraft set down on the same helipad they'd taken off from yesterday.

The same aide approached, and if he was surprised that his King had returned just a day after leaving, he didn't show it.

Bodyguards didn't bar her way this time. In fact, she was—to her amazement—treated to the same reverent greetings as Tahir. It was probably why she didn't fully take note of her surroundings until she was led into another lavish living room.

And she came face to face with her parents.

'Mum? Dad? What are you doing here?'

'Your mother told me about your conversation,' her father replied, his voice just short of a sneer. 'It was clear you were getting nowhere, and Matt needed us to be here. But we didn't quite think we would be meeting you here.' He sent a puzzled glance at Tahir.

Lauren ignored the puzzling last response and addressed the main one. 'So you came to light a fire under my feet because I wasn't moving fast enough for your liking?'

He stiffened in surprise, then annoyance.

Yes, this was the first time she'd used a less than cordial tone with him. She could excuse herself with the overwhelming emotions coursing through her. But regardless of the circumstance, this conversation was long overdue.

'You look pale. Are you quite all right?' her father said, after a quick, pandering glance at Tahir.

Lauren wanted to laugh but she was mildly terrified she would drown in hysterics. She swiped her hand across her eyes, praying for strength. 'No, I'm not all right. I haven't slept for more than an hour in the last day, and you turning up here because you think I'm…' She stopped to swallow the surge of emotion in her throat. 'You know what? I don't care any more.'

Her mother gasped, her eyes widening before turning cool with disapproval. 'That's hardly the way to talk to your father, Lauren.'

'Oh, no? How about the way you talk to me? The way you treat me?'

Charles cast another glance at Tahir as if gauging his

reaction to her outburst. 'I'm not sure what's up with you, but this is hardly the place. Perhaps His Majesty might give us a private—'

'No. He stays. This concerns him, after all, doesn't it? Don't you want to know how I got on with trying to convince him to help Matt?'

'Well, we were told our presence would hasten things. Although we were under the impression that His Majesty was arranging for Matt's lawyer to meet us at our hotel, not be brought here.'

She frowned. Tahir had arranged this?

Her gaze swung to him. He stood with his hands tucked behind his back, his profile formidable as he watched her father. 'You'll be taken to where you need to be in due course,' he said. 'First, you need to finish this conversation with your daughter.'

'You should know I wasn't successful,' Lauren said bluntly. 'Tahir isn't going to step in. My presence here changed nothing. Matt's on his own.' She sensed Tahir stiffen but kept her gaze trained on her parents. 'And so am I.' Something cracked open within her then, but, amazingly, what was left behind wasn't as awful and devastating as she'd feared.

Her father frowned. 'So are you? What does that mean?'

'It means my days of lessening myself for you are over. I resign.' She switched her gaze to her mother. 'And I'll be moving out as soon as I get home. I'm grateful that you gave me a home, but I can't...' She stopped and cleared her throat, bunching her fists so she wouldn't shake so much. 'I'd rather have no love than conditional indifference.'

'This is all absurd. Are you sure the desert heat hasn't got to you? Look, let's settle this properly when you're back—'

'I've never been clearer, Dad.'

His face went florid, his eyes colder than she'd ever seen them. 'I always knew you were an ungrateful child. After all we've done for you—'

'Does that include encouraging her to betray those she cares about? Consistently taking your other child's side instead of hers? What about emotionally blackmailing your own child, Winchester? I don't think that's quite in the parenting manual,' Tahir said.

Lauren's shocked gaze swung back to him. He didn't love her, and yet he was defending her? Was he trying to make it impossible for her heart to ever forget him? 'Tahir, you don't have to—'

Tahir's nostrils flared and she spotted mild rebuke in his eyes before he shifted his attention back to her father. 'Yes, I do. What your father forgot to say was that when I arranged yesterday to have them brought here, he tried the same tactic with me, believing I could be manipulated. Now you're here, perhaps you can elaborate on your intentions?'

Her shocked gaze swung back to her father. 'You really thought you could manipulate Tahir? Don't you know that my desire to have a better relationship with you was your only leverage over me? That I sacrificed...' She stopped unwilling to bare the true state of her tattered heart in front of Tahir, the man who'd decimated it.

Her father squirmed, and his mouth gaped but no words emerged. No words to dispute anything she'd said. Or even attempt to heal her heartache. Foolish tears brimmed in her eyes and she dashed them away.

After a minute, her father pressed his lips shut and shook his head.

'It's time for you to leave,' Tahir decreed, his tone stone-cold.

Charles Winchester nodded after casting a chilling look at Lauren.

With a flick of his hand, Tahir's aide stepped forward. Within seconds, her parents were gone.

She turned on Tahir. 'You arranged this! You wanted it to happen, didn't you?'

He shrugged. 'Yes, I did.'

She couldn't even summon the temper to grit her teeth. All her emotions were locked into the *why, why, why*?

'Men like your father respond predictably to one thing—power. He thought me summoning him meant he could manipulate some out of me. He discovered differently.'

'So this was all another game to you?'

His gaze hardened. 'No, it wasn't. I wanted you to be free of them once and for all.'

'Why? What do you care?'

He stiffened as if she'd knifed him with the words. 'You still don't get it, do you? I can stand many things, but not watching you live a half-life. You needed to take back your power.'

'And that's all it comes down to, is it? Who holds the most power?'

His chin lifted and he cast her a look so pitying she shrivelled where she stood. 'Don't disparage it. Without it, you wouldn't be here. You love what it can do for you. Once upon a time, you lobbied for it because you knew what it could do for the causes you upheld. And admit it, you love it moving between your legs when I take you.'

Heat and cold drenched her. 'It didn't do me a lot of good in the long run, though, did it? Just in case it wasn't clear before, I heard what you said about not helping Matt. About me.'

Regret flashed in his eye and his jaw tightened. But in the next instant, it was gone. 'That's unfortunate. But it's not why you're running back to London. You've already washed your hands of your brother. As for what you overheard, perhaps you shouldn't take things like that at face value.'

Before she could ask what he meant, he was walking away. He returned moments later with the hourglass tray.

'What are you doing? Our twenty-four hours is over. I'm leaving.'

'Not quite. Midnight approaches. Spin the tray one last time, Lauren.'

'Why? What does it matter any more?'

His eyes blazed and this time something contained in them set her insides alight. 'Because I want my life to begin, Lauren. I want *our* lives to begin.'

'I...what do you mean...our lives?'

His nostrils flared and for the first time in a very long time, he seemed at a loss for words. At a loss, full stop. But his eyes...oh, God, his eyes devoured her. In a way that siphoned all of her breath. Risked dampening down the righteous anger she should be fanning—

No.

'You know what? It doesn't matter what you mean—'

'Doesn't it?' Soft words, no less ground-shaking for their impact. 'You've freed yourself from the shackles of conditional love. Don't you want to fight for what you truly want now?'

'Tahir.'

Those eyes burnished brighter. 'I believe you when you say you didn't wish for things to unfold and end the way they did. So do the present and future not really *matter*?'

'I can't...they can't.'

'Why not?'

'You know why not. I'm—'

'If you call yourself a nobody one more time, I'll commission my best architect in Jukrat to build a dungeon just to throw you in until you come to your senses,' he promised through gritted teeth.

Her head snapped up, a little bit of that anger igniting to life. 'I wasn't going to call myself a nobody. I am somebody. I'm my own person. That person is a realist. This…whatever is going on between us…it's a fairy tale. I've woken up. You need to wake up too.'

His chest expanded on a deep breath, his jaw softening a touch. The flames in his eyes morphed. No less powerful but deeper. The kind that promised to burn brighter. Longer. Eternally? 'There she is. The woman who owned me even before I ever clapped eyes on her. The woman no other has ever been able to hold a candle to.'

She gasped. 'Tahir.'

His fist curled hard as if he was physically restraining himself from reaching for her, from acting on the possessive need surging like rip tides in his eyes. 'You keep saying my name like that and I won't be responsible for my actions. We need to clear this up once and for all because I never want to revisit it again.'

Warmth rushed at her, threatening to overwhelm the cold loneliness. But could she trust it? She shook her head. 'Did you not hear what I just said? This isn't real. It can't be. You went from preparing to say goodbye to me in a matter of hours to asking me to be your queen. And you know what changed within those hours? The tiniest possibility that I might be pregnant. Tell me why I shouldn't think it was a knee-jerk reaction triggered by the need to claim your child. Tell me how that's not another form of conditional possession that makes me surplus to requirements?'

'It wasn't,' he answered, his voice as deep as the earth's crust and just as unshakable. 'Do you want to know the first time I imagined you wearing my crown?' he challenged again. He took a single step towards her then froze again. 'I knew within a minute of meeting you twelve years ago that you were exceptional. Bold and unafraid and so damned alive, I couldn't not fall under your spell.' He took a long, deep breath. 'More than the sex and the conversation and the giving heart I knew you possessed, you gave me hope. Made me believe I could be a better version of myself, a better version for the woman I wanted to be my queen, even back then. That hope…that spell hasn't waned, Lauren.'

She shook her head again. 'That's just it, don't you see? Spells by their very definition don't last for ever! We put ourselves in a pressure cooker of twenty-four hours. You'll be a fool to believe it'll be sustainable beyond—'

'Beyond what? Twenty-four hours? Twelve years? A lifetime? I'm prepared to test it. Are you?' he dared.

'No! I can't… I won't do that to you.'

He exhaled harshly. 'Why not? Why are you so hell-bent on saving me from this perceived path you think will lead to misery?'

'Because I…' She froze. Her throat locked tight. She wanted to squeeze her eyes shut, pretend his eyes weren't blazing at her. That he wasn't closing the gap between them, leaving her no room to escape her thoughts. Her very real, far too potent emotions that shook every cell in her being.

'Because you what, *habibti*?' he crooned softly, his breath washing over her forehead as he leaned close, fusing his essence with hers.

When she shook her head, her eyes wide open because, self-preservation be damned, she wasn't going to miss a moment of this, the tiniest self-deprecating smile kicked up the corner of his velvet-smooth lips before he was all purpose and danger again.

Before his lips were caressing her face, lingering on her lips, taking another breath before he said, 'I'll go first, shall I?' He didn't wait for her response. Every muscle in his body was set on one purpose. 'Personally, I think twelve years is more than enough. Don't you? I regret, deeply, that most of it was wasted being bitter and unforgiving and far too invested in feeling aggrieved. Believing the future you hoped for has been taken away from you for ever has a way of doing that to a man.'

Lauren knew her mouth was gaping but she couldn't quite bring herself to correct herself. Tahir didn't seem to mind though. The ferocious look in his eyes didn't abate one little bit.

'I told you that my family lawyers took care of shutting down most of the tabloids within weeks of what happened. What I tried to say back in the desert tonight was that there was nothing to forgive because *I* should've acted differently too. I had the palace PR machine and a team of investigators I could've used to discover the real truth. But I let my father deal with it. I marinated in my bitterness to justify everything that was done to me when I knew deep down you weren't capable of such duplicity. For that, we lost a dozen years. I didn't need a year to know the kind of ruler I would be. Or that those months with you were special. My deepest regret through it all was being separated from you.'

That crack came again, sharper. Harder. And again it was replaced by something stronger. Durable. The everlasting kind that said it wouldn't break or be subject to conditions or whims. It was so overwhelming, tears filled her eyes. 'Oh, God. I can't believe... Tahir.'

He closed the gap, finally. Brushed her tears away with his thumbs before lowering his head to kiss them away. 'No tears. Never again. Stay with me,' he pleaded.

The possibility that this was a dream she'd wake up from soon rendered her speechless. 'I...'

'I know you want to return to London, but give me a chance to show you the best of Jukrat? To make a home here with me? We can spend part of the year in London if you truly miss it...'

Her eyes widened. 'You'd do that for me?'

'For the chance to build a life with triple the happiness we've denied ourselves all these years? I'd do just about anything, *habibti*.'

Hope threatened to soar but, like him, she'd endured having it dashed to grasp it. 'Am I truly your beloved, Tahir?'

The expression that came over his face threatened to blow her away. 'I know what you heard me say about you and about Matt didn't do me any favours, but it was just for my cousin's sake. I instructed Ali to speak to the prosecutor the moment we got to the riad. Your brother has been given another month to prepare his case.'

She gasped. 'Tahir... I don't know what to say.'

His large hands framed her face, his eyes fervid on hers. 'Then listen. There was only ever you, my heart. I want you whether you're carrying our child or not. I want you beside me, ruling our people, dazzling me with that brilliant mind, stunning my senses with your incredible body. I want it all, Lauren. Do you?' he demanded thickly. Ferociously.

She threw her arms around him. 'Yes. Oh, please, yes!'

When she strained towards him, eager for his kiss, he held her back. 'And? Is there something you want to say to me, my heart?' The question was cocky, bordering on imperious, but the vulnerable look in his eyes said he wasn't sure she felt the same. Wasn't sure of the solidity of the ground beneath his feet.

She vowed then that she would never give him cause to doubt her love.

'I love you, Tahir. I've loved you from the moment we met. I loved you even when I thought you hated me, and I'll love you triple hard now I know it's returned. Please, please, let's build that life you promised together?'

He kissed her then. A deep, soul-shaking, life- affirming kiss that began to restore all the broken cracks of deprived affection they'd suffered.

When they parted, she placed his hand on her belly. 'I've learned not to wish for much because it may be denied me. But I wish with everything that I have that this is true. That I'm carrying our child.'

She'd thought it impossible that his eyes could blaze brighter. But in that moment, they did. Dropping to his knees, the Sheikh of Jukrat placed a soft, reverent kiss on her belly.

Then, the most beautiful eyes in the world gazed up at her, love burning deep and true.

'I'm the King. If I will it, it will be so.'

EPILOGUE

One year later

IT TURNED OUT that they had made a baby together that night in the desert.

Crown Prince Malik Al-Jukrat came screaming into the world nine months later, to his parents' utter joy and the kingdom's jubilation. He didn't care that he'd put his mother through thirty-six hours of labour and his father through bouts of feverish cursing and making promises to every deity he could name.

He was adorable and that was all that mattered.

'If you stare at him with any more adoration, he'll become even more unbearable. And I have plans for those fingers you're letting him wrapped his around so tightly,' Lauren joked as her husband rocked their son beneath the nursery window overlooking the royal gardens.

She'd just finished feeding him in time for his debut at his christening. Like their royal wedding and her coronation as Queen Lauren, Sheikha of Jukrat, Humanitarian Ambassador to the United Nations, the guest list for Malik's christening had grown from several hundred to thousands. Lauren's complaint had been met with an implacable response. One Tahir now liked to trot out every time they hosted a state function or even a private party.

'You're the love of my life. I can't let a day go by without showing the world what a beautiful treasure I've found. Don't deny me.'

And truly, what was a girl to say to that level of adoration? She lapped it up, of course. And because it did her heart good, she gave it back tenfold.

She approached the two loves of her life now, dropping a kiss on her son's head before peering up at Tahir.

His blinding smile awaited her, followed by a kiss that she felt all the way to her toes.

'Does everything look ready?' she said, glancing into the garden where the palace decorators had gone to town with the event planning. Boldly coloured chairs and flowers were spread out in cosy groupings, inviting guests to mingle. Lauren had taken inspiration from Tahir's desert home—their desert home—and the result was breathtaking and relaxing.

'They will be unless they want to incur Maman's wrath,' Tahir responded dryly.

As if on cue, the decorator and event planners rushed into view, trailing an older woman dressed in the sort of stylish French elegance that shrieked her royalty. She tossed out instructions, her hands flicking left and right as she navigated the decorations.

Lauren grinned. 'She thrives on occasions like these, doesn't she? She's already planning Malik's first birthday party.'

Far from discarding Lauren's urge to look deeper into his mother's behaviour and how it'd dictated his relationship with her, Tahir had taken it to heart. A quick detour via Paris on their way back from their honeymoon in Zanzibar had laid the groundwork for a new relationship. His mother's confession that the lump sums paid to her had been at her father's instigation and that he wouldn't take no for an answer had led her to believe that was the relationship he wished her to have with his children. She hadn't been proud of it, but she'd reasoned that a skewed relationship was better than none at all.

Tahir's scepticism had eroded with continued contact, and Malik's arrival had finally brought about a complete change of heart. Malik's grandmother adored him and wasn't afraid to show it one little bit.

'Any thawing from Javid?'

Her brother-in-law hadn't been receptive to Tahir's urgings to renew *his* relationship with his mother. In fact, they'd had a heated row about it.

'He'll come around in his own time,' Tahir said. His gaze drifted to the far side of the grounds where Javid paced while on a phone call. The problems with the trade agreements had taken longer to fix in Riyaal, a fact Javid grumbled about every chance he got. Her brother-in-law had moaned at dinner last night that he hadn't had a girlfriend in months, a fact Lauren had warned him not to remedy at his nephew's party.

His grin and I-Make-No-Promises response had filled her with dread.

'Or he'll find a woman half as incredible as my wife and she'll help him embrace every aspect of love, as I have.'

She blinked back sappy tears, even as she teased, 'Only half as incredible?'

Tahir's tawny gaze burned into hers. 'No one holds a candle to you, my heart. They can try, but no one ever will. It's why I'm grateful every single day for you. For the life you've given me and the love I'll cherish for ever.'

She rose on tiptoes and pressed her lips to his, uncaring that tears streamed down her face and she was ruining her make-up.

'As I'll cherish you too, Tahir. For ever.'

* * * * *

CINDERELLA'S SECRET BABY

DANI COLLINS

MILLS & BOON

To my sisters, Donna and Maggie,
who live far away, but are always here for me.

I love you both very much.

CHAPTER ONE

AMELIA LINDOR COULDN'T fathom what had gotten into her father, Tobias. He had come straight back after leaving on his morning constitutional with a fire in his belly, insisting Amelia drive him from Goderich to Niagara-on-the-Lake. *Right now.*

It was a three-hour trip that her daughter, Peyton, had *not* enjoyed. The two-month-old believed any car ride longer than twenty minutes was intolerable torture and made sure everyone knew it. After fussing on and off for two hours, she had finally settled into a hard nap.

The silence was a blessed relief, but it threw off the schedule Amelia had finally started to establish with her. Peyton was meant to be nursing by now. As Amelia parked and bent into the back seat of her dusty but trusty sedan, her breasts were already heavy and tight. Should she wake the baby and coax her to feed? Or risk a public letdown?

"How long will we be here?" Amelia asked her father, but only got a slammed door in response. She stood and called, "Dad?"

"I told you, I have to meet someone," he grumbled over his shoulder as he hurried through the full parking lot toward the door of the winery's tasting house.

"Who?" she said with exasperation.

He didn't answer. Or wait. Tobias had arthritis and a

heart weakened by grief, but seconds later he had heaved open the wide door and disappeared inside.

This didn't make sense. When her father met someone, it was usually his fellow retirees from the salt mine. Six mornings a week, he rose to take his medication, record the temperature in his weather journal and listen to the early news. He left as soon as it was light, joining his buddies at the café two streets over where they nursed coffee and grudges against politicians and potholes.

This morning, one of his cronies had said something that sent him home to snap orders like the maintenance supervisor Tobias had once been. *Let's go. This can't wait.*

Since Amelia's only plan for the day had been drop-in infant yoga, she had hurriedly dressed, and here they were.

Tobias had refused to talk in the car, so she had bounced through the music stations, trying to calm Peyton, remaining ignorant as to what this was all about.

Releasing an irked sigh, she carefully skimmed the limp Peyton into her arms. Since the seat weighed more than her baby did, she only threw a receiving blanket over her shoulder and cradled Peyton there, not even bothering with the diaper bag so she could hurry after her father.

A couple came out the door as Amelia approached, both dressed to the nines. The man wore a dapper suit; the woman was in a strapless amethyst gown. Bridesmaid. Who else dressed like that at eleven twenty in the morning? Was that why there had been purple and pearl balloons on the welcome sign?

The woman abruptly halted before crashing into Amelia. She offered a strained smile that suggested a supreme effort at politeness when she was barely holding on to her temper.

"Hello. Vienna. Sister of the groom." She touched her bare upper chest, then gestured into the tasting room. "Go all the way through and out the back. You'll see the pergola by the shore. Everyone is sitting down. We're about to start."

"I'm not here for a wedding." Amelia grimaced an apology as she realized they were intruding on a ceremony. "My father is—" On a rampage of some sort. "Inside. Looking for someone."

"Oh?" Vienna cocked her head. "Who? We've reserved the entire place for the wedding. I might know them."

"I'm not sure, but we'll get out of your hair right away. I promise." Amelia turned her friendly smile up to the man still holding the door. Cool, conditioned air beckoned from inside. "Thank you."

"My pleasure," he said in the very creepy tone some men used when they thought they were being charming by sexually harassing a woman. His gaze slid down to ogle the stretched neckline of her T-shirt. The pink cotton was straining across her nursing bra, but one breast was squashed by her *newborn baby* so, *Don't be gross, man*, Amelia thought crossly.

Behind her, Vienna was saying an impatient, "Okay, Neal. What's so important you had to drag me out here when it's about to start?"

The door closed behind her, and Amelia blinked in the shadowed interior, turning over the name Vienna in her mind. It was unusual, but she had heard it somewhere, which caused a prickle of premonition.

At the same time, the sounds and smells of the tasting room were provoking a flashback. Last summer, Amelia had taken a job at a microbrewery not far from here. On her off days, she and her workmates had toured the local wineries on their bicycles, getting tipsy inside tasting rooms like this one with its brick floor and post-and-beam ceiling. This was a bigger vineyard, so the tasting room had two bars, one on either side. Behind each were rows and rows of bottles, while the space between was full of shelves displaying knickknacks and branded tea towels and specialty wineglasses.

Amelia automatically blocked the other memories that tried to invade from last July. The ones containing a brooding man who had kissed her in the moonlight and warned her against coming to his room.

My life is a mess right now. It won't be more than tonight.

She shifted the weight of that encounter to her other shoulder as she searched for Tobias. He wasn't among the guests scrambling for a glass of wine before they headed out the doors to the ceremony. Had he gone to the lawn? *Was* he meeting one of the wedding guests?

"Grandma. There's one more. Would you like to sign the guest book?" An adorable girl of eight or nine reopened the book she had closed. She stood behind an upended barrel near the door and wore a demure version of the bridesmaid's dress. Her hair was gathered up in a bundle of tight black curls on her crown, and she wore a hint of soft pink makeup on her lips and cheeks. She had clearly been given this Very Special Job and was taking it *very* seriously.

An older woman wearing a stylish royal blue dress gave the girl an indulgent look before saying to Amelia, "Welcome. Friend of the bride or groom?"

"I'm not here for the wedding." That ought to be obvious from her very casual clothes. Her stomach was starting to sour at how ill-timed her father's mission was. "Did you see an older man come through? He's wearing a yellow shirt and brown pants. He has a bushy gray beard?"

"I think so." The little girl's face screwed up quizzically and she looked to her grandmother. "He didn't sign, either."

"He said he had an important message for the groom. I sent him to the guesthouse." The older woman pointed down a hall where a glass door led to a covered walkway.

"The groomsmen were gathering for a sip of courage in the breakfast room." She winked. "Would you excuse us? Hannah and I need to take our seats."

"Of course. Thank you." Amelia turned to start down the hall, but her gaze was snagged by the chalkboard behind the bar.

The stark black slate was adorned with a border of silk orchids in purple and white. Calligraphed letters read Congratulations Hunter and Eden.

Amelia's heart jolted to a stop, then slammed into a panicked gallop.

No. No, Dad. No.

Nooooo.

"I've always presumed I would get married at my aunt's vineyard," Hunter Waverly's fiancée had said when their engagement became official. "Weddings are their specialty. She'll pull out all the stops for me."

Hunter had gone along because a groom didn't override his bride when she set her heart on an outdoor wedding at a vineyard on a lake. Holding the ceremony here had been one less decision. Simple, if not ideal.

By anyone's standards, everything about this wedding was perfect. Bright June sunshine beamed from a cloudless sky. There was a soft breeze coming off the water, just enough to keep Hunter from overheating in his suit as he walked out to the pergola. If any of the typical day of disasters had occurred behind the scenes, solutions had been found before Hunter heard a whisper of it.

The guests were taking their seats, the bride was said to be ready, and the officiant was motioning to the string trio to wrap up their current piece.

It was unfolding flawlessly, but Hunter was tense enough to snap in half.

PTSD, he thought dourly. For most of his life, every special occasion had turned into an embarrassing disaster. He had been tempted to insist on a small ceremony with Eden, but that would have been cowardly.

The officiant checked in with his best man. Remy nodded, patting his lapel, smile tight. Something had been eating at him for months. Hunter noticed it at the engagement party, but Remy didn't want to talk about it and Hunter had lived with so little privacy in his own life, he didn't invade others'.

Through the amplifier that would allow the guests to hear their vows, he heard Eden's voice ask, "Is it working?" Her tone was a fraction higher than normal.

Wedding jitters. A bride was entitled, and Hunter refused to catch a case of it. This marriage was advantageous for both of them.

Eden had inherited controlling interest in Bellamy Home & Garden last year. Its stock value had languished in recent years, but it was a trusted Canadian icon, especially in rural communities. Eden would right the ship once she had Waverly cash at her disposal. The fact that their marriage merger included a plan to use Bellamy as a road map to bring Wave-Com's next generation of wireless technology into all those remote locations wouldn't hurt, either.

For his part, Hunter was repairing the Waverly reputation by attaching himself to the Bellamy name. Wave-Com had suffered in the years after his father died, plagued by ugly legal fights and a takeover attempt as his stepmother had sought to steal the corporation from her husband's children, throwing mud every chance she got.

Today would turn the page on those perpetual scandals. With this sophisticated wedding, brimming with homegrown celebrities and dynasties from abroad, Hunter was setting a tone of respectability, family values and stability.

Dare he add, *class*? Because Eden was intelligent, cultured and accomplished. She was well known for her philanthropy and admired for her Canadian-made fashion choices. Her grandfather had been a beloved voice on the national radio waves, and her mother still contributed weekly gardening tips to one of their programs.

Eden was suitable in other ways, too. Vienna had introduced them, implicitly promising that family gatherings would always be pleasant and civilized. Eden wanted babies right away, and Vienna was ready to start her family, too. Their children would grow up together.

Best of all, Hunter found Eden attractive, but not *too* attractive. They would have a foundation of friendship and respect, not fickle love or treacherous lust. Hunter wouldn't be tugged around by his fly the way his father had been, subjected to spectacles every other week while making excuses for the source of his humiliation.

This marriage was exactly the right thing for all concerned.

Yet his gut was full of gravel, and he couldn't shake this sense of impending doom.

It was the location. As Hunter breathed the scent of newly mown grass and heard the ducks on the lake and the buzz of bees, more prurient memories were accosting him. A musical laugh and a soft shoulder under his lips. Fine hair that carried a fragrance of sunshine.

That one night had been an escape, he often reminded himself. In some ways, it had been a narrow escape, because the heat in his blood had nearly made him say rash, embarrassing things. *Don't go in to work. I'll stay another night.* For sex.

Stop it. What kind of groom awaited his bride with a one-night stand clouding his thoughts?

Maybe it was the natural reckoning of a wedding day.

He was saying goodbye to freedom and flings as he committed the rest of his life—his sex life—to one person. That heaviness in his gut wasn't misgiving. Or regret. It wasn't.

The music faded to expectant silence. The murmuring crowd quieted.

The officiant covered her lapel microphone with her hand and asked, "Ready?"

Hunter drew the device from the pocket of his coat and turned it on, noting the green light. He nodded and brushed his jacket straight again. He looked over the guests. There were roughly two hundred arranged on either side of the carpeted aisle, all smiling with anticipation.

The first notes of their wedding playlist were plucked from the harp. He looked to the top of the stairs from the terrace where his cousin's tot of three years appeared in a flouncy dress. A bridesmaid of fourteen, one of Eden's cousins, kept a firm hold of the little one's hand and used the other to hold the rail as they began to descend.

"You!"

The gravelly bellow cut through the sublime moment, creating a stillness that silenced the angelic notes and the rustling leaves on the nearby rows of vines. Even the lap of water on the shore seemed to hold its breath.

Then a higher, feminine, anguished voice broke in.

"Daddy, no. *Please.*"

CHAPTER TWO

It was the sort of wedding Amelia's blue-collar roots could only dream of.

As she glanced from the walkway, she saw pots of gardenias and begonias stationed at the ends of rows of white chairs. The posts and slatted roof of a pergola were draped in wisteria. The backdrop was a stunning view of the lake and a hazy glimpse of Toronto's skyline, like a tiny floating island, sat on the horizon.

To the right of the pergola, there was an arched walking bridge over a trickling creek, perfect for photos of the bride and groom before they made their way to the pavilion filled with rustic tables set with linen and china and sparkling crystal.

It was fairy-tale-perfect, and her father was *ruining* it.

Amelia swerved off the walkway to intercept Tobias as he came out of the guesthouse and charged toward the pergola. Everyone swiveled their attention to her, making her feel extra clumsy as she kept a firm hold on Peyton while trying not to trip on the grass.

Oh, God, look at him. Hunter Waverly was so blindingly handsome in his morning suit, clean-shaven and tall with his wide shoulders and his stern, narrow face, he made her eyes sting. From the concrete pad of the pergola, he was even taller and looked down his bladelike nose at Tobias before shifting his gaze to Amelia as she rushed up behind her father.

Hunter stood in dappled shade, but she thought he jolted as he recognized her.

She felt naked then. And small. Smaller even than when she'd left his guest room last year. Her face was blistered by that old humiliation and this new one. Her heart was cracking down the center, falling open to pulse unprotected because her *baby* was exposed. Here. In front of hundreds of eyes where their very different positions in life were even more pronounced than they had been then.

Hunter had bought out a vineyard for his bride. He had only offered *her* what was in his wallet.

"You," her father said again, voice dripping with contempt. He avoided Amelia's attempt to catch his arm. "You ignore your own flesh and blood, leave the mother of your child to fend for herself while you…" His impatient hand waved with disdain at the guests, the tranquil setting and the loving union that was about to be blessed.

"Daddy, *please*. I am *begging* you." Amelia managed to catch a fistful of his sleeve and tugged. "Come on. We're leaving. I am so sorry."

The kindly grandmother was staring at Amelia as though she was a skunk that had waddled into the kitchen. Amelia couldn't make herself look at anyone else, especially Hunter. Her stomach had risen to churn in the back of her throat.

"She's better off without you." Her father shook off her grip. "But your friends and family ought to know what sort of man you are. Your *wife* should know what she's marrying. And I'll be damned if you won't even feed and clothe the child you made." Her father shook his finger at Hunter. "Judging by this, you can afford to, so quit being a bum."

"Dad!" she cried. "He didn't know. Okay? I never told

him." And if she didn't have the helpless bundle of Peyton snuggled in her arm, she would wish herself dead right now. She really would.

Someone in the crowd guffawed a curse of enjoyment.

Her father snapped a look at her. "A man has a right to know, Amelia."

"*I* have a right to decide what happens to *my* baby." She was furious with him.

"I care what happens to *my* baby," he barked straight back.

He did. She knew that. He was a dear, loving father, but *such* a dinosaur sometimes. Old-school and old-fashioned and so protective after losing Jasper, but how did he even know Hunter's name? How had he known Hunter would be here?

"Is it true?" Hunter's voice was deep and tight and sounded like it came out through clenched teeth even as it boomed from a speaker off to her left.

Oh *God*.

With an appalled snarl, he ripped the wire from his lapel and pulled something from his pocket, handing it to the man beside him.

"Is it?" he demanded of her without the bullhorn effect.

"Of course not," she lied blatantly. "This is all a horrible misunderstanding. I'm very sorry for the interruption," she added to the crowd. Her face was about to combust, it was boiling so ferociously in embarrassment. Her head was dizzy. She could hardly see straight.

"You just said you didn't tell me. That I didn't know," Hunter pointed out with subdued outrage.

Take the free pass, you idiot.

"Hunter." The man beside him—Remy, Amelia recalled—nudged Hunter.

Hunter lifted his gaze over Amelia's head.

Amelia looked over her shoulder and up.

The bride had come to the rail of the terrace. She was red-carpet-gorgeous with midnight-black hair and luminous golden shoulders accentuated by the stark whiteness of her strapless satin gown. Her veil caught the sunlight so it created an angel's halo effect around her astonished yet beautiful face.

Could this moment get any worse?

Hell, yes, Peyton assured her. She began to stir and whimper, rubbing her face into Amelia's neck, rooting for the nipple she wanted.

Amelia's full breasts were ready. So ready.

No. Please no.

But the tightness in her heavy breasts became a hard sting. A rush of tears rose to her eyes as letdown happened. Damp warmth began soaking into the pads of her bra, leaking around the edges to stain her shirt.

Mortified, Amelia spun and started back to the walkway.

Behind her, she heard something drop like a shoe.

She glanced back to see that the bride's bouquet, a spray of ivory rosebuds interspersed with baby's breath and lacy fronds of spring ferns, had landed on the grass.

Hunter wished he were a stranger to outrageous public displays.

Sadly, this pageantry was all too familiar. His sister was equally familiar. With a sharp nod from the terrace, Vienna assured him she would stay with Eden and followed his bride back into the honeymoon suite.

Through the speakers, Eden's voice cried, "Is it *true*?"

With a squeeze of his arm, Remy also conveyed, *I've got this*. He cut a sharp line across his throat, indicating to the wedding planner that the microphone feeds should be cut.

Hunter left the pergola and brushed past the older man

still working his mouth in search of further words to be-rate him.

As he went after the woman who may or may not be holding his baby, Hunter's mind raced. No fully formed thoughts seemed to stick. That wasn't like him. He knew how to grasp hold of catastrophe and mitigate it. He'd been doing it since his eleventh birthday party, the first occasion his stepmother had ruined with her obscene behavior and the last time he had celebrated that annual milestone.

Get things back on course, he kept thinking, but his "course" was marriage. To Eden. He couldn't let that be derailed by a woman he had fooled around with once. Okay, three times. It had been a very active night, but it had only been sex. Not conception. Surely not.

"The woman with the baby," he snapped at one of the servers in the tasting room even as he looked to the exit to the parking lot. "Did she leave?"

"She asked for somewhere to sit and—"

Hunter stopped listening and followed the pointed finger around the corner, stalking through a closed door labeled Operations Manager.

"Excuse me." Amelia glared from the love seat crammed beneath the window.

Her face was bright red. The dark roots of her hair were so long, only the fraying bun on the top of her head was still blond. She looked a lot younger without the makeup she'd worn when he'd met her. Her brows were pulled into a knot of affliction, her wide mouth pinched.

"Get out," she said more insistently.

While nothing was on show, she was clearly uncomfortable as she cradled the nursing baby against one breast and held a pink blanket against the other.

Hunter swore, but he'd seen a baby nurse before, and this was more important.

"Is it true?" he demanded.

"Get out!"

He rolled his eyes and turned to face the closed door, stepping forward to lock it.

"I'll insist on a test either way, but I don't have time for games. There's a woman next door who deserves to know." *He* deserved to know.

Amelia muttered something and said, "Ouch. Yes, I know." She seemed to be talking to the baby because there was a cry of protest then, "There. All better." She sighed.

Silence resumed, broken by loud gulps.

As he warily turned back to face her, Hunter was doing some quick and dirty math, trying to work out if this was even possible. Nine months from July would take the birth to April.

Amelia had draped the blanket over her shoulder, and the baby was now hidden beneath the tent. One bare foot was kicking out from beneath it, working an invisible pump. Amelia kept her glower aimed at his shoes.

"How old is…?" He? She? Check that gender bias, he reminded himself. A child. Could he have made this baby?

"Nine weeks. Almost ten," Amelia admitted sullenly.

May. *June.*

Hunter swore again, using a clear, all-purpose curse that encompassed the act that had brought him to this point and the complexity of his reaction. It spanned everything from resignation to disgrace. Irony to self-disgust. Anger to injustice. Remorse.

And, flittering around the edges, a nascent curiosity coupled with a small resentment that she had hidden the baby for months. From his eyes right now.

"I didn't mean for this to happen," she mumbled. "Any of this."

"Why didn't you tell me before today?"

"I tried." Her voice grew tougher. Belligerent. "I called your office, trying to reach you. You texted back that you were engaged. You told me not to text again."

"That's not trying. For God's sake, Amelia. I wanted to hear *that*. Why did you wait… What? Five months after we were together?" He had been engaged by then. "Why didn't you tell me as soon as you found out you were pregnant?"

"I did."

He snorted, never quite believing those *I didn't know I was pregnant* urban legends.

Her lashes finally came up. Her lake-blue eyes were pools of sorrow.

"Do you remember I left that morning because Dad got the news my brother had disappeared? That's all I could think about. Finding him. When the company quit trying, I decided to go to Chile myself. I needed shots to travel, and the doctor had to screen me for pregnancy before he could administer them. I thought stress was making me sick and stopping my periods. I wasn't doing anything except sitting at a computer, writing emails, so the weight gain didn't seem unusual. We used condoms," she reminded, waving between them. "It didn't occur to me I could be pregnant."

He always used condoms and didn't recall one breaking. It seemed far-fetched that she could have gotten pregnant by him, but he was having trouble hanging on to his skepticism in the face of how upset she seemed.

"I wanted to have her, even though it meant I couldn't travel." She rubbed her brow, mouth pulled down at the corners with deep sadness. "It was the hardest decision I've ever made, but I knew Jasper would never expect me to give up a baby to go look for him, especially if…"

The catch of torment in her voice struck Hunter straight in the chest, rocking him back on his heels. He tried to imagine making a decision between his unborn child and looking for his sister. His mind refused to go there. The idea of it, the fact that Amelia had chosen to keep his baby rather than search for someone she loved, caused a visceral shift inside his chest, one that hurt in a way he didn't understand.

He brushed aside trying to untangle that emotive knot, focusing instead on the word "her." Such a tiny detail, but now he knew that little foot belonged to a girl. His daughter?

"I thought I should tell you, but you blew me off," Amelia said in a lifeless tone. "Given all I was going through, it seemed like a blessing that you didn't want to be involved. One less person to worry about."

You didn't ask *me if I wanted to be involved*, he nearly growled, but she was obviously still in deep pain, so he bit that back.

"And your brother?" he probed carefully.

"Presumed dead."

Hunter rubbed the cynicism from his expression. "I'm sorry, Amelia. That's rough."

"It is. Dad was in pieces. I moved back into his house, we pulled up the drawbridge, and we've been looking after each other ever since. Peyton's been a bright spot, though." One side of her mouth went up a little as she caught the bare foot that was still working thin air. "Dad's been more like his old self since she arrived."

Peyton. He had a daughter named Peyton. It didn't seem real.

"And maybe we don't live like you do, but we're *fine*," she insisted. "He shouldn't have made it sound like we're starving. Dad has a pension, and the house is paid for. I get maternity benefits that I supplement by tutoring. I'm finishing my Bachelor of Ed online. In a year or so, I'll be a teacher. That's a perfectly good living for a single mom."

"But you let your father believe *I* don't care if you're starving and destitute." That rankled. A lot.

"I don't even know how he found out your name! I didn't tell anyone. Not even Cheryl— You remember her? She's the one Remy—"

"I remember," Hunter dismissed, vaguely recalling a bubbly redhead.

"I haven't really talked to her since I left," Amelia continued in a distracted mumble, lashes lifting warily. "I don't post about Peyton. No one knows you're her father."

Yeah. Not even me.

"But Dad got after me to make a will the minute she was born, especially since Jasper didn't have one. I finalized it a couple weeks ago. Maybe he read the copy I left in the freezer? I only mentioned you as a last resort. My cousin agreed to raise her if something happens. She lives in Ottawa, but she and Dad would work something out."

"I'm a last resort for custody of my child? Wow." Very few things got under his skin. Hunter had been exposed to every possible slight at one time or another. He was jaded and impervious, but that was a kick in the stomach. "What about her birth certificate? Is my name on that?"

"No." Her reply was prompt and remorseless. "I would have needed your permission, so it didn't make sense to add you. Can you turn around again? She's finished and I need to put myself back together."

He turned his back and absorbed everything she'd said, but kept coming back to that phrase, "last resort." He'd been tangled up in a legal mess for the last few years, but did that make him so objectionable a person she didn't want him to have anything to do with his own child? He was gainfully employed and didn't have a criminal record. He was about to marry—

He swore and pinched the bridge of his nose.

What the hell was he supposed to do? Parts of the merger might be salvaged if he called off the wedding, if Eden could stand to speak to the man who jilted her. She didn't deserve this humiliation any more than he did.

"I need a paternity test," he muttered, grasping at the off chance this was a stunt organized by his stepmother, but he knew. Deep down, he already knew the truth.

"I'll agree to that, but I don't expect anything from you. If you want access, we can talk about it, but please don't feel obligated."

"Of course I'm obligated, Amelia. Do you know who I *am*?" He pivoted around again to see her shirt was down and she held the baby against the blanket on her shoulder.

Peyton's fine brown hair was thin on top and turned up in feathery ducktails around the fringe, like a balding old man on a hot summer's day. In response to Amelia's pats, she released a robust burp.

Amelia was glaring at him with resentment.

"Please don't accuse me of getting pregnant for money. If that's what I wanted, I would have come after you a lot sooner."

"I've already deduced that." Everything she was saying added up to preferring to keep this baby from him. Which made him furious. And uncomfortable.

"Please don't sue me to try to take her." She tucked her chin, brows low with warning.

"Is that why you didn't tell me? You think I would try to separate my baby from her *parent*? I'm not like that, Amelia," he said pointedly.

Her scowl deepened. "I'm not going to apologize. You are in love with someone else, Hunter. About to be married. I did what I thought was right."

"By whom? Not our daughter," he scoffed. "My life comes with a lot of comfort and privilege. Your father is right. My child deserves to benefit from what I can give her."

"Her needs are met," she insisted. "She's chubby and

happy and sleeps in a dry diaper under a sound roof every night. I love her to death. So does my dad. She wants for nothing."

"Except the father who wants to be part of her life. Were you really going to wait until she was old enough to ask about me before you sprang her on me?"

"I refuse to feel guilty over the choices I've made! You told me not to text you."

He brushed that aside. "If she's a Waverly, she's entitled to live like one." That much he knew.

"Fine. Organize a paternity test. Make whatever arrangements you want for her. For *her*," she stressed. "I need to live with Dad and look after him." She inched to the edge of the love seat. "And, um, don't think this is me being a jerk or anything, but I plan to talk to a lawyer and find out my rights. She's still nursing. I genuinely think it's better if she's with me full time. I'm open to something more balanced after she weans. I want to be reasonable."

"Nice to know," he said facetiously. "But nothing about this is reasonable. It's outrageous."

She sighed. "You're right that I should have told you sooner," she admitted grudgingly. "I'm sorry it happened like this. I'll get Dad and we'll leave and—"

"And what? The damage is done," he snapped.

"To the wedding? Why? This isn't your fault. You didn't know." She blinked incredibly naive blue eyes.

"I know *now*. Everyone does." The press was going to have a field day. The clock in his head was warning that he was losing his chance to get ahead of this. The feeding frenzy had likely already started. Despite his best security precautions, there had been several boats on the water. He would bet at least a few guests or staff were already texting or posting. This was a situation ripe for one of those real-time threads that went viral.

The groom's sidepiece just showed up. Her dad brought his proverbial shotgun.

Hunter slapped a hand to his lapel, double-checking he hadn't been on a hot mic this entire time.

What would be said about this relationship? Nothing flattering. Amelia wasn't the sharp-witted, confident woman he'd met last summer, the one with straightened blond hair, cat's-eye liner and long tanned legs beneath a saucy skort.

She'd become a disheveled and distressed new mother. Her complexion was wan, and she had dark circles under her eyes—standard for new parents from what he'd heard, but it made her look extra vulnerable, and that faded T-shirt and her bargain yoga pants screamed neglect on his part.

She looked hellish, really, but there was still a clench inside him that he was fighting to ignore. *Want.* The baby weight made her curvier, which he found intriguing. The huskiness of emotion in her voice kept calling up the sensation of her soft cries spilling against his ear. From the second she had appeared, some animalistic part of him had growled with satisfaction at being near her again.

No. She had just turned his life into a mile-long train wreck. This woman was dangerous. She was everything he *didn't* want.

"What?" Amelia's gaze grew apprehensive as she realized he was staring at her. She pressed back into the love seat, cradling the baby closer.

A knock at the door had him snarling, "Busy."

"It's me," Vi said.

Amelia sucked in a worried breath, perhaps expecting Eden, but he swung around to let his sister in.

"Eden needs to know what's going on." She looked at Amelia with curiosity. "The B-Team is assembled online when you're ready."

Hunter would have given up his firstborn to never hear those words again, he thought with dark irony, but he was grateful Vi had put their PR bomb squad on standby.

The clock had run out. Decisions had to be made.

He squeezed Vi's arm and left.

CHAPTER THREE

AMELIA WATCHED VIENNA close the door and lock it. She came toward her, then leaned over her to drop the blinds down the window behind her.

Amelia snorted. "Are you *hiding* me?"

"I'm protecting the newest member of our family." Vienna's brows went up with indignation. "If it's true? Please be honest, because I'm about to bond with my niece or nephew."

Now that Amelia was clued in, she saw Vienna's resemblance to Hunter in her tall bearing and dark brown hair. She had his high cheekbones and darned if her cupid's bow of a mouth wasn't exactly like Peyton's. That's where she had heard her name. Remy had said it last year. *What does Vienna think?*

Peyton was fully charged after her nap and meal. She was digging her toes into Amelia's stomach and pushing her little arms against Amelia's chest, causing her downy head to bobble against the hand Amelia kept protectively cupped behind her neck.

Vienna was looking at Peyton with hungry wistfulness, so Amelia turned her and sat her in her lap.

"It's true. This is Peyton. She turns ten weeks on Tuesday."

"Oh." Vienna's tension melted as she sank to a crouch

before them. "Hello, sweet pea." Vienna beamed at Peyton and touched the baby's hand, gently clasping tiny fingers when Peyton reflexively closed her fist around her finger. "You're just the most perfect thing, aren't you?" Her thumb stroked the back of Peyton's dimpled knuckles.

Amelia's heart turned over at how tender Vienna sounded. It gave her hope they might— Well, it was probably a stretch to imagine they could become friends.

"*Please* let her know I didn't mean to ruin her special day."

"Eden?" Vienna's expression cooled and became unreadable. "It's better she knows before they marry."

"Does that mean—?" Amelia's heart lurched. "She still wants to marry him?" That was good, wasn't it? Then he wouldn't blame her for ruining his future.

So why did she feel as though her own future had just dropped into the bottom of that lake out there?

Vienna carefully withdrew from Peyton's grip and gave Peyton's round cheek a last caress before she pushed to stand over them.

"I don't know what they'll decide. I do know that calling off a wedding isn't as easy as it sounds." She bit her lip pensively. "Especially when there's so much at stake."

Amelia suddenly recalled the conflict she had walked through on arrival. She had an urge to ask Vienna if she was all right, but Vienna was smiling at Peyton again, catching her foot to give it a gentle squeeze.

"Whatever happens, I'm happy to meet you, Peyton. Every cloud has a silver lining, and you are today's."

Did that make Amelia the ominous, unwanted thunderhead?

She mustered a weak smile, growing overwhelmed as she realized Peyton had more than a father now. She had an extended family and, if Hunter married Eden, there would be step-relations who were all strangers to Amelia, yet they would all imagine they had a right to tell Hunter how he ought to raise *Amelia's* daughter.

Her pulse rate picked up, and adrenaline returned to her veins.

"Do you know where my dad is?" Amelia rose, trying not to let her voice reveal her panic, but she heard how shrill she sounded. Her shock was wearing off, and she was starting to fall apart. "I should make sure he's okay. I can't believe I left him out there with everyone."

"He's having a drink with my grandfather," Vienna said, as if that was a totally normal thing after objecting to a wedding.

"Okay, well, Peyton needs the diaper bag," she lied.

"Let me hold her while you get it." Vienna started to extend her arms.

"You can't ruin your dress. What if the wedding is back on? Dad and I should really go." Really.

"But Hunter will want—"

Amelia didn't care what Hunter wanted. She needed to get the hell away from here. She walked back to the tasting room, which had filled up with excited, babbling guests.

The walk of shame had never been so literal as when she approached her father at the bar. He was talking to a man his age in a pin-striped brown suit. They faced each other, elbows propped on the polished quartz, holding glasses of red wine. Amelia heard something about lake trout as she approached.

"Dad? Sorry," she threw at the other man, aware she was being rude. "But if you're coming home with me, the car is leaving."

She ignored his admonishing, "Amelia," and headed for the exit.

Outside, she walked through a handful of people who

were smoking and laughing. One said, "Oh, hey. Can I talk to you for a minute?"

She veered around the man, fighting to wait until she was in her car and driving away before she let the tears overflow. Her throat was on fire with suppressed anguish, though.

The damned car was too hot! She had forgotten to put up the reflecting screen, so the full sun had beamed through the back window onto the car seat, heating up all the plastic and metal parts. The car itself was an oven.

With a whimper, Amelia shifted to squeeze behind the wheel long enough to start the car and set the air-conditioning to high. She closed the door and left it slightly ajar so she didn't lock herself out.

The man had followed her and tried to approach her as she stood in the shade of a nearby tree. Was he really recording her with his phone? Her heart tripped and she turned her back on him, sheltering Peyton with the angle of her body.

Thankfully, her father came out, but he only wanted to lecture her on her manners.

"What was that about? Ubert was being very decent about all of this. We thought you would need time to work something out with Hunter, so why are you leaving?"

"Dad," she hissed. "Remember how you refused to talk about this until we got here? I'm not talking about it until we get home. Also, those people are listening," she added, glaring past him at that hideous man who was edging closer like a feral dog hoping for a dropped sandwich.

Tobias glanced over his shoulder and grunted his disgust.

"How did you know he was here anyway?" she was compelled to ask, but she kept her voice pitched low. She deliberately didn't stalk Hunter online, only occasionally reading headlines in the news related to Wave-Com.

"I gave Mo the details from your will. He used that tablet his son gave him, told me Hunter was here last year when you were working here. Then he saw the notice he was getting hitched today. It seemed my best chance to catch him in person and give him a piece of my mind. How have you not told him about Peyton? It's not like you to lie to me. Is it?" His good eye fixed on her.

"It's complicated." And humiliating enough to turn her voice vehement. "I don't need his money, Dad. Why would you *do* this?"

"It wasn't right that he wasn't helping. You make children, you look after them."

"Exactly. That's what I'm doing!"

"With my help. But I won't live forever," he added in a grumble. "I need to know you'll be all right after I'm gone."

Her heart sank. "Dad."

"Amelia." Hunter pinned her with his silver-bullet gaze as he came through a bed of petunias, trampling the pink and white and indigo trumpets. His unbuttoned jacket flared open to reveal his gray vest and amethyst tie.

Her heart lurched in a painfully bittersweet relief. She had been fairly convinced he was patching things up with Eden and the wedding would continue.

Maybe it would. She searched his granite features, but couldn't read what his pursuing her to the parking lot meant. As much as *The Runaway Groom* sounded like an uplifting rom-com, it was actually a nightmare to be the cause of something like this. She felt sick and guilty and very much the target of his resentment.

The man with the phone turned to catch Hunter's approach and Hunter seemed to ignore him, but as he got close enough, he grabbed the phone and spun it back the way he'd come, sending the phone into the sea of petunias.

Oh. Amelia covered her mouth.

"Hey!" The man swore and ran toward the flower patch.

The people at the door began to squeal and laugh. Some of them were holding up their own phones, recording every second of this interchange.

"I have to take Dad home." This was worse than a nightmare. She moved to the door of her car. "My number hasn't changed. Reach out when you're ready to talk."

"I'm ready right now."

"I'll go finish my drink," her father said.

"Don't you dare," Amelia hissed.

Hunter intercepted Tobias and shot out his hand. "Hunter Waverly. I appreciate you coming today. This was important. Something I needed to hear."

"Tobias Lindor." He shook Hunter's hand. "Yes. You did. You two take as long as you need."

"We will, but not here."

"Pfft." Damned right she wasn't staying here. Not one second longer.

But as she opened the back door, intending to strap Peyton into her seat, Hunter leaned into the front from the passenger side. He turned off the car and stole the keys, straightening to hand them to her father.

"Stay as long as you like. They'll start serving food soon."

"What are you doing?" She popped out again, still holding Peyton as she scowled across the roof. "Dad doesn't drive." Only on the streets he knew, because of his bad eye. Not at all if he'd been drinking.

"I'll work something out," her father insisted, pocketing the keys and walking back to the tasting room.

Men.

"I'm not going anywhere with you." She had to lean in to talk to Hunter across the back seat where he had begun to fiddle with Peyton's seat. "Leave that alone."

"We can't talk here." He paused to remove his jacket, revealing perspiration stains on his shirt, perhaps not as impervious to all of this as he seemed.

"We don't have to talk *now*," she said with exasperation, switching Peyton's weight to her other arm. "This isn't a national emergency. We can both take a beat and process, can't we? I'll have my people call your people." After she found people.

"I would love nothing else." His tone was weary and patronizing. He yanked the seat out, slammed the door and came around to her side, forcing her to straighten and face him. "But look around."

The one man was still feeling around in the petunias, searching for his phone, but everyone else had fanned out to record them. They were keeping their distance, but it was still disgusting.

"I don't want strangers taking photos of my baby." She cradled Peyton closer.

"Neither do I. That's why we're leaving. Do you need that?" He pointed at the diaper bag on the seat.

"Yes, but—" She didn't want to be railroaded.

She didn't want to become an online meme, either.

"Here's Denis." Hunter retrieved her bag and slammed the car door, then he opened her driver door, pressed the lock button and slammed that, too.

An SUV stopped behind her car and a wiry, middle-aged man leaped out, leaving it running as he efficiently installed the car seat with a click and a smile.

Conflicted, Amelia climbed into a deliciously cool and roomy back seat. She buckled Peyton in, tucked her blankie around her, then clicked her own belt, blowing a stray tendril of hair from her eyes.

It will be okay, she assured herself, even though her stomach was churning with misgiving.

Maybe she could have believed it if Hunter hadn't looked so remote and menacing. Rather than take the passenger seat up front, he took the spot on the far side of Peyton. His tanned face was like carved and polished maple. Smooth, but hard.

"Where to, sir?" Denis asked as he wound his way out through the parking lot toward the exit.

"Goderich," Amelia said while Hunter spoke over her.

"The apartment." Hunter frowned at her. "It's in Toronto. Closer."

"It's kidnapping," she pointed out.

"Only if I ask for a ransom." He was texting as he spoke. "What kind of security do you have in Goderich?"

A dead bolt and venetian blinds.

"Why? Those people won't bother me in my own home, will they?" She twisted to look out the back window. A car was following them.

"In my experience, those sorts of people will climb on a trash can and photograph you on the toilet if they think they can earn a buck for it."

"Then why did you invite them to your wedding?"

"I didn't. This wasn't the easiest place to secure. *You* got in."

Ouch. But… "Is this some of the 'everything' you can give Peyton?" she asked with facetious bite. "You're right. I should have told you sooner."

"This will go more smoothly if we stick to what needs to happen rather than what has already happened. Yes, I'm here." He gave his attention to whoever he had just called.

He was talking to a group, Amelia realized as he began listing out assignments.

"Zudora, I need a paternity test. Have a nurse meet us at the apartment. Kimi, get everything a two-month-old needs. Leave it in one of the guest rooms. Who has the number for the wedding planner? Let her know that Denis will come back for Amelia's father and will arrange for his car to follow, but find him a hotel room if he prefers to stay the night. Carina, let me hear what you've got so far. No, don't say that."

"Say what?" Amelia prompted. She would really love to know what the heck was going on. Had his wedding been called off or merely postponed?

She didn't ask, not sure she was ready for the answer.

"No. Call it a brief relationship that ended before I met Eden. I want it to be clear I wasn't involved with her at any time while I was dating Eden."

Amelia's breath was punched out of her by that. She blocked out the rest and turned her face to the window.

She had no reason to be surprised or offended, she reminded herself. He had warned her not to come to his room if she expected it to go beyond that night.

"Tonight is enough," she had said, believing it in the moment. She had believed a lot of silly things that evening—that he respected her as a person, rather than seeing her as an object of entertainment. That he was rich, but grounded. That they had a connection that went beyond physical.

All of that delusion had been on her side. Worse, the infuriating awareness of him was still tingling and alive within her, making her feel his presence like a force that both pushed and pulled against her. Magnetism? Was that what it was?

It was agonizing and juvenile, and it was what had made her agree when Cheryl had said with excitement, "Table Fourteen invited us for drinks after we cash out."

The management had frowned on servers fraternizing with customers, but they didn't forbid it. Even so, Amelia usually kept things simple. She knew players when she saw them. She'd been involved with one already, and it hadn't ended well. A pair of men in upscale golf clothes with gold watches and aviator sunglasses were *not* looking for love. Besides, while one of them had a sexy French accent and a slow, lazy smile, the other was contained and remote and intimidating. Amelia had learned to gravitate toward golden retriever types, not men with energy that was brooding and coiled and dangerous.

"They probably have wives to get home to," Amelia had said, even as reluctant interest had been unfurling inside her.

"Don't you recognize them? That's Hunter Waverly. Wave-Com? And Remy Sylvain. Can-Carib airlines. I would do anything for a private flight to Turks and Caicos." Cheryl had waggled her brows.

Cheryl would do anything for a laugh and a pleasant roll in the hay. She had broken up with a long-term boyfriend and was determined to sow her oats before settling down again.

Amelia was the opposite. Her one serious relationship had left her wary and suffering a crisis of confidence. She'd been mad at men and had been hanging on to her virginity with stubborn defiance that had begun to feel like martyrdom—especially when an order took her past the men's table on the patio and she caught Hunter checking out her legs.

In that moment, she had seemed to walk from a gloomy fog into a bright, verdant day. A sharp sensation had pierced her, like a hunger pang, but lower. Her skin had warmed, and her heart had been in her throat that she had caught his interest.

It's only one drink. That was another thing she had allowed herself to believe. One drink was harmless. She hadn't already been in bed with him, mentally, before she'd given him her name.

Which was what made the whole thing so cringey. That's why she'd been glad to never see him again. He hadn't even had to seduce her. With nearly no effort at all, she had offered herself up. Here. Take me. Take my *virginity*.

Do you need money?

She would have buried her face in her hands, but Peyton began to whimper.

"You're okay, baby. It won't be long," she murmured and set her hand on Peyton's round belly.

It didn't work. Nothing did.

As Peyton worked herself up, Hunter stopped speaking to send them a distracted frown. "Is she okay?"

"She doesn't like long car rides." Amelia shrugged, defensive, but also passive-aggressively smug that Peyton was turning into a pill. Babies fussed. Figuring out why and solving it was Parenting 101. If he couldn't handle that, he should walk away from the gig right now.

"It might get loud here," he said to his minions. "See what you can get done. I'll check in when I get to the apartment." He ended his call.

Amelia tried to coax Peyton to take the pacifier, which she never took, but this time she sucked long enough for Amelia to ask, "Are you, um, still getting married?"

"You didn't notice the marquise-shaped dent in my face?"

She had forgotten he had that talent for arid remarks. She bit her lip, refusing to be amused. Or blamed. Or relieved.

Peyton spat out her pacifier and began to wail. Amelia gathered her patience and tried again, but Peyton turned her head in rejection.

"Are you seeing anyone?" Hunter asked.

"With this as my profile?" She waved at the growing tantrum Peyton was staging. "They're lined up out the door.

Why?" Amelia barely heard him over their daughter, but a blush of hopefulness rose across her chest.

"Because this mess is big enough with just the two of you."

And that was the real reason she hadn't told him about Peyton. He didn't want either of them.

"No." She ignored the scorch in her throat that strained her voice, compelled to defend her daughter. "The two of *us*—" Amelia pointed between herself and Hunter "—made her. And she is not a mess. My life is not where I thought it would be, either, you know."

She might have pulled off that moment of righteousness if she didn't look like a carton of eggs dropped on the sidewalk and their daughter hadn't drowned her out by arriving at full nuclear meltdown.

"Is there something I can do?" Hunter asked impassively.

"No," she mumbled, wanting to fold over Peyton and cry just as hard.

Because this was a mess. It was a giant awful mess, and she couldn't help feeling it was all her fault.

CHAPTER FOUR

"STILL THINK BRINGING us here was a good idea?" Amelia taunted under her breath as she unclipped the car seat and allowed Hunter to lift it out the other side.

He wouldn't pretend the last hour hadn't been an exercise in endurance. Talking had become impossible. Peyton didn't like the car seat. She said so. Denis had put in his earbuds while Amelia had tried a dozen ways to soothe her. She had rubbed the silky border of the blanket on the baby's cheek and given her a snuggle toy and a pacifier, put socks on her feet and kissed her waving fists, but the infant had craned her neck and squirmed against her restraints and bellyached the whole way.

Hunter sympathized, strapped into his own inescapable situation.

The wedding had been off the minute Amelia appeared. He had resisted admitting it right up until he was walking into the Honeymoon Suite where Eden had waited for him, still in her gown. "It's bad luck to see the bride before the wedding," she had reminded him through semi-hysterical tears.

She had been prepared to go through with the wedding. They both needed their marriage and probably could have rescued the day. The interruption could have been spun into a farce and his surprise baby sold as a blessing. But after that?

After that, his daughter would have had a stepmother. As much as Hunter respected Eden and had been prepared to share parenting with her of whatever family they might have made together, he couldn't start Peyton's life that way. He couldn't start his own relationship with his child by bringing in another stranger, not that he spelled all of that out to Eden.

He had said the words. "We can't get married."

She had suggested postponing the wedding, but he rejected that, too. It had felt too much like postponing the inevitable, because there had been that other, shameful relief under his skin that he barely wanted to acknowledge.

It had become unpleasant at that point. "Quinn warned me not to marry you," Eden had spat hotly. "She said your family is addicted to scandal. She said you would take my ship down with yours. I chose to believe Vienna. I believed in you, Hunter."

That last remark had lashed deep across the place where he believed in himself. Where he knew himself to be a decent human being. Honorable. Not given to selfishness or callous behaviors that harmed others. *I'm doing this for my child*, he had wanted to assert, but to his chagrin, there was a grim gratification sitting in the pit of his belly. Amelia was back in his life and couldn't slip away so easily this time.

He loathed himself for being pleased by that. It was too much like his father. However, marrying Eden at the expense of what was right for Peyton would also be too much like Frank Waverly.

It was an untenable situation with no easy answer, making Peyton's screams of protest kind of cathartic while he brooded on the mistakes he'd made.

As if she understood that the shift of the carrier and the glimpse of blue sky between the skyscrapers meant freedom was imminent, she quieted, but her baby breaths were still catching.

God, she was tiny. If she didn't have this protective shell of a car seat and a handle that Hunter could grasp in a strong fist, he'd be terrified to hold her at all.

He waved off Denis and slipped the doorman a bill, asking him to order a late lunch for him and Amelia.

"You'll eat sushi?" he asked Amelia.

She nodded, slowing as they entered the lobby. She glanced from the security desk to the chandelier suspended three stories above, then to the spacious visitors' lounge with its silk rug and fresh floral arrangements and colorful aquarium built into the back wall.

When the elevator dinged, she hugged herself and ducked her head, hurrying to enter with him.

"Don't be like that," he said as he used his thumbprint to access his floor. "You knew who I was when we met." But it was hitting him that she wasn't someone like Eden or Vienna who took this level of comfort for granted.

"Is this, like, a company building or something?"

"I am the company." It was an exhausting truth and a reality that couldn't be changed. Especially not after he'd fought so hard for the privilege.

He felt her gaze lift to touch the side of his face. "What about Vienna?"

"She prefers that I vote her share." Neal had been after Vi to give him her proxy. Their stepmother had soured both of them on spousal involvement in the company, and Vi had always had other interests. She left the company to Hunter and always backed up his decisions, but the fact that she didn't trust her husband told Hunter all was not well with her marriage. Between their father's death, the court case and the wedding, however, Hunter hadn't had a chance to dig into it with her.

Now he had this—he looked at the baby—circumstance.

The doors slid open and Amelia said with great cheer, "Guess what, Peyton? You get to come out of your car seat!"

Hunter set the seat on the wide bench in the foyer and watched as Amelia released Peyton. If anything, some of her tension seemed to dissipate as she gathered up the baby and kissed her cheek. She closed her eyes and made a contented noise as she nuzzled the baby, behaving as though she had missed her daughter when the kid hadn't been out of her sight for a second.

It was cute, though, especially when Peyton let her head snuggle into Amelia's shoulder and opened her mouth against her own fist. All seemed right in her little world now, too.

Through a vague sense of being shut out, Hunter still had to acknowledge how beautiful they were, like a Renaissance painting with the baby's lashes drooping and light stealing in to frost the wisps of hair framing Amelia's face. She was wan, but her skin was clear and smooth, her mouth pink and somber. Angelic.

He had the urge to kiss her. Not in foreplay, but in greeting. Maybe foreplay, too. Despite only knowing her the one night, she had stayed in his thoughts along with a near constant ache of want. He wanted the right to touch her and kiss her when her eyes were closed and open his mouth across hers with more purpose—

Amelia's lashes lifted, and she caught him staring.

He looked away, annoyed with himself. This was battle conditions, not a time to let his libido cloud his judgment.

"We have a lot to discuss. We're losing our chance to control the narrative. Come." He led her into the lounge. "Do you want anything? Coffee? Something stronger?"

"I'm breastfeeding," she reminded. "I try to stay sober when I'm in charge of another life."

"Is that a dig?" Because as appealing as getting blackout drunk sounded, he didn't usually have more than two or three himself. He was charged with the lives and livelihoods of thousands of workers. Also, his stepmother had covered the ground of public drunkenness pretty thoroughly. He didn't need to contribute anything to that cause.

"It's a fact," she murmured, wandering the open plan, taking in the Italian marble and twenty-foot ceiling and floating stairs to the upper floor. She paused to study the Casson and the Carmichael before moving to the wall of windows that stretched to the upper floor. Beyond was the spacious terrace, the city skyline and the horizon where the blurred line of Lake Ontario met cloudless sky.

"You play?" She nodded at the grand piano.

"Vienna does."

"She lives here, too?"

"She and Neal have a place on the waterfront that they use when they're in town."

"You bought this for you and Eden," she said in a tone of realization, tilting the engagement photo on the end table.

He had an urge to take it from her and throw it in a drawer. He would do that. Later.

"No, we're—" He swore as he remembered something and brought out his phone, texting his real estate agent to put a hold on the house in Bridle Path. "This is mine. It's a good location and convenient for entertaining." The kitchen noise was tucked behind closed doors, the big screen was a button-touch from descending from the ceiling, and the building was in the city center.

Amelia gave him a befuddled look. "You don't strike me as a partier."

"This doesn't scream raves and orgies?" He waved at

himself, still in his tailored but very traditional morning suit. "I hold charity events and host those who expect it."

"Like?"

"Celebrities." He shrugged. "Athletes in town for a game. VIPs from overseas."

She tucked her chin. "That's the kind of people you invite for supper?"

"Sometimes." He shrugged it off, never starstruck. They were people. Some pleasant, others vapid. Either way, he didn't want to talk about them right now. "I'll start the coffee and get changed. I have decaf and soft drinks." He led her into the kitchen. "I usually have a housekeeper, but most of my regular staff were given the next two weeks off since I expected to be on my honeymoon."

She made a noise halfway between a choke and a cough, pausing at the autographed photo that hung inside the door to the kitchen. "I've seen him on the celebrity chef Bake-Off thing. He cooks for you?"

"He does the annual benefit for our foundation." He poured beans into the grinder and pushed the button, nearly missing what she said because of the noise.

"Of course he does," she snorted.

"Why is that funny?" he asked when the grinder silenced.

"It's not. Is that filter real gold?"

He turned from setting it and filled the carafe from the tap. "You're judging me."

"No."

She was, and it annoyed him. Was that why she hadn't told him he had a kid? Because she was a snob who disdained wealth? In case she hadn't noticed, she wasn't his first choice to share parenting, either.

"I'll make a call, find out when the nurse is supposed to get here." He glanced at the clock. "The paternity test will inform a lot of our decisions." He finished filling the coffee maker, swiveled the filter into place and pressed the button. "Here." He opened the refrigerator and waved at the door. "See if there's something you might like."

She turned the labels on the soda bottles. "Lime and jasmine, rhubarb and cardamom, fennel…" She gave her head a shake. "I didn't even know these flavors exist."

"Try the cola with pear. It's good. Actually, it probably has caffeine. There are organic juices, too."

"Can I, um, use the washroom?"

"Sure. It's through there." He pointed.

"Thanks." She offered Peyton.

For two thudding heartbeats, his brain couldn't make sense of what she was doing. Then a bolt of realization struck him. He took the baby, stomach pitching because holding her was like trying to cradle a soap bubble without popping it.

Amelia walked away, and he swallowed a reflexive, *Wait. Come back. What do I do?*

Hunter knew to protect her neck, but that was where his familiarity with babies ended. What else were you supposed to do? Feed 'em and clean 'em and keep them from being eaten by wild animals, he supposed.

This felt a lot like holding a freshly caught fish, given her absent wiggling. The average salmon weighed more than she did, though, and they didn't have delicate limbs that looked like they could snap in a stiff breeze.

Her wandering gaze found his, and she smiled.

Why that hit him like a kick in his chest, he couldn't say. Maybe because that dimple high on her cheek was exactly like Vi's. Maybe it was her oblivious joy. Her unconditional welcome at finding someone new. That smile of hers was so happy and pure it hurt to see, like looking into the sun.

Maybe it hurt because this was the moment he'd been

avoiding. Holding her and seeing her forced him to acknowledge her. She was his. He didn't need a test. He would do his due diligence, but too many things pointed to the obvious. He had made this child with Amelia.

With acknowledgment came the repercussions, all deeper than he'd been prepared to face until he had to. Here they came, though. Even as he smirked back, guilt washed through him because Amelia was right. Peyton *had* been better off not knowing she was a Waverly. His name would impact her from now until the end of time, and all the five-star meals and chartered planes in the world couldn't protect her from it.

His arms instinctually enfolded her in apology and a desire to protect.

As her achingly delicate weight met the wall of his chest, his heart slammed hard enough he feared he might bruise her, but his arms contracted, holding her closer still.

What the hell was happening to him? A ferocious strength was gathering in him, the kind that would step in front of a charging grizzly to protect her. At the same time, he felt so damned vulnerable a cold sweat lifted on his skin.

A few hours ago, he hadn't even known he had created this life, but he was suddenly sick with the knowledge that life would happen to her. She would fall off swing sets and get her feelings hurt by some jerk at school. She would have a fender bender and go on spring break to Florida and face sexism and fall in love only to have her heart broken. Those bumps were inevitable, and he already couldn't forgive himself for letting them happen to her.

She gurgled and wiggled and batted her fist against his Adam's apple, gently hammering herself into his heart and blood and soul.

She took all the labels he had applied to himself through

the years—son, brother, friend, man, CEO… Today, he had even been prepared to call himself a husband.

He had never once imagined the power and humility in calling himself a *father*.

He swallowed, shaken to realize he had been reacting as he did to any iceberg strike against his ship. Contain the damage, deploy a team, salvage what was valuable. Recover.

Recovery wasn't possible. That hard truth impacted him like a brain-jarring uppercut. Peyton wasn't a scandal to be contained. She wasn't changing his life. She was changing him. *He* had to rise to this new role and rethink all his objectives, because his child had just become his top priority. His next steps weren't about spinning what had happened today. They were about shaping his future and ensuring that future held plenty of room for Peyton.

And therefore Amelia.

A sensation like a shot of whiskey went straight to his gut and radiated into his pelvis.

He turned his thoughts from where they had automatically gone. Did he want to sleep with Amelia again? Sure. On a base, randy level, of course.

Sex would complicate an already complex relationship, he reminded himself, trying to cool his jets. They would share custody and he would have to make Toronto his home base so he could be more accessible to his daughter—

Unless…

He absently rubbed Peyton's back, trying to be objective about the thought that had popped into his head. Was he *trying* to completely level his life? Because a traditional wedding to someone like Eden had made sense. A spur-of-the-moment marriage to Amelia would come across as a wild impulse driven by the sort of horny passion that had motivated his father's marriage to Irina.

Or it could be the spin that saved him from looking like a philanderer who preyed on hapless waitresses. From a practical point, moving Amelia and Peyton into his home would provide both of them the most security possible.

He would need a watertight prenup, obviously. For Peyton's sake, they would have to make an honest effort at a real, successful marriage.

He ignored the fresh spark of heat that kindled in his lap. That's not why he would propose. He was warming to the idea in other ways, though. It solved a lot of issues very neatly.

"Thanks," Amelia said in a subdued voice, returning with dampness around her hairline. She came across and held out her hands.

Still raw and self-conscious at how thoroughly Peyton had reconfigured his view of himself, he gave up the baby and watched Peyton brighten and grin. She knew her mama, and it caused the envy bug to nip into Hunter. He wanted his child to react to him like that. Which meant becoming a part of her daily life.

Amelia's expression softened briefly, but when she transferred her attention to him, she sobered, and her tone became resolved.

"I've decided to go to my cousin's."

CHAPTER FIVE

ONE OF HUNTER'S dark brows pulled down and in. Not in an aggressive or angry way. More an indication that he was concentrating or trying to solve a puzzle. It was as though he were studying the behavior of an animal that didn't make sense to him.

"This is too much," she expounded.

He lived in a two-story mansion in the top of Toronto's most expensive building. The toilet lid had lifted as she entered the powder room, for heaven's sake. The seat warmed itself. He had bought out a vineyard and owned real art. Not cheap prints, but actual originals by famous dead people.

No wonder he had set a one-night limit when he invited her into his room at that B and B. No wonder he had never tried to call her and had brushed her off so unceremoniously when she reached out to him. Bringing her here wasn't about trying to "protect" her and Peyton. He was *hiding* them. He was trying to protect himself and this lifestyle of his.

"You and Dad are making decisions for me that aren't yours to make," she added, resenting it all over again. She kept thinking, *If I had just said no, if I had insisted on going to yoga, none of this would have happened.* Her father would have been forced to tell her what he wanted to do and none of this would have happened.

Hunter's lips parted as though he was about to say something.

"This isn't fair. It's not *right*." She hurried to talk over him, but she was distracted by his mouth. She had forgotten how full his bottom lip was. It was wide and undeniably masculine. Powerfully sexy. Everything about him was screaming superiority and affluence and seductive appeal, from his clean-shaven jaw to his shiny shoes. It was disconcerting. Intimidating.

His natural air of authority tempted her to trust him and let him take over, which scared her. This baby they'd made had already consumed her life, and Peyton had come about because Amelia allowed herself to leap into a brief infatuation. At least when Hunter had offered one night and that's all she'd given him, it had been an even exchange.

Today she was seeing the endless resources he had at his disposal. Independence was one of the few she had left, so she was exercising it.

"You can't take over my life," she insisted, even as she felt as though she was talking to a cat. A big, dangerous jungle cat that only noticed her because she was making noise. He was flicking his tail with boredom, letting her chatter and squawk because he wasn't hungry yet, but he had the weight of his paw on her, making it impossible to get away. "We share a baby, but we can work out how to share her in a way that doesn't involve you keeping me here like some prisoner in a tower."

His chin dipped in the barest hint of *You think not?*

"My cousin's husband works in Parliament. He'll know how to handle reporters and keep photographers off the lawn."

Hunter only brought out his phone and dialed, setting it to speaker when someone named Carina answered.

"Status update," he prompted.

"They're calling my flight. One sec." Presumably, Carina found a place to speak where she wouldn't be overheard. When she came back on the line, her tone was hushed and rushed, pulling no punches. "It's trending. Obviously, there's been a race for scoops by the online editions. The general tone is that Eden is a victim, you're a cad, Amelia is the other woman."

Amelia's mouth fell open with affront.

Hunter touched his lips and nodded, indicating she should stay quiet and listen.

"Eden has put out a brief statement confirming the wedding was called off. We've requested she coordinate a more detailed statement with our team, but we'll see if she complies. We have also confirmed the wedding is off, making no comment on the baby rumors. We're promising further information in due course and have requested privacy at this time. We'll know better on Monday how this affects stock prices. The anticipation is a drop of six points. There's an emerging narrative that the Waverly scandals are more of a family-wide issue, not just Irina, so recovering stock value could take time. Most of the directors were at the wedding. Did you talk to any of them? Some are asking for an emergency meeting."

"I know who's asking," Hunter said. "Put that off at least a week so stock price can level."

"Will do. The nurse should arrive within the hour. How confident are you that the baby is yours? Vienna had the idea for your grandparents to take Amelia's father to their cottage."

"Confident," he stated, holding Amelia's gaze so unwaveringly, her breath halted in her lungs. "They should do that and plan to stay at least a week, likely two."

"Done. When can I sit with Amelia? We need everything they might dig up on her family so we can get ahead of it.

And photos. The ones from the winery are making it too easy for attack. Once we're on an apology tour, we'll get family photos and a feature, but right now I suggest staging something for paparazzi that shows her being a protective mom and you being the helpful dad."

Amelia recoiled, unable to find adequate words to express her outrage and disgust.

"See if Vienna's stylist is available," Hunter said. "If not, find someone and come straight here when you land. See if one of the visitor units is open so you can stay in the building."

"Will do. Final call for boarding. See you soon."

He ended the call, brows lifting in a very annoying, supercilious way.

"Carina was also on vacation, visiting family in Nova Scotia."

"Now it's my fault her vacation has been interrupted?"

"I'm saying it would be rude if you decided not to be here when she's on her way to meet with you."

"Like I have a choice!" she cried, becoming teary as she heard again, *Amelia is the other woman.*

"You always have a choice," he said in a tone that sounded patronizing. Pitying. "You can leave if you insist, but until I know otherwise, Peyton is my daughter. Therefore, it's incumbent on me to protect her. If your leaving puts her in danger—"

"Don't you dare threaten me," she warned, insides beginning to quake.

"It's not a threat. It's reality. This is what we're up against." He indicated his phone and everything Carina had revealed. "Let me protect both of you."

She refused to believe her life was spiraling this far out of her control. Surely Carina was exaggerating?

"Where's the diaper bag?" she asked, looking to the door to the lounge.

"You should find everything you need for Peyton upstairs."

"I want my phone."

"To confirm what's being said?" He shook his head gravely. "That wouldn't be productive, Amelia."

She held his stare while pressure built in her chest and throat and behind her eyes. *I'll do what I want. You're not the boss of me. This doesn't have to happen this way.*

"This is all your fault!" she blurted childishly.

"And I'm taking responsibility."

"Oh—!" She spun and hurried back to the foyer where she hovered her hand over the bag, then snatched it up before starting up the stairs.

Peyton was overdue for a change and was still wearing the short-sleeved onesie Amelia had put her in this morning. Here in this air-conditioned palace, she needed warmer clothes.

At the top of the stairs, Amelia glanced in the first open door and found a tastefully decorated guest room brimming with deliveries. Boxes and shopping bags were spilling out of the floor of the closet. Clothes in infant sizes hung from the rail. A playpen was set up in the corner and next to it stood a high-end changing table with a bumper around its padded top. Its shelves were stocked with diapers and creams and wet wipes—all the organic, biodegradable, skin-sensitive brands. *Big spender.*

She pulled a cotton sleeper from her diaper bag and placed Peyton on the table.

Hunter leaned in the doorway. His long jacket was abandoned somewhere, but he still wore his snug vest and tailored trousers. The suit emphasized the power in his shoulders and wide chest. His shirt strained against his biceps as he folded his arms.

"You're just going to stand there and continue to intimidate me?" Amelia asked.

"Is that what I'm doing? I thought I was observing a caretaking procedure."

"You want to learn how to change her?"

"So I can evaluate the nanny's competence once I hire one, yes."

"I look after her myself. If you're not prepared to do that, why would I grant you any access at all?" she asked with peevish superiority.

"It was a joke." He came to stand on the pedal of the waste basket, holding the lid open for her. "And, look. You're allowed to be angry."

"Gosh, thanks." The wet diaper landed with a dull thud in the bottom of the can.

"But it doesn't change anything. I'm furious, too," he said in a tone that was almost conversational. *Nice weather, eh?*

Behind his eyes, however, there was a flash of incendiary fury that made her suck in a breath that burned.

"Gaining custody and the right to provide for her is something I *have* to do," he said in an implacable tone. His pensive look skimmed her face, then shifted to Peyton. "It's not performative. I didn't arrive here the way I thought I would, but I've always known what kind of father I wanted to be."

Amelia's pulse skipped, and she paused in securing the fresh diaper. "What kind is that?"

"Present," he said flatly. "One who does the right thing. One who protects his child instead of putting his own whims and desires first."

Her umbrage against him eased a notch. She tried to remember what she knew of his family, but it wasn't much. His father had died a few years ago and there'd been a drawn-out court battle with his stepmother over control of Wave-Com. He'd been in the middle of that when they'd met, not that he had talked about it. Remy had made some remark about the golf weekend being necessary to help his friend unwind, though.

In the weeks after, Amelia had been consumed by her search for Jasper. She hadn't followed the twists and turns of Hunter's journey to legal triumph. By the time she realized she was pregnant with his baby, he was out of the headlines and she was turning inward with grief.

To her mind, though, all of those things reported on TV had happened to someone else, not the Hunter Waverly she knew. The man she had slept with had been surprisingly human while the one on TV was a mythical legend from a dynastic family. That one had wealth and power and little empathy for mere mortals like her.

That was the one who confronted her today. He had no compunction about sweeping her into his world and mercilessly making her face how impossible it was for her to go back to the life she knew and loved. He was so armed and armored, she couldn't touch him.

But for a second, one tiny second, she saw the man who had held her hand and called her amazing and made her feel incredible things.

She blinked, and he was turning away.

"I'll change and meet you downstairs. Our lunch will be here any minute."

"You said you liked sushi." Hunter's voice broke into Amelia's introspection. "Do you prefer a fork? I'm not a purist."

"Pardon? Oh." She adjusted her grip on her chopsticks and blinked at the array of seafood before them. While she

had taken a couple of rolls, Hunter had polished off half
the platter and most of the teriyaki chicken and seemed to
be eyeing the last of the yam tempura, which she had yet
to taste.

"I'm not very hungry." She glanced to where Peyton
had just kicked a jangling toy on the play gym arched over
where she lay on an activity mat.

What was she going to do? Things were so much worse
than she had feared.

"You looked," Hunter said with heavy disappointment.
"Didn't you?"

"What?" She flashed her gaze back to his, then dropped
it guiltily.

This was what she got for searching his name online. She
had only wanted to know more about his father and stepmother, but that hadn't come to the top of the page. Her own
name had. Apparently, she was ruining Eden Bellamy's life.

The Bellamy family was considered a national treasure.
Amelia knew that, so maybe she should have been prepared
to be vilified, but it wasn't as if she had done this on purpose! Her baby was completely innocent in all of this, yet
there had been some very sickening things said about Peyton as well. Things awful enough to make her want to cry.

"They're trolls, Amelia. Not worth thinking about."

"But I had messages from friends. They want to know
what's going on and why I never told them you were Peyton's father."

"What did you say?" His words came out fast and crisp
enough to lash like a whip.

"Nothing. I don't know what to say. Other than mind
your own beeswax," she added in a grumble.

He let out an exhale. "That's why we're bringing in a
team. They'll clean up your timeline and craft stock an-

swers to the most awkward questions. You'll feel back in control very soon."

"Will I?" she scoffed. "Or will you? Because if you're going to tell me what to say, that's not really me in control, is it?"

"This is a very big bus, Amelia. I already know how to drive it. I won't ask you to lie, only stay on message."

She snorted and picked up a round of BC roll, swirling it in soy sauce and wasabi before popping the morsel of barbecued salmon and cucumber in her mouth. She chewed and swallowed, chasing it with a salty sip of her miso soup.

"I'm predisposed to hate PR people," she explained once she'd swallowed. "The company that sent Jasper to Chile did everything they could to quiet his disappearance. It made them look bad. I would sit with a reporter for hours, pouring my guts out, hoping to get some attention and support. The story would be watered down or outright killed before it posted. If I got a government official to take an interest, they would suddenly ghost me and I'd be back to square one. I can't prove it, but I know his employers were behind the obstruction. I realize people like Carina are a necessary evil for you, but to me they're just evil."

"Understood." His cheeks went hollow. He had changed into cream-colored pants and a checked shirt. The short sleeves were rolled up once, revealing more of his tanned upper arms. "For me, they've always been more necessary than evil. My life has been one publicity nightmare after another since my mother died."

That's what Amelia had wanted to learn more about. She stopped chasing a clump of rice and gave him her full attention.

"I remember the odd headline about a wardrobe malfunction and some Twitter feuds. Were there other issues?" she asked.

"So many," he said with disgust. "You can still find a lot of them online if you look hard enough, even the affairs."

"She cheated on your father?"

"I don't know if it can be called cheating if he knew about it and put up with it. Maybe it was her kink to step out, and he got off on being cuckolded. It's none of my business if that's the case, but she slept with married men when Dad was in the middle of cutting deals with them. Their wives would find out and everything would go to hell, so it affected the company. That *is* my business." He tapped his chest.

"Because you knew the company was coming to you? Or were you working there by then?"

"Both. I barely remember a time when I wasn't getting a paycheck from Wave-Com. Even before Mom died, Dad would pick us up from school and take us back to the office. We were sitting through high-level meetings before we had our times tables memorized."

"That sounds like he was at least trying to connect with you and your sister."

"In his way, maybe. Once Mom was gone and he was married to Irina, going to the office was the only way I could see him without her there. I was fourteen when the first board member came to me, complaining about her and asking me to 'talk to' my old man."

"That's a terrible thing to ask of a kid."

"It was, but someone had to. It helped me in the long run. I had relationships with all of them. They backed me when Irina tried to take control of Wave-Com after Dad died."

"Did she really think she had a chance? Did she have experience?"

"God, no. But ignorance of little things like the law never stopped her from doing what she wanted. At one point, she decided she didn't have to pay her maid. Dad didn't find out until the human rights tribunal got involved."

"Oh, *no.*"

"Oh, yes. She did childish, tacky things, too. When Vi got married, Irina had a penis cake brought out instead of the wedding cake. She thought it would be funny. She was always doing things like that. If there was an occasion where one of us was being celebrated, she had to bring us down a peg and grab the spotlight for herself. Today, when your dad showed up, I honestly thought for a minute that she'd hired him, purely to embarrass me."

"Really?" Amelia lost her grip on her chopsticks. They skewed, sending the round she held rolling off the edge of her plate.

"Really." He caught it with his fingers and ate it.

"Does she have mental health issues? Trouble processing appropriate behavior?"

"Perhaps." He shrugged. "That's no excuse for being mean. And greedy. And criminally irresponsible. She has never tried to curb her own behavior. Trying to help her was a no-win situation. If anything, she enjoys the control of inciting chaos. Of making others fix whatever she breaks."

"Why didn't your father divorce her?"

"Great question. *He didn't want to.*" Hunter's rage was so cold and condensed, his clothing should have frozen and shattered, dropping off his body. "I genuinely don't know what he saw in her. Can anyone be that good in bed that you would let them humiliate your kids on a regular basis?"

An acute pain stabbed in the middle of her chest. "I'm so sorry, Hunter."

"It's nothing to do with you," he dismissed brusquely. "Thankfully our grandparents—the ones who are taking your father to Lake of the Woods—took us as often as they could. They're my mother's parents. Prairie folk. Steady as you get. And Irina is in Palm Springs now, married to some other unfortunate twit. You don't have to worry about her."

"No, I mean I'm sorry for today. Like, really sorry." So sorry, she felt sick. "You must hate us."

"No." Shadows shifted behind his eyes. "But don't do it again." There was no levity in his flat order. He meant it.

Peyton started to fuss, allowing Amelia to escape the intensity of his hard stare.

Peyton immediately began to root, so Amelia brought the receiving blanket with her and sat back at the table, settling Peyton to nurse before she picked up her chopsticks again. Her stomach was still in remorseful knots.

"The truth is, I was glad when you brushed off my text," she admitted. "I didn't know how to face you. I felt stupid for getting pregnant." She had felt like a cliché. Who got pregnant on their first time in this day and age? "I thought you'd be angry, or think I did it on purpose, and I was grieving Jasper so hard." Her eyes stung and her chest burned whenever she talked about him, but she pushed on. "I didn't have the energy to work out custody. I *needed* her to be mine." She cradled Peyton closer and breathed through the ache that sat like a knife in her breastbone. "But if I had known you would find out like this, I would have come to you sooner."

"I believe you." He nodded, but a small spasm flickered across his face. His voice became gruff. "Thank you. I would have loved for Irina to apologize just once. To mean it."

"I do."

"I know." He looked to the window and flicked his hand with weariness. "I make it a policy not to apologize for Irina's history because it implies I'm responsible for her behavior, but I realize her notoriety colors all of this, making it that much more difficult for you."

"Why couldn't you just be the guy at the hardware store?" she said, but bit her lip. He was probably thinking *Why couldn't you be rich and influential like me?* "I will play ball with your PR people," she assured him. "We can do photos or whatever, so you look like a helpful dad. I realize it's in Peyton's best interest."

"Amelia." Her name was tinged with exasperation. "I intend to *be* a helpful dad. *That's* in her best interest."

"Nanny remark notwithstanding?"

He didn't crack a smile. He ran his tongue over his teeth behind his lip, watching her and seeming to consider his words. He picked up his coffee and sipped, then stared into it.

"My marriage to Eden was supposed to demonstrate that I wasn't like my father. That I'm a steady man who is a paragon of family values."

She sat back. "Do you hear how cold that sounds? Weren't you marrying because you love each other?"

"We like each other. Past tense on her part, I imagine." His mouth curled with self-deprecation. "But our marriage made sense in concrete ways. You're judging me again." His eyes narrowed. "There were sound business reasons, and we were both ready to start a family. Arranged marriage is not forced marriage. You feel a lot more comfortable merging fortunes if it will go to children you make together."

"It's none of my business." She tried to sound as though she meant it. Believed it. "I just wouldn't sign up for a loveless marriage myself. That's all."

"No?" His tone had the precision of a scalpel. "Because it's an effective way to address needs that go beyond romantic delusions."

"Excuse me," she huffed. "If you weren't in love with Eden, that's fine. In fact, I'm glad." A little too glad. "It means you won't blame me for your broken heart, but love isn't a delusion."

"That kind isn't," he said, waving at the blanket.

Peyton had fallen asleep, so Amelia anchored the blanket with her chin and wrangled to cover herself while trying not to wake her daughter.

"But what did you tell me last year?" Hunter challenged lightly. "That you had recently broken up after a long relationship. You thought you loved him, but you were wrong. Delusion."

"That was a very specific case." Of a man who had led her on because he was trying to get her into bed. When she had asked him to wait, he had cheated on her. She didn't like revisiting her naivete, and she didn't appreciate having her words thrown back in her face.

She loosely wrapped the blanket around Peyton and adjusted the infant's position on her bent arm.

"I'll take her so you can eat." He rose, and Amelia was too bemused to protest as Hunter picked her up. He was careful not to wake her, and he made sure the blanket was smooth, not bunched beneath her.

He looked surprisingly confident, as though he had been settling Peyton in the crook of his arm since the day she was born. There was even a ruefulness in his gaze as he sat and looked at his daughter in a way that made Amelia's heart swoop.

She picked up her chopsticks and shoved a bite in her mouth, but couldn't swallow past the lump in her throat. In her heart of hearts, she had wanted him to look at Peyton that way, but witnessing it was too much to bear. It sparked a panicked sense of threat in her, forcing her to face that they *would* share custody. She already begrudged him the time she would miss with her daughter.

"What is your vision of marriage? Fall in love with the guy from the hardware store and hope it works out?"

"What's wrong with wanting to fall for a decent guy with a decent job? My mom worked at the sewing store and fell for the guy from the salt mine. They…" She shrugged, growing teary again because it had seemed like a very simple, common dream that should be attainable by anyone, but it had eventually turned to ash. Now it seemed further beyond her reach than ever. "They were very happy, and I always thought I would have what they had. The house wasn't fancy and our cars were always used and practical. There were tough times when interest rates went up and Dad was laid off, but it was a very loving home. My brother was my best friend, and he made me boxed mac and cheese when Mom had to work late. Dad taught me to ride a bike and built us a tree house."

"That's what you want for Peyton?"

"Now who's judging?" She lifted her chin, but after a moment, her spine softened and she found herself drawing patterns in a smear of soy sauce with the tips of her chopsticks. "It was what I wanted when I was growing up. I wanted to be a teacher so I could have summers off with my kids. Mom would take them on weekends so I could go on date nights with my husband. She would make cookies and Uncle Jasper would take them fishing with Dad."

Don't. Cry.

She sat up straight and took a big gulp of cold water.

"I can still have pieces of that," she reminded herself. "Maybe I'll still fall for the hardware guy. Maybe he'll already have a child of his own. Hopefully Peyton will be as close to his kids as I was to Jasper. It's not a lost dream, just a different one, but I'm not ready to think about it, so I don't."

"I don't want that."

"Yes, I know. I saw what you want." God, Eden was so beautiful. Everything about that wedding had been first class. They would have had their whole lifetime planned, from skiing in Europe to going on African safaris over spring break. Their children would have gone to all the top schools, starting in preschool all the way to the best university. Then they would marry another elite like they were and the legacy would continue.

"No." His features grew craggy with tension. "I don't want her to have a stepfather. I want her to have *me*."

She opened her mouth, made herself pause and grasp at her patience, but there really was a limit to how much of her life she would let him dictate.

"I can see why stepparents would be a sore spot for you. I get it. I do. Plus, you're only starting to bond with her so you don't want me dating anyone and messing with that. I'm not planning to. If I did, I would wait ages before introducing them to her and I swear I would let you meet them first, so quit feeling threatened."

"No. Amelia." His smile was so patronizing she wanted to roll her eyes. "I want her to have both of us. In the same house. We can give her as many brothers and sisters as you want."

"I—" She scratched her brow, genuinely lost because he couldn't be suggesting what she thought he was suggesting. "What?"

"I want us to marry."

"No," she said reflexively.

"Think about it."

"No."

There was a ring of some internal bell.

"The nurse is here." He rose and walked away while Amelia kept thinking, *No*.

CHAPTER SIX

THE TEST WAS a cheek swab that Peyton slept through. Hunter gave his own sample and showed the nurse to the door.

"I'll put her down and have a shower if you don't mind," Amelia said, still cradling the sleeping baby.

She was trying to avoid him and the proposition he'd put forth. Hunter could tell. Was she disappointed he hadn't been more romantic about it? The hardware guy would have gone down on one knee and offered a diamond worth two months of his salary, he was sure, but what did that prove?

Their marrying made sense. He wanted to keep talking until she saw that, which was how he behaved in most business negotiations, but Amelia's hollow cheeks suggested she was on her last nerve. He would have to give her a little time to process and come around to seeing the wisdom in it herself.

"Do you want something clean to wear? I think Vi left a dress here that might fit you." He waved her to precede him up the stairs.

"*Vi* did," Amelia said skeptically.

He bit back a sigh, not used to being disbelieved or having to make explanations for himself, but he could understand her suspicion that it belonged to Eden.

"Vienna was shopping and brought it up when she came

for lunch. She wanted to try it on again because she thought she might return it, then she forgot it in the foyer. I left it upstairs for whenever she comes by again." He veered into the other guest room to fetch the flat box with the embossed scroll of the boutique's name.

When he came back to the room full of baby gear, Amelia was reading the back of an unopened baby monitor. Peyton was in the playpen, fast asleep, wrapped in a duck-print blanket snug as a tortilla around a burrito.

"I can figure out the monitor," Hunter said, setting the box on the bed. "Helpful dad, remember?"

"This isn't a reality show. I'm not going to marry you for TV ratings." She handed him the monitor, though, and lifted the top off the box, peering at the dress.

"I'm not trying to portray myself as a better father than my own. I want to *be* better. You would still get a decent guy with a decent job." Actually, his position was demanding as hell, but it had its perks—designer dresses like that, for instance. "Auntie Vienna will make cookies with her niece," he added with a nod to Peyton. "Actually, they'll probably finger paint. I realize that's not the same, but it's something. Uncle Remy would love to take her fishing with your dad." In Martinique. Was she open to outright bribery? Because he could go on.

"We don't even know each other. You didn't want to get to know me," she reminded him as bright red spots arrived on her cheekbones. Her voice quavered with degradation as she added, "It was a one-night hookup, and you tried to *pay* me."

He recoiled as though she'd slapped him. "That's not what happened."

"Do you know what gaslighting is?" She scowled at him.

"You were upset, and I was trying to help." He squeezed the back of his neck, still embarrassed at how that morning had gone. "You said—" He couldn't remember what she'd said. Something about having to get home right away because her brother was reported as missing. He'd asked, "Do you need money?"

She had looked at him like that. Like he was the lowest form of life.

"I was trying to help. Money solves a lot of problems. I won't apologize for being wealthy," he stated. It wasn't as if he hadn't been punished for it.

"Clearly it creates them, too," she said sweetly. "Because I didn't want anything to do with you after that. I still don't."

She walked into the bathroom and firmly closed the door.

It was one of the best showers of her life, damn him.

Amelia was feeling grotty and sweaty from a very tumultuous day, but was revitalized as the showerhead rained gently upon her face. The water was soothing and cleansing as it ran down her naked skin. Hotel-sized shampoo and other products were already in the bathroom, and they smelled amazing, producing bubbles that caressed her scalp and skin.

When she came out and moisturized with an equally delicious and fragrant lotion, she couldn't bear to put on her stained T-shirt. She gave in and tried on the blue-and-yellow polka-dot summer dress that had supposedly been purchased by Vienna, not Eden. Either way, it still had the tags and—

"Good grief," she muttered, eyes popping at the price.

It fit, though. Her bra straps showed beneath the tie straps and the bodice strained across her ample, padded breasts, but it would be easy to nurse in. The fall of soft cotton felt so lovely as it brushed her bare legs, she couldn't bear to take it off.

It also gave her a little more confidence when she went downstairs to meet the exquisitely put-together Carina and the even more chic Unity, Vienna's stylist.

Unity took Amelia's measurements and finger-combed her hair and held a few fabric swatches against her skin, then promised, "I'll pull some things together and come back in the morning." Unity departed, and Amelia went to the lounge.

Carina looked up from her tablet and smiled.

"Baby still sleeping?"

Amelia nodded and set the monitor on the end table as she curled into the corner of the sofa across from Carina.

"Where's Hunter?" Was she doing this alone? Amelia looked around.

"He promised me coffee, but the service in this place is terrible. Oh, you didn't hear that." Carina bit her lips in pretended chagrin as Hunter appeared from the kitchen.

"Tip better," he suggested, setting a mug on the coffee table before seating himself next to Amelia.

Amelia looked at her nonexistent manicure and wished the sofa cushions would swallow her. The banter wasn't flirty. It was more like the comfortable trashing between longtime colleagues, but it still seemed to exclude her.

"Okay, so…" Carina tapped her screen. "Hunter brought me up to speed on the fact that you're considering marriage."

Amelia glared at him. "I didn't agree to that."

"I said we're talking about it," he said mildly. "We are."

"*You* are," she muttered.

"Obviously, we'll wait for the paternity results before making any announcements of that sort," Carina said in a soothing tone. "In the short term, we don't want anyone painting you as a home-wrecker. We'll circle back to talking about your family, but first I need all your best qualities, volunteer work, any friends in high places who might be willing to offer a quote? This is not a time to be modest. Gossip rags will approach your neighbors and anyone else they can find who might talk about you."

Amelia swallowed a thick lump of revulsion. Something touched her elbow and she snapped her head around as Hunter slid his fingertips down her bare arm, pulling goose bumps onto her skin before he captured her hand in his warm grip.

"It's okay. That's why we're doing this. To counter that sort of thing."

It was still awful, but she closed her hand around his. Clinging to his solidness made it a little easier to dredge up a few people who would say nice things about her. She made sure to mention that she tutored refugees online through a nonprofit organization, volunteering to help with their English as part of building her teaching résumé.

When Carina moved on to asking about past lovers, Amelia pulled her hand from Hunter's and tangled her fingers together in her lap.

"There's not much to tell. I dated in high school, but I had an overprotective brother so…" She shrugged wryly.

"I have one of those myself," Carina said with amused empathy.

Amelia experienced a stab of envy because Carina still had hers.

"What about university? Anyone serious there?" Carina asked.

"Just one. Gareth Bedford. He was a TA on another course and, um, cheated on me so I don't think he'll come out and say rotten things about me." She defensively slouched deeper into the corner of the sofa.

"You'd be surprised what people will say for their fifteen minutes of fame. When exactly did it end? Because speculation could emerge around Peyton's paternity. These sorts of things can linger. We want to be very clear there's no doubt."

Amelia snorted. "I'd like to see him try claiming he was her father when we never even had sex. If anything, he'll continue complaining about what a frigid prude I was."

"Oof. I'm sorry he was a jackass. I've met a few of those as well." She tapped her screen briefly. "Anyone else? Casual dates?"

"Like, coffee? What are they going to say about me? We traded notes from classes?" She shrugged. It had all been friendly, but benign.

"I'm not prying out of salacious interest, Amelia. This works best when we know who and what might come out to bite us."

"Us," Amelia repeated with a sniff of disdain.

"You," Carina acknowledged, taking on a kinder tone. "I'm only saying that this works best if you tell me about any intimate partners of any gender who might be brought to light and used against you. Forewarned is forearmed."

"I don't have any." She *really* wished she had stayed in bed this morning. To think, when Dad had come back and insisted on getting in the car, there had actually been a part of her that had latched on with enthusiasm to getting out of the house. She had thought the drive might be nice. Maybe they would pick up some sandwiches and eat them on the beach.

"Are we talking about the same thing?" Carina cocked her head, seeming perplexed. "Are you saying you've only slept with… Hunter?" Her voice rang with acute disbelief.

"I—" Amelia's heart lurched as she realized how much she had exposed of herself.

She could feel Hunter drilling holes into the side of her face with his gaze. Her cheeks started to sizzle, and her chest grew tight.

"Yes." Her voice cracked in the middle of the word.

"I see." To her credit, Carina didn't make a big deal of it, only said casually, "I'm not sure why you bothered with the paternity test, but it's good to know it will come back as expected. Let's talk about less favorable publicity. I haven't had time for a deep dive online, but I saw something about your brother walking away from his job site—"

"That is *not* what happened!" Amelia cried, lurching forward on the sofa cushion.

She was already wound tight enough to break in half. Now tears crashed into the backs of her eyes. She was suddenly short of breath, teetering on the verge of falling apart.

The cushion sank beside her as Hunter slid his hip right up against hers. The warmth of his body seemed to encompass her as his arm came around her hunched shoulders and he tipped her into his chest.

"This topic will be handled with the absolute, utmost care, Carina."

"Yes. Yes, it will," Carina assured him gravely. She nodded slowly and swallowed before she offered a tight smile. "I'll freshen my coffee and give you a minute, Amelia."

"I don't need a minute," she lied as she pressed her face into the hollow of Hunter's shoulder, but Carina was already gone and she was relieved. "I can talk about him," she insisted, even as she crushed the fabric of his shirt in her fist. "It's just been a really emotional day."

"It has." He shifted so she wasn't twisted quite so hard. He scooped her legs across his and dragged her into his lap. Then he just held her, light fingers drawing circles against the back of her shoulder. His chin rested on her hair.

She was shaking with the effort to fight grief and sorrow

and despair. She slid her arm around his neck and clung to him as she clung to her composure. *Breathe*, she reminded herself. Breathe and let the wave of grief come up as high as it needed. It would recede in its own time; she just had to endure it while it was on her and in her.

After about four breaths, she realized he was inhaling and exhaling with her, guiding hers to become slow and steady. She clenched her eyes, and a tear squeaked onto her lashes. She sniffed.

"This is what I should have done that morning," he murmured, breath stirring the part in her hair. "I just wanted to help, Amelia. I swear that's the only reason I said what I did."

The money. If she hadn't been so distraught, she might have knocked her fist into his shoulder, but this felt so comforting, that old bruise faded into a vague memory.

"I don't want to cry," she said with a frustrated pang in her voice. "That has never helped. Not once."

"Stay right here as long as you need, then." He smoothed her hair and continued to rub her back.

She could have stayed like this forever, but hiccuped a few sobs before getting hold of herself and climbing out of his lap.

"It's okay. Tell her she can come back. I can do this." She just had to step into the hard shell she had worn every time she had picked up the phone or sat down to write yet another email that had wound up being ignored.

Hunter rose and invited Carina back into the living room.

"I'm really sorry, Amelia," Carina said as she retook her seat. "I thought— Well, it doesn't matter what I thought. You'll tell me the truth and we'll go from there."

Amelia started from the beginning. Jasper had been working in northern Alberta for a company that specializes in rare earth metal exploration. He was dispatched to Chile, where he was surveilling for a new project.

"The last time I spoke with him, he was excited because he'd realized they could sift through tailings from hundreds of dams. It's a greener endeavor than pit mining. The cost for the rights was dirt cheap, he said." She smiled faintly at that remembered pun. "The soil had already been displaced, and once the rare earth metals were extracted, it could be moved to better locations than where it had been left by the dam projects. He saw it as win all around. A couple of weeks went by and the next thing we heard, the company said he walked away with his interpreter. But why would he? He *wouldn't*. Something happened."

"No ransom demands?" Hunter asked.

"No. And no body." She clung to her elbows, still feeling so bewildered by this turn of events.

"Which company?" Hunter asked.

"REM-ex. Their HR manager told me—"

"I'll speak to their CEO." He pulled out his phone.

"Oh, good luck," Amelia huffed. She'd never gotten higher than a letter from the operations manager for South America advising her that they considered the matter closed.

She expected Hunter to leave a message with a recording or, at best, some low-level receptionist. He had it on speaker and set it on the coffee table.

"Hunter!" The male voice boomed into the living room. "I'm not taking work calls, but if you're on your honeymoon and want to meet up, we're anchored off Mykonos."

"I'm calling about Jasper Lindor, Orlin. You may have seen correspondence from his sister, Amelia?"

A pause, then, "Oh. Her. I'm familiar with the name, yes. Is she becoming a pain in your ass, too?"

"She's the mother of my child," Hunter said flatly. "Our

marriage will bring her brother's disappearance back into the spotlight. You'll want better answers ready than the ones your people have been giving her."

There was dumbfounded silence, then a curse and a resigned, "I'll see what I can find out."

"Do," Hunter commanded. He ended the call without saying goodbye.

One call. Amelia had made thousands and had written a million emails and gotten absolutely nowhere. Hunter had made one call and got the man on vacation and got him to *promise* something.

Fresh tears welled in her eyes. Such a pressure grew in her chest, she couldn't speak. She didn't know if she was touched or outraged or hopeful or all of the above. Hopeful. Definitely hopeful. Her lips began to quiver. Her breath shook.

Hunter said to Carina, "Go check in with the team, see what you can get done with what you have so far."

"Sure thing." Carina flashed her a look as she quickly gathered her things and slipped away.

Amelia grabbed the tissue box like it was a lifeline and pulled some out. She jammed them against her running nose and brimming eyes.

"That's not a quid pro quo," Hunter said quietly. "I said we're marrying because it will light the largest fire under him."

"You'd think a man's life would do that, but…" She used the heels of her palms to hold the balled tissues against her wet eyes.

She didn't even care if Hunter had said it to blackmail her or make her feel beholden to him. She *was* beholden. She would marry him a dozen times over if it would give her the tiniest inkling of a clue as to what had happened to Jasper.

Apparently, he was right. Money could solve certain problems.

"Why—?" He cut himself off.

She blew her nose and dropped the tissues onto the table.

Hunter was looking toward the window, profile twisting with self-deprecation.

"What?" she prompted.

"Why didn't you tell me it was your first time?" His brows were bunched into a perplexed angle. When his gaze came back, it was filled with apprehensive concern, "Did I hurt you?"

"Not too much."

He winced. "You should have said."

"I thought you'd think I was a weirdo, never having done it. I was twenty-three," she reminded him, and waved toward the elevator. "Did you see Carina's face? She thinks I'm a total weirdo."

"There's nothing weird about being a virgin. You haven't had sex and then you have. It's weirder that we make such a big deal of it. On the other hand..." He studied her. "If someone is holding off, there's usually a reason. Which makes me wonder, why that night? Why me?"

Her heart turned over in her chest. She buckled defensively over her folded arms, rocking slightly.

"This is a day when every single detail of my life has to be torn open and examined, isn't it? Do you want to hear about the day my period started and Jasper had to buy me supplies? Spoiler alert, he also bought a cake mix. It fell after he baked it and iced it too soon. It was literally the ugliest cake ever made, but I ate so much of it I still can't stand lemon-flavored desserts."

Tears leaked from the corners of her eyes down her temples. She clenched them shut.

"You don't have to talk about this, Amelia. I didn't mean to upset you."

"No, it's okay. I've never told anyone that, but it always makes me laugh when I think of it." She was smiling through her tears. "That's what he was trying to do, make me laugh. We'd lost Mom a few months before and he knew I really, really needed her that day."

"You miss him a lot."

"I really do." She picked up her head and cleared the thickness from her throat, swiping one more tissue across her face and resolving she was finished breaking down. "He also put the fear of Jasper into any boy who looked twice at me, mostly because he'd been through a pregnancy scare himself." She wrinkled her nose. "The girl actually went away with her aunt and only told him after she came back that it was all dealt with. She expected him to be relieved, but he was kind of messed up by it. Her body, her choice. He understood and supported that, but he was really adamant that if I was going to put myself in the position of having to make a choice like that, I should be serious about the guy. Not some random, you know?"

A harsh laugh cut from his throat.

"The irony, right?" She drew a pillow into her lap and hugged it. "When I started seeing Gareth, I explained that I wanted to go slow, that I needed to know we had a future before we had sex. He said he was fine with that, but whenever we fooled around, he was always pushing me to go all the way. He would pout when I made him stop, laying on a guilt trip. Some of that was my fault—"

"None of that was your fault," Hunter interjected firmly.

She waggled her head. "You're right. I know you're right, but I always think I should have seen him more clearly. There were other issues. He was controlling, but in a subtle way so I couldn't really argue with him. If I did, he would make me feel as though I was being petulant rather than standing up for myself. He wanted to tell me what to wear and who to talk to and what to say."

"Is that how you feel with me? Because I convinced you to stay here?" He drew his head back as though bracing for an unpleasant answer.

"No." She gave herself a moment to really consider the question, able to say truthfully, "I'm not thrilled that I feel stuck here, but you talked me into staying with facts, not manipulation. He always made it about him. He would say that if I genuinely loved him, I would want to make him happy. I knew I was putting too much pressure on myself to make my wedding night some big, romantic culmination, but I also didn't like feeling pressured by him. Even so, I was starting to think about doing it so he would shut up about it."

"That's a terrible reason to have sex."

"I know. Fortunately—I use that word loosely—a fellow student told me she was sleeping with him. She had just found out he and I were in a relationship and she was really sorry she had helped him be unfaithful to me, but she thought I would want to know. I did. I told him to kick rocks and he said it didn't count as cheating. He said we weren't really together since we hadn't consummated our relationship, but also, that's why he slept with her, because I wouldn't satisfy him."

"And you didn't order a hit? There's an app for that." Hunter curled his lip in disgust.

"Under self-help, I know. I made an account, but didn't go through with it."

"Ha," he barked. "At least you can laugh about it."

He eyed her with something like admiration, making her tingle.

"I did at first, yes." She brought her knees up and hugged

them, resting her chin on top. "Then he spread rumors that I was frigid and uptight and whatever."

"What a piece of work. What's his name again? His Wi-Fi is going to become very spotty."

"Appreciated."

"Was it limited to campus, that gossip? Or online harassment, too?"

"Mostly on campus and it was embarrassing, but it wasn't untrue. Mostly. It meant that only two kinds of men approached me after that. The ones who thought I was a challenge—I'd been there, done that and no thank you to the headache. The other types were also waiting for their wedding night. They were nice, but I never met anyone who intrigued me enough to consider marrying him purely to find out what all the fuss was about."

Hunter had the one brow down again as he tried to make sense of all she had said and, perhaps, the things that she hadn't.

"Then I met you and you made me want to know what the fuss was about." She lifted a defensive shoulder. "You were open about it being only one night, which was refreshing honesty. I didn't know when I would meet someone else who made me feel like that, so I let it happen. And even though we ended on a sour note…"

His somber gaze reiterated that it had been a misunderstanding, not a payoff.

"I didn't regret it. I kind of thought, at least I had that one happy memory before we lost Jasper. Then I got *pregnant*, which made me feel like a world-class *idiot*."

"You're not an idiot. From what I've been told, sex is the leading cause of pregnancy. We both took the risk, and here we are. You still could have told me it was your first time, though."

"Then I would have had to tell you all of that and we only had the one night, Hunter. I wanted to get to the good part."

"Oh." He smirked. "Same." He studied her, expression sobering. "Was it good? Worth the wait?"

She was dying, curled up as small as she could get, holding in not just self-consciousness, but that odd mix of excitement and sweetness and joy and unfettered lust that had exploded between them. It had been a good memory, one she had clung to through a lot of bad. One that made her daughter a precious gift.

"How would I know?" she asked wryly. "I had nothing to compare it to. You tell me." A hard, stinging blush heated her cheeks. Yes, she was fishing for a compliment. Some sign that it had meant something to him.

"I thought you were amazing," he said, voice pitched one note lower than usual. Shadows of conflict chased across his expression.

"Then why—" Her voice cracked, and she averted her face, not wanting him to see how badly she'd yearned for more from him. For some tiny sign that she had not been used and discarded.

He sighed. "I was in the middle of that mess with Irina. That's why Remy insisted I needed a weekend away. I didn't have the bandwidth for a relationship, especially one long distance. And..." He winced. "Vienna had already been nagging me to meet Eden."

"And you already knew she was more suited to you than a waitress who owed more than she owned. I get it." She nodded, devastated, but not surprised.

"Amelia."

"It's true. And you need to think about that before you spout off to Carina that we're getting married," she hurried to add. "It's one thing for me to privately feel that I'm not good enough for you. It is quite another for you to put me on the front page so everyone else can think it, too."

"Stop it," he said curtly.

"Don't pretend it's not true, Hunter! What would I bring to a marriage that even comes close to what Eden offered you?"

"Our daughter," he said sternly. "She outweighs all other considerations. She's the reason I'm not married to Eden right now."

"Listen to yourself!" She shot to her feet and took a few agitated steps away before she whirled on him. "You walked away from your wedding for *Peyton*. Not for me. I've said I'll work with you to have access. That doesn't mean we have to get married. What would I bring to our marriage besides potential for another child? Because this isn't Victorian England, Hunter. I need to be wanted for something more than my fertility. We don't love each other—which you've made clear isn't something you want—so what do I have that you want?"

He started to speak, clacked his teeth together, then abruptly shot to his feet and walked away in the other direction. "Sex. All right?"

She choked out a laugh and waved a helpless hand. "You can get sex from anyone. If that's all you wanted, you should have married Eden. You could be having sex right now."

"I don't want sex with her. I want sex with *you*." He shoved his fingers through his hair, leaving it mussed. "I had to tell you not to text me. I was engaged. But if I hadn't been—"

Her ears strained to hear the rest. She actually took a few steps closer, trying to catch whatever he might say. Trying to see his expression behind the troubled hand that scrubbed across it.

"What?" she prompted.

"I haven't stopped thinking about you, Amelia." He dropped his arm to his side, the movement so heavy, it was as if he dropped a broadsword to the ground.

"Really?" She hugged herself. She wasn't even who she had always planned to become. That woman who was gainfully employed and living independently and confident in herself was far in the distance. She was still a stumbling, scuffed version of her. She was on her feet, but she was far behind where she wanted to be.

And that woman couldn't touch the Edens of the world—the ones with more than an education. A family name and a seat at the head of a corporate table and so many big-name friends, Amelia would have been starstruck today if she hadn't been the one in the spotlight.

"I want to ask how you could doubt it when that night was so fantastic, but…"

A humorless rasp sounded in his throat as he came toward her. His light touch grazed her elbows, thumbs sending goose bumps up her arms and down into her chest by barely caressing her biceps.

"I don't do that, you know. Pick up women. I wanted to believe I was blowing off steam, but even when it was happening, I knew it was more than that."

"What was it?"

"I don't know." His hands continued to caress her arms and shoulders, making her shake. "But I'd like to find out." His chin dipped so they were eye to eye. "Wouldn't you?"

In what she had thought were very twisted, messed-up fantasies, yes. She had longed to see him again and had felt wretched for it, as if she were that easily taken in again by a man who only wanted one thing.

That uncertainty still pulsed within her like an electric fence, keeping her holding a part of herself at a distance, but another part—the physical connection that had unraveled her that night—unfolded her arms and shifted her feet closer to his. She set light hands on his chest and felt herself nod jerkily. Her searching gaze slid from the stormy ocean of his irises and landed on his mouth.

Look at that beautiful mouth. That uncompromising bottom lip held a stern line as he brought it down on hers and *consumed* her.

A jolt, a savage blast of need, swirled around her, catching her up in a claw of acute passion. Maybe that was his arms closing around her, claiming her while he gently yet thoroughly ravished her mouth.

Had she expected some hesitant reunion? Not from Hunter. His confidence and his undisguised desire for her had drawn her last July. When he had looked at her, it hadn't been in a way that suggested she was a potential conquest. There'd been curiosity and heat and that wonderful control that said, *I want you, but I won't take you. You have to give yourself to me.*

Nothing and no one else made her feel like this. Hunter's embrace was unbreakable, but who would want to get away? She wanted to be closer and twined her arms around his neck, one hand splaying in his short hair so she could press him to kiss her harder. *Devour me. Make me yours. Forever.*

Now.

A noise that didn't make sense caused Amelia to gasp and shove her hands against Hunter's shoulders, pressing him to let her go.

He had to consciously tell himself how to do that, because he'd fallen into a purely animalistic state that wanted to hold on to her for the duration of whatever was about to happen between them.

That noise was Peyton. Her cries were coming through the monitor.

As Amelia hurried away, Hunter bit back a groan that was both pain and relief. Pain because he was so aroused by their kiss, the denial of stopping physically hurt.

He was glad it hadn't gone further than that kiss, though. He had already revealed too much of himself. Too much hunger and—no. He refused to call it a need.

He couldn't believe he had confessed to all of that. It was lowering and left him feeling vulnerable that she knew how much he had craved another encounter with her. That night of theirs had kept talons in him for all these weeks and months since. He'd been thinking of her when he had finally given in to Vienna's prodding and asked Eden to dinner. His mind had been split between the past and the present when he proposed. From the moment his ring had gone onto Eden's finger, he had fought to forget a single night with a waitress he was convinced he would never see again.

Then she had reached out in November.

The temptation to say more than he had, to bring her closer rather than push her away, had been acute.

The very fact that he would think it, while engaged and moving down a far more sensible life path, had told him that Amelia was becoming the sort of obsession for him that Irina had been for his father. The same sort of weakness.

He had feared she would upend his life if he wasn't very, very careful, so he had told her he was committed elsewhere.

Don't text me again.

She hadn't.

That should have allowed him to put her firmly in the past, but it hadn't. The moment the first rows of grapes had appeared as he'd driven into the vineyard this morning, his libido had come alive with memories of sexual heat and shy touches and greedy lips and passionate cries. With the feel of her soft skin against his nude frame as he stretched awake.

That last, intensely satisfying tumble had been the hook. His orgasm-drugged mind had begun rearranging his world so he could bring her into it. He clearly remembered his sense of entitlement. *Why not?* He had mentally brushed aside duty and the importance of meetings with lawyers. He was a powerful man. The boss. He could do what he wanted. He could *have* what he wanted. He worked hard and *deserved* to have what he wanted. He wanted Amelia.

Into that slumberous arrogance, she'd picked up her phone and released a torn cry. Minutes later, she had dressed and left with that final, wounded look.

And she'd been a *virgin* that night?

He pinched the bridge of his nose, still trying to comprehend how he'd missed that salient detail. She'd been bashful, obviously feeling awkward, but the first time with any lover was always a little awkward. He hadn't thought anything of the nervous laughs and hesitant touches.

No, he remembered her passion. She might have been unschooled in the way she touched him, but her small gasps and moans and the way she had clung to him had told him she liked the way he touched her. That had turned him on like nothing else could. Her first climax had been against his hand, and her abandonment had almost taken him over the edge with her.

Maybe he should have realized her lack of experience when she had apologized for peaking so unexpectedly.

He recalled chuckling hoarsely, bemused, so horny he'd thought he would combust.

Had he rushed her at that point? He always wore a condom, always asked. She had said yes, she wanted him inside her, but he'd been aware of her tension as he pressed into her.

He'd thought maybe she wasn't as aroused as he was, having just climaxed, so he had paused and slid his touch between them, nearly losing it again when he found her dewy and taut. Her breaths had shortened as he teased her. She had clenched around his tip and her knee had come to his ribs and she had opened her mouth against his neck. Her moan of need had sent a vibration through his blood, straight to where he was penetrating her.

Slowly, slowly, he sank all the way in. It had been heaven and hell to hold himself still, hold back. He wanted to let loose, yet wanted it to last. Her arms had twined around his neck and she'd released a shaken sigh, pressing a tremulous smile to the corner of his mouth.

That was the moment he should have realized it was her first time, but his mind had been fixated on the feel of her. His pulse had hammered in his ears, and his breath had been fire. They had started kissing and he began thrusting and she moved with him in perfect synchronicity. Her hands had been in his hair and across his shoulders and danced across his spine. Her legs had hugged him; her heels had been in his buttocks, encouraging him.

Pure torture and absolute paradise. His whole body had been a tense line of delicious self-denial, but he was determined to last for her. It had been hard not to give in to the pleasure crashing like waves over him, so hard the effort knotted his breath. The tingles of culmination had been gathering in his tailbone when her ragged breaths had become sobs of desperation.

Come, he had ordered roughly, as if he had the power to command it.

She had. Her inner muscles had clamped around him

and released into the fluttering contractions that tripped his own powerful release. He'd nearly been ripped in half by the force of it. And loved it.

He ran his hand down his face, finding himself back in his Toronto penthouse with a rattled shake of his head. He was hard. Muscle memory, he thought ironically. He remembered every millisecond of their lovemaking, because he still replayed it in his highlight reel. She *was* his highlight reel.

She was his weakness, exactly as Irina had been for his father. Had he already forgotten that Amelia had ruined his *life* today?

On the baby monitor, he could hear her cooing to Peyton, laughing softly.

"How can you be hungry again? Okay, okay. Don't panic. I'm right here." Her voice faded as she moved away from the monitor, but he still heard her as she murmured, "So demanding. I wonder where you get that from?"

There was only amused indulgence in her voice, though. She loved their daughter without reserve. Did she really think that wasn't something he *required* in his marriage? Her capacity for loyalty toward family had tremendous value to him.

They had to marry. He still saw no other course of action that accomplished as many goals in one swoop, but he would have to be mindful of how easily she could influence him.

He would have to hold her at arm's length even when he was buried deep inside her.

Amelia had the fearful sense that if her daughter hadn't woken, she would be courting another pregnancy right now.

She gently smoothed her daughter's fine hair, thinking

she would happily have a dozen more of his babies. This one was so lovably perfect, it was ridiculous.

Amelia was genuinely scared for Peyton, though. Hunter's world was as dangerous as it was luxurious. As she pulled her mind out of sexy kisses and back to everything Carina had said, she knew that marriage was the only way to spin their affair to keep Peyton from being crushed by the fallout.

Lust and a baby were not the strongest pillars on which to forge a marriage, though. The sort of marriage she had always seen for herself had been built on love and respect and liking. Friendship. Equality.

She didn't have any of those things from Hunter. Even his respect for her must be a thin version of it, given how she had forced this one-eighty on his life plan. Equality? Pah!

She drew the bodice of Vienna's dress back into place and shook out a fresh receiving blanket from the package of a dozen.

This was Peyton's life, she acknowledged as she gently swaddled her. Money wasn't everything, but it was something. Plus, as someone who had lost a parent, she knew the value in having a good relationship with the one who survived. She had to marry Hunter, for Peyton's sake. She knew that.

And she wanted to marry him. For her own sake. For the sex.

She clenched her eyes shut as she admitted it to herself. That kiss had been the same wild magic as their night last July. It was wonderfully exciting and dangerously disturbing. He made her feel weak. Helpless to herself and to him.

He made her want things he wasn't likely to give her, which made her deeply afraid their marriage wouldn't last. Maybe she was best thinking of it as a continuation of their affair, one that would be a little messier to end than most.

Cradling her daughter against her shoulder, she found him downstairs taking the dishes from the living room to the kitchen.

"Everything all right?" he asked with a flicker of his gaze from her tense expression to the firm grip she had on their daughter.

"Sure. I'm dandy as hell. You?"

"Point taken." He set the dishes in the sink.

"Look. I know we have to get married," she began carefully.

He turned and leaned on the counter, arms folded across his wide chest. His expression was an absolute study in poker faces.

"Peyton needs your protection. I suppose I do, too." She chewed her lip, feeling hollow as she spoke of marriage so clinically, rather than with the excitement she had always anticipated she would feel. "It goes against everything I believe in to marry expecting to divorce, but that's what I think will happen."

"That's the spirit," he drawled. "Positive thinking is the secret to success."

"Do *you* think we have what it takes to go the distance?" she scoffed.

"I'm pretty stubborn when I set my mind to something."

"Like running a marathon even if it makes you vomit? That's the spirit," she mocked.

"We'll have a prenup," he said as if that was obvious. "If we divorce, it will be very civilized. I'll make sure of it."

That was the spirit she expected from him, she thought dourly.

"I don't care about your money. I need you to believe that. But I am concerned about what my life will look like."

"Finish school. Teach if you want to." He shrugged that off.

"I was worrying more about whether we would have more kids. I don't think that's a good idea. Not right away. I'm not ready to be pregnant again anyway. But I'll go on the pill or something. Obviously, condoms don't work for us."

"Oh. Yeah, of course." He pushed off the counter, all dynamic motion as he started back to the living room. "Whatever you're comfortable with."

CHAPTER SEVEN

THEY MARRIED THREE days later in the apartment.

Hunter offered to plan something bigger for another time, but Amelia brushed that off. She really did believe this union would be temporary. That's why she didn't take him up on the offer to fly her father in for the ceremony. Tobias had only just settled into the cottage at Lake of the Woods. He sounded content, so she would tell him after the fact.

Maybe she was also punishing Tobias for putting her in this position. He wanted Peyton's father to do the right thing? Fine. She acquiesced, but she wouldn't let her father see it and be all smug about it.

She wouldn't raise his expectations, then dash them in a year or two when she and Hunter admitted it wasn't working.

She asked Hunter to keep it to a bare minimum. Vienna was their witness, along with Carina. Apparently, Remy had read Hunter's invitation to be his best man again, but hadn't replied. Amelia could tell he was confused when his friend ghosted him, but the ceremony went on—not that it was very ceremonial.

She kept reminding herself that it was her choice to keep it so unsentimental and bureaucratic. Unity had shown her a dozen beautiful dresses of various lengths. Amelia had settled on a muted yellow pantsuit that Unity persuaded her to dress up with a satin camisole and a few sprigs of baby's breath in her hair.

Even that much froufrou nonsense bothered Amelia. She couldn't help recalling the vineyard and the string trio, the multitude of guests and linen-draped seats and the pavilion of fine china. That vision carved a hollow cavern into the pit of her stomach. Not because she wanted that. Not really. A thrown-together civil union would have been completely satisfying if she was marrying someone she loved, but she and Hunter didn't have that. *That* was the reason she felt cheated and unattached to anything that happened today.

Maybe if they had spent the last three days getting to know each other she might have felt differently, but they'd only come together for meals, and invariably someone had joined them. He had constantly been taking calls or meeting with strangers whom he would introduce very casually as, "Your driver while we're here," or "She's with the nanny agency. They're pulling some candidates together."

Amelia had been equally busy and inundated with decisions. Did she like this cut of neckline? Would she rather have her hair corrected to brunette or re-streaked to blond? Which brand of crib would she prefer for Peyton, and was there anything she needed from the house in Goderich?

She had left the penthouse only once for a visit to the doctor. She took Peyton because she was due for her first immunizations. That left the infant fussy and running a low-grade fever. Amelia had opted for an IUD, so she had cramps and was up with Peyton half a dozen times in the night.

Hunter came in at four, concerned that Peyton wasn't settling. He took her and walked her until she cried herself out, allowing Amelia to finally get some sleep.

They both had sunken eyes and a distinct lack of spirit as they repeated their vows.

When the officiant pronounced them husband and wife and urged, "You may kiss if you wish," Amelia felt teary, and not in a good way. She was still angry about all of this. She was sad that her life had become so much less than she had wanted for herself. She felt cheated and raw and second-best.

Why had she agreed to this?

Hunter's strong hand cupped her cheek and his mouth slanted across her own. It was a chaste kiss, but the warmth of his palm brought heat to the surface of her skin. The brush of his lips made hers buzz with subtle electricity that pulsed in signals down her throat, through her heart and into her loins. Her lips unconsciously caught at his, wanting him to linger.

The tip of his tongue brushed the seam of her mouth, and she opened to welcome a deeper kiss. A more thorough seal of their mouths and their union. His touch on her arm firmed, and her hand fisted into his jacket. She ran the other up and behind his neck. His arm went behind her back and crushed her into the hard wall of his chest.

This, she thought distantly, as desire swept through her like fire through dry grass. This was why she had agreed. She wanted the sex, too. She wanted the run of his palm to her lower back and the shift of his body so she felt the brush of his growing erection against her stomach. She wanted to be wanted.

But even as she melted, Hunter abruptly lifted his head, setting Amelia back a step. He checked his mouth for smudged lipstick.

She pretended to care about her hair and used her raised elbow to hide whatever hurt might be showing in her expression. Then she sat to sign all the paperwork including a form to have Hunter added to Peyton's birth certificate.

She took Peyton from Vienna while they had their photo taken and accepted congratulations and sipped champagne when it was handed to her.

"It's a shame you didn't have time to get Peyton's passport sorted. A proper honeymoon would have been nice," Vienna said as they ate a light brunch. "The cabin is off-grid, though. At least no one will bother you there."

"I've never seen the Rockies. I'm looking forward to it," Amelia said politely. She had never seen Greece, either, but she was glad not to be subbing into the honeymoon Hunter had planned with Eden. "What time do we have to be at the airport?" she asked Hunter, already dreading the long flight with Peyton.

"The plane is ready when we are," he said absently.

That wasn't an answer, but she bit back saying so.

A short while later, they said goodbye to their few guests. Amelia combed out her hair and changed into more comfortable travel clothes. When she came downstairs, Hunter was putting Peyton into her car seat.

"Ready?"

"No," she said with frustration. "I packed the diaper bag, but now I can't find it. Did you put it somewhere?"

"Everything has gone ahead. I've got the ticking time bomb— Yes, I know you hate being in this thing," he said patiently to Peyton as she squawked a complaint. "It's only a few minutes. I promise."

"I usually put my phone and wallet into it," Amelia grumbled, looking at both in her hands.

Unity had supplied her with a number of accessories, so she fetched a small purse with a long strap and only noticed the monogramed design after the fact. Goodness, the purse was worth ten times the amount of cash she was ever likely to carry in it.

She hurried to join Hunter on the elevator. "This doesn't feel right. The two times I went south for vacation, I was weighed down with bags and the stress of whether I had my passport and tickets. Do you use one of those first-class concierge services I've only heard about?"

The doors opened onto the roof, where a helicopter waited.

"Something like that," Hunter said drily.

The helicopter whisked them over the midday traffic to a private jet that was, indeed, waiting for them at the island airport.

Amelia had only seen planes like this in movies about drug lords and corrupt politicians. The interior was styled like a comfortable one-bedroom apartment with a king-size bed in a stateroom. The galley held a real stove, and the main salon had armchairs, a sofa, a big-screen television and a dining area toward the back. The decor was all polished wood and gleaming chrome.

The flight attendant brought champagne and gave Amelia the Wi Fi code, instructing her to ring for anything she needed. After they got under way, she hung a swing seat for Peyton, but Peyton didn't care for it. Hunter wound up holding her. He urged Amelia to lie down in the stateroom, which she did, and she had the best nap of her life.

When they landed in Calgary, they hopped onto another smaller plane that took them to Banff. Only then did they travel by road—in a tricked-out four-wheel-drive SUV. A young man handed Hunter a key fob, and Hunter drove them through a winding route onto roads that weren't well-marked, but he seemed to know where he was going. Peyton must have been as enthralled with the scenery as Amelia, because she stayed quiet the whole way.

They arrived at massive iron gates that Hunter opened with a touch of a button on his phone. He parked in front of a stone structure that was no modest cabin. It wasn't even a chalet. It was a castle with split levels and a round tower, angled roofs and massive windows that reflected the surrounding granite peaks.

"Why do you call this a cabin?" She had expected something far more rustic.

"It was a log home when my father bought it. He called this the cabin, and the lake house was the cottage, so we knew where we were going on vacation. Irina tore down the cabin and built this monstrosity about eight years ago. Way over budget, obviously. Vi and I still call it the cabin because we're very mature. But I told you it was a real house."

He hadn't told her it was a palace with *staff*. The caretakers were a young couple who volunteered on the ski patrol in the winter, "For the free ski pass," Kyra confided over her shoulder with a cheeky grin.

She showed Amelia into a room converted to a nursery, where Amelia put down the sleeping Peyton.

"I can listen for her if you and Mr. Waverly want to relax. There's a short walk down to a viewpoint. It has a picnic table. I could throw together a happy hour basket in five minutes if you like."

It hit her that she was Mrs. Waverly. That's why this young woman was treating her with deference even though Amelia was younger than she was and was technically still a jobless student.

"I'll, um, ask Hunter what he wants to do." She peeked into the hall.

Mr. Waverly had gone to change his shirt because Peyton spit up on him during the flight.

The double doors to the master suite were closed, and

she almost knocked before entering, then slipped inside like a thief because she definitely did not belong here.

The room was huge with hardwood floors and a vaulted ceiling. There was a sitting area with a box window that thrust out, creating an impression of being suspended over the tree-filled valley where the turquoise line of a river snaked in the bottom of the crevice.

Hunter emerged from the walk-through closet that seemed to lead to what looked like a massive bathroom. He was shrugging on his shirt, fixing the collar. He froze when he saw her.

"Kyra said she would listen for Peyton if we want to go for a walk."

"We can do that." He finished straightening his collar, then lifted his head, eyelids growing heavy over his steady gaze. "If you want."

His voice dropped several octaves, hitting her like a stimulating vibration between her thighs.

She swallowed and looked to the window. Hugged herself. She was nervous about the sex, mostly because she was so eager. Embarrassingly eager. What if it was awful? What if they were married and stuck with each other and that night last year had been a combination of moonlight and ovulation?

"How long will she sleep?" he asked.

"An hour?" If they were lucky.

"Do you want to lock the door?" His voice was making her scalp tighten. All of her skin had grown sensitized. Nerve endings prickled beneath the surface. The air in her lungs thinned.

"I do, but—" She didn't move except to squinch up her eyes in a cringe of self-consciousness. "I don't know how it will be. My body is different. I'm worried it won't be good."

"I'm not." He spoke right in front of her.

She snapped her eyes open to see him reaching past her to click the lock.

"If something doesn't feel good, we'll stop and find something that does. For instance, that kiss the other day…" He cupped her face. "Felt very, very good."

"It did," she whispered, and watched his mouth come closer.

Then his lips were brushing hers, capturing. Her hands found his neck and the crisp line where the fade of his haircut met the hollow at the base of his skull. In seconds, they were back in that passionate kiss, and she was lost.

They both groaned, and he shifted his hands to the door behind her, flattening her there with the press of his body.

She gasped as she felt the shape of his erection press against her stomach.

"Yeah," he said against her ear, nuzzling her neck in a way that weakened her knees. "I think this new body of yours is really freaking hot."

She couldn't help but slide her hands beneath the open edges of his shirt to explore the warm skin of his torso. She followed the ripples of his rib cage and found the lines of muscles in his lower back on either side of his spine. As they continued to kiss, she crept her touch back to the hard beads of his nipples.

He sucked in a harsh breath and lifted his head, pressing his hips into her, nostrils flaring as he looked down at her. He cupped her chin again.

"I'm trying to take this slow," he admonished through his teeth.

A thrill of power went through her, giving her the confidence to hold his gaze as she deliberately pushed back on him with the thrust of her hips, gently crushing her pelvic bone into his erection.

He made a supremely sexy sound, eyelids flinching before he swooped, gathering her up like she weighed nothing. Her stomach dipped and her head floated. She blinked and clung around his neck, trying to get her bearings, but she was disconcerted by his strength and the razor-sharp lines that had come into his intense expression.

"Did I hurt you?" she asked in surprise.

"In the best possible way, yes," he said grittily as he placed her on the bed. "Brace for payback."

Oh. She scooted to sit and drew her knees up. "I should, um, tell you that the doctor said I might need lubri—"

He withdrew a tube from the night table.

All her sexy feelings fell off a cliff. "Kept that handy for Eden, did you?"

"No." He scowled. "I did my research. You think I wasn't interested in how soon a woman can have sex after a baby?" He caught her ankle and tugged.

She let him drag her down onto her back and remove one sock, but had to say, "I'm a little nervous. It's been a while for me, and you've been having sex with someone else—"

"I haven't." He threw her sock away and removed the other.

"But " She was surprised. She let him pull her bottom all the way to the edge of the bed. "Sorry, I just assumed. You were engaged."

"She wanted to wait until we were married. Now quit talking about her."

She set her hands on the sides of his head, needing him to look her in the eye. "Is that true?"

"Yes. You're the last woman I slept with, okay?" There was such banked discomfort in his eyes as he revealed that, she couldn't doubt it.

"Okay," she said dumbly.

He threw off his shirt and dropped his trousers, his hurry implying it had been a while for him. She hid a smile at that thought and let him dispense with the fly on her wide-legged trousers. She lifted her hips so he could more easily peel them off her hips, then sat up to pull her shirt over her head.

He studied her as he absently dropped her clothes atop his own.

She bit her lip as he looked her over. Unity had bought her matching underwear with nursing bras that were a lot prettier than the boring white cotton ones she had gotten for herself. This one was gray satin with pink rickrack and a closure between her breasts that she found a lot more convenient than the strap snap of her old bras.

"I'm afraid to take this off," she said truthfully. "I don't want to spoil the mood if they decide to misbehave, but maybe a quick look?" She teasingly opened the cups to expose the heavy swells and the deep cleavage between.

"I think I have a kink for denial." He groaned as he sank to his knees between her feet. His gaze never left her chest. He grazed his tickling touch from her hips up her waist, making her nipples sting before he stole the edges of the cups from her fingers.

With great tenderness, he pressed a kiss to each inner swell, pooling his hot breath against her skin as he promised, "Another time."

He took great care securing the cups closed, then he made a noise of concern as he traced his fingertip up the flame-shaped mark on her abdomen. "Stretch marks?"

"Yes." She started to cover it with her hand, but he brushed her hand aside and gave her sternum a light nudge, encouraging her to lie back. He kissed and nuzzled along the marks, smoothing his lips across her abdomen and licking suggestively against the narrow waistband at her hip, then against her bikini line.

She was still a little tender from being waxed the other

day, but when he opened his mouth and scraped his teeth over the silk covering her mound, such an exquisite spear of sensation went through her she nearly leaped straight up in the air.

"Hurt?" His eyes were laughing at her.

"No." But her legs had turned to jelly. Quivering jelly as they tried to decide if they wanted to clamp onto his torso or relax open for him.

"Do these have to stay on for some special reason?" He hooked his finger in the gray lace against her hip.

Only because it was daylight, rather than the shadowy intimacy of midnight.

"You can take them off if you want to," she said, voice husky with nerves.

"I do want to. Lift your hips."

He peeled the silk away, then stroked his hands up and down her thighs. Her stomach jumped and quivered, and her muscles trembled. When his thumbs came up to gently caress on either side of her sex, her folds grew heavy and hot and sensitized. She groaned and tried to twist.

"Do you want my mouth here? Because I'm dying to taste you again." The pad of his thumb was tracing a line, barely, barely touching her. The most agitated, excited point on her body felt each pass of his fingerprint like a lightning strike.

"I do," she admitted with a pang.

He drew her ankle onto his shoulder, kissing the inside of her calf. "Do you think of that night?"

"Yes," she sobbed, throwing her arm over her eyes.

"What do you do when you think of it?" His mouth was traveling to the inside of her knee, arriving at the thin skin of her inner thigh. "Show me," he coaxed.

She was *dying*. Keeping her eyes hidden by one forearm, she slid her free hand down to relieve the ache he was stoking.

He groaned and his hair brushed her leg, then his mouth was against her, displacing and replacing her fingertip. His thumb circled her entrance, then eased in.

"Okay?"

"Yes," she groaned, digging her heel into his back and lifting her hips, losing herself to the sort of pleasure she hadn't known she could feel until she had met him. She had fooled around here and there. She wasn't a *strict* virgin, but that had been a biology class. This was…

She groaned out her enjoyment.

It was earthy. Erotic. Carnal in the way he turned her body into one receptive nerve ending. Filthy in the way he held her thighs open. Exquisitely pleasurable as climax swept up suddenly and crashed across her.

She realized belatedly that a cry had been torn from her throat. Had Kyra heard her? She might wake Peyton. Hunter didn't let that stop him. He aroused her anew, making it impossible for her to find breaths that didn't scrape and shake. Her breasts ached and her skin burned and a terrible, needy emptiness gripped her.

She licked lips that were dry from panting. "I want you inside me."

He turned his head and opened his mouth on her thigh, biting softly against the tendon there. Then he kissed her stomach and along the underside of her bra, her sternum and her collarbone and her chin.

"I don't think you're going to need this, but let's be sure." He reached for the lube and kicked away his boxers before smearing some on his erection with blatant confidence, fascinating her as she watched.

Then he lined himself up and played his glistening

tip against her, pressing with incremental pressure at her entrance.

"It's okay," she gasped. There was a small pinch, no worse than their first time, which had had this same quality of hot friction and gratifying stretch.

As he filled her, the deep intimacy of the act made her eyes sting. This was the most vulnerable she'd ever felt, lying beneath him with his flesh inside her, but also the most alive and animalistic and, when he gently brushed her hair from the corner of her mouth, cherished.

"No condom," he said shakily. "I may not last long."

"I'll try to keep up."

"Do." He kissed her softly once, then more deeply, as if he couldn't get enough of her.

She shifted so he sank a fraction deeper, and he grunted with pleasure. Then he gathered her beneath him and watched her as he withdrew and returned.

"Okay?"

"Yes," she breathed, tracing his ear and arching sensuously. "It feels really good."

"It does." He combed a hand into her hair and kissed her deeply, moving with more purpose. "Really good."

They were made for this, she thought as she began to meet his thrusts, matching the pace he set. They were made for each other, because she was suddenly approaching another peak.

"Hunter—"

He paused.

"No, don't stop. Never stop," she gasped, so close. Almost there. "Don't stop, don't stop."

"Damn, woman." He kept thrusting, increasing his power.

Another profound orgasm rolled through her, nearly

painful in the strength of her contractions, but so good she could only moan her pleasure.

"I thought I remembered this wrong." He made a sound between gratification and suffering as he gathered her and rolled her so she was above him.

For a few moments, she could only remain splayed atop him, nuzzling her nose into the crook of his neck while his hands stroked over her back and hips and backside.

He remained a pulsing presence inside her, so hard she couldn't help tightening around him. Soon he was subtly lifting his hips, and the pressure and slight friction brought her senses awake all over again.

She rose to sit straddled across him and roamed her hands over his chest, luxuriating in the right to do this.

His lips were pulled back against his teeth gritted in control. His hands firmed their grip on her hips as he urged her to ride him.

She did, watching through the screen of her lashes. The tendons in his neck stood out along with a vein on his arm. He might leave fingerprints on her buttocks, he was so fully in the grip of near orgasm.

"Let go," she urged, wanting to feel it, to watch him. She wanted to know she could make him unravel the way he kept devastating her.

"You first," he said in a voice so tight it was nearly menacing. He swept his thumb in and down, pressing between them so she couldn't escape the pressure as she rode him.

She didn't want to escape. Everything fell away except that pinpoint of exquisite sensation where he penetrated her. Her flesh tightened around him and shot shivering waves through the rest of her body.

"Hunter—" As her pleasure rose, she dug her nails into his chest and the marble-hard strength of his forearm. This shouldn't be happening again, but it was. She was nearly there. She lost her rhythm and ground herself against him, needing that. Him. Deep and hard within her as sparks danced behind her eyes and culmination reached up like a hand to grab her.

It was him. His hand caught behind her neck and drew her down so they were kissing. Her cry was muffled by his own sharp groan as they shattered in unison.

CHAPTER EIGHT

"THAT WAS..." AMELIA'S voice faded as though she didn't have words.

Hunter didn't. His brain was nothing but fried wires. He was spent and gratified, still joined with his wife, who was sprawled upon him. *His wife.* Why did that satisfy him as deeply as the sex?

"A long time coming," she decided, then burst into giggles, stirring the hair on his chest and turning her smug laughter at her own pun into the hollow of his shoulder.

Tightness invaded his chest, but it wasn't a chuckle. It was a yank of discomfort at the truth in her remark.

"I'm sorry. Was that tasteless?" She abruptly lifted her head, sobering as she realized he wasn't as amused as she was.

"It was terrible. Worse than a dad joke. You're stepping on my territory." He smoothed her hair back from where the ends were tickling the edge of his jaw.

She searched his eyes, then gave him a smile as pale as his own. When she shifted away, Hunter didn't try to stop her.

She slipped into the bathroom and he stayed where he was, throwing his arm over his head as he mentally probed at why he was so dismayed by something that was exactly the sort of dirty private joke a couple ought to share in the afterglow.

He didn't brag about conquests and had never been embarrassed by dry spells between lovers. On the contrary, it was a point of pride for him that he could go without sex, unlike his father.

But it felt too revealing that Amelia knew he hadn't slept with anyone since her, probably because self-discipline wasn't the reason he had put off having sex with Eden. Eden had broached the subject a couple of times, very cautiously. There had been a necessary timeline on their marriage, but they hadn't known each other well. He'd assured her there was no rush for intimacy.

The stark truth, however, was that he hadn't desired Eden the way he wanted Amelia. At that point, it had only been the memory of Amelia, interfering and preventing him from rousing to desire for Eden.

And once Amelia had been back in his life, it had been all he could do to wait the three days until they were married and she had some reliable birth control in place. How long had they been here? Not even an hour, and he'd been all over her. If he'd been able to manage it, he would have made her come three more times before he let himself finish.

He almost wished it hadn't been as good as he remembered. If he was disappointed right now, regretting this marriage, he wouldn't feel so raw. Instead, the sex had been *too* good. He was already impatient for her to emerge from the bathroom. Maybe they wouldn't have sex, but he wanted to touch her. Cover her. Kiss her.

He bit back a groan, flesh stirring with recovery. With want.

He didn't know her well enough for this to be an emotional connection. It was pure chemistry and hormones, which made it worse. His libido didn't care about little things like whether he could trust her.

If he wasn't very careful, he would become as besotted and stupidly indulgent as his father.

"I should unpack." Amelia reappeared wearing a fluffy white robe. She paused in the walk-through closet to stare at the suitcases that had been left there.

"Kyra will do it." Hunter made himself rise and find his briefs. They needed to get out of here or he'd have her on her back again before either of them knew it. "Let's walk. If Peyton is awake, we'll bring her with us."

Amelia wasn't sure what she had expected from her honeymoon—probably that she would get to know her husband better, but small things got in the way.

The most persistent small thing was their daughter. That didn't bother her. She enjoyed seeing Hunter bond with Peyton. He wore her in a sling while they took short hikes, never shied from changing her and even brought her to Amelia, saying, "That sounds like her hungry cry."

Other times the obstacles were more dismaying. They were out in public, where they could be overheard. Or even in the house, Kyra and her husband were always nearby.

When she did get a minute to ask him something personal, Hunter always seemed to deflect. He was comfortable telling her facts—his mother had died from a blood infection when he was nine—but he didn't tell her how he felt about it.

"That must have been so hard. I'm really sorry." Amelia's heart ached for him.

"Vienna barely remembers her. That's why our family foundation raises money for treatments and cures for sepsis. The gala is next month, actually. I'll have my PA send you the details." He walked away to find his phone and issue that command.

He worked on and off, taking calls at odd moments and disappearing to sit in on video meetings, which formed yet another thin wall between them.

Amelia couldn't help wondering if he would have done the same to Eden if he'd been sailing the Greek islands with her. Then she felt churlish because she was the one he had married.

She still didn't know what to think of his celibacy between July and their wedding night. It probably wasn't significant. Maybe Eden hadn't wanted to be intimate with someone who didn't love her.

Amelia wondered if there was something wrong with her that she did, because the other thing that came between their communicating with words was the constant sex.

She wouldn't call it lovemaking, because in a strange way, it felt almost like a sensual battle. They both triumphed, yet she always felt defeated. Sometimes it was a stolen quickie during naptime, sometimes it was a lazy, sleepy midnight coupling, and sometimes it was a lengthy contest where Hunter seemed determined to hold back through sheer strength of will while he found every single way he could wring moans and sobs and gasps from her.

She exulted in it, but also felt as though she was losing a piece of herself every single time.

She might have felt less dismantled if they had had a lazy day watching TV in bed, talking to no one but each other, but they went out every day. She didn't mind. It was beautiful. They walked to see waterfalls and ambled the shoreline of glacier-fed green lakes. They went up on the gondola one afternoon, and he took her out for dinner another evening. They lingered over dessert to listen to a folk musician. It was her first time leaving Peyton, but it all went fine.

They must have been recognized, though, because they visited an art gallery the next day and Amelia became aware of the stares they were garnering. Celebrities were common in Banff, but usually came in the winter months for ski vacations. That meant the paparazzi who made their living with candid photos had slim pickings this time of year. They were more than happy to settle for the Wave-Com cad and his strumpet wife.

That night they made the six o'clock news when it was reported that they were on honeymoon in Banff. The next day, they were photographed getting out of their SUV at the base of a hiking trail.

They got straight back in, not wanting to be stalked for the next two hours.

"It's okay," Amelia said as Hunter turned back toward home.

She was disappointed and feeling threatened and exposed, but she didn't think it warranted such a hard scowl as the one he was wearing. It made her feel the weight of being responsible for this scandal.

"I've been meaning to check in with Dad," she continued evenly. "Maybe I can catch him before he's out on the water again." He was fishing every day and loving it.

"Hopefully they're not at the gate when we get there," he said grimly.

Her phone pinged at that moment and so did Hunter's. Here in the mountains, they were in and out of service constantly. It wasn't unusual that both of their phones would buzz for attention simultaneously, but this seemed like more noise than usual.

Amelia glanced at her screen. Her messages were filtered, but she had set up an alert for Jasper's name. It was only a clickbait headline teasing his disappearance as a family trait. The article claimed Hunter was "hiding" his "runner-up wife" and her "money baby."

She told herself it was okay that she was getting raked over the coals so long as Jasper's situation was getting renewed visibility.

"What's wrong?" Hunter asked.

"Nothing. Just a nasty headline."

"Those aren't supposed to come to you."

"I can't keep from seeing all of them," she said, but he was already commanding his phone to "Call Carina."

"You got my message?" Carina asked as she answered. "I just confirmed it."

"Confirmed what?" Hunter snapped, glancing sharply at Amelia.

A pause, then in a confused voice, Carina said, "That Eden married Remy."

"Sylvain?" Hunter asked out of sheer astonishment.

Carina's swallow was audible. "Yes."

Hunter was quiet. Too quiet. Amelia couldn't tell if he was scorned or betrayed or embarrassed or furious or all of the above.

His only reaction was to say flatly when they got home, "The attention here is about to get worse. We'll go to Vancouver where security is easier to manage."

Within a few hours, they had landed in a drizzly Vancouver. After crawling across the bridge into West Vancouver, they arrived at a modern two-story home that, frankly, didn't look as welcoming or posh as the chalet. It was kind of boxy and had stone columns and a brick drive and a fancy front door, but Amelia was thinking that everyone who had ever complained about West Coast weather and traffic and the price of real estate was justified in their disparagement.

Then they walked inside, and she was confronted by one hundred and eighty degrees of windows. With suitable drama, Mother Nature turned off the rain. The clouds parted to allow rays of sunshine to crash onto platinum water. As she walked out to the terrace, a warm breeze that was sweet as pineapple kissed her cheek in greeting.

"Oh. Kay," she murmured. "I get it."

She walked back into the living room of white leather sofas. They were arranged to face a fireplace that looked through to the dining area furnished with space-age chairs and a glass table. The kitchen had a pass-through like a restaurant, but it was currently shuttered.

The house was built into the mountainside so there were several terraces at different levels, one overlooking the pool, another that offered a view of the inlet and the city skyline and a land mass in the misty distance.

"Is that Vancouver Island?" She squinted against the sheen on the waves.

"Yes. And always glance down there for orcas." He pointed.

"Get out of town!"

"True fact." He had pulled Peyton from her seat and was following her around, watching her reaction, but now said, "I have to make some calls. I'll show you where my office is so you can find me if you need me."

The housekeeper had whipped their luggage up the spiral staircase, not that there was much of it. Hunter had assured Amelia she should leave most of her clothes in Banff, claiming Unity had stocked *all* his homes with appropriate selections for the climate. *What did that even mean?*

He carried Peyton as they started down the spiral staircase. It also wound upward so the hollow space took up three floors and had spheres of modern art suspended in the column of empty air.

"Is Remy one of your calls?" she asked.

"If he wanted to talk to me, he would have called by now." Hunter spoke with so much frost, she sealed her lips.

They stepped off the stairs into a rec room tricked out like a pub with a full bar, a dance floor, a pool table and a dart board. There were comfortable pockets of seating and three televisions hung at convenient angles. Four sets of glass doors appeared to fold back upon themselves, opening the room to the patio and pool area. There was a hot tub out there as well. Hunter showed her a switch that ignited a semicircle of fire surrounding an outdoor eating area.

"Dramatic."

"It was built by a musician." He popped her eyes by naming one of Canada's most successful vocalists. "I bought it not long after I met you, actually."

"Did he let it go for a song? I couldn't resist." She bit her lip again.

"He did not." He didn't crack a smile.

She sighed inwardly. Did he blame her for his best friend moving on his bride? Was he concerned that any hope he'd had of salvaging the business side of his marriage to Eden was now circling the drain?

"After the court case was over, I was ready for a change of scenery. Vi is in Calgary so I was planning to make that my home, but this came up. Then I spent three weeks out of four back east so I was planning to unload this and make Toronto my home again."

Because of Eden.

"You might prefer something closer to your father. We can talk about it as time goes on. That's salt water," Hunter said of the pool, continuing his tour. "Home theater." He moved to a windowless room at the back. It sat twelve in three rows of four recliners. "Gym." He opened and closed a door on a room full of equipment.

"Nanny suite." He flicked a wrist toward the back corner as he crossed behind the bar. "This is my office."

It took up the corner and was enormous. Two sets of French doors and a plethora of windows looked onto a garden that was in full bloom. The interior wall contained shelves filled with books and awards and art pieces. His desk was a shiny slab of ribbon-grained wood across two blocks of marble that were so big, she suspected the house had been built around them.

His phone rang so she said, "I'll leave you to it."

She took Peyton back upstairs, wondering if Hunter had bought this thinking he would raise his family here. The top floor held three bedrooms, all with walk-in closets and full bathrooms. One room was a nursery, and she thought the big one on the far end was the master since it had such a lovely view, but the closet only held a guest robe.

She went to the other end of the hall and *this* was the master. The walk-in closet here was a dressing room. It was lined with sliding doors and held a wall of shoe shelves, and there was a round upholstered bench in the middle. There was even a tailoring platform placed before a trifold mirror in the corner.

"I'm starting to think we're not in Goderich anymore," she whispered to Peyton.

The bathroom was as extravagant as everything else with French doors leading onto a private veranda and a massive shower that looked more like a sci-fi transportation device with nozzles and buttons and glass. In a bowed window, a jet tub invited her to relax and contemplate her life choices.

Amelia was questioning them. Big-time. Misgivings had been creeping in at every turn. While they'd been in Toronto, she'd been in shock, not fully appreciating Hunter's wealth until they had married and she had climbed aboard his private jet. *His*. Vienna had one, and there was a corporate one as well. In Banff, she had fallen into an illusion that she was visiting an all-inclusive upscale resort. It was a nice place to visit, but it wasn't her life. No one actually lived like this.

Except Hunter.

And her?

Things grew even more surreal as the day wore on. People arrived. She met her personal assistant and her West Coast stylist. The housekeeper asked her questions about menus, and a prospective nanny arrived.

Amelia had chatted with the agency a few times through the week, shortlisting résumés, but it hadn't hit her that the decision to hire someone would rest with her—as it should, but it still freaked her out. She barely felt qualified to be a mother. Suddenly she found herself interviewing an accomplished woman her own age who had a degree in early childhood education, held a lifeguard certificate, and was fluent in English, French, Punjabi and Spanish, "Because my last family spent their winters in Mexico."

Matinder was not only more highly educated than Amelia, she was more prepared for Hunter's lifestyle.

Amelia introduced her to Peyton, who loved her, and Hunter, who asked questions around whether Matinder was prepared to travel internationally and whether she had pediatric first aid. She did. Of course she did. She had also worked briefly with a toddler who was hearing impaired. She knew basic ASL that she said would be useful for Peyton before she became verbal.

They arranged for her to start the following day.

"Because we have that party tomorrow night," Hunter added.

What party? Amelia recalled her PA asking if she wished to accept the invite while her stylist had promised to pull a few outfits together. She had told them to ask Hunter whether they would attend. Apparently, he had said yes.

Great, she thought with dread.

Hunter was still withdrawn at dinner, and Amelia thought a few times that she ought to try harder to discover how he was feeling about his best man marrying his bride. She kept thinking that if she couldn't bring sophistication and social cachet to this marriage, at least she could offer him emotional support.

He didn't seem to want that, so she began to quietly hyperventilate. Until now, all the pressure on her had been from the outside. Paparazzi followed them and people judged her, but she was mostly able to shrug it off because they didn't know her.

Tomorrow, however, she would have to step into a role that was completely foreign to her. When she organized a dinner or spoke at a fundraiser, she would make missteps and be critiqued on her decisions and actions.

No wonder he had wanted to marry someone like Eden. Amelia was going to embarrass him as badly as his stepmother had, and she wouldn't even do it on purpose.

When she got Peyton settled for the night, she found him waiting for her in their bedroom.

They barely spoke. She was so desperate for reassurance she went straight into his arms. Whatever emotions were churning within him translated into white-hot passion. His hard arms caught her close, and his hungry mouth ravished hers.

She sobbed with relief. Here she didn't have to think about what a misfit she was in his life. Here they were equals.

At least, that's what she thought as he carried her to the

bed. As they stripped and he came down to cover her, she pressed his shoulders, urging him to fall onto his back.

She was no shy virgin any longer. They had become familiar enough with each other's bodies that she didn't hesitate to pour herself over him, slithering her nudity against him and sweeping her hands over his shoulders and ribs and stomach. She was being more aggressive than she ever had been, caressing and kissing across his chest. His rib cage expanded beneath her lips as he drew a deep, shaken breath.

She loved it. She smiled and stroked her hands lower, caressed his powerful thighs and the flesh between, hearing him growl in pleasure. When she shifted lower to take him in her mouth, his hand on her shoulder tightened and he groaned like she was his salvation. Like he needed this. *Her*.

Excitement and sweet exaltation poured through her. She did everything she could to drive him wild, reveling in the intimacy. In the trust it implied. She was always the one to break first, but this time she would take him into that vulnerable place and know that she gave him *this*.

"Stop," he said in a jagged voice.

She lifted her head, feeling almost drugged, she was so lost to the act. "What's wrong?"

"What do you want?" His harsh question, delivered in that gravelly tone, didn't make sense.

"You." Wasn't that obvious?

"Take me, then." He dragged her up and atop him. "Do you need— No," he said with satisfaction as he caressed between her straddled thighs and found her slippery with desire. "You're more than ready, aren't you?"

So ready. She was shivering, holding still for his explorations because it felt so good. So necessary.

He held himself for her to impale upon and she groaned out as his thickness filled her.

This was better, she agreed hazily. She wanted them to

be together when they finished. She began to move, losing herself in these rhythms they had taught each other. This was where they were not just equal, but the same. They wanted and sought as one. They reached and rose and lifted each other toward that pinnacle, arriving—

She shattered, dimly aware of his hips lifting hard beneath her. His hands gripped her waist, firm and unyielding. His grimace was one of ultimate control as he withheld his own release, leaving her to shudder and cry out and lose herself while he watched.

As she folded limply onto him, he rolled her beneath him and slowly began to pump, bringing her still-quivering senses sharply back to life. He knew exactly how to touch her, when to scrape his teeth on her neck and where to trail his fingertips on her breasts to make her nipples peak and sting. He knew how to lift her hips so the angle of his penetration hit a spot that had her arching with acute pleasure, a cry of anguished joy torn from her throat.

Then, only then, when he had her again on the brink of another explosive orgasm, did he allow himself to let go and take her over the edge with him.

That culmination, shared with him this time, was so powerful and glorious, it brought tears to her eyes.

But the sting lingered behind her eyelids when they were both weak and panting on the sheets. They weren't equals, she acknowledged, trying to swallow back the lump in her throat. She might be helpless to the chemistry that gripped them both, but he was impervious to it. Or at least, not as susceptible.

Maybe he had reasons for refusing to give up his control to her. Maybe he was determined to control *something*, given he was blindsided and helpless to do anything where his best friend and former bride were concerned.

Maybe she would know if he told her, but he only

spooned her into his front and exhaled as his arm grew heavy across her waist.

Despite her physical satisfaction and growing lethargy, her lashes stayed wet and her mind continued to churn with angst. She was hurt and she was frustrated that he wouldn't share with her and she knew why it ate at her so relentlessly.

She was starting to fall for him.

Oh, who was she kidding? She had begun falling for him last year, when she had let a man she'd only just met take her virginity. She had been angry and scorned and deeply hurt when he didn't want to see her again. When he had told her he was marrying someone else, the rejection, the sense of a chance missed, had leveled her. She had blamed her weepiness on losing Jasper, but a large part of her depression at that time had been because there had been no more chance with the only man who interested her.

Then she had had his baby and had felt even more connected to him. That's why she had let him put her on this bullet train into his life. Here was her chance to see what they might have had.

But they had nothing.

That was the harsh reality she was beginning to face.

Perhaps not nothing, but a lot less than she had dreamed of.

As she realized what sorts of romantic ideals she had let form over that week of their honeymoon—that he might come to love her—she quietly cringed at how childish that vision had been.

This was her life. And she would have to live up to it.

CHAPTER NINE

HUNTER GOT UP with Peyton and was handing her over to the newly arrived nanny when Amelia came to find them. She was dressed, but her hair was in a messy clip and she was still befuddled with sleep.

"Why didn't you wake me? Isn't she hungry?"

"I gave her a bottle." Amelia had started pumping so he could feed her. "And we'll be out tonight, so I thought you should sleep in."

He tried reading her expression, but she became wrapped up in chatting with Matinder, so he left them to it.

The truth was, he had left her sleeping because she'd almost killed him last night. He'd awakened wanting her—that was constant—but he'd also been disturbed by how close he'd come to simply letting go last night.

He'd been tense after a long, restless day of ruminating over Remy and Eden. The oddest thing about that news was, once the initial shock had worn off, he discovered he didn't care.

He cared about them as people, especially Remy. Hunter had met Remy in their first year of university. They had both been bored with the basic prerequisites they'd been forced to endure, going through the motions of earning paper credentials for work they already did. Unlike their classmates who were learning the theory of business, they had been deep in the practical trenches of their respective family corporations. Hunter had been leading Wave-Com's R&D team. "You're young," his father had told him. "Keep us ahead of everyone else." Remy had been running his family's airline with his grandfather. He'd been flying planes longer than he'd held a license to drive a car.

Aside from the tragic fact that Remy had lost both his parents while still in high school, Hunter had always envied him. Remy's family, spread among Paris, Montreal, Martinique and Haiti, was closely knit and very supportive of one another. Remy was good-looking, charming and smart. Everyone admired him for being a pilot and a talented vintner among his many other accomplishments.

"Chin up. No one likes the cable guy, but we all need him," Remy had noted once, proving himself sarcastically funny as well.

Remy was, simply, a good friend. As the court case had begun taking its toll on Hunter, when he'd still been reeling from his father's death, trying to keep the wheels from falling off the bus while fighting legal eagles and his dragon of a stepmother, Remy had insisted, "You need to unwind."

The weekend was supposed to be golf, a few drinks and no phones. When the server at a microbrewery had flirted with Remy, Hunter hadn't been the least surprised. He'd been taken aback that Remy suggested, "Ask your friend to join us."

Hunter had been lousy company and said so, but Remy had said, "For God's sake, man. Buy a pretty woman a drink and let her smile at you for an hour. That always cheers me up."

Now he came to think of it, that was the last time Hunter had spent any time with Remy. He had congratulated Hunter on the legal win. Vienna had hosted a small party to celebrate and Hunter had invited Eden since they had begun to date. Remy had arrived, but quickly mentioned another engagement.

When Hunter had called to ask him to be his best man, there had been a brief pause and a cryptic remark about a business rivalry with Eden's brother Micah. It had sounded like old news and something that happened across the pond.

"Who else would I ask? No one else would put up with me," Hunter had insisted.

"Then it would be my honor," Remy had assured him.

He had made an appearance at the engagement party, but hadn't lingered. He had attended Hunter's bachelor party, which had been another golf weekend, this time in British Columbia's wine country. Remy had jokingly had "the talk" with Hunter, asking, "Are you sure about this marriage?"

At least, Hunter had thought he was joking.

As far as he knew, Remy and Eden had only met once before Hunter had reintroduced them, but now Hunter wondered. And even though he found the pair's rushed marriage strange, he discovered that he felt no envy for Remy. He should. His friend was marrying the woman Hunter had thought would be his ideal match. Hunter could no longer imagine being married to Eden, though. Not now that he was with Amelia.

He wasn't sure if he'd been misguided in his thinking when he had proposed to Eden, or was falling into the trap of self-indulgence with Amelia. Either way, it seemed he couldn't and shouldn't trust his own judgment.

That inner conflict had been eating at him when he met up with Amelia in their bedroom.

She had leaped on him in a way that had been gratifying. Too gratifying. His cynical brain had wondered if she was beginning to recognize her power over him and exercise it. Yet when he had asked her what she wanted, she had said, *You.*

Possibly the most ominous demand of all.

He mentally balked at letting down his guard. The barriers he had erected against her had to stay in place, for his own peace of mind, but he could tell she was nervous about tonight. He felt her agitation as she handed Peyton off to him, heading into a spare bedroom to have her hair and makeup done.

Hunter felt guilty for putting her through this. He had a learned aversion to parties, but a man in his position had no choice about attending at least some of them. Vi had always been a sport about going in his place when it made sense, but there was no avoiding this one.

This first appearance as a couple was inevitable, he reminded himself. He couldn't do anything about the clouds hanging over them, so he and Amelia would just have to power through.

He was nervous, he realized as he poured himself a second drink while waiting for her. This was the first time in a long time that he was escorting someone so important to him.

He shrugged against that word. *Important*. It wasn't wrong. Not only was Amelia the mother of his child, she was his wife. He cared about her, which was only right. A person ought to care about their spouse, but he didn't like how vulnerable his depth of caring made him feel. He didn't like how helpless he felt taking Amelia to a party where she would be measured against Eden.

He wasn't concerned for his own sake. He didn't care what people thought of him. If there had been a bright side to Irina's constant scenes, it had been to forever inoculate him against embarrassment. His depth of concern for public opinion only went as far as caring how it affected the company. It was his job to watch for bad publicity and fix it.

Amelia, however, was not so impervious to censure.

He'd seen it when she had caught glimpses of online troll dung. She wanted to reflect well on him and Hunter wanted to say a weary, *It doesn't matter*. People would talk behind their hands regardless.

He heard her on the stairs and turned, catching a glimpse of her legs. Never mind stopping traffic. Those stems stopped his heart, playing peekaboo through the uprights as she picked her way down in a pair of gold sandals with rhinestone buckles against her ankle and a lethal heel.

The rest of her appeared in a short, sleeveless dress in a nude color with gold beading in geometric patterns. The weight of the beads caused the fabric to rest against her curves in the most arresting way.

Her hair had been cut before the wedding, removing the blond, leaving a rich brunette curtain that landed on her shoulders and flipped up with a vintage flair. Her makeup was only slightly heavier than what she applied herself, but it managed to make her eyes look bigger and darker, her lips plumper, and her skin radiant.

"Unity picked it out," she said self-consciously as she came to a halt halfway toward him. "I thought it disguised the fact that I was still carrying some baby weight, but it's too short, isn't it? Now that I've put on heels?"

"Define 'too short.' Because I think you look hot as hell."

"I'm supposed to look like your *wife*." She plucked at the hem.

"My wife can't be hot? Change if you're uncomfortable, but I think that's perfectly on brand. For you, actually, not just for my wife. You were wearing something much shorter when we met, and it suited the hell out of you, same as this."

"Big surprise that all you can remember about me is my legs." She flicked her hair behind her shoulder.

"Excuse me, but your legs are not the only thing I remember. They're not even the first thing that drew my attention." They were the second. "I heard you laugh and it was so engaging, I turned my head to see what the joke was." Then he had caught an eyeful of her smiling profile, her pretty legs and ample breasts and straw-colored hair. He had immediately tried to pretend to himself and Remy that he wasn't mesmerized.

She made a noise of uncertainty, looking down. "You really think this is okay? Because I feel like people are going to talk about me behind my back."

"They absolutely will. Let's give them something to talk about." He waved her to come closer and reached for the box he'd left on the end table.

"Oh," she murmured as she realized it was a jewelry box.

"This is where I went today." He opened it to show her the necklace with rose-gold links in a basket weave pattern. Seven pink and white stones were interspersed between them across the front half.

"It's beautiful, but— Wait," she said, balking when he drew a circle in the air, indicating she should turn and lift her hair. "Those aren't real, are they?"

"You think I bought you glass and plastic? They're diamonds and pink sapphires, yes. Why? Don't you like them?"

Her eyes grew wide enough to swallow her face. "I'm already nervous, Hunter. I can't walk around wearing something so expensive. What if I lose it?"

"It's insured. And I don't know any jewelry designers who go to the trouble of making art hoping it will sit in a safe. Show it off. Turn around."

She did, and he set the chain against her throat, closing it behind her neck, then setting a kiss there, wanting to linger and breathe in her fragrance of almonds and whipped cream.

"Is it a special designer? Why are people going to talk about it? What should I say if they ask?"

"That it's your push present."

"What? Hunter!" She whirled to face him. "Push presents are a fad created by advertisers to sell stuff to gullible dads."

"It worked. But I am very grateful for our daughter, you know." He traced a line along the inside of the necklace so it was a perfect arc beneath her collarbone.

She shivered, and he would bet this necklace that her nipples had just peaked behind her nursing pads. It was a heady enough thought to have him considering blowing off the party and heading back upstairs.

"I'm grateful for her, too," Amelia said with a hint of impatience. "Does that mean I owe you a trinket for your manly effort in punching through a condom?"

"Ha!" The remark caught him so off guard, he couldn't help laughing. Damn, but she knew how to lift him out of whatever ruminations he was trying to wallow in. "I appreciate the thought, but no."

"Well, I didn't need anything, either, but thank you." She set her hand on his lapel and lifted her mouth to invite his kiss. Her pleased smile at making him laugh was so cute, he took a mental picture.

For one second, he thought, *I don't need anything else, either. Only you.*

"There's more," he said, eschewing the kiss and clearing his throat. He stepped back to take her hand while he fished in his pocket. Then he slid the diamond ring onto her finger.

"No. Hunter. We talked about this. Oh, gosh," she said helplessly. Covetously.

When they had prepared for their wedding, she had said she only wanted a plain wedding band because she didn't want to accidentally scratch Peyton. They hadn't been engaged, she said. It would be silly to wear a ring to signify the handful of hours before they married. They had settled on a platinum band with three baguette diamonds, and there hadn't been a matching ring, anyway.

Hunter had spotted this one today, though, while he'd been picking out the necklace. Seven baguette diamonds stood at different heights like a miniature city skyline. When it sat nestled against her wedding band, the effect was not unlike the hazy silver shape of Toronto against the glittering water as they'd stood on the shoreline last year.

That sounded far too sentimental and romantic to admit, though.

"People will expect you to wear one, so put it on when we go out. I'll give you the combination to the safe in the bedroom. You can store it there when you take it off."

"Okay. Thank you." She made a micro adjustment to the ring, lashes lowered, voice subdued. When she lifted her face, her smile wasn't as warm or bright as it had been, making his stomach pitch.

"Careful of my makeup," she said as he lowered his head to kiss her. "Let's not give them *that* to talk about."

Amelia was so nervous her hand was clammy in Hunter's as he drew her into the party.

As if the pressure couldn't get any worse, their host turned out to be a television personality. His wife held this solstice party every summer to celebrate the longest day of the year. The point was to arrive before sunset, so it was eight o'clock. The rain had ceased and the cloudy horizon was turning pink and pale gold.

Conversation lulled as they entered. Several pairs of curious eyes turned on them.

Amelia felt a pinch on her ring finger and realized she

had tightened her grip on Hunter's hand, causing her new ring to dig into her flesh. What a scaredy-cat.

She didn't want to think about that ring, either. For a few seconds, she had been charmed and delighted. If the necklace affirmed his joy at having a daughter, the ring must be a symbol of his gladness at marrying her, right?

Then Hunter had reduced its significance to carrying an umbrella in case it rained. *People will expect it.*

"Hunter!" Their hostess approached with a beaming smile. "We're so glad you both could make it."

"So are we." He introduced Amelia, and they began making the rounds.

Her on-and-off career in the service industry came to her rescue. The ability to gauge when and how much small talk to make was a surefire way to improve tips.

Each time she met someone new, she asked a variation of, "Where's home?" or "Where do you plan to travel next?"

She liked to make the other person feel superior, too. She said, "I'm dying to get to know the Okanagan labels. Which wineries do you recommend?" and, "That's my father's team. He would disown me if I didn't root for them, but he's not here so I'll secretly agree with you. They're playing terribly this year."

Hunter stood by, interjecting with his own droll remarks, making her feel safe and funny and pretty. She began to relax and enjoy herself.

That's why she was so aghast when a viper struck.

A woman who had had one too many leaned in to ask, "What do you think of this sudden marriage between Eden Bellamy and Remy Sylvain? Sounds like Hunter wasn't the only one stepping out. What can you tell me about it?"

"Nothing," Amelia blurted, falling back on something her mother used to say. "There's no such thing as harmless gossip. It always stabs someone." She wanted to cringe as soon as the pompous words came out of her mouth. Who did she think she was?

Clinging to her last shred of dignity, she said, "Would you excuse me? I should check with our nanny."

She hurried away without even looking at Hunter, far too mortified that she had done the one thing she had sworn she wouldn't. She had embarrassed him.

CHAPTER TEN

AMELIA WAS SITTING in a quiet window seat on a landing, trying to compose a text to Carina to explain her behavior, when she realized with a lurch of guilt that Hunter was coming up the stairs toward her.

"Is Peyton all right?" he asked. "You've been gone a while."

"Totally fine. Fast asleep. Matinder showed her to me over video chat." Which had made Amelia feel like a helicopter mom, among other things. She gathered her courage and just blurted it. "I'm really sorry I embarrassed you. I shouldn't have said that to that woman. She took me by surprise, but that's no excuse. I'll keep my cool next time, I promise."

"Is that what you're doing up here? Self-flagellating? That woman embarrassed herself. For God's sake, Amelia. There is a vast difference between standing up for yourself and tearing someone else down." He leaned his shoulder against the wall. "I'm the furthest thing from humiliated. I'm glad to know you can hold your own when someone crosses a line."

"Really?" Her vision blurred she was so relieved.

"Yes, really. Come here." He drew her to her feet and into a warm hug. "And thank you for refusing to gossip about them."

"It was the truth," she said with a scrape in her throat. "I barely know them. Their marriage doesn't affect me, so I have nothing to say."

"Except?" he prompted, as if he heard the word silently tacked to the end.

"Unless…" she corrected into his tie, then lifted her gaze to his, making herself put this into words. "Unless their marriage makes you regret ours?"

"No," he said firmly, frowning with confusion. "Why would it? My only regret about our relationship is that it caused me to hurt Eden. I feel like I led her on." His mouth curled with self-disgust. "That wasn't fair. If she has since found consolation with Remy…" He shrugged. "More power to them."

She studied his expression, searching for shadows, but he looked and sounded as though he was being completely frank. She offered a crooked smile.

"Thank you. I was feeling really sick about that." She nodded toward the party. "I felt like I'd been rude to a customer and was about to be fired."

He snorted. "First of all, if one of us tries to fire the other, a lot of lawyers will get involved, so let's save it for a truly heinous offense, like leaving the cap off the toothpaste. Also, that woman isn't your customer. She is definitely not always right."

"True, but…" She slid a finger along his tie. "I feel like I have to impress people and I'm not… impressive."

"I was thinking the complete opposite." He rubbed her back. "You're better at putting people at ease than I am. They enjoy chatting with you."

"Oh, please," she scoffed.

"Hey. *I* wanted to spend more time with you. That's the reason you wound up in my room last year. If I'd found you boring or unpleasant, I wouldn't have invited you to join me there, killer legs notwithstanding. Be yourself, Amelia. Be polite until someone breaks that social contract, then do what you did and stop giving them your time."

She was so touched, she hugged him and the words almost came out of her. *I love you.*

For an extra second, she held on to him, eyes closed as she absorbed the rainbow of refracted emotions that shot into every corner of her being. Sparkling gold and passionate pink, earnest orange, possessive green and a true blue edged with dark indigo shadows of knowledge that he didn't love her back.

He kissed her temple.

"And listen. I don't care if people think I sneaked away with my wife to neck in a stairwell, but if that's what you want to do, we should go home and do it properly."

"We'll stay for another twenty minutes. Let's not be obvious."

"Deal."

Over the next weeks, things settled into a comfortable routine.

Hunter went into his downtown office a few times a week, but worked from home on the other days. He took her to Calgary for a two-night trip, mostly so she could visit with Vienna while he was at work. Auntie Vi suitably spoiled her niece with dozens of outfits and toys, admitting while Amelia opened them that she and Neal had been trying to conceive for two years.

"I'm so sorry." Amelia let the panda-patterned romper drop into her lap. "It must have hurt so much when I came along with my unplanned, first-try surprise."

"Not at all. I'm happy for my brother. And I'm only twenty-five," Vienna dismissed with an overly cheerful smile. "We have time to explore options if it doesn't work out naturally."

"I'm sure it will." Amelia left it at that, but it was a good reminder that even someone like Vienna, who seemed to have everything she could ever want, still struggled with things that felt basic to existence.

Amelia mentioned it to Hunter when they were back in Vancouver a few nights later, enjoying a rare evening at home. "Did you know Vienna and Neal are trying for a baby?"

"I did." He hesitated, as though not wanting to say too much. "She's wanted to start their family for some time."

Does Neal? She closed her mouth against saying it, but while Vienna had taken every opportunity to cuddle Peyton, Neal had barely looked at his niece. Not everyone liked other people's children, Amelia understood that, but for a married man starting a family, he talked an awful lot like a bachelor on his way to a sporting match with his toxic friends.

"How long have they been married?" she asked curiously.

"Four years." He mentally calculated. "Coming up to five."

"Gosh, she married young."

"Unlike us," he mocked drily, then sobered. "I tried to keep her from rushing into it, but Vi had her reasons."

"Such as? You don't have to tell me." She immediately corrected herself. "It's just that she said something at, um, the wedding. I keep thinking about it."

"What was that?"

"That it's not as easy to call off a wedding as it sounds. I feel like only someone who has actually contemplated doing it would say that."

"Little did she know it's easy as hell. Just walk away,"

he said with a darkly ironic curl to his mouth, then he grimaced. "I wish she had called it off. She had a more complex relationship with our father than I did. He assumed I would take over and I was interested in the business. No matter what else went on, what disagreements we had, we always had that common ground to come back to. Vi didn't have the same connection with him, but she wanted to feel like she was contributing to our collective benefit. Her marriage to Neal looked very good on paper. His family made their fortune in video rentals, eventually expanding into entertainment tech and home computers. It was a good fit to merge that under our umbrella, and Neal is a savvy salesman. I can't deny he closes deals."

"But?" she prompted.

"But I can't stand the man. He cheated on her at his bachelor party. I told her to call it off. Dad told her to get over it and finish what she started. She listened to him." He stabbed a breaded oyster and ate it.

"He didn't have much sympathy because his wife cheated on him?" she guessed.

"Or didn't care that she did? I don't know why he thought Vi shouldn't be upset, but I had a chat with Neal. He understands that any future infidelity won't be tolerated by *me*, though he still finds ways to be a jerk to her. I support her having a family if that's what she wants, but I also want to tell her to cut her losses. It's a tough line to walk."

His protective older brother act always made her wistful for her own.

Which reminded her in a roundabout way of something else they needed to discuss.

"Vienna told me your birthday is coming up—"

"I don't celebrate it," Hunter cut in flatly.

"She told me that, too." She smiled faintly at how firm he sounded. "She didn't say why."

"We're cleaning out the entire family closet tonight?" He sighed and picked up his wine, taking a healthy gulp. "When I was turning eleven, Irina arranged my birthday party. It was the first time she had done something nice for me. My whole class was invited along with their parents. I realize now, as an adult, it was an excuse for her to stage a raging party for day drinkers. At the time, it felt like I was cementing myself as Most Popular Boy heading into middle school."

Another big gulp, then he set his glass aside.

"You also have to realize that I wasn't as inured to her behavior as I am today. This was the first time I'd really seen that side of her. She got worse over the years. Much worse, but this was my first exposure to her being a sloppy drunk and making off-color jokes about how long I spent in the shower."

"Oh, no. Hunter, I'm so sorry."

"I'm not even there yet," he assured her, holding up a hand. "Dad thought it was hilarious. All the other parents were laughing. I felt like the biggest tool alive when I was forced into the decorated chair, the center of attention as I opened all my gifts. I didn't want anything except for the day to be over. I didn't open her gift. I pretended I didn't see it and, once everyone went back to eating their cake and ice cream, I took it into the house. I was going to throw it away in the laundry room, but there they were."

Amelia sank back in her chair, asking a dread-filled, "Who?"

"Irina and one of the dads. I didn't even have a full grasp of what sex was. I sure as hell didn't know you could do it by dropping your pants around your ankles and bending a woman over the washing machine."

"No. That's *wrong*. A child isn't equipped to process that!"

"Tell me about it. I felt like I was in the wrong for seeing them. I didn't know whether I should tell my dad. I was sick about it."

"Was there anyone you could talk to? Your grandparents?"

"I would have taken it to my grave," he said grimly. "But about a week later, Dad got on me about how I was treating her. I couldn't even look at her. She told him I was sulking because I'd caught her in the laundry room. She told him flat out in very blunt terms what she'd been doing and with whom. Like it was a joke that I'd seen it and was upset about it."

"What did your father do?" There was an ache behind her breastbone as she watched old emotions paint across his face—anger and humiliation, impotence and disillusion.

"He blustered about how I should have knocked."

"No," she breathed.

"I heard them arguing in the bedroom later. It didn't last long, and she was still there the next morning. She was always still there." He took another gulp of wine. "And somehow that other man's wife found out. I didn't tell anyone, but the kid blamed me for his parents' divorce. It was my party where he cheated. That stuck to me for years."

"I'm so *sorry*."

"Not your apology to make. And like I say, her antics grew worse. I learned not to give her opportunities. No more birthday parties."

"And your father stayed married to her." She couldn't believe it.

"He did." He nodded.

Amelia felt so sad for both him and Vienna, having to grow up and grow a thick skin when they should have been able to make their own mistakes and have their father be there for them the way hers had for her.

"Thank you for telling me. I just thought it was contradictory. Vienna said you don't celebrate, but when she told me the date, I thought it must have been the reason for your golf weekend last year."

"No." He shook his head. "That was a mental health break that happened to fall on my birthday. But that's *our* anniversary," he realized. "We can celebrate that. We'll go for dinner. Or would you rather make a weekend of it? Visit the Okanagan?"

"Actually…" She folded her arms in front of the plate she had yet to finish. "It's also the anniversary of Jasper going missing. I'd rather spend it with Dad, if you don't mind. He's heading back to Goderich this week."

Hunter swore and sat back. "Of course. I didn't even think. I need to spend a few weeks in Toronto anyway. We'll visit him from there. Let me know if he has any trouble with paparazzi once he's home. The security system was installed, but that will only protect his privacy while he's inside the house."

"Thanks. I will." He was doing so much for her father. For all of them. She hated to ask for more, but, "Since we're on the topic… Have you heard anything from your friend? About Jasper?" There had been a few brief news pieces that had coincided with the coverage of their marriage.

Amelia Lindor, sister of Jasper Lindor, who went missing in South America last year and is presumed deceased…

She was glad his disappearance was being noted again, but it didn't seem to be pushing anyone to investigate further.

"To be clear, I golfed with Orlin at a charity tournament once. That's as well as I know him. He sent their internal investigation to my PA, but it doesn't say anything more than what you've already told me. They do mention a life insurance policy," he said in a very neutral tone.

"And that I've pushed them to pay it out? I know how that looks." She picked up her fork, but had lost her appetite.

She could feel the weight of Hunter's suspicion in his gaze.

"Think about it," she rushed on with subdued fury. "They say we have to wait seven years for that money because there's no proof he's dead, yet they want us to believe there's no reason to investigate further. They know I'll use that money to hire someone to go there and look for him so they refuse to pay it."

He blinked, but not before she saw the shadows of pity behind his eyes.

"I know I'm grasping at straws," she muttered, dropping her fork with a clank. "But you don't know what it's like to come up against someone like you! All the power is weighted on your side. All the money and information and..." She picked up her napkin and pressed it to her stinging eyes, lungs seized by injustice.

"You want someone to blame. I understand that, but I have nothing to do with this, Amelia."

"I know that." Her mouth still quivered with futile anger. With frustrated loss. Her heart was cracked in two and there was a part of her that felt as though marrying him was consorting with the enemy. "But if Jasper suddenly reappeared, he would find me living like this. He would think I had completely forgotten about him. What if he's hurt, Hunter? What if he can't get home and I'm not even trying to help him?"

She was going to fall apart.

"I have to check on Peyton." She rose abruptly and threw her napkin over her half-eaten meal.

"Amelia." She had the sense his hand came out behind her, but she hurried away.

Hunter's first reaction when he had read that Amelia was pressing for the insurance pay out had been a cynical one. Money fueled all things, all people. That's what he'd been taught, and it was borne out by his lived reality nearly every day.

Nearly.

Amelia wasn't motivated by financial gain. He had known that when she'd thrown his money back in his face as she walked out of his room last year. Amelia ran on love, especially where her brother was concerned.

Hunter didn't take it personally that she had flared up at him. He understood. Grief had its own cycles, and he still became moody in April, which was the time of year when his mother had passed.

Also, he might not be at fault for Jasper's disappearance, but he felt some guilt as he brooded on it. He *was* the type of Goliath she and her father were up against. More pertinently, he could have done more for her that morning when the disappearance happened. He hadn't wanted to involve himself in someone else's drama, having enough in his own life.

Her anguish ate at him. He asked her to send him her file of correspondence and spent several days going through it.

It was a relentless and heart-wrenching effort on her part, shaking every tree she could find without success. His own grim conclusion was that Jasper was gone. Her brother had been sent to Chile to survey specific terrain. Against instructions, he had gone a different direction. This was the source of their "walked away from the job site" claim. A month or so into his disappearance, there had been a landslide. His interpreter had been among those found in the rubble.

Amelia's argument was that Jasper understood the dangers of the mountains. He had worked in avalanche control for several winters. He would recognize dangerous conditions.

Hunter was skeptical that anyone could have such a heightened sixth sense, but he couldn't shake the contradiction she had pointed out. Why wouldn't REM-ex pay out the insurance if they were so confident her brother was dead?

He made discreet arrangements for boots on the ground in Chile. At least his own conscience would be satisfied that he had done all he could for her.

He didn't tell her, though. He would wait for the report. The last thing he wanted was to tease her and Tobias with false hope.

Amelia was subdued when they arrived at her childhood home two weeks later. It was a small bungalow in a modest neighborhood, well maintained with a tidy yard. Peyton's bedroom was filled with secondhand furniture, but it had clearly been assembled with care.

The somber reason for their visit was lightened by the baby. Peyton was becoming a real character with an infectious giggle and an expressive face. She always wiggled and crowed with excitement when one of her parents reached to pick her up and, cutest of all, she remembered Tobias. He sat down in his chair and held out his arms. As Amelia bent to place her in his lap, Peyton gave Tobias a brief look of confused anxiety, almost seeming about to cry, but the second he took her, she folded right into his chest.

"It's that scratchy beard," Amelia teased, pinching her father's whiskers. "I would know a hug from you blindfolded. Like a baby duck imprinting on its mother's feathers."

"This little duckling is sure getting strong," Tobias said with gruff affection. "I can barely hold on to her."

It was a touching moment that put smiles on all their faces, but later, when Hunter came back from changing Peyton, he found Tobias trying to comfort Amelia through a very weak moment.

She was sobbing uncontrollably, and Tobias was saying gruffly, "No, chicken. He wouldn't want you breaking your heart like this. Shush now."

Something cracked in Hunter's chest, ringing a hard enough ache through him that he had to take Peyton back into her bedroom and breathe through it.

As he rocked his child, he had to wonder how he would cope in Tobias's shoes. Not well, that was for damned sure. This little sprite was so much a part of him, he couldn't imagine his life without her. As for her mother...

He couldn't stand that Amelia was hurting. He did have all the money and power and influence, as she had accused him, yet he couldn't fix what was wrong for her. He had a half dozen homes, all big enough to fit this one inside it, and she didn't care. She only wanted what he couldn't give her. It was humbling.

She slipped in to join him, wiping a balled-up tissue under her eyes as she asked in a tear-hoarsened voice, "Is everything okay? You didn't come back."

"It looked like you and your dad needed a minute." He lifted his arm with invitation.

She pressed herself to his side, slipping one arm behind his back. The other encircled their baby, who sleepily left her head on his shoulder.

For a few breaths, they stood quiet, both watching Peyton chew her fist.

"Sometimes I wonder if Jasper's spirit made her happen," Amelia confided softly, brushing a tender hand over

Peyton's fine hair. "Maybe he knew she would give me and Dad a reason to keep going after we learned he was gone."

Hunter hugged her closer and pressed his lips to her forehead.

Then he had to admit, "I don't actually find the idea of your brother being in the room with us last summer very comforting."

She hugged herself into him and shook with laughter, muffling it against his chest.

He smiled past the ache in his tight throat, pleased he could give her that at least.

CHAPTER ELEVEN

BEFORE THEY LEFT, Amelia tried to convince her father to move to Vancouver. He wanted to stay in his home and continue to see his friends every day, but he agreed to visit soon.

Wistful, Amelia hugged him goodbye and left for Toronto with Hunter.

"You'll have time to pop out and see him again before we go back to Vancouver," Hunter reminded in a consoling tone. "Would you feel better if we moved here so you would be closer to him?"

"I'm not sure. I like Vancouver." She had started to make a network of friends there through a baby group. "But I worry about Dad feeling lonely, even though I think he found it stressful for us to live with him. He felt a lot of responsibility to provide for Peyton and keep up with her, but he's not as spry as he was when Jasper and I were her age."

"That's why he found the man who is responsible for her," Hunter noted. "I'm glad he did." He looked down at Peyton with such tenderness, Amelia's heart fluttered. "We don't really have to decide until she starts school, but give it some thought."

"Are you being considerate? Or do you really not care where we live?" It seemed laughable to her that he would leave such a huge decision up to her.

"Both. I can tell that your father's house is what home means to you—retreat, security. Memories, I suppose." He shrugged. "You want to be deliberate about where you make one with me and Peyton so you can foster those same things, but I don't have that same desire for attachment to the place where I sleep. Comfort and convenience are my priorities."

Because he didn't have any *good* memories of home?

She felt such pity for the child he'd been, unable to *be* a child who felt safe and happy in the place where he slept.

"What?" His gaze sharpened and his expression stiffened at whatever he read in her eyes.

"Nothing." She looked away, hiding the melancholy she felt on his behalf. "I'm just wondering if I'm comfort or convenience?"

He snorted and picked up her hand to kiss her knuckle. "You're the luxury touch that makes one place more appealing than another."

"Ooh. Nice recovery," she teased.

They arrived at the penthouse then and kicked off a busy schedule of Hunter disappearing for meetings and other work commitments while Amelia planned dinner parties and attended engagements with him most nights.

When she had a moment, she conducted a discreet search online to see if Remy and Eden were in town. They seemed to be in France, and Amelia wasn't sure if she was relieved by that or not. Hunter was still being circumspect about that strange twist, but when Amelia looked at photos of Eden, the other woman looked so beautiful and put together, Amelia felt inadequate all over again.

She was getting better at this role of society wife, though. She enjoyed hosting a dinner for some of Hunter's executives and meeting their spouses. Thanks to her father, she was enough of a basketball fan that, when she and Hunter were invited to watch a game from the private box of a famous rap star, she had a great time.

Still pondering whether to make Toronto their home, she arranged a brunch for a handful of her old friends. She had lost touch with many of them in the last couple of years. They had finished school and started their careers while she had stayed home with her new baby and concentrated on finding Jasper.

It was fun to catch up, but she felt…different. Not better or worse than any of them. She was picking up the bill with a credit card her husband had given her and she didn't have a job of her own, so their opinion of her could have gone either way, but she knew she wasn't the person they had known a year ago. Jasper had changed her. Peyton had. *Hunter* had.

She had been raised to be independent, yet she relied on him. He could have made her feel small or resentful of that, especially after the way she had ruined his life plan with Eden, but he empowered her with decisions like where they would live. He made an effort to do his share with Peyton, saying, "I'll bathe her," leaving her to finish her book.

And sometimes, he did ridiculous things to spoil her, like when he took her to a charity gala aboard a restored tall ship in the harbor.

Amelia was feeling proud of her marriage and confident in her new self. She wore a sassy gold evening gown with a cutout at her cleavage. The skirt turned to fringe past her knees, showcasing her sling-back brass-colored sandals. Her hair was in a loose topknot with a few tendrils around her face, something that drew Hunter's gaze to her diamond stud earrings right before he made an obscene bid for a pair of chandelier earrings set with a half dozen pear-shaped yellow sapphires.

"You just called them gorgeous," he said when she nearly

choked on her champagne. "They would suit that gown better than the ones you're wearing, and it's a good cause. You want to support them, don't you?"

"As if I could say no when you put it like that." The charity was a children's hospital foundation. It was a very good cause.

"Okay, then. Buck up and accept them."

What an absurd man. She had to laugh as she leaned into him, giddy. It wasn't the earrings. It was the way he looked at her with amused affection while making his illogical argument, as though he knew how to tickle her funny bone and was smug that he'd found it.

In that moment, she loved him so much, the declaration lifted like helium in her chest, expanding in her throat. The words formed against her tingling lips.

"I lo—"

"Amelia?" a male voice interrupted.

She drew back and turned with a polite smile that faltered as her new life collided with an old one she had escaped via a painful wormhole.

"Gareth. It's nice to see you." Not. She could have lived her whole life without ever seeing this particular man's smarmy face again. He was handsome, no doubt about it. A regular Viking god with blond hair and golden stubble and a shiny tailored suit.

Most of the men had removed their jackets because the heat of the day lingered, even here on the water after the sun had gone down. Gareth still wore his double-breasted jacket buttoned closed, and Amelia knew why. His shoulders were padded and the cut gave him the wedge shape that he coveted, but didn't naturally possess. Gareth was all about how things looked, his female companions being of particular importance to his controlling eye.

"This is my husband, Hunter Waverly," Amelia said. "Gareth was a TA at my university."

"Professor now," Gareth said as he shook Hunter's hand. "Philosophy and English Lit."

"Ah. Good evening," Hunter said in a circumspect tone that Amelia had learned to read. His instincts were far better than hers. He already saw Gareth for what he was. She had been far too easily impressed by Gareth's superficial gleam.

She smiled at the woman by Gareth's side, expecting him to introduce her.

Gareth continued holding Hunter's cool stare. "It sounds like a quick trip to the altar. I've seen the news." He shifted his razor-sharp gaze to Amelia. "And you have a baby? How did that happen?" He made it sound like friendly teasing, but Amelia was still sensitive to that honed edge in his "jokes." How had Hunter pried open her legs, Gareth was asking.

She stifled a flinch of old scorn.

At the same time, she saw the young woman's smile fading into insecurity at being overlooked. Amelia saw *herself.* The other woman was twenty if she was a day, exactly the age Amelia had been when Gareth had impressed her with parties like this. He didn't have money, but he leaned on calculated social connections for invitations to things like this. He loved to seem wealthier and more popular than he really was. All of it was designed to elevate his ego and make others feel worthless.

"I'm Amelia." She thrust out her hand at the woman. "How are you enjoying the evening?"

"Chelsea. Hi." She grew flustered now that she'd been noticed.

"We're having a great time," Gareth said, throwing a possessive arm around Chelsea and speaking for her.

"You're one of his students?" Hunter asked as though he already knew she must be.

"No!" Chelsea's eyes widened in horror.

"It's summer break," Gareth reminded him smoothly. "We met at the end of last semester. She's not going back so…"

So it was okay for him to prey on her, even though Amelia estimated their age difference to be at least twelve years. She had every confidence that Chelsea's decision to put off going back to school had been Gareth's decision more than her own.

"You're enjoying the auction," Gareth noted, narrowing his eyes at the bid sheet for the earrings. "Driving up the bids." *As usual*, his tone said as he slid another look at Amelia.

What are you holding out for?

A future. Do you want to marry me or not?

Today, the idea of being married to Gareth made her sick. What a narrow escape she'd had! Poor Chelsea was still stuck in his quagmire, though.

"What were you studying?" Amelia asked her.

"Oh, um, marketing?" Chelsea flickered a glance at Gareth, who had no doubt been critical enough that she now questioned any passion or talent she'd had for the field.

"That's good luck." Amelia looped her hand around her husband's arm. "Hunter was saying yesterday that there would be positions opening up at the Toronto office once the interns left in September. You should apply."

"You should." Hunter didn't bat an eye at Amelia's fabrication. He reached into his pocket for a business card. She had never felt so connected to him on a purely psychic level. "Call that number and leave your name with my assistant."

"That's not necessary." Gareth tried to take the card.

Hunter held on to it and said very frostily, "I'm not talking to you." *Ever*, was the implied period on that sentence.

"Thank you." Chelsea swallowed and read the card.

Amelia instinctually knew Chelsea was memorizing the number because she fully expected Gareth to take it from her, costing her an opportunity.

"DM me on social media if you lose that," Amelia said with a warm smile. "It will take me a few days to get back to you because I don't check it myself. Some people are trolls." She dropped her smile and looked to Gareth. "Would you excuse us? I should check with our nanny." It had become her code to Hunter that she wanted out of a given conversation.

"Let's find a quiet corner. Good night." He nodded at Chelsea and turned away from Gareth without another look.

Hunter was jealous. It was a new color on him and one he didn't care for. At all. Especially because it wasn't even warranted. It had been plain as day to him that Amelia couldn't stand her ex. Also, he knew for a fact that her physical relationship with that egomaniac hadn't been as intimate as the one he currently enjoyed with her.

Even so, she had given that other man enough of her heart to leave it bruised. He recalled her talking about how Gareth had controlled and manipulated her. She gave that other man time he hadn't valued. Time he hadn't deserved.

Hunter wanted that time back. For her and for himself.

He was affronted, too. Disgusted that a professor had moved on her. He remembered her vaguely mentioning he was a TA during that first meeting with Carina, but it had slipped his mind with so many other things going on. And maybe Gareth had been a teaching assistant at the time and not on her course, but it still seemed wrong. Hunter was already planning to make a call to the chancellor. His family name was on the business program, and he signed off on generous donations every year. He sure as hell wouldn't be associated with a school that allowed its faculty to con students into dropping out so they could screw them.

"I feel like I should apologize," Amelia said as she returned to the bedroom from feeding Peyton. Their daughter had seemed to sense their return, waking as Amelia had been changing out of her gown. She had hurried down the hall in her robe, hair still up and jewelry still on.

"I feel like *I* should apologize," Hunter muttered. "He's the kind of man who makes all of us look like scumbags."

"He makes me appreciate that you're *not* like him. You must be wondering how I could have had anything to do with him, though." She sat down on the edge of the bed and removed her earrings, dropping them into the dish on the bedside table.

"I know how," he said with a snort. "You were young and inexperienced and *kind*. You give people the benefit of the doubt, always wanting to see the best in them. It annoys the hell out of me that he took advantage of that."

"That's a nice thing to say. I think." Her lips wobbled in a rueful smile. She looked at her fingers as she worked her engagement ring off. "I was gullible, but I became cynical after I stopped seeing him. I didn't believe any man was who he pretended to be."

"Is that what you thought when we met? That I was pretending to be someone else?"

"Kind of. I knew who you were so I knew you were rich, but I didn't think you were rich like this." She looked to the ceiling. "When I got into your room, I thought you had only booked it to impress whatever woman you brought back to it."

"I wasn't planning to bring anyone back to it," he said, insulted.

"I know that now." She lifted a shoulder. "And at least you were up-front about your lack of intentions."

"That wasn't my best moment," he noted with self-disgust. "I shouldn't have invited you to my room at all. We weren't as equal as I thought at the time." Virgin. He still couldn't fully grasp it. "I can't help feeling I took advantage of you."

"No, that's the thing. It was the first time a man had made a move on me who wasn't trying to make me feel guilty if I refused. I genuinely knew it was my choice whether to go with you or not. Weirdly, I felt like if I said no, I would be saying no to myself. It's hard to explain. I just knew I would regret it more if I didn't go with you than if I did. I had never felt like that with anyone else."

"Then you did regret it because you thought I was trying to pay you for it."

"I did hate you a little bit for that," she admitted, pulling her hair free. "It confirmed my worst suspicions of men, but thinking the worst becomes a habit that paves a straight road to despair and depression. With Jasper missing, I needed hope. I made myself look for the good in life. REM-ex gave us the runaround, but so many of our neighbors and friends were supportive and generous. Then Peyton became such a blessing. She's a little joy machine, so how could I stay a pessimist?"

"True." He chuckled, but drily. Amelia might have been disillusioned by Gareth, but Hunter hadn't exactly redeemed his sex. "I was in a terrible headspace last year. Still grieving Dad and even though I wasn't the least bit surprised by Irina going after the company, I couldn't believe it went as far as it did, legally. There was even a part of me that thought, hell, take it. The idea of not being responsible for Wave-Com sounded like heaven."

"You did mention that you were grumpy. Maybe Remy

said that." She fiddled with the tail on her robe's belt. "I just remember Cheryl and Remy doing all the talking while I sat there wondering if you were interested in me at all."

"That's funny." He released a gust of laughter as it suddenly came back to him. "I remember waiting for *you* to show some sign of interest. I don't know if you know this, but I'm rich and reasonably good-looking. I make great babies that come with all the latest features."

She snorted. "That *is* news to me."

"I'm used to women making it clear when they're interested, but you played it pretty damned cool."

"Oh? Tell me more about the women who come on to you. Maybe text it from one of the other bedrooms," she suggested with a flutter of her lashes and a sugary smile.

He ignored that. "Your friend was throwing herself at Remy, but you were quieter. When you did speak, you were funny, but you didn't say much about yourself. I wanted to know more. That's why I suggested we walk down to the water after they left. All you said was that it was a pretty night."

"Oh, gosh. Big surprise you weren't interested in more than a night with that brilliant conversation going on," she muttered with self-deprecation.

"No. I remember thinking how refreshing it was." He had the sense of a time slip. For a moment, he was there on the shore with her, coated in quiet blue light. "Everyone wants something from me." Attention or money or favors. Conversation. A diaper change, he thought ironically. "Even Remy, with the best of intentions, insisted I give myself a break to golf with him. You said it was a pretty night. It was a simple observation that didn't require me to agree or decide or do anything except stand in it with you. That made you precious."

He had held her hand, and there had been music in the distance and sweetness on the breeze. It had been the first time since childhood that he'd felt so unencumbered. So at ease.

Then they had kissed, and his brain had wanted to know her better in the more biblical sense.

The way she was looking at him made his heart seesaw in his chest. Having her in his life was like having potent wine and spring sunshine and hope on tap at all times.

Skepticism had been his stalwart friend for so long, he didn't know how to replace it with her, but he wanted to. She was softness and peace, and she brought light into the gloomy caverns inside him. She was a gift, and he didn't know how to make her understand how precious she was except to show her.

Hunter pressed his mouth to hers in the most tender way, achingly gentle so Amelia felt like the most treasured thing in existence. He cradled the back of her head and worshipped her with his touch, shaping the hills and dips of her figure, setting small fires across her skin that licked their way into her erogenous zones.

They made love often, but this was the first time it *felt* like love. As she basked in the sweet way he kissed across her cheek to her ear, as he blew softly against her neck and made her hair stand on end, she closed her eyes and pressed more deeply into him.

It meant so much to her that he'd wanted to know more about her. *Her.* Their baby might have brought them back together, but their connection had been there from the beginning, the tiny, barely visible strands as strong as they were fragile. Precious.

When his lips came back to hers, she poured her soul

into their kiss. Her passion. Her love. It felt so good to let it release without fear, holding nothing back.

His chest expanded as though he felt it. He squashed her breasts as he held her closer and deepened their kiss. She swore she could feel his heart pounding behind his rib cage, matching the urgency that was taking hold in her quickening blood.

This moment felt urgent yet not. She needed more of him. All of him. But they had their whole lives to discover every last thing about each other. They were still learning how to share their bodies and their hearts, and this was one of those times where they had moved into a new level of intimacy. Of caring and adoration.

Maybe he felt the same contradictory urges. He yanked at his shirt, then jerked open her belt, dragging her bared chest into contact with his.

She shivered and went on tiptoe, offering a deeper kiss, accepting his tongue and rubbing her hips against the steely shape behind his fly. She wanted him to know what he did to her. Only him. It had to be him.

"I want to be inside you," he rasped as he skated his damp lips down her throat. "I could lose myself in you. I really could."

"Yes." That's what she wanted, for all of him to overwhelm her. Fill her up and dissolve any barriers between them. "I'm yours." *Be mine.*

They skimmed away their clothes, and he pressed her to the mattress beneath his naked heat. She opened her legs in welcome, but he only guided himself against her wet folds, teasing and readying both of them before he slowly entered her.

They both released shaken sighs as he sank deep and held himself there.

Now the urgency subsided. They were where they

needed to be. She looked at him through vision that was hazed by love and lust. His green-gray eyes were equally glazed by passion, and his kiss was soft again. Tasting of benediction.

Now they existed in a place of pleasure and profound connection. Love. She loved him so much. And he was hers. Forever. She stroked her hands possessively across his shoulders and traced her fingers down his spine, smiling when she caused him to draw a breath of delight. She rolled her thumb across his nipple and slid her hand to where they were joined, making him growl as she played her hand there, pleasuring them both.

"You'll make me lose it before you're even close," he warned, dragging her hands up beside her head.

She would love to. Just once. "Would that be so bad?"

A shadow moved behind his glittering gaze, just enough to tell her that it would be. For him. She didn't understand that reservation in him. Weren't they surrendering to each other right now? Didn't he trust her as completely as she trusted him?

She would have cupped his jaw, but he kissed her and began to move with more purpose. She groaned, luxuriating in the powerful way he thrust and withdrew, driving both of them toward the pinnacle.

This was all she needed in life, this man moving within her, making her feel exalted as he sent shuddering reverberations of pure joy through her nerves and muscles and blood.

"Hunter," she gasped, arching in the throes.

"Let go, angel. Come so I can."

As if she could hold back. She was there, clinging to him as her vision turned to gold and her skin caught fire and her inner being melded with his.

"I love you," she cried as the world fell away and orgasm crashed onto her like a hundred-foot wave. "I love you. I love you."

His answer was a tortured noise of agony and a crushing embrace as he pinned his hips to hers and his whole body shuddered in his own defeat.

CHAPTER TWELVE

HUNTER'S HEART COULDN'T seem to settle back into his chest. As the thunder of climax subsided, his heartbeat shifted into an uneven, more suffocating rhythm.

Amelia came back from the bathroom and slipped on her nightgown before she slid into bed.

Most nights he was sorry for that thin barrier between them. She wore it so she could rise and go to Peyton if needed. Tonight, it was a necessary layer in the wall he was trying to shore up between them as she snuggled close into his side, resting her bent knee across his thigh. She settled her arm across his tense abdomen. Her head found the hollow of his shoulder and fine hairs caught against the stubble coming in on his jaw, exactly as it always did.

He smoothed it with his free hand, letting his other arm curl around her.

But he wouldn't fall into a dead sleep the way he usually did. An underlying tension ate at his core.

I love you.

She wasn't as boneless as she usually was, either. She didn't sigh and drift off. He felt the blink of her lashes tickling his skin.

I love you.

From the very beginning, he had sensed she could wield untold power over him if he wasn't careful. The very fact that they'd wound up in bed that first night when he'd had no intention of taking her to his room had warned him that he had a weakness where she was concerned. That's why he continued to fight the depth of passion she was able to wring out of him. That's why he held on to his control every single time they came together physically. He never let go until it was on his terms, not hers.

His fear had always been that if she gained the upper hand sexually, she would exact something from him—concessions and indulgence like his father had offered to Irina time and again. Hunter didn't want to be humiliated by his wife. He didn't want to be controlled by her.

Slowly, he had begun to believe Amelia would never ask anything from him that he wasn't prepared to give, but now he realized she would. Had. She wanted his heart.

Once he gave that up, there would be nothing left of himself. She would own him completely.

"Should we talk about it?" she asked with soft apprehension.

He could have pretended he was asleep, but that would have been the coward's way out. And it only would have prolonged a conversation that would have to happen regardless.

Trouble was, he didn't know what to say.

There was a long stretch of silence where neither of them moved. Then she swallowed and moved away to her side of the bed.

"It's fine if you don't want to say it back." Her voice broke in the middle of that statement, proving it wasn't fine at all.

He silently swore and set his arm across his eyes, wishing it hadn't come to this because he was going to hurt her. There was no way he would lie to her, though.

"You have to remember where I come from, Amelia.

What we have here, in this bed, is incredible. But it scares the hell out of me. I've seen what sexual infatuation does to a man."

Her breath was sucked in harshly, and she withdrew even farther across the mattress, so he couldn't feel the silk of her nightgown or the heat of her body.

"That's all you feel for me? You called me precious. I thought that meant you liked me. That you had feelings for me."

"Of course I care about you." His heart lurched at how precarious everything felt all of a sudden. He sensed he was on the verge of a public disgrace when there was only the two of them here in the dark, barely able to read each other's expressions. "I care about you a lot. I *trust you.*" To a point, but far more than most people in his life.

She didn't move, but he could feel her gaze trying to penetrate the shadows and read his expression. He felt her confusion and disappointment hitting him in chilly waves.

"I'm not trying to hurt you, Amelia. I'm explaining why I'm careful how deep I let myself fall. This is why someone like Eden seemed a safer bet. I knew I would never feel like this about her."

"Then you shouldn't have tried to marry her!" Her disgust hit him like wet muck. "And thanks for *that* heartfelt compliment. Do you know where *I* come from? A man who reminded me daily that there were other women out there who were better for him, exactly like you're doing right now. Gosh, I'm sooo lucky you picked me, though. Aren't I? Except you *didn't.*"

"Amelia." He tried to reach across to her, but she batted his hand away and sat up, throwing off the blankets.

"Do you know what's ironic, Hunter? Gareth kept telling me he loved me and I thought that meant he should want to marry me. When I asked if he would ever propose, he always dodged. You and I *are* married, but you don't love me and you have no plans to do so."

He came up on his elbow. "Do you want me to lie about something like that? The way he did?" Defensiveness shot the question out of him, sending his finger pointing toward the window and the boat on the water while a trail of fiery guilt went down his throat and expanded through his chest.

"No," she acknowledged with a huskiness in her voice. She swallowed, keeping her back to him. "Once again, you're warning me against having false expectations. That's pretty decent of you. I mean it," she added when he swore under his breath.

She stood.

"Where are you going? I'll sleep somewhere else if you're too angry to share a bed."

"I'm not *angry*," she choked out. "I'm hurt. Crushed. Maybe that's all it is," she said with a pang of weak hope. She sniffed and brushed at her cheek. "Maybe it will wear off in due course and won't hurt so much."

That hit him like a knee in the stomach. He lifted his hand, wanting to grab back something he felt slipping away, but he was too far away. There was only empty air between them. He let his hand fall back onto the blanket, and heaviness coated his heart.

"Lie down. We shouldn't argue about something like this when we're so emotional."

"Oh, are you emotional? How do I tell?" she asked over her shoulder. "You know, it would have been fine if you had simply said you weren't there yet. That you needed more time, but no. You had to tell me that you begrudge the great sex. That it makes you uncomfortable because you think I'm going to use it against you. I don't know what to do with that, Hunter. I only know I can't sleep beside you. Not tonight." She walked out.

He swore again, throat thick with the words he didn't know how to find. He didn't begrudge the sex. He respected it as the force it was. And he cared for her enough that his chest felt hollowed out and achy that he'd hurt her. That she'd chosen to leave their bed and go to Peyton's room.

He glanced at the baby monitor as he heard the soft rustle of her movements in the nursery as she climbed into the bed there. After a moment, he heard a shaken breath. A sniff.

Ah hell. He clenched his eyes shut. That's why she'd left. She wanted to cry. Alone.

CHAPTER THIRTEEN

THE NEXT FEW days were rough. Peyton was cutting her first tooth, crying on and off all day and night. That gave Amelia an excuse for her wan expression and red eyes, as well as a reason to sleep in the nursery.

She wasn't trying to punish Hunter or even avoid him, she just didn't know what to say or how to act around him. She half expected him to accuse her of withholding sex as some sort of power play, but he only asked if she wanted him to cancel his meeting to help with Peyton.

"There's nothing you can do," she said wearily. "She wants me."

Poor Matinder was constantly hovering with teething gel and frozen face cloths at the ready, wringing her hands with helplessness.

"I'll be home by five," he promised, and was.

When he walked into their bedroom and found her pacing before the windows, trying to soothe Peyton, he said, "Still fussing? I'll cancel dinner."

Amelia stared at him, mind blank. It was a broadcast thing, she recollected. A pretty big deal, actually. He was supposed to present awards.

"Did you mention that this morning? I completely forgot." She looked at the clock, noting that she should have started getting ready an hour ago. "You can go without me."

"You've had her all day. I'll take her so you can have a break."

"She doesn't want anyone else to hold her," Amelia said with exasperation.

"You need a break," he said firmly. "Go run a bath." He gently stole Peyton, who began to sob with fresh misery, but she flopped her head onto his shoulder in a bid for comfort.

Amelia didn't want to be alone with her thoughts. She would dwell on things like this, how her husband could make her feel so scorned, yet show her such consideration. It was maddening, but she couldn't help loving him more for it.

As it turned out, she was so shortchanged on sleep, she fell asleep in the tub, waking with a start to tepid water and a still-full glass of wine.

For the first time in days, she spent more than five seconds on her appearance, pulling both thoughts and emotions back together as she dried her hair and touched up her eyebrows and worked moisturizer into her hands and feet.

Was she putting off a difficult conversation? Yes. She and Hunter were due to fly back to Vancouver tomorrow, and she didn't know if she should go with him or if they ought to take a break.

She dressed in wine-colored pedal pushers and a sleeveless mock turtleneck, then went looking for them.

He was in the den off the main lounge that he used as his home office when they were here in the penthouse. Peyton was asleep in his arms, and he was talking on his phone.

"Try that and call me if—"

Some inner radar had him glancing at the door, almost as if he had been watching for her, concerned he might be overheard. Wary stillness came over him.

"I'm in Toronto," he continued evenly, holding her gaze.

"We'll stay here until I hear from you. Call me anytime on this number." He ended the call. "Feel better?"

That had sounded exactly like any of his business calls, but something had her skin prickling. "Was that Remy?"

"No." The question seemed to surprise him. "He's in France as far as I know."

"Mmm." She searched his expression, which seemed deliberately stoic. "I thought you had meetings in Vancouver this week?"

"Right. Thank you for the reminder." Was he deliberately avoiding her eyes by glancing at his phone screen? "I have to make some calls to push those back. I'll put Peyton down, then do that. The table is set on the terrace. Start without me." He brushed past her.

She had worked up her courage to address the elephant that had been trampling all over their separate bedrooms for the last few days, and he disappeared before she could even acknowledge it.

Frustrated, she sat down to eat, but he didn't join her. When he finally did, he seemed distracted. Then Peyton woke and Amelia's chance to have an adult conversation with him was gone.

For the first time since their argument, Amelia went to bed in their bedroom as a sort of peace offering, but he wasn't there, and she couldn't get comfortable. Her mind spun for two hours with all the things they weren't saying.

She could have gotten up to find him, she supposed, but she suspected he was sleeping in another room and that was such a painful death knell on their marriage, she didn't want to face it.

He wasn't there when she rose at three to feed Peyton and she flopped straight back to sleep after, still playing catch-up from her recent sleepless nights.

She was bordering on a coma when he gently squeezed her shoulder. "Amelia."

For a moment she was disoriented and only felt the warm joy that always filled her when she opened her eyes to him.

Then she took in the daylight and the fact that he looked like ten miles of dirt road, eyes sunken and face lined.

"Have you been up all night? Is Peyton okay?" She hiked herself onto an elbow.

"She's fine. I changed her and gave her a bottle. Matinder has her."

"Okay. Um…" Her heart lurched. They were really close. His hand was still on her shoulder. It was all she could do not to press her cheek to his hand. Her throat began to burn with apprehension at what might come of this, but… "Should we ta—?"

"I got a call," he said over her. His hand tightened on her shoulder as though he braced her for something. "Jasper is alive. He's on his way here."

If she hadn't been lying on the bed, she would have dropped like a stone. Everything fell away. Wind seemed to rush around as she plummeted through blurred, empty space.

A cold ghost sat in her throat, turning her voice to crushed ice. "Pinch me."

"It's real." He rubbed her shoulder with enough friction to assure her that she was awake.

She was still afraid to believe, but her body reacted, sweeping back the covers. She slapped her feet onto the hardwood floor and stood so fast, her head swam.

"Easy." He steadied her. "He only left Santiago a few hours ago. He won't get here until late tonight. Okay, I know, I know."

She only realized she was shaking and growing limp, breathing so fast her vision was fading, when his arms went around her, catching her before she crumpled to the floor. The tears came so hard and thick, they made her cheeks ache, but there was no stopping them.

"I know, I know," he kept saying, rubbing her back and smoothing her hair.

He didn't know. He couldn't. But when he eased onto the bed and drew her into his lap, cradling her, she clung to him, weeping out all the loss she'd carried this last year.

When she was weak and wrecked, head too heavy to lift, she only had one thought. "I have to phone Dad." Her voice was a rusty nail on a chalkboard.

"I've sent a car for him. I didn't tell him why. Listen." His arms tightened around her. "I didn't know for sure that Jasper was alive until he was in the air. That was his instruction. They had to sneak him out because somewhere in the REM-ex chain of command there are people who don't want him alive. He thought it better to let them think he was dead. Otherwise, they might have come after you and your dad."

She tilted her face up, searching his grim expression, trying to take that in.

"He said he would tell you as much as he can when he gets here, but we have to keep his return secret."

"Anything," she vowed.

He nodded. "Good. Get dressed. I'll dismiss the staff for the day."

She moved through the rest of the day as though walking through gelatin.

A few times she caught Hunter looking at her. They had so much to talk about, but her mind was consumed by Jasper, by willing his flight to arrive safely. Maybe she was even embracing this momentous occasion to avoid thinking about what would happen next with her husband.

Peyton finally, *finally* cut her two bottom teeth. Her

swollen gums settled and two sharp white lines appeared. She smiled again, but Amelia still held her for her own comfort, pacing restlessly, arms aching, mind nothing but cotton balls.

Her father turned up, and they had a long hug and a good cry, then it was more waiting. Each minute was a ratchet on a torture device until Amelia was utterly, emotionally exhausted.

Finally, when she was yawning because it was growing late, the elevator dinged.

She stood and held her breath.

A man she barely recognized stepped off the elevator. He wore a bushy beard and was thinner than he'd been even in his high school beanpole days. He had a scar cut into his eyebrow, and his clothes were hanging off his wiry frame, but it was him. It was Jasper. Her brother.

She handed Peyton to Hunter and followed her father across the floor into a big hug that nearly broke her in half. Both of the men closed her in so strongly she couldn't breathe, but she was completely okay with that.

Her father was saying, "Son. My son," and Jasper was whispering a jagged, "I'm sorry. I'm so sorry."

Tobias broke away first, trying to regain his composure by wiping his handkerchief across his cheeks.

Amelia wasn't ready to let go and wrapped both her arms around her brother. He smelled like he had showered in chlorinated water, maybe on the airplane? She didn't care. The chemical smell imprinted on her as the best fragrance in the world, one that swelled her heart with joy.

"I can't believe you're really here."

Jasper nearly lifted her off the ground as he squeezed her. "All thanks to that flop of a cake I made for you when you hit puberty."

"What?" She lifted her wet face, vaguely remembering telling Hunter about that.

"A stranger turned up claiming to work for your husband, but I didn't even know you were married. It felt like a setup, so I told him he had the wrong guy. Then he told me about the cake. I knew you wouldn't have shared that with anyone you didn't trust completely."

She looked to Hunter, starting to realize exactly what he had done for her. He stood there all gorgeous and tailored, even though his expression was pulled into an emotive grimace while he watched their reunion. He cradled their daughter, always the tender, attentive father he had told her he wanted to be. In fact, his dedication to her and her family was so deep, he had found her brother and reunited her with him.

She'd been so hurt after their fight, and now it seemed like a huge waste of her energy to be angry. If this was Hunter's version of caring, his unfettered love might be too strong to withstand. She was having trouble bearing the emotions swamping her as it was.

Just then, Tobias blew his nose with the goose honk that had been a mainstay of her childhood. It was such a familiar sound of home, it didn't even alarm Peyton and busted Amelia and Jasper into laughing so hard, they doubled over, breathless and crying. It was too strong a reaction for such a silly thing, but it broke the tension and allowed her to draw Jasper the rest of the way into the apartment.

"You must be Hunter," Jasper said, offering his hand.

"Good to meet you. And this is your niece. Peyton."

Peyton was a sturdy little bundle these days, keeping her head up and her attention alert. She fixed her eyes on Jasper, fist in her mouth.

As if she recognized one of her own, she pointed her

wet hand at Jasper and smiled, showing off the glint of white on her gums.

"Hey," he said shakily. "We have the same name." As he took her, Jasper glanced at Amelia with a gentle scold for being so sentimental as to give her daughter his middle name and for bringing fresh tears to his eyes.

"I was going to come to Chile and look for you myself, but I found out I was carrying her—"

"I was doing my best to stay lost. You wouldn't have— *Ouch.* That's quite a grip, kid." He pried her fist loose from his beard and shifted her against his shoulder, letting her curl her hand around his finger instead.

"Why did you have to hide?" Tobias demanded, easing into a chair.

"Sit," Hunter invited with a wave.

"Thanks. I'm exhausted."

Jasper sank onto the sofa, and Amelia perched right beside him.

"I am *so* sorry I let you believe I was dead." Jasper included both her and Tobias in his remorseful look. "I can't explain it all. Not yet. I can't even stay. The man Hunter sent—I won't give you his name. Hunter has arranged for him to take me to an undisclosed location. Thanks for the lawyer, by the way," Jasper said to Hunter. "I'll swear some statements into evidence before I go public that I'm alive. It's easier to leave a man for dead in remote mountains a continent away than it will be once there are charges pending. It'll be dangerous for me at first, and ugly for all of you for a while. That's why I want you at arm's length. Hunter knows how to reach me if something happens, but until I go public, I'm still dead. Got it?"

"I guess." Amelia's lips wouldn't stay steady enough to speak. "I really missed you, though. I don't want you to go away again."

"I won't go far. I missed you, too." He looped his free arm across her shoulders and hugged her into his side. Then he let her take Peyton. "But it has to be this way."

"Okay," Amelia hiccuped, recognizing his stubborn look. Arguing would be futile.

"Dad?" Jasper asked, moving toward Tobias.

"You're alive, son. That's all that matters to me." Tobias stood and hugged him. "Come home as soon as you can."

"I will." With a final pet of Peyton's hair and a kiss on Amelia's cheek, Jasper left.

"Was that even real? It feels like a dream." Amelia sank back onto the sofa, still holding Peyton, face pale, but with a light behind her eyes that Hunter hadn't seen since he'd met her.

He squeezed her shoulder.

"Can I get you a drink, Tobias?" he asked as the older man slumped back into an armchair as though he'd run a marathon today.

Tobias rubbed his face.

"I'm trying to decide if I'm sleeping here or catching a lift home so I can sleep in my own bed."

"I'll take you in the morning," Amelia said. "Peyton and I will come stay for, um…" She glanced uncertainly at Hunter, then down at their daughter.

Hunter's heart swerved in his chest. The morning after she had told him she loved him, he'd gotten the first inkling that Jasper might have been found. Hunter had wanted to tell her, but after disappointing her so badly that night, he couldn't bring himself to raise her hopes if they were about to be dashed again.

With Peyton so fussy, Amelia had had her hands full without his toying further with her emotions. He had focused on relaying what information he could to convince Jasper to trust his emissary and come home.

Hunter was glad, so glad that he'd been able to find Jasper, but he was aware that Jasper's brief visit didn't undo the hurt he'd caused Amelia.

"You'll be heading back to Vancouver, won't you?" Tobias was saying.

"That was the plan," Hunter said carefully.

"It bothers me you're alone at home," Amelia said in a subdued voice.

"We have plenty of room if you want to come to Vancouver with us," Hunter said, not for the first time. Or the last. "There's a room ready for you."

"I'm not alone in Goderich. I have my coffee with the boys every morning," Tobias reminded her, then grew sheepish. "And I've taken to having pie with Mo's sister, Ola, on Sunday afternoons. Sometimes we have the early bird special at Thursday's on Thursday. Don't get any ideas." He shook a warning finger. "She's a widow with kids who have grown and left the nest, same as me. We keep each other company, is all. It's someone new to talk to who hasn't heard all our same old yarns, but I wouldn't want her feeling lonely if I weren't there." He wore a self-conscious blush on his cheeks.

"Oh. That's nice. I'm happy if you're happy, Dad." Amelia blinked in bemusement.

"And we'd be happy for you to bring her for a visit if that works sometime, too," Hunter said. "I can make arrangements anytime. Just let me know."

"I will, thanks. I've decided to hit the hay," Tobias said, standing and heaving a sigh. "It's been a long day, and it's catching up to me."

Amelia rose, and they said their good-nights. Then she disappeared to put Peyton down for the night.

Hunter poured himself a drink, bracing himself for the reckoning that couldn't be avoided. *Peyton and I will come stay...*

She didn't want to come to Vancouver with him.

His guts roiled with the dark irony of her rejection. His greatest fear had been that Amelia would hold some sort of power over him, and she did. Knowing she was angry with him, and worse, knowing he deserved it, had been eating into him like acid.

He was every bit as enamored with and susceptible to her as his father had been Irina.

The difference was, Amelia was sensitive and supportive and *loving*. How had he seen that as a threat? Her heart was the most precious thing she could offer him, and he'd been a blind fool to throw it back at her the way he had.

No wonder she wanted to leave him.

Now he'd ruined it. He'd seen how completely she loathed the last man who hadn't given her the respect her love deserved.

Her footsteps on the stairs had him turning to pour her wine and top up his scotch.

"Oh my God. Thank you," she sighed as he handed her the glass. She took a sip. "And *thank you*." Her eyes glossed with emotion. "I don't know how to even process that you brought my brother back from the dead."

"I threw money at a problem and hoped for the best. Fortunately, that's what we got."

"I'm still very grateful," she said sincerely.

Grateful enough to stay? The pain down his breastbone was sharp as a fracture.

"I can't imagine what it cost you," she was saying, as if he cared about the money. "Finding him. The chartered flight... And his legal bills?" Her brow twisted with anxiety. "That's not your responsibility, Hunter. Dad has said many times that he can remortgage the house—"

"Don't even think it. There will be a settlement. It will be huge. Trust me. Anything I give Jasper will be a loan." It stung that she didn't want his money. How was this still a bone of contention between them? "You would help my sister in any way you could. I know that."

"I would," she agreed absently, then winced. "But it sounds like our family will drag yours into the spotlight *again*. That's why I thought going to live with Dad would be a good idea. Wouldn't it be better for you if we said we were on a trial separation—"

"Better?" he choked. "How would it be better for me if my wife and daughter leave me?"

"I…" Her shoulders slumped. "I know you want Peyton close to you, but—"

"I want you!" he shouted, then clacked his teeth together. He glanced toward the stairs as he recalled that her father was trying to sleep. Pressure filled his head and his throat and his chest. Urgency. *Fear.*

"Dad wears earplugs so Peyton doesn't wake him." Amelia hugged herself as she eyed him warily. "I know that we click, chemistry-wise. I just don't know how that can be enough when you're going to all this trouble on my behalf."

"Enough?" He ran a hand down his face, wondering how she could make him feel so callow and misunderstood. "I didn't search for him so I could get laid, Amelia. It was the right thing to do and it might not have worked out as well as it did, but I wanted answers for you, one way or another."

"Because you care about me." She sat down, hand shaking as she abandoned her wine on the coffee table. "I know you do and I've been churlish, acting as though you don't give me everything I need when you *do*. I realize that.

Words are cheap. Actions are real and the way you act is…loving. It's okay if you don't say the words or feel it the way I do."

"Don't be so damned forgiving!" he burst out, hating himself in that moment. "Do you know how I would have reacted if I told you I loved you and you said, *That's nice*? I would throw up my heart and wonder what reason there was for continuing with my sorry life. I would call you a coward when I can see with my own eyes that you love me." He pointed at his eyes. They were stinging with gathering tears. His throat was on fire, barely able to mutter, "Even if you were too stubborn and scared to say the words."

She tucked her chin and bit her trembling lips into a line, blinking wet lashes.

"Actions *are* real," he noted. "The things you do for me… I don't need a business partner for a wife. I need *you*. By my side. *Taking* my side. You keep me grounded and give me someone to come home to. You make every one of my houses feel like a home. If you're not here, then I guess I'm moving to Goderich, because my home is wherever you are. I need you in my life. I need you to keep me from being a distrustful jerk and to help me see the good in this world. You *are* the good in this world. You're the good in *my* world."

The tears brimming her lashes began to trickle down her cheeks, but she managed to sniff, "And Peyton."

"She wouldn't be here without you, would she?"

She released a shaky chuckle. "I'm starting to think you really do love me."

"I'm starting to think so, too," he said humbly. Contritely. "I think I love you more than either of us realize."

He waited for the cavernous vulnerability to hit him, but saying those words didn't make him feel defenseless.

They filled him with something strong and certain and right. Like lifeblood. Like air. Necessary and energizing.

He had been so afraid of what she would take from him if he let himself fall for her. Instead, he wanted to give her everything. Not in a foolish way. Not as an infantile means of keeping her, but because he wanted her to know what she meant to him. Because he wanted her to thrive so she could be with him always.

He walked across and knelt before her, cupping her cheeks.

"I love you," he said, feeling the words vibrate from the depths of his chest, radiating outward to his fingertips and toes. The only way it broke anything inside him was to crack the wall around his heart. Rather than feeling unguarded, he felt *free*.

"I love you, too." Her mouth trembled. "So much."

He stood and drew her up with him, closing his arms around her, needing as much of her touching him as possible. He needed the taste of her unsteady lips against his. The dampness of her tears against his cheek and the press of her heartbeat to his chest.

Her thumb swept across his clenched eye. There was dampness there, and he only held her closer, unashamed by how much of his love was seeping out of him to land on her.

"I thought I would lose you," he confessed. "I didn't know how I would bear it."

"I'm here. I will be. Always."

"Same. Always."

They kept making promises between kisses, slowly making their way up the stairs to their room. To their bed.

And when they made love, it was pure love, each caress and kiss a vow. It was a celebration of their bodies and their soul-deep connection.

When the shimmering clench of climax began to grip

them, she traced his ear and said with a pang of doubt, "You're still waiting for me."

"Because I'm a gentleman, love."

Which made her laugh. She twisted and he was lost to the throes of climax, groaning and thrusting, dragging her with him into the delirious storm.

EPILOGUE

Two days later

HUNTER ARRIVED IN Goderich as they were sitting down to dinner. Amelia hurried to rise and meet him at the door even though they'd only been apart the one night. She had wanted a little more time with her father after the upheaval of Jasper's return, so she had driven home with him yesterday.

She had also been anxious to vet her father's sweetheart. Mo's sister, Ola, was an absolute doll. Amelia would worry about him a lot less when she returned to Vancouver, knowing the pair were keeping each other company.

"Hey." Hunter greeted her with an intimate smile and a warm tone and a lingering kiss that curled her toes against the welcome mat. "Traffic getting out of the city was a nightmare or I would have made better time."

"It's okay. Supper's almost on the table, so this is perfect."

"You must be Ola," he said as he greeted the woman with gray hair and a tender touch as she cradled Peyton. "Tobias." He nodded at her father, then touched his daughter's hair. "Hello, bean sprout. I missed you."

Peyton picked up her head, but her eyes were still heavy from her recent nap.

It was a pleasant meal with plenty of chatter as Amelia and Ola continued getting to know each other, but Amelia noticed Hunter wasn't saying much.

After he drove Ola home and her father had gone to bed, she put Peyton down for the night and joined Hunter on the couch.

"Are you okay? You've been quiet."

"Plotting my revenge against your father if he decides to marry Ola," he claimed wryly, staring into the drink he had yet to finish.

"Just desserts," she said lightly, taking heart from the fact that he was making jokes.

She brought her knees up under her and leaned into him, wrapping her arm across his shoulders as she kissed the side of his face.

"How did it go with Remy?" she asked gently.

"Fine." He chased it with a swallow of whiskey.

Okay. She wouldn't press. Today had been the only window of time for the men to connect. Hunter had been planning to come with her yesterday, but heard at the last minute that Remy and Eden had come into Toronto. He had sent Amelia ahead and lingered to catch up with his friend.

She started to withdraw her arm from around him.

"Don't do that." He set aside his drink and swiveled her into his lap. "I'm being cryptic because he told me some things he never shared before. I don't want to break his confidence."

"I don't expect you to." She nestled her shoulder beneath his arm, relaxing as she understood his walls were protecting his friend, not himself.

"Also, he gave me Eden's engagement ring. What am I supposed to do with that?" He shook his head in baffled annoyance. "It's in the safe at the penthouse. I'll unload it as soon as I can."

"It doesn't bother me. I'm just glad you're on speaking terms again."

"We weren't *not* on speaking terms. He had a lot going on and wasn't ready to talk until now. I respect that," Hunter summed up pensively.

"Are he and Eden happy?" She discovered that she hoped they were.

"Not happy the way we're happy." Hunter dragged her bottom more fully into his lap and dropped his smug smile onto her lips, turning it into a tender kiss. "But who could be?"

"I know, right?" She played with the buttons on his shirt, thinking about releasing them.

"The whole drive here, I was thinking how lucky I am." His hand traced absent circles on her back. "Lucky Remy dragged me away that weekend last year. Lucky you joined us. I'm damned lucky your father interrupted my wedding to the wrong woman. I don't want revenge against him," he assured her with a grave look. "I want to give him a kidney if he needs it. I owe him a lot."

"We gave him a grandchild. That's a pretty close second." She was grinning with amusement, but growing misty with emotive tears. "I'd suggest we give him another, but honestly, I need this one weaned and sleeping through the night before we have that conversation."

"I want that, too. The second baby and the uninterrupted sleep." He grew more contemplative, tucking her head beneath his chin as he absently sifted his fingers through the curtain of her hair before warming the back of her neck with his palm. "I want to go through the pregnancy with you and be there when you're swearing at me through labor. I want time with *you* before we bring another personality into the mix. I do love you, you know. So much, I can hardly breathe sometimes."

"I do know." Her eyes were wet and stinging, her smile wide and unsteady. She felt his love with everything in her and could hardly breathe herself. "But I don't get tired of hearing it. Or feeling it." She pressed closer suggestively.

"Allow me to demonstrate, then."

"Please do."

He lifted her into his arms and carried her to the bedroom, where he did exactly that.

* * * *

COMING SOON!

We really hope you enjoyed reading this book. If you're looking for more romance, be sure to head to the shops when new books are available on

Thursday 27th October

To see which titles are coming soon, please visit
millsandboon.co.uk/nextmonth

MILLS & BOON

MILLS & BOON ®

Coming next month

HER CHRISTMAS BABY CONFESSION
Sharon Kendrick

His words were as emotionless as his expression and Bianca couldn't deny a twist of pain as their coldness washed over her.

But what else had she expected? Joy? Excitement? Surely she hadn't anticipated Xanthos would behave in the way would-be fathers were supposed to behave. Get real, Bianca.

"You're not suggesting I planned this?"

"I have no idea," he drawled, dark eyebrows shooting upwards. "Did you?"

"Please don't insult me!"

He nodded, as if her anger and indignation were in some way reassuring. His gaze rested upon her face. "What do you intend to do?"

"I'm k-keeping my baby, of course!"

"Good."

The word took the wind right out of her sails and she blinked at him in confusion, before reminding herself that she didn't need his approval. But that didn't prevent the sliver of hope which shot through her, like sunlight breaking through a dark cloud. "I know you never intended to be a father—"

"No, you're right, I didn't." His words effectively killed off that brief flash of optimism. "So what do you want from me, Bianca?"

Continue reading
HER CHRISTMAS BABY CONFESSION
Sharon Kendrick

Available next month
www.millsandboon.co.uk

MILLS & BOON

THE HEART OF ROMANCE

A ROMANCE FOR EVERY READER

MODERN

Prepare to be swept off your feet by sophisticated, sexy and seductive heroes, in some of the world's most glamourous and romantic locations, where power and passion collide.

HISTORICAL

Escape with historical heroes from time gone by. Whether your passion for wicked Regency Rakes, muscled Vikings or rugged Highlanders, aw the romance of the past.

MEDICAL

Set your pulse racing with dedicated, delectable doctors in the high-pre sure world of medicine, where emotions run high and passion, comfort love are the best medicine.

True Love

Celebrate true love with tender stories of heartfelt romance, from the rush of falling in love to the joy a new baby can bring, and a focus on emotional heart of a relationship.

Desire

Indulge in secrets and scandal, intense drama and plenty of sizzling h action with powerful and passionate heroes who have it all: wealth, sta good looks…everything but the right woman.

HEROES

Experience all the excitement of a gripping thriller, with an intense re mance at its heart. Resourceful, true-to-life women and strong, fearle face danger and desire - a killer combination!

To see which titles are coming soon, please visit

millsandboon.co.uk/nextmonth

LET'S TALK
Romance

For exclusive extracts, competitions
and special offers, find us online:

- **f** facebook.com/millsandboon
- 🐦 @MillsandBoon
- 📷 @MillsandBoonUK

Get in touch on 01413 063232

For all the latest titles coming soon, visit

millsandboon.co.uk/nextmonth